P9-COP-075

the
heiresses

SARA SHEPARD

the heiresses

A NOVEL

HARPER

www.harpercollins.com

HarperCollins books may be purchased for educational, business, or sales promotional use. For information, please e-mail the Special Markets Department at SPsales@harpercollins.com.

Produced by Alloy Entertainment, 1700 Broadway, New York, NY 10019.

FIRST EDITION

Library of Congress Cataloging-in-Publication Data has been applied for.

ISBN 978-0-06-225953-0 (Hardcover)
ISBN 978-0-06-235758-8 (International Edition)

14 15 16 17 18   OV/RRD   10 9 8 7 6 5 4 3 2 1

To Michael

Whether we fall by ambition, blood, or lust,
like diamonds we are cut with our own dust.

—JOHN WEBSTER

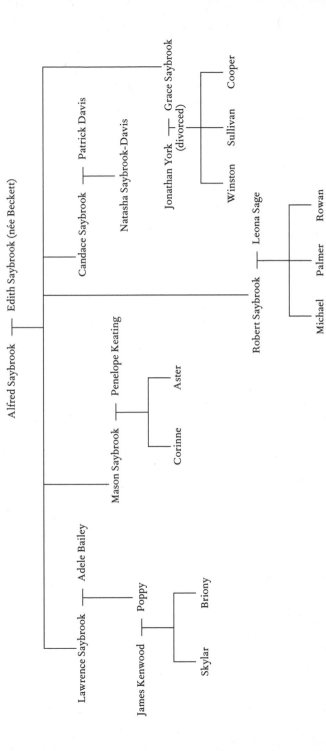

FAMILY TREE

Alfred Saybrook — Edith Saybrook (née Beckett)

Lawrence Saybrook — Adele Bailey

Mason Saybrook — Penelope Keating

Candace Saybrook — Patrick Davis

Robert Saybrook — Leona Sage

James Kenwood — Poppy

Skylar   Briony

Corinne   Aster

Natasha Saybrook-Davis

Jonathan York — Grace Saybrook
(divorced)

Winston   Sullivan   Cooper

Michael   Palmer   Rowan

PROLOGUE

You know the Saybrooks. Everyone does. Perhaps you've read a profile of them in *People* or *Vanity Fair*, seen their pictures in the society pages of *Vogue* and the *New York Times* Sunday Styles. When walking along that choice block on Fifth Avenue, you've been tempted to enter the ornate limestone building with their family name etched into the pediment above the door. At the very least, you've paused at their ads, pictures of Aster Saybrook's stunning face framed by a galaxy of baubles, the diamonds so flawless and clear that even their glossy images make you dizzy. *They* make you dizzy too, for the Saybrooks are a family of beauties, entrepreneurs, debutantes, mavens, and mavericks, the type of people for whom doors open and restaurant tables open up. If you live in New York City and happen to catch a glimpse of them doing something normal, like walking into the office in the morning or rounding the Reservoir on an evening jog, you feel like you've just been touched by a sunbeam, a magic wand, a stroke of luck. They're sort of like me, you think.

Only they aren't. And be careful what you wish for, because if you *were* a Saybrook, you'd be haunted by secrets as deep as a mine and plagued by a streak of luck just as dark. You'd have to go to a hell of a lot of funerals too. Larger-than-life though the family might be, they also have to contend with a lot of death.

TEN HIGHLY POLISHED town cars idled in front of St. Patrick's Cathedral on the clear early September morning of Steven Barnett's funeral, and at least five more had parked around the corner on Fiftieth Street. The church steps had been swept clean, the railings gave off a high shine, and even the pigeons had found somewhere else to roost. The activity on the sidewalk across the street continued apace. There were so many people that they seemed to move in one long, silken scarf of color. But when the town car doors opened simultaneously in a perfectly choreographed ballet, all movement stopped and the gawking began.

Edith, the venerable matriarch of the Saybrook dynasty, was already inside the church along with her children. Now it was the younger generation's turn to step out of the cool darkness of their cars into the flash of cameras and the screaming crowds. First to emerge was twenty-nine-year-old Poppy Saybrook, perfectly styled in a black Ralph Lauren sheath and showing off a large diamond engagement ring—a Saybrook's, naturally. Her new fiancé, James Kenwood, trailed behind her casting unassuming smiles at everyone in the crowd—especially the women.

Next were Poppy's cousins, sisters Corinne and Aster. Though Corinne looked impeccable in a black wrap dress and taupe heels, her skin was ashen, and her balance seemed slightly off. Rumor had it her boyfriend, Dixon Shackelford, had broken her heart at the beginning of the summer. Maybe that was why she'd taken a yearlong assignment in Hong Kong as a Saybrook's business liaison. Word was she was leaving the next day.

Aster wore a dress that could have doubled for a negligee, her blond hair mussed. The eighteen-year-old, who had spent the summer modeling in Europe, didn't lift the Dior frames from her eyes as she hugged Poppy. Maybe she'd been up all night crying. Or, more likely, partying.

A door slammed on the corner as twenty-seven-year-old Rowan, Saybrook's newest in-house lawyer, stepped onto the curb. Her two brothers, Michael and Palmer, were not in attendance—they hadn't joined the family business and didn't know Steven. Rowan looked up at her cousins, only to flinch as she caught sight of Poppy and James. Her pale blue eyes were bloodshot, and her nose was red. No one had realized that Rowan and Steven Barnett were close . . . or was she upset about something else?

And finally eighteen-year-old Natasha Saybrook-Davis hurried over from the subway stop on Fifty-Third, her wild mess of dark curls pinned off her face, her lips twisted into a surly frown. The other cousins glanced at her cagily, no one knowing quite what to say. The fact that Natasha had recently disinherited herself was the subject of much speculation. Why would one of America's heiresses give up her fortune?

Flashbulbs popped. Poppy shaded her fine-boned oval face with her quilted Chanel clutch. Aster squeezed her eyes shut, looking positively green. After a moment, Poppy, Aster, Corinne, and Rowan clutched hands. This was the first time they had been to-gether since Steven was found on the shoals of their family's summer property on Meriweather, a sunny island off the coast of Martha's Vineyard, one week earlier, after their annual end-of-summer party. This year they'd celebrated Poppy's promotion to president of the company.

"Excuse me?" said someone behind the four women.

They turned and peered into the flushed, eager face of a reporter. A cameraman in jeans and a Yankees T-shirt stood behind her.

The woman smiled brightly. "Amy Seaver, Channel Ten. How well did you know Steven Barnett?"

Corinne ducked her head. Poppy shifted awkwardly. Rowan balled up her fists.

Amy Seaver barely blinked. The cameraman leaned in. "It's strange," the reporter went on. "First your grandfather, who ran the Saybrook's empire, and now his protégé, the man who was rumored to be next in line for the job . . ."

Rowan frowned. "If you're trying to connect the two deaths, you shouldn't. Our grandfather was ninety-four. It's not exactly the same thing."

"And *Poppy* was named president, not Steven," Corinne jumped in, pointing to her cousin. Mason, Corinne's father and the company CEO, had made the last-minute decision, saying he wanted to "keep things in the family." It had been a huge surprise, but everyone knew Poppy was up to the challenge.

The reporter kept pace with them as they walked toward the church, Natasha a few steps behind the rest of the cousins. "Yes, but didn't Mr. Barnett row for Harvard, surf in Galápagos? Don't you think it's odd that he drowned in *shallow water?*"

Rowan thrust an open palm toward the camera.

"No comment," Poppy said quickly, then hustled Rowan and the others toward the church. "Try to hold it together," she whispered.

"You *know* what she's getting at, though," Rowan whispered.

"I know, I know," Poppy answered. "But just let it go, okay?"

It was something they never liked to think about—the family curse. The media had invented the concept long ago, and oh, how they adored it—there was even an anonymously run website called the Blessed and the Cursed that documented the Saybrook calamities and misfortunes, and it received thousands of hits a day. No one could get enough of the legendary American family that was so blessed with fortune and beauty, yet cursed with a string of mysterious sudden deaths.

When the girls were little, the curse had been their go-to ghost story when they camped out in the backyard in their family compound in Meriweather. *It all started*, they'd begin, flashlights positioned under their chins, *when Great-Aunt Louise fell off a balcony at a New Year's Eve party. She fell twenty stories, holding her martini the whole time.* After Louise, a great-uncle was trampled at a polo match. Then a second cousin's plane was lost at sea. Their now-divorced aunt Grace, the youngest of Edith and Alfred's children, had a son who was kidnapped from their front yard.

Though Steven Barnett wasn't technically a Saybrook, it *felt* like he was. Alfred, who was always looking for new talent, had plucked Steven straight from Harvard Business School nearly fifteen years prior, impressed by his business acumen and poise. Steven was efficient and brilliant, with a keen business mind and a knack for PR, able to talk about anything from the hottest diamond bauble for the holidays to the future of socially responsible mining. He'd ascended the ranks quickly, a constant fixture at Alfred and Edith's town house in the city or at the family's island beach estate on long weekends, becoming a trusted adviser and honorary son. Now he'd suffered the same fate as all those other Saybrooks, claimed by the great gray cloud that followed their family. Yes, his drowning in the shallow water of the marina was strange. But Steven's blood alcohol level had been sky-high, and the police had deemed it a tragic accident.

The reporter finally fell back, and the cousins continued into the cathedral. An organist played a Bach fugue, and an empty pew waited for the cousins near the front of the church. In the first pew Steven's wife, Betsy, dabbed her gray eyes, though her grief looked rehearsed. His brothers sat shoulder to shoulder, like fun-house mirror versions of the deceased. Two red-haired women stood in front of the casket, hands folded in prayer. One wore a diamond tennis bracelet the Saybrook women recognized immediately.

"Danielle?" Corinne said.

The woman turned, her expression shifting. "It's so awful," she whispered.

Aster inched away, but Corinne pulled Danielle into a hug. Danielle Gilchrist was the daughter of the caretakers at the Meriweather estate, and she'd been around so much when they were kids that she was practically like family. She and Aster had been the closest—Aster had given her the bracelet—though Aster refused to look at her now. Danielle's mother, Julia, stood next to her daughter, dressed in a black sheath that showed off her slender figure. Though she was nearly fifty, with her lithe physique and the same stunning red hair as her daughter's, she could almost pass for Danielle's sister.

"I still can't believe he drowned," Danielle said as Natasha approached the group.

Natasha placed a hand on the casket. "It *is* a convenient explanation," she murmured, "given everything that happened that night."

Poppy whipped her head around. Aster pressed her lips together, looking caught. Corinne visibly paled. Even Rowan seemed nervous. They hadn't exactly talked about what *they'd* been doing the evening Steven drowned—or much else that had happened that summer. Maybe there had been too many other things to discuss, or maybe they'd avoided it on purpose.

Julia touched Danielle's arm. "Come on," she said sharply. "Let's leave them be."

The organist broke into the opening bars of "So My Sheep May Safely Graze," and they all took their seats. Supporting their grandmother, Edith, the priest walked slowly down the aisle. He grasped her dripping-with-diamonds, liver-spotted hand, although she kept trying to swat him away. Despite the humidity inside the church, Edith pulled her sable even tighter around her, as though it were a brace to hold her neck in place. She pushed her large, dark, round-framed glasses higher up her face and smiled coolly at the mourners.

When she reached their pew, Edith gave each of her granddaughters a papery kiss. "All of you look lovely."

Then she sat, crossing her slim legs at the ankles, and folded her hands in her lap, as though she assumed all eyes were on her. And likely, they were. She always gave her granddaughters one piece of advice: *You, my dears, are the heiresses. Remember that, always. Because no one else will ever forget.*

The girls were the future of Saybrook's Diamonds, and they had to act accordingly. They were to live their lives with the utmost decorum, smile for the cameras, speak several languages, hold many

degrees, cultivate the art of conversation, and, most important, refrain from doing anything that might bring scandal upon the family.

And yet they had. All of them. It had been a summer of secrets.
Secrets that set them apart and made them tighten inside—secrets
that they hadn't even told one another. As they glanced around the
sweeping cathedral, they each suddenly feared a bolt of lightning
from above. They were the heiresses, all right, the sparkling princesses of a family that might or might not be doomed. But by Edith's
standards, they hadn't been behaving like heiresses at all.

And it was only a matter of time before the world found out.

FIVE YEARS LATER

I

On a late April morning, as rain smeared the windowpanes, washed the dirt off the sidewalks, and slowed traffic on every block in New York City, twenty-seven-year-old Corinne Saybrook stood barefoot in a dressing room, talking on her cell phone in clipped, precise Turkish.

"So we have permission to establish the liaison office?" Corinne asked Onur Alper, her contact at the Turkish branch of the General Directorate of Foreign Investments, whom she'd met the last time she'd visited.

"Yes, all of the documents are in place," Mr. Alper answered, the phone connection crackling. "We'll still need you to register with the tax office, but Saybrook's International is cleared to set up a branch of your business in the Republic of Turkey. Congratulations to you and your company, Miss Saybrook."

"Thank you so much," Corinne said smoothly, adding a salaam before clapping the phone closed. She smiled at her feet, feeling the satisfying swell of victory. Her family's jewelry empire was one of the most prominent retailers in the country, both for the masses and the fabulously wealthy, but it was Corinne's job to make it number one in the *world*.

Then she gazed down at herself, almost startled to see where she was—and what she was wearing. She was clad in an ivory Monique Lhuillier gown. The Chantilly lace fabric clung to her body, accentuating her porcelain skin. The hem ended neatly at the floor at the front and spilled into a long, romantic train at the back. A diamond necklace, on loan from her family's private collection, sparkled at her throat, the jewels cold and heavy against her skin. Today was the final fitting for her wedding dress. Corinne had already canceled several times because of work obligations, but with the wedding in a month, time was running out.

There was a knock on the dressing room door. Corinne's cousin and matron of honor, Poppy, poked her head inside, dressed in a classic white shirt, khaki trench, skinny black pants, and a pair of bright red Hunter boots that only Poppy could pull off. Poppy had grown up on a farm in the Berkshires, spending as much time picking wild berries and milking cows as she did learning French and playing tennis.

"Everything all right, honey?"

Corinne turned to her and broke into an exuberant smile. "I just secured the liaison office in Turkey," she said excitedly.

"That's wonderful." The corners of Poppy's mouth eased into a smile. "Although you *are* allowed to take a break, you know." Poppy gazed down at Corinne's dress and swooned. "*Gorgeous.* C'mon. Let's show you off." But just before she led Corinne out of the dressing room, Poppy touched her arm, her expression shifting to one of concern. "I meant to ask you," she said in a low voice. "Tomorrow is May first. How are you . . . feeling?"

Corinne sucked in her stomach and looked away. She was about to say that she was fine. But then she felt a peppery sensation behind her eyes. "Sometimes I wish I'd just told him," she blurted. "It seems so selfish that I didn't."

Poppy clutched Corinne's hands. "Oh, honey." A timorous look crossed her face. "You know, there's still time."

Corinne straightened up and looked at herself in the three-way mirror. Her skin was flushed, her eyes a little dilated. "Forget I mentioned it, okay? I can't believe I even said anything."

She grabbed her cell phone from the ottoman in the corner as Poppy gathered up her train. Her mother, Penelope, and her wedding planner, Evan Pierce, sat on an ivory divan in the main salon. Both women turned at the sound of Corinne's swishing skirt. Penelope rose and walked shakily across the room—she had been in a skiing accident in Colorado that winter and no one had seen who hit her. It was just yet another incident chalked up to the Saybrook curse. The press had had a field day with that, especially as it was common knowledge that Corinne's father, Mason, was supposed to have been on the private plane that had crashed two years earlier, killing Poppy's parents and the pilot. He'd canceled at the last minute to attend a work meeting. Two near misses for the Saybrook patriarch and his wife in as many years.

Penelope took Corinne's hands.

"Darling." She smoothed down Corinne's hair, fussed with the lace straps on the dress, and then stood back. "It's simply beautiful."

Corinne nodded, tasting the waxy lipstick she'd just applied a few minutes ago. It wasn't lost on her that her mother had said the *dress* was beautiful, not Corinne.

Bettina, Lhuillier's tailor, smiled proudly. "The alterations are perfect," she murmured.

Evan inspected the dress too. "Good. Fine," she said in her nasal voice, her bluntly cut black hair falling across her sharp features.

Poppy shook her head. "You're so hard to please."

Evan shrugged, but Corinne knew it was just about the best compliment Evan could give. She was Poppy's old roommate from boarding school; Corinne had never really clicked with her, but she was a shark in the Manhattan wedding industry, getting her way even if she had to step on a few pedicures along the way. Corinne appreciated that ferocity. Evan also kept all details about Corinne's upcoming wedding a secret from rabid reporters and bloggers, even the anonymous masterminds behind the Blessed and the Cursed.

Bettina fluffed Corinne's skirt and met her gaze in the mirror.

"So. What is it like to be the bride in the wedding of the century?" Her thickly accented voice was rich with admiration.

A rehearsed smile snapped onto Corinne's face. "Please. The century has only begun."

"Yes, but *Dixon Shackelford*." Bettina shuddered with delight.

Corinne pushed her dirty-blond hair behind her ears. She'd been with Dixon since their sophomore year at Yale. Well, except for that one summer just after graduation—but Corinne had always liked a story with a happy ending, and she'd neatly trimmed that interlude from her personal history. His mother was British, his father Texan, and Dixon himself was her mother's dream come true—a blue blood on both continents, heir to the Shackelford Oil fortune, affable to a fault.

Bettina lifted Corinne's veil from its dark-blue box on a nearby sideboard. "And now you're going to be a *princess*!"

Corinne waved her hand. "There's not much of a chance of that. His mother is the queen's fourth cousin twice removed. Or something," Corinne said, feeling she had to add the *or something* even though she knew precisely where Dixon's mother fell on the royal family tree.

Bettina put her hands on her hips. "That makes you more of a princess than any of us. Now, let me see that ring again."

Corinne held out her hand. Dixon had given her a large, canary-yellow diamond set in platinum—an homage to the Corona Diamond, the very first stone that her beloved grandfather, Alfred, had acquired when he fought in World War II. Before that, Alfred had owned a fledgling jewelry store in Boston, but the acquisition of the Corona had launched the business into a new stratosphere.

"Stunning," Bettina gushed, staring at the ring. Then she pinned the veil on Corinne's head. Poppy rose to help, and together they pulled the veil over Corinne's eyes and let it trail in front of her face. "This is how Dixon will see you on your wedding day."

Your wedding day. Corinne's smile wavered a tiny bit. With all the pomp and circumstance, Corinne sometimes forgot this wasn't another charity event committee she was heading up, and that she was actually getting . . . *married*.

Before she could let the notion truly sink in, the door to the salon flung open, bringing with it a gust of wind and a few sprinkles of rain. A woman in a black trench coat stood in the doorway, battling with an inside-out umbrella. She wrestled with the metal spokes and flimsy fabric, a thin curl of cigarette smoke appearing over her head. "Mother*fucker*," she grumbled, finally winging the crumpled umbrella to the sidewalk just outside the door. Then the tall, blond, beautiful woman turned to face them.

Corinne sucked in her stomach. It was her sister, Aster.

Aster teetered in on jet-black five-inch laser-cut booties. A hand-rolled cigarette dangled from her lips, the stench of tobacco overpowering the salon's light floral scent. Her wet trench dripped puddles on the mahogany floor. Her fuchsia dress, also wet, clung high on her thighs. Though Aster would have still been striking even after a roll in a city Dumpster, there were circles under her large, luminous blue eyes, and her ice-blond hair was matted. She had a disoriented, used-up look about her. Corinne wondered if her younger sister had just emerged from a stranger's bed after one of her typical all-night bacchanals.

"I'm here!" Aster announced in a husky, slurring voice. Then she stopped in the middle of the room, her gaze on Corinne. "Whoa, mama," she said. "That dress should *not* be white."

Corinne tried to speak, but she didn't know what to say. Aster took a drag and exhaled blue-tinged smoke toward the vaulted ceiling. "Nice choice, by the way. Love the lingerie look—you can skip straight to the wedding night." When she leaned toward Corinne to inspect the lace, her breath smelled of cigarettes, booze, and orange Tic Tacs.

A prickly feeling shot from Corinne's core all the way to her fingertips. "Have you been drinking?" she hissed, glancing at the clock on the wall: 10:30 a.m.

Aster lifted one shoulder. "Of course not!" She lurched sideways in an attempt to sit down, but missed the large leather wing chair completely, her legs going out from under her. "Oops!" she cried. Bettina and Poppy rushed forward to help her up. "I'm okay!"

Corinne shut her eyes and tried to stay calm, but all she felt was hot, pulsing embarrassment. As soon as Aster was on her feet again, Corinne shot her arm forward and plucked the cigarette from Aster's lips. "You can't smoke in here," she snapped.

Bettina rushed forward. "It's fine," she said in a meek voice.

But Corinne dropped the still-lit cigarette into a glass of water. It fizzled as it went out, the only sound in the suddenly still salon. "Actually, Aster, I think you should leave," she announced, her voice wavering.

Aster blinked, then scoffed. "You *asked* me to come."

"An *hour* ago," Corinne said coolly. "And now we're almost done."

Aster shrugged. "So I'm a little late."

Corinne shifted her gaze to the right, focusing on the cigarette butt in the water glass. There was a tinge of pink lipstick on the filter. Her throat welled with words, but it wasn't as if she could say them. She glanced at her mother for support, but Penelope just sat there, gripping her knees.

Poppy appeared next to Aster and touched her arm. "Maybe you should go, honey," she told Aster in that kind, gentle-but-motherly voice Poppy had mastered but Corinne could never quite pull off. "Sleep it off. You'll feel much better."

Aster stuck her lip out in a pout, but didn't resist when Poppy took her arm and guided her away from the pedestal. The two of them walked toward the door, and Poppy scooped up her own Burberry umbrella from the metal basket and placed it in Aster's hands. In moments, Aster disappeared and the door slammed behind her.

Poppy walked coolly and confidently to Corinne's side, smiling brightly. "Come on," her cousin said, lifting the veil from Corinne's eyes. She guided her back to the dressing rooms. "Show us your reception dresses. It'll be okay."

"I *know*," Corinne said grumpily. Then she looked down at her dress. She'd worried off one of the pearl embellishments on the bust. Bettina rushed forward with a needle and thread and quickly sewed it back on.

Once Corinne was back in the dressing room, she stared at herself in the mirror, something she often did after being side by side with Aster. Even in a wedding dress, Corinne couldn't compete with Aster's radiant beauty. Corinne spent enough money on her looks, but her long forehead, square jaw, and thick eyebrows equated to something more handsome than pretty. Her shoulders were broad like her father's, her chest small like her mother's, her legs too thick and pale even after hours of Pilates, countless meals uneaten, and thousands spent on spray-tanning. You're good stock, her mother had told her when she was eleven years old. She meant it as a compliment, but it made Corinne think of a prizewinning heifer in a county fair. Penelope had certainly never referred to Aster as *stock*, no matter what she pulled.

It had always been that way. Her parents made excuse after excuse for Aster. Corinne used a knife and fork at eighteen months, Aster threw her food against the wall well into preschool. Corinne studied during recess, while Aster bought test answers on the playground. But their parents always looked the other way. Mason had actually favored Aster, celebrating when Aster got a B, as if she had to do little more than show up for class to earn it.

Corinne preferred her mother's company anyway, enjoying long, girly weekends of tea at the Plaza and spa trips to Elizabeth Arden when Aster and Mason took one of their special trips to Meriweather or the Berkshires. But with her mother's attention also came her criticism and instruction. Penelope had come from old money, made a hundred years ago on railroads, and she was very specific about how her daughter should behave. *Study French. Attend Junior League. Dress in classic lines. Marry well.*

Did they instill any of those values in Aster? Corinne doubted it. The two of them had gotten along as kids—one of Corinne's favorite memories was holding tightly on to Aster's hand as they stared, transfixed, at the Macy's Thanksgiving Day parade floats from a friend's penthouse on Central Park West. They grew apart as they got older, though . . . and when Aster stopped listening to her. Did their parents give Aster a wide berth because she was beautiful? Did they figure she'd get by anyway, even coarse and unfinished? Well, *that* hadn't worked out: when Aster was a year into college, she'd dropped out and settled into the life of a socialite. In the first year of Aster's downward spiral, whenever Corinne visited their parents at their Upper East Side town house, the air seemed fraught, as though she'd just interrupted an argument. They still made excuses for Aster and bankrolled her life, but they were clearly stressed, especially her father, who suddenly wouldn't even look at Aster anymore.

The only thing Corinne could do was to follow her mother's advice to the letter. While Aster took off on a whim to Morocco or went on monthlong bar crawls around Ireland, Corinne shot up the ranks at Saybrook's, conquering one emerging market after the next. While Aster never took another modeling job, barely showed up for Saybrook's PR events, and frittered away her allowance, Corinne dutifully invested, acquired, and got engaged.

Now she leaned against the dressing room wall and took breath after breath. Her heart began to slow. Her nerves no longer felt snappy under her skin. She always got so worked up about Aster, but really, what was the point? She gazed at her first reception dress on the hanger, a long sheath in ivory satin and beading. Corinne's *second* reception dress, a shorter one she would wear for dancing, hung behind it. Just the sight of them lifted her spirits.

"Are you sure about three dresses for one wedding?" her mother had asked, raising a skeptical eyebrow—as an heiress to Saybrook's name and fortune, Corinne was expected to dabble in luxury without seeming tacky. But Dixon's mother had done the same thing, and *she* practically was a princess.

True, Dixon was more swaggering Texan than mannered British, but Shackelford Oil was just as much American royalty as Saybrook's Diamonds. They'd become a couple effortlessly, and shortly thereafter a plan was put into place. Well, it was Corinne who'd instated the plan, but Dixon good-naturedly went along with it. Once they graduated from Yale, Dixon would work on the trading side of Shackelford Oil on Wall Street. Corinne would work at Saybrook's. They would move into separate apartments in the same condo building, and then, once they were engaged at twenty-five, they would move into the three-bedroom penthouse. They would marry by twenty-six, have their first child at twenty-nine, and their second at thirty-one. And then they'd spend the next thirty years building their careers and raising the family.

Besides the blip when Dixon took off to England—and, well, the *other* incident Corinne tried never to think about—life had proceeded exactly to plan. Only, somehow, whenever Dixon proposed a wedding date last year, Corinne had found reasons to wait—the estate in Meriweather, where she insisted they have the wedding, was undergoing renovations last summer. Fall was her least favorite season, and spring was just too muddy and unpredictable. But no matter. In a month, they'd finally do it. Evan had made all the arrangements, with Corinne's blessing. Every detail was in place.

Corinne stepped out of the gown. As she carefully hung it on the satin hanger, laughter sounded from outside. "Corinne, darling?" Evan called. "Come out! We're going to have a toast!"

Corinne pulled the first reception dress from the hanger. Her reflection in the mirror caught her eye once more, and her gaze drifted to the scar below her navel. It was something she rarely looked at, the sight of it still surprising after all these years.

Slowly, carefully, her fingers traced the puckered skin. She'd told

Dixon—she'd told everyone—that it was from emergency gall-bladder surgery when she'd worked in Hong Kong five years ago. It was amazing what people believed. No one even suggested that the scar might be too low for that procedure. Not even Corinne's mother guessed it was from something else. Only Poppy knew the truth.

Stop thinking about it, a voice in her head demanded. *Stop it right now.*

Corinne pulled on the reception dress, slipped on her satin kitten heels, and opened the dressing room door. *Smile*, she told herself sternly as she strode back to her family, remembering all she had to be thankful for. She would twirl in her reception dresses and let everyone ooh and ahh. *Thank everyone for coming. Get married. Don't look back.*

She picked up a clean champagne flute. "To happily ever after!" Corinne toasted. She was marrying Prince Charming; her entire future was ahead of her.

So long as her past didn't catch up.

2

Later that night, Aster Saybrook settled on a pouf inside a large Bedouin-style tent as a waiter peeked through the flap. He wore a batik-print sarong and had a fez cocked to one side on his head. "Can I get you anything, miss?" he asked, looking to Aster as the clear leader of the group.

"Another bottle of Veuve for each of us." Aster waved to indicate the rest of the table, her Hermès bangles gleaming in the dim light. "And by the way," she added as the waiter started to retreat, "we have a bet going. Are you wearing anything under that sarong?"

The waiter looked taken aback, then straightened and mischievously shook his head. Aster's side of the table erupted in cheers. "Looks like this round's on you," Aster said, nudging Clarissa Darrow, the tall brunette who sat to her left. Clarissa grinned and shrugged good-naturedly.

As the table erupted in conversation, Aster sat back and twirled the stem of her champagne glass, glancing around at her best friends. Well, "best friends" might be a slight embellishment; some of them, Aster had only met tonight. But Aster collected people the way other girls collected shoes or handbags or cocktail rings—though Aster collected all those things as well. Across from her sat Javier, an artist whose most recent show involved coat hangers, fluorescent light-bulbs, and pictures of Hollywood starlets cut out of *Us Weekly*. There was Orlean, a tall, sinewy writer for *Rolling Stone* whom Aster had met in Europe. He was Aster's shopping buddy these days, though Aster suspected he liked her company primarily because stores gave her special treatment. There was Faun, a friend from Tangiers who'd dragged Aster through building after building on her Manhattan real estate quest, always complaining that the closets weren't big enough. There was Nigel, Aster's latest fling, the drummer and head song-writer of the British band Lotus Blackbeard. She'd picked him up last week at Gray Lady, and he'd spent every night at her apartment since. His long, thin fingers drummed on the table, probably com-posing a brilliant new song.

And then there was Clarissa, Aster's rail-thin best friend and maybe frenemy, daughter of a hedge fund billionaire. Aster had met Clarissa at Spence in second grade, yet Clarissa still spoke with an affected British accent. She was always up for getting in trouble—or making trouble. Aster suspected that some of the blind items on Page Six about her were tips from Clarissa.

The waiter reappeared with their champagne, and Aster held her glass out for a refill. "Cheers!" she exclaimed as she clinked glasses with Clarissa, then downed her pour in a single swig. "To the hottest place in town."

They were at a restaurant called Badawi, which had been carved out of an old warehouse in the West Twenties and transformed into high souk glamour. It was decorated to look like a bazaar in Mo-rocco, with hanging lanterns and brightly colored tents and couches. Aster had started out the night at SoHo House, but half the tables had been empty, the music was all from last year, and several guests looked like they'd come straight from New Jersey. After consulting Instagram and Foursquare and texting a few of her model friends, she and her entourage had arrived here.

Aster's nights often took on this spontaneous spirit; she couldn't predict at the beginning of the evening where she'd be at the end. It had been this way since the summer she'd spent in Europe, right after high school. She had some great stories for the memoir she'd write—well, dictate—someday: the time she and her rotating posse piled into a private plane and flew to Ibiza; the time they pooled their cash to buy a Porsche Carrera and drove to someone's upstate chalet at 2:00 a.m.; the time she stayed in a mansion in Harlem for a week and partied like people in the Jazz Age. Once she flew a friend's twin-prop plane around his Connecticut airfield on a dare, even though her last lesson had been years ago. She'd water-skied naked on an ice-cold lake in Maine, and mountain-biked down dangerous trails in Sedona. Recently, someone had even dared her to chop off her signature long, white-blond hair. Aster had turned to her friend Patrick, a stylist, and handed him the scissors. He'd cut it all off, leaving the front at an exaggerated, crooked angle over her left eye—Aster never knew whether that was on purpose or a drunken mistake, but the press loved the new look as much as her father hated it.

For Aster, every thrill needed to be more thrilling, every high higher, and every song louder and more danceable. A psychoanalyst might suggest that she had daddy issues or was doing this for attention—or perhaps that she was running away from something. But Aster never went to therapy. She wasn't a sad girl who self-medicated by drinking too much and staying out too late; she was a daredevil who'd have lots of interesting stories for her grandchildren.

When the girls were growing up, Aster and Corinne's parents had forced them to memorize poetry; the ones that made sense to Aster were by free-spirited women poets from the 1920s. She was a huge fan of Edna St. Vincent Millay, who allegedly loved to party and tended to her lush blueberry farm in upstate New York totally in the nude. *My candle burns at both ends; / it will not last the night; / but ah, my foes, and oh, my friends— / it gives a lovely light!* Hells yeah, Edna St. Vincent Millay.

Mr. No-Knickers Waiter reappeared with several lit sparklers and a bottle of Grey Goose L'Orange. Aster joined in everyone's squeals of excitement as she reached for a sparkler, waving it in the air as some R&B artist crooned over the speakers.

She reached for her phone, seized with the desire to invite more people out. The first person who came to mind was her cousin Poppy. It rang once, then her cousin's sleepy voice broke through.

"Pops!" Aster called out over the noise of the club. "What are you doing right now?"

"I'm home." Poppy yawned. "What are *you* doing?"

Aster held out her champagne flute for a refill. "I'm out. Will you come? Please?"

When they were growing up, Aster prided herself on not trying too hard to be like Poppy, like her sister Corinne always did. Poppy was her friend—like a cool big sister who didn't give Aster shit about her choices. Well, most of the time. She had given Aster a pretty harsh talking-to after Aster confessed she'd seduced her European history teacher at NYU for a better grade, then dropped out of college altogether. But Poppy pried because she *cared*.

"Ugh, I'm beat." Poppy sighed through the phone. "I'm in back-to-back meetings for the rest of the decade, Briony's been up every night this week, and I'm losing my mind planning this birthday party for Skylar. I'm such a buzzkill. But why don't you call your sister? Maybe she'd like to come."

Aster burst out laughing. "You were there today, Poppy. She's probably not going to speak to me ever again."

She rolled her eyes, recalling Corinne's gown fitting that morning. Who scheduled a fitting at 9:30 on a Saturday, anyway? She had woken up with a start, remembering the three messages her sister had left her the day before, and wriggled out from underneath Nigel's arm. She hadn't even taken the time to shower or explain where she was going, instead just throwing on her clothes and sprinting out of her apartment with her shoes only half on. Only in the cab did she realize she still smelled like the tequila shots from the night before.

At least the rain might help with that, Aster had thought wryly as she raced down Lhuillier's block under the shitty umbrella she'd bought from a bodega on the corner. But when she walked into the salon, she'd seen the look on her sister's face. Corinne wasn't happy that Aster was there or worried at all about her soaked appearance. She just wrinkled her nose in that way she always did, as if Aster had ruined everything.

Poppy heaved a sigh. "I think she just had an idea of how she wanted things to go, honey. And you sort of threw a wrench into that."

"Well, she's got to learn that sometimes life throws you wrenches," Aster shot back, crossing her arms over her chest.

"You should try to see things her way," Poppy said quietly.

Aster scoffed. "What about her seeing things *my* way? Has she *ever* done that?" Aster already knew the answer: No. Corinne didn't like things she couldn't understand. And she had never understood Aster.

Poppy yawned. "I'm sorry I'm so old and lame. Do you want to grab a drink later this week?"

Aster cradled the phone, touched. Even when Poppy was up to her eyeballs in work and family duties, she *always* made time for Aster. Even in the aftermath of Poppy's parents' death in that freakish plane crash two years ago, Poppy had come to brunch with Aster for her birthday just days later. She was always so . . . *solid*. Unflappable. "Of course," Aster said. "Just let me know when you're free."

She hung up and took another swig of champagne, then another. She was feeling warm and distinctly fuzzy at the edges; she'd drained almost the whole bottle. She hiccuped loudly, watching as her friends stood to dance. "Are you coming?" Nigel asked, extending his hand.

Aster closed her eyes for a moment, imagining what it would be like to fall into her thousand-thread-count bed—alone. To sleep for a full eight hours, get up at a normal hour, go for a jog, stand in line for coffee. Actually *make* one of Corinne's bridal activities tomorrow—surely there was one scheduled—instead of whirling in horribly late, only to be kicked out. Kicked out, she thought angrily, by her own fucking sister. What Corinne didn't know was that Aster had *protected* her all these years. She'd preserved Corinne's perfect little view of their family. Oh, there'd been plenty of times when

Aster had almost blurted out what she knew, but something inside her had held back, knowing it would shatter her sister even more than it had shattered Aster. And what did Aster get in thanks? Rejection.

She grabbed the Veuve and drank it straight from the bottle, hoping to silence the thoughts that flitted around her mind like sharp little birds. All at once, she *wanted* to black out—to drink so much she forgot herself, forgot everything except the dance floor and the sound of the music. She held out her hand to Nigel, and he pulled her to her feet.

The crowd on the dance floor parted for them, leaving them space in the middle of the room. "You forgot your drink," Clarissa yelled over the sound of the music, pressing another glass into her hand. Aster downed it without realizing what it was, then closed her eyes and raised her slender arms over her head, letting all the grimy memories and barbed comments from today wash down the drain. The only thing that mattered right now was having fun.

My candle burns at both ends, it will not last the night, Aster thought defiantly as she swayed slowly to the beat. Aster didn't believe in the curse, but she did know that if another Saybrook died young, she'd be the one. Her reckless, feckless lifestyle was a ticking time bomb. Deep down, she worried she wasn't long for this world.

But maybe that was okay, Aster thought, stumbling forward into Nigel's arms. She'd rather be the quick-burning firecracker than a slow-to-die ember. Everyone knew it was far more fun to go out with a bang than with a whimper.

3

On Sunday afternoon, Rowan Saybrook sat in the corner of a living room in the Dakota on Central Park West and watched twelve princesses meet and greet one another. Each was adorned in a taffeta ball gown, crystal slippers, and a tiara. They plucked hors d'oeuvres from a silver tray with grace and poise.

But then Jasmine stepped on Ariel's foot. Aurora raised an eyebrow at Sofia the First, declaring that she wasn't as real a princess because the Disney cartoon had only started a few years ago. Rowan, sensing disaster, tiptoed out of the room and into her cousin Poppy's kitchen, reaching for a bottle of cabernet. It was Poppy's daughter Skylar's third birthday, and it was probably best to let the little princesses work things out for themselves.

The kitchen was large and airy, with new marble countertops and Brazilian cherry cabinets. Poppy, dressed in a gauzy batik-print silk popover and skinny pants that made her legs look a million miles long, stood at the island, arranging the tray of chopped-up locally grown vegetables she'd bought at the Union Square farmer's market, her twenty-month-old, Briony, balanced on her hip. She noticed Rowan pouring the wine. "The kids driving you to drink, huh?"

"I've never really understood the whole princess thing," Rowan said, recorking the bottle.

"Of course *you* don't," Rowan's mother, Leona, said good-naturedly, smiling at her daughter from across the kitchen. "This one was all about climbing the highest trees in our backyard when she was Skylar's age. And sometimes falling out of them."

Aunt Penelope paused from making a plate of food for her husband, Mason, the CEO of Saybrook's, and laughed. "You could climb higher than most of the boys, Rowan. I still remember when you beat your brother at the ropes course; he sulked for days."

Corinne, who had been leaning against the counter, sidled over to Rowan and eyed the wine. "Can you pour me a glass? I need it after the week I've had."

"I heard about Turkey," Rowan said. "Congratulations." Then she lowered her voice. "I *also* heard what happened with Aster."

Corinne's eyes narrowed to slits. "Yeah, well. I guess we shouldn't be surprised." She peered around the room, probably searching for her sister, who'd been here a few moments ago but was now absent. "She's probably passed out in Poppy's bed right now," she spat angrily.

"Don't worry—I'll make sure she's on time to the wedding," Evan said, taking a break from directing the housekeeper's cleanup efforts. She hated messes, especially kid messes. "Believe me when I say I've dealt with worse."

"Worse than the Saybrooks?" muttered Natasha from her perch near the pantry.

"Natasha!" Natasha's mother, Aunt Candace, snapped from the corner, where she was helping Poppy with the hors d'oeuvres.

Rowan glanced at Natasha cautiously. Not so long ago, she and Natasha had been so close. Rowan was nearly ten years older than Natasha, but she'd happily played bit parts in Natasha's one-act plays and cheered when Natasha put on karaoke concerts on the back porch at Meriweather. But after Natasha disinherited herself from the family—never explaining why—she treated Rowan and the others like irritating pedestrians taking up the whole sidewalk on Fifth Avenue.

Rowan knew her cousins were wary of Natasha too. Except Poppy, who'd begun to mend fences with Natasha a few years ago, after Poppy's parents died. But perhaps that was because Aunt Candace and Uncle Patrick had served as Poppy's surrogate family after the plane crash, smothering her, James, and their girls with love, help, and baked goods for months.

Luckily everyone ignored Natasha's comment, even the perfectly groomed moms Poppy knew from Episcopal, where Skylar attended preschool. To Rowan, those poised Manhattan mothers with their matching Bugaboo strollers were a different species. They compared notes on organic cloth diaper vendors, bragged about sleep training, and rated their friends' live-in nannies. But as judgmental as they were of one another, they seemed to judge nonmothers most of all. "Jealousy masked by superiority," Poppy always said. "They envy your free time, so they pretend you're selfish for not having kids to feel better about playing patty-cake all day long."

And that was the beauty of Poppy. She had the Bugaboo stroller and made her own organic baby food, but she'd never behaved as though motherhood was a special, exclusive club.

"What's going on, ladies?" Poppy's husband, James, appeared in the doorway, dressed in a vintage T-shirt and well-cut jeans that, when he raised his arms, revealed just a half inch of his Brooks Brothers boxers. He swept across the room and pulled Poppy into a hug.

Poppy wriggled away and turned toward the fridge. "Did you get the hummus from Zabar's?" she asked briskly. "I can't find it anywhere."

"Right here." James reached in and produced a container.

"Perfect." Poppy grabbed it from him and placed it on the table, next to the veggies.

"Thanks, James," Rowan called out, when Poppy didn't.

James gave the moms an exaggerated bow and an irresistible grin. "Just doing my job." Then he grabbed his wife once more and kissed

her cheek. Poppy squirmed away again, and James disappeared to the
den. A whistle bleated from the flat-screen TV. James, Mason, and
a few other fathers were back there watching the Djokovic-Federer
French Open match.

A mother named Starla, her infant Baby-Björned to her torso,
sighed. "Poppy, he's such a doll."

"How do you keep other women away?" another woman named
Amelia teased.

"Oh, he wears an ankle bracelet so I can keep track of him,"
Poppy said absently.

"Poppy has it all," said Amelia, a little unkindly. "And we all kind
of hate her." She tapped a manicured nail against the window. A biathlon was taking place in Central Park, and hundreds of runners
thundered past toward the finish line. "Do you know what Beth-
any said when we came in?" she murmured, changing the subject.
" 'Mommy, can I be in the bisexual next year?' I was like, 'Don't you
mean *biathlon*?' But she said, 'No, I want to be in the bisexual!' "

Poppy smirked. "Skylar said 'douche bag' to the doorman."

Darcy, a blond mother, shifted her weight. She had Pilates-perfect
balance even in her five-inch heels. "My daughter's favorite word is
prick." Then she looked at Rowan. "What about yours?"

"Oh, um—"

Before Rowan could answer, Poppy clutched her arm. "Rowan is
the best aunt in the world," she said in a loud voice.

"Thanks," Natasha said sardonically.

"*Tied* for best aunt," Poppy corrected herself with a smile, squeezing Rowan tighter. "*And* she's Saybrook's senior counsel. She was
first in her class at Columbia Law."

Rowan suddenly felt too tall and too visible, all elbows and angles.
Poppy meant well, but boasting about what Rowan *was* seemed to
highlight what she *wasn't*: a mother.

Fumbling to change the topic, Rowan turned toward Natasha.
"So . . . how's the studio?" she asked. After Natasha decided she

no longer wanted to be a Saybrook, she'd moved to Brooklyn and reinvented herself, running a yoga studio for the borough's bourgeoisie.

"It's great, thanks," Natasha said, lowering her long lashes. She was darker than the other Saybrook girls, with olive skin, sleek, dark hair, and almond-shaped eyes. "How are things going with . . . Charlie, is it?"

Aunt Penelope leaned on the cane she'd used ever since her skiing accident. Rowan's mother set down her water glass. "Are you seeing someone, Ro?"

"Oh, we're just friends," Rowan said quickly.

Aunt Candace and Aunt Penelope exchanged a glance, as if to say, *Oh, no. What's wrong with* this *one?*

Rowan's skin prickled, and sensing more questions on the way, she excused herself, darting into the hall. She hurried past the line of Warhols, Picassos, and an Annie Leibovitz portrait of Poppy's parents, her mom in a long, breezy dress, her strapping, tanned father in jeans and a polo shirt, in front of a ramshackle red barn. They'd always been Rowan's favorite aunt and uncle. In middle school she'd spent several summers on their farm, shearing the sheep with Poppy and exploring the cavernous attic in their refurbished farmhouse. Uncle Lawrence hadn't gone into the family business, but he had several old photo albums of the family from back before Papa Alfred found the Corona Diamond. Rowan and Poppy used to marvel at snapshots of Edith without her now-ubiquitous fur.

When she reached the bathroom, Rowan slipped inside and slammed the door hard. A little wooden plaque hanging from the doorknob rattled. "Go Away," it read. Rowan's thoughts exactly.

Rowan stared at her reflection in the mirror. She had an oval face, bow-shaped lips, a long forehead, a sloping nose, and the signature Saybrook blue eyes. Her tall frame was lithe and toned from long runs and hours on the tennis court. She knew she was pretty; plenty of people said so. And she was as successful as Poppy said—senior counsel at Saybrook's just five years out of law school, and she sat on several review boards and charities. She loved her family, and she adored her two dogs, Jackson and Bert. But she was nearly thirty-three, and still on her own.

It was, of course, the same conundrum she'd pondered for years. Thanks to her two older brothers, who now lived across the country and overseas, Rowan had no trouble with men. Growing up, she was always up for a game of hockey or freeze tag at the end of their cul-de-sac in Chappaqua, and she beat up on Michael and Palmer as much as they beat up on her. As she got older, she and some of her cute guy friends did more than just play touch football. Girls in her class talked about only having sex when they were in love, but Rowan thought that was just about as naive as believing that putting on a satin gown made you Cinderella.

Of course, in time those were the girls who got steady boyfriends, while Rowan had just acquired a string of make-out buddies. She tried to change her ways, copying what she saw in the paired-up girls she knew, but becoming a softer, needier, whinier version of herself just didn't work. And so she settled into the role of the quintessential guy's girl. The one who'd go to a strip club on a lark. The one who'd match you shot for shot. The girl who didn't give a shit about getting mani-pedis with her girlfriends, who didn't care if porn was on, who almost seemed like she didn't need a guy.

It didn't mean Rowan didn't want what those other girls had. But now, she felt too old to change who she was—nor should she have to. Her parents didn't give Rowan a hard time about being single. Her mother, Leona, had been an essayist in her pre-Saybrook life, exploring open marriages and same-sex rights—much to Edith's embarrassment. Her father, Robert, treated Rowan the same as his sons, pushing her to be ambitious and successful over everything else. And her brothers always told her not to settle. It was Poppy who eagerly shoved eligible guy after eligible guy Rowan's way. Though they were nice and cool and Rowan had remained friends with quite a few of them, none of them exactly . . . *clicked*. Rowan had felt true love once before, and she wouldn't settle until she felt it again.

There was a knock on the bathroom door, and Rowan looked up.

"Rowan?" someone whispered. "You in there?"

Rowan opened the door a crack and saw James's curly brown hair, light eyes, and slightly crooked smile. "No fair that you get to hide out in here," he said mock-sternly.

James's skin smelled like peppermint soap. A fleck of glitter from one of the princess's wands was stuck to his cheek. Rowan refrained from brushing it away.

"I just needed a minute," she told him.

He glanced down the hall. "Princesses getting you down? The grown-up ones, I mean?"

Rowan stared at the monogrammed towels hanging on the silver bar across the room. One bore Poppy's initials, the other, James's. "You could say that."

"Do you want me to smuggle you out of here, Saybrook?" James asked, his gaze shifting conspiratorially. "We can escape out the balcony. Use the gargoyles as a ladder."

She pictured the two of them scaling the Dakota, dropping to Central Park West, and falling in with the biathletes. They'd laugh together, like in the old days.

James slipped into the bathroom. "Is there room for another?" he asked, shutting the door. "I'm princessed out too."

Rowan sniffed. "Please. All the men are just watching tennis."

James leaned against the sink and made a face. "Have you ever hung out with Mason for any length of time? He's the biggest princess of them all." Then he picked up a remote sitting on the edge of the soaking tub and pointed it at a small TV in the corner. "And anyway, we get the match in here too."

The French Open appeared on the screen. Rowan remained planted in the middle of the bathroom, her arms wrapped tightly around her torso. Though she saw James regularly, she couldn't remember the last time they'd been alone together.

They'd become friends at Columbia, when they lived on the same floor freshman year. Rowan's father had offered to buy her an apartment, but she liked the idea of being like everyone else, even opting for a double instead of a single. She'd spent most of the time in James's dorm room, playing video games and chatting about the people in their building, especially the girls. They'd stayed on for graduate programs at Columbia, James for business school—he had always wanted to be an entrepreneur—and Rowan for law. They had a standing Monday-night dinner date at a Mexican dive on Broadway with spicy guacamole. On weekends, they played pool at SoHa, the dingy bar on Amsterdam whose bartenders made potent Long Island iced teas. As usual, Rowan had fallen into her role as the perennial guy's girl, James's wingwoman. Plenty of times Rowan had consoled James's date at the end of the evening when she caught James making out with someone new in the unisex bathroom.

"You're such a dog," Rowan had always teased him over brunch on Sunday mornings. To which James just shrugged and bared his teeth. "Woof."

Now James stared at the mini TV over the tub. It was the third set, the match tied. "Okay, Saybrook," he began, pointing at the screen. "Djokovic or Federer?"

Rowan swallowed hard. It was an old game they used to play—one of them would name two people, and the other would have to pick which they'd have sex with. Sometimes it had been a geek showdown, like Sylvia Plath versus Emily Dickinson, or Shakespeare's Iago versus Oberon from *A Midsummer Night's Dream*. Other times they named people in their lives—Veronica, the busty registrar, or Colette, the waifish French exchange student. More often than not, James would actually go home with the hot exchange student.

Sometimes Rowan thought James had forgotten their old friendship entirely, now that he was married to Poppy. Although maybe he didn't want to remember part of it—especially the part about all the girls. James had reformed for Poppy. Poppy was much too beautiful and perfect for anything less. Any guy would fall in line for her.

Rowan looked at the players on either side of the court. "Federer for sure," she decided. "Djokovic is too cocky."

"Tall, dark, and European. I like it." James tilted his head down, his expression mock-serious. "So tell me: Who do you have on tap these days?"

Rowan pretended to rub out an invisible water spot from the sink. "I plead the Fifth. I've already been asked that question a few too many times today."

James sank down to the edge of the tub. "You have to give people a chance, Saybrook. Actually go out with someone more than once."

"I go out," Rowan insisted.

"I know you do." James laid his hands in his lap. "But who have you actually *liked*?"

Rowan stared intensely at the TV screen, trying to recall the last time she'd gone out with someone consistently. Someone she'd actually felt something for.

"See? You can't even remember." James playfully nudged her calf with his toe. "They can't all be like *me*, you know," he said, spreading his arms wide and giving her a boyish grin.

Rowan froze. He was kidding, wasn't he? Her pulse thudded in her palms.

Five years ago, when they were at SoHa just before finals, James had taken a deep breath and looked at Rowan over his beer. "So, Saybrook. I was thinking about checking out this Meriweather place you always talk about."

"Oh?" Rowan cocked her head. "Do you want to visit? There's room."

"Actually . . ." James fiddled with the straw in his drink. "I rented a place on Martha's Vineyard. For the whole summer."

"What?" Rowan blurted.

James's gaze bored into her. "Yeah, I was thinking it would be nice to hang out together outside the library or dive bars."

His eyes and smile were so damn dangerous, instantly sucking her in. But Rowan *knew* what he was like. She'd seen him work his magic on other women. And yet when he looked at her, she was just as weak as all the rest. That night, when she went home, she fantasized about the shape their summer would take. The meals they'd cook, the things they'd talk about, the family members he'd meet. And then . . . what? After hours and hours of talking and laughing, in that beautiful setting, with the stars twinkling all around them, what would happen next?

She knew it wasn't wise to think that way. She was being naive, one of the many pitiful girls who fell under James's spell. She was afraid of her feelings for James, mostly because of how strong they were. But there was such a big *if.* If James felt the same way, well . . .

She'd thrown him a party the night he arrived. All the cousins, even Natasha, lined up in the foyer to greet him. Poppy strode up first and extended her hand. "Rowan has told me so much about you," she gushed. "I'm her cousin, Poppy Saybrook."

"Another Saybrook," James had said, smiling that wolfish smile, his eyes skimming her up and down. It was the same thing he'd done to countless girls in Rowan's presence, but something inside Rowan still lurched. He wasn't supposed to do that *here*, to her cousin.

That night James gave a toast on the patio, thanking everyone for giving him such a warm welcome, especially his "best friend, Saybrook." Every time she turned around, he was chatting with Poppy, and soon she realized that he wasn't just being polite. Rowan had to duck behind the bar that had been set up on the edge of the patio to collect herself, feeling that infrequent hot sting behind her eyes. She felt so blindsided. And stupid. To make matters worse, she felt someone staring at her from the other side of the yard. It was Natasha. Her gaze slid from Rowan to Poppy and James—as if she had it all figured out.

Knowing she was going to lose it, Rowan had retreated to a bedroom, sat down on the bed, and stared at the diamond-printed wallpaper, seeking refuge—much as she was now, in James and Poppy's powder room.

Blinking the memory away, Rowan turned to James and *ts*ked. "If you keep saying things like that, I'm going to have to hide from you too." She opened the door. "C'mon. We'd better join the royal court."

The party had moved into the dining room. Streamers and glittering tiaras surrounded the tiered buttercream-frosting cake on the table. Corinne's mother was placing three little candles in the center, and all the young mothers stood around, oohing and ahhing. Aster had finally appeared, looking tired but still managing a smile. Rowan looked around for Poppy and found her standing in the corner with Mason. Mason's face was red, and Poppy's mouth drawn. Rowan had never seen them argue—since Poppy's parents died, Mason had taken her under his wing, much as Candace and Patrick had, treating her like a third daughter.

They were talking so heatedly that Poppy seemed oblivious to the cake lighting. More important, she didn't seem to notice that Rowan had just come out of the bathroom with her husband.

But someone else had noticed. Natasha stood at the end of the hall, her head cocked, her gaze squarely on Rowan's face. She raised one eyebrow, just as knowingly as she had that night Poppy and James met. Rowan looked away, watching James kiss his beaming daughter on the cheek.

They can't all be like me. Little did James know how true that was. She'd known James for nearly fifteen years, and she'd loved him every minute.

4

A few days later, Aster sat down in her parents' Upper East Side
town house for the dreaded but obligatory weekly Wednesday
dinner. The enormous table in the baroque-style dining room was
set for twelve, with silver candlesticks in the center. The high-
backed mahogany chairs were so huge and heavy they could have
served as kings' thrones. The blocky mahogany china cabinet, an
heirloom from the eighteenth century, took up a whole wall and
bore priceless Sèvres plates, artifacts from her parents' world trav-
els, and a silver tea set that had once belonged to a queen. There
were lots of portraits of dead relatives, landscapes showing a fox-
hunt on the moors, and a huge painting of Edith and Alfred with
their young children, standing on their staircase. On the top step
were Mason and Lawrence, Poppy's dad, both with slicked hair;
then Rowan's father, Robert, and Natasha's mother, Candace, at
the bottom. Candace, probably no more than four at the time,
struggled to hold Grace, a fat, grumpy-looking baby. Years ago
Aster had loved this room, and made up stories about the people in
the paintings and the previous owners of the artifacts. She would
tell tales to her father over breakfast in the morning. He always listened attentively, and laughed at all the right parts. "Maybe you'll
be an author someday, Aster," he'd tell her.

"Thank you so much, Esme," Penelope Saybrook murmured as
their private chef placed a roasted chicken in a red wine reduction

next to a platter of grilled asparagus and Brussels sprouts. As usual,
Aster's mother stood, rearranged some of the garnishes, and added a
dash of pepper to the bird. You don't get to pretend you cooked it just
by playing with the pepper, Aster thought.

"Yes, thank you, Esme," Corinne echoed. Dixon, who was sitting
next to her, nodded his thanks, and Poppy, who was next to Mason,
smiled sweetly. Ever since Poppy's parents died, she'd had a standing invitation to dinner. Sometimes Aster wondered if Poppy's recent
closeness to Mason stemmed from her father's survivor's guilt; he
was supposed to have been on the plane that killed Poppy's parents.
Usually Poppy brought James and the kids, but today she had come
alone. She'd brought with her a homemade strawberry pie, using the
berries she'd picked the previous week during a visit to her family's
rural estate in western Massachusetts. Only Poppy, who probably
worked twenty-three hours a day, could also find time to bake a pie.

"You rock, Esme!" Aster yelled enthusiastically, adjusting the
strap of her jacquard bustier top. Her father eyed it disapprovingly.
Whatever—everyone and her grandmother were wearing bustiers
these days. Well, except Corinne, who sort of looked like a grandmother in a Wedgwood-blue sleeveless silk dress and Mikimoto
pearl earrings.

Aster eyed her sister across the table. Corinne hadn't even glanced
in her direction yet, and Aster certainly wasn't going to make the first
move. Her gaze then wandered to another portrait on the wall, this one
taken about ten years ago. It was of herself, Corinne, Poppy, and all
the other first cousins, including Rowan's brothers and Aunt Grace's
young sons, Winston and Sullivan, who lived in California with the
now-divorced Grace. Natasha was there too, front and center.

Just looking at Natasha irritated Aster. The girl had acted like
their best friend for years, hogging the spotlight, begging them to
come to every school play she was in, even once dragging Aster to
accompany her to an open-call Broadway audition when they were
both fourteen years old. And then, suddenly, she just . . . didn't need

them anymore. Aster still couldn't believe Natasha was in Corinne's wedding; Poppy had somehow talked her into it.

"Is that *blood*?" Aster's grandmother Edith asked, pulling her mink stole tighter around her shoulders—she never took it off, even though it was uncharacteristically warm for May. Her white hair was slicked back from her face, showing off her good bone structure, the high cheekbones and tiny pert nose that Aster had thankfully inherited. Jessica, the personal-assistant-slash-nurse who accompanied Edith everywhere, leaned over to examine the plate.

Mason, who was thinner now that he was working out with a personal trainer, inspected it as well. "No, Mother," he said wearily.

"It's just the sauce," Poppy added helpfully, taking a bite. "See? Yum."

Edith considered it for a moment, probably only because Poppy was her favorite granddaughter and she hated to disappoint her. Finally she pushed the plate away. "Well, this is too undercooked for my liking." She looked accusingly at Penelope, just as she always did when she found fault in something in her daughter-in-law's house. Penelope snapped for the chef, who rushed to take Edith's plate away. "I'll have a soft-boiled egg in an egg cup, please," Edith brayed loudly.

After the offending chicken was gone, Corinne cleared her throat. "So I checked the registry, and a *lot* of people have donated to City Harvest."

"That's wonderful, dear," Edith said approvingly.

Aster took a fresh roll and bit into it. It was warm and flaky from the oven, and tasted like butter. "I can't believe you guys didn't register for gifts," she said between mouthfuls.

Corinne moved her chin to the right, her gaze on her mother. "We've raised almost ten thousand dollars," she went on, as though Aster hadn't spoken. "And I'm sure we'll get much more."

"You could've gotten some amazing stuff from Bendel's, Barneys, ABC Carpet . . . ," Aster continued.

Edith wiped her mouth. "It's very respectable to ask for charitable donations, Aster."

Aster wrinkled her nose, wondering if she'd been switched at birth. When she was little, she used to have fantasies that her real parents were actual rock stars. Like Keith Richards—Aster had seen an amazing photo shoot of his family in St. Barts in last month's *Vanity Fair*. They knew how to party.

She peered questioningly at Dixon across the table. Corinne's fiancé was wearing a boring gray business suit, but Aster had always liked Dixon—he had a cute Texas accent, he and his friends were usually game for late nights, and he could turn anything into a drinking game. Surely he'd want presents. But he just shrugged. "I don't care what we do, as long as we still go on the honeymoon."

"Where are you going again?" Aster asked.

Dixon brightened. "Safari. But also Cape Town. I've already got tickets to a football match."

"That sounds amazing," Poppy said warmly.

Corinne's fork scraped noisily across her plate. "I'm going to meet with my contacts in Cape Town and visit a few of the mines," she added, still to her parents. She must have caught Aster rolling her eyes, because she sighed loudly. *"What?"*

Aster blinked, surprised at Corinne's break in demeanor. "Are you seriously going to work on your honeymoon?"

"My thoughts exactly," Dixon said, raising a glass.

Corinne shot him a look. "Don't *agree* with her!"

"Girls!" Mason blustered. He looked at Poppy helplessly. "I apologize on my family's behalf."

"Oh, stop," Poppy said, swatting him playfully. Aster felt the teensiest stab of jealousy. Poppy had always been close with Aster's family, but ever since her parents' death, she had become Mason's favorite—a spot Aster used to hold, once upon a time.

Then Aster's cell, which sat on the table next to her, chirped to

indicate a new text from Clarissa: *We're heading to PH-D after this.*
Aster gritted her teeth. They were all at dinner at Catch without her,
probably drinking her favorite lavender-and-yuzu martini. *Be there
in an hour,* Aster furiously typed back.

It's a theme night, Clarissa replied. Trashy housewives. *I'm wearing
my leather minidress.*

Aster caught her breath in excitement. She *lived* for theme nights.
She was so excited that she didn't even call Clarissa out on the fact
that the dress in question was actually hers; Clarissa had just never
returned it. *Awesome,* she wrote back. *Too cray-cray if i stuff my bikini
top?*

"Aster," her mother said sharply. "Don't text at dinner."

"One sec." The cell chimed again. *No, go for it!* Clarissa wrote
back.

*I'm thinking Missoni bikini, white cutoff jeans, and wedges. And
maybe hair extensions?* Aster typed quickly.

"Aster." Mason slammed his hand down on the table. When Aster
looked up, her father's eyes were steely and cold. "Put. The phone.
Away."

Aster slipped the phone back into her bag. Get over yourselves,
she wanted to say. All of you.

When Aster was a little girl, everyone told her that she was lucky
to be an heiress, and that her life would be extraordinary. She had
a floor-through playroom, a rotating staff of nannies, and private
planes. But being an heiress also meant fitting a specific mold—one
to which Aster could never quite adhere.

When she was eight years old and their second cousin Madeleine
got married, Aster had been the flower girl in the wedding. She would
never forget how she had complained to her mother that her white
patent leather shoes were hurting. "Can't I wear something else?"
she'd begged. "No, Aster," her mother had hissed, her lips pursed in
frustration. "No one ever said this would be easy." "No one ever said
what would be easy?" Aster had asked—but Penelope was already

sweeping out of the room, rolling her eyes. "Being an heiress, silly," Corinne answered from the corner, doing pirouettes in the narrow white shoes that didn't seem to bother her at all.

It had been Mason who came to Aster's rescue at that wedding, pulling her into his lap at the dinner and feeding her an extra slice of cake when Penelope wasn't looking. "What your mother means, Aster," he tried to explain, "is that being an heiress isn't always easy. There are good parts, and there are bad parts."

"Do I have to be an heiress?" Aster had asked.

"Oh, sweetie," Mason had said, and leaned forward to kiss her forehead. "You're a Saybrook."

There are good parts, and there are bad parts. Aster just hadn't realized that the bad parts would often outweigh the good—and that her once-beloved father would turn out to be the worst of it. She met his eyes across the table and felt herself flush with anger. He had no right to be angry with her, not after what he had done to this family. Not after all these years of Aster keeping his secret.

"Aster, I need to speak to you," Mason said, staring at her as if he'd been witness to her thoughts. "Let's go to my office," he added, and stood up.

Aster squinted at her mom, then Corinne, Dixon, and Edith, but all four of them looked away. The moment felt fraught, as though everyone was in on a joke Aster didn't get. Only Poppy was looking at her encouragingly, nodding in the direction of the office.

Aster got up from her chair, suddenly shaky in her strappy leather pumps. Esme appeared from the kitchen to whisk away her uneaten food. The classical music Aster's family always played during dinner faded as she followed her father from the dining room to his office at the back of the town house.

The room smelled like cigar smoke and cedar, just the way Aster remembered it. She hadn't set foot here in years, not since she and her father fell out. There was the same bearskin rug on the floor, the same cutting tools and old loupes on the desk, and the various vintage rifles from the Civil War through World War II mounted on the walls. On one shelf was a line of old photographs, including one of Papa Alfred in his World War II uniform. Standing next to him was Harold Browne, a friend he'd made during his time there. Next to that was a picture Aster hadn't noticed before, of Mason and other Saybrook's execs on a golf outing. Steven Barnett stood off to the side, his handsome smile broad.

Aster looked away. It seemed strange that her father would have a picture of Steven in his office after everything that had happened. But then, her father always did have a way of compartmentalizing things.

Lined up on another wall were the taxidermied animal heads from his favorite hunts. An enormous elk, a long-horned ram, even an African elephant, with fanned ears and an extended trunk. There were glass marbles where its eyes had been. As a child, Aster had been afraid of that elephant; but Mason had brought her into his study and asked her to look at it. "It's like the elephant at the Museum of Natural History," he said, holding her up to face it. "What if I let you name him?"

"His name is Dumbo," Aster announced. "But I still don't like him." To Aster, Dumbo was completely different from the elephants at the museum—or the cartoon. The elephant was dead because her father had killed it.

Aster glared at Mason, then plopped onto the overstuffed leather couch. "So what's up?" she asked stonily.

Mason lit a cigar. "I'm ending your allowance."

"Excuse me?" Aster barked a laugh.

"I guess you haven't seen this." He set the cigar in an ashtray and tilted his computer screen toward her. The Blessed and the Cursed was front and center. Aster almost burst out laughing—she would never have guessed her dad read the gossip site.

Then she saw the pictures. The first shot was of Poppy ushering her from Corinne's dress fitting, her makeup smeared and her hair a tangled mess. The second was of her dancing at Badawi later that night. The strap of her dress had fallen off her shoulder, showing what little cleavage she had as she stared into the camera vacantly. She looked as wasted as she'd felt.

"Aster Saybrook Is Out of Control," read the headline.

Aster felt the blood drain from her face. This wasn't the first time that she'd been featured on that stupid website, but this was the first time her father had called her out on it. She felt for her phone. Had Clarissa sent the Badawi picture? Backstabbing bitch.

Her father sighed. "You ruined your sister's fitting. For her *wedding* dress. And this business at the club—come on, Aster. You're better than that."

Aster blinked hard. "Better than what?"

Her father just stared at her. She searched his face for a sign of her dad there, of the man who used to carry her on his shoulders and tell her that everything would be okay. All she saw reflected there was disappointment.

"Deanna can handle it. She can get those photos taken down," Aster tried next. Deanna was the family's publicist; she could make almost anything go away.

Mason shook his head. "I don't want Deanna to *handle* it—that's not the point. You need to learn some responsibility." He had another puff. "It's time you got a job. I've talked to HR, and they're finding an assistant position for you in one of the departments."

"A *job?*" Aster sputtered.

Mason stared at her. "You start next Wednesday."

"As in a week from now?" Aster shrieked. "You had no right to do that!"

"I have every right. I'm the one who pays your bills." Mason stood, the discussion clearly over. "You've got to grow up sometime, Aster. And that time is now."

Spots formed in front of Aster's eyes. "What department am I working in?" she asked. *Not Corinne's; please don't let me be working for Corinne.*

"I don't know—HR is handling it," Mason replied. "And frankly, I don't care."

Aster headed toward the door, feeling tears in her eyes. She turned back so that her father could see her crying, but he just stared at her stonily. That trick didn't work on him anymore.

She envisioned going to work at Saybrook's, getting bossed around and gossiped about because of her last name. For a moment, Aster thought of revealing her father for the liar he really was— running back into that dining room and announcing what she'd discovered about him five years ago. But then the anger deflated from her like air leaving a balloon. Telling the truth about Mason wouldn't solve anything.

"Fine," she snapped. "I'll take your stupid job. But I'm warning you, I'm going to suck at it."

She walked out of the office, down the hall, and to the front door without even saying good-bye to anyone. Why should she? They were probably snickering about her in the dining room. Or doing the proper-person alternative to snickering, whatever the hell that was. Tut-tutting. Tongue-clucking. God, she hated all of them.

A job. Jesus. She hailed a cab and gave the driver her downtown address, then leaned against the window and closed her eyes. For the first time, it felt as if the family curse was real. Because starting next week, Aster would be living it.

5

The following evening after work, Corinne got out of a cab on the corner of West Tenth and Bleecker in the West Village. Spring had sprung all over the city. The trees were fragrant with new cherry blossoms, everyone had pots of flowers on their stoops, an old Gwen Stefani song, which always reminded her of cruising around Meriweather in the vintage Jaguar convertible they kept there, wafted out of an open window a few stories above. As she stepped daintily onto the curb, careful not to scuff her python and suede pumps, she tucked her phone between her ear and shoulder.

"I don't think Aster knows what hit her," Poppy said on the other end of the line. "I mean, Corinne, she is really freaking out."

Corinne waited at the curb for the light to change, absently watching the crowd across the street. A couple of guys in cutoff jean shorts chatted with a woman in a neon maxidress, pretending not to notice a famous actor who lived nearby. People in the Village looked so different from everyone on the Upper East Side, and she always felt like a tourist here. Her gaze focused on an old lady in a bright pink trench coat on the corner. She was wheeling a small portable cart full of groceries from D'Agostino's, a toothy smile on her face.

She sighed into the phone. "I think Aster will be okay," she told Poppy, though she wasn't sure if she believed that. She had an unexpected wave of sympathy for Aster: she'd wanted her parents to stop enabling Aster's ridiculous life, but now that they had, her father's ultimatum seemed so dramatic. Corinne was hurt too that Aster had called Poppy instead of her. Then again, her sister still hadn't apologized for wrecking the dress fitting—or for the Blessed and the Cursed post about the behind-the-scenes drama in her perfect wedding. Corinne had had to give a short, fluffy interview to *New York* magazine's online editor this morning, saying how *helpful* her cousins and sister had been in the planning process. "My sister really knows how to do a party," she'd tittered. Problem solved, without Aster's help. As usual.

But that was how Corinne sailed through life; the waters were choppy, but she was steady, never veering off course. She wondered sometimes how she and Aster had wound up so different, how much was a reaction to the other and how much was built into their DNA. From the time she was a kid, Corinne had been goal-oriented—to make a best friend, to get an A, to meet the right kind of people. The only time she'd strayed was at boarding school, when a group of older girls in her hall had enlisted her to help steal a bronze horse statue from the headmaster's desk. It was something students attempted every year, and even though getting caught could mean disciplinary action, those girls were the right ones to get in with. In fact, when her parents had moved her in, her mother had pointed out some of these very girls, saying Corinne should introduce herself. But when she'd gotten caught, her mother also told her how disappointed she was in Corinne. "I expect more from you," she'd said. Corinne still carried that memory in her mind, even now. It was a small thing, but it encapsulated so much more. Sometimes it was hard to make the right choices especially when everyone was watching.

Now Corinne spied the awning she was looking for, a restaurant called Coxswain. "Hey, Poppy, I have to go," she said, picking up the pace. "I'll talk to you later, okay?"

"Sure," Poppy answered. "But listen, maybe you should talk to Aster. She probably needs you right now."

"Talk to you soon." Corinne dropped her phone back into her

bag and walked past the potted plants and wrought-iron figurines on Coxswain's doorstep. The inside of the restaurant was dark and cool, the vibe like someone's living room. The chairs didn't match, nor did the tables—some were round tile-tops, others were wood, and the bar was made of chipped marble. Hundreds of oars made a latticework on the ceiling. Every table and stool was full, but then she spied Dixon waiting at the bar with a beer. His suit jacket was off, his tie was loosened, and his floppy brown hair had been pushed off his head. Sitting next to him was another oxford-shirted Wall Street type, whom she recognized as Avery Dunbar, one of Dixon's fraternity brothers.

She sighed inwardly. It seemed like they *always* had company when they went out.

When Dixon saw Corinne, he gave her an enthusiastic wave, his gray-green eyes crinkling at the corners. He leaped off his stool and kissed her cheek, then gestured to Avery. "He was in the neighborhood. *Loves* this place. It's cool, right?"

"Sure," Corinne said; she was too tired to care. She'd called Dixon out on his dinner-crashing friends before, but he'd just seemed confused. "The more the merrier, right?" he'd said once. And then, "Wait, that bothers you?"

She looked at Avery. "So you suggested this place?"

"Actually, Evan Pierce told me to try it," Dixon said, signaling to the bartender. A chardonnay for Corinne appeared in seconds. "*Gourmet* says it's a restaurant to watch. Or maybe it was *Bon Appétit*. One of those."

Avery, who had a square jaw and a thick platinum wedding ring on his fat finger, laughed. "Look at you. Quoting *Gourmet* magazine."

A waitress in a gingham shirt and tight dark-wash jeans appeared and told the trio their table was ready. Dixon laid down a few twenties— Corinne wondered how long they'd been drinking—and both of the men loped behind the girl to a corner seat. She sipped her wine as she followed behind, listening to them chatter about a major IPO that had happened during trading that day, and then about whether they'd get a house in the Hamptons in August. As they slid into the chairs at a small, round corner table, Dixon smiled. "Could be fun—nice to get away for the weekends? After the honeymoon, I mean?"

Corinne shrugged. "I still prefer the Vineyard."

Then she looked up at Dixon, who had just been given another beer. "Wait. Why were you talking to Evan Pierce about restaurants?" Corinne had handled every wedding detail thus far, aside from Dixon's upcoming bachelor's golf weekend.

Dixon cut his gaze to the right. "Oh. Uh, I had a question about the accommodations for the guests. For my parents, I mean."

Corinne squinted at him. "I had a long conversation with them about that last week." She'd invited Herman and Gwendolyn Shackelford to stay at the estate in Meriweather, where the rehearsal dinner and wedding would take place, but they'd decided to stay in Edgartown instead.

Dixon tugged at his collar. He looked like he was about to say something, but he was interrupted by the return of the waitress, this time bearing three plates of food. "Lobster soufflé," she said as she set them down.

Corinne frowned. "We didn't order these." The waitress smiled mysteriously. Corinne peered at Dixon and Avery. "You guys ordered without me?"

Avery just shrugged. Dixon's throat bobbed. "Try it."

Corinne shrugged and took a bite. The consistency was creamy, and the lobster was fresh and perfectly seasoned. It reminded her immediately of something she'd eaten in Meriweather. "Amazing," she murmured, scooping up another bite.

Dixon glanced at Avery, and his friend gave him a knowing nod. "I'm happy to hear you say that, because the chef is going to do our wedding."

Corinne set down her fork. "But we already have a caterer. The chef from L'Auberge." Everyone wanted the new French chef on the

Manhattan culinary scene. His three unmarked restaurants around the city had already been awarded Michelin stars. Evan had secured him more than a year ago.

Dixon cleared his throat. "Don't freak out, okay? But there was an issue. That's why Evan called me today. He had to back out."

"Back out?" Corinne's heart sped up. "But our wedding is in less than a month!" Her fingers sought out the hem of the tablecloth. Slowly she began to pick at a loose thread.

"I know," Dixon said calmly. "Evan knows too. Like I said, she sent us here. Everyone who's been to this place loves it. And get this: the chef used to *work* on the Vineyard—he knows the local fishermen, he knows all the good spots for produce, *and* he's free the weekend of the wedding. He and I have already talked, and everything's set as long as you're cool with it too."

"Seems like a decent guy," Avery piped up, and then had the good sense to stand and excuse himself for the bathroom.

Once Avery was gone, Dixon peered into Corinne's eyes. "Problem solved, right? *Right?*"

"I don't know," Corinne said, feeling scattered.

"Well, *I* do. This is going to be great." Dixon handed Corinne her fork. "Now, take another bite of soufflé."

Corinne did as she was told, chewing it thoroughly before swallowing. "You and Evan have known about this *all day*, and you didn't tell me?" she asked, hurt. She looked at Avery's empty chair. Even he'd known. She imagined Dixon prepping him beforehand. *Man, she's going to panic. Help me talk her down.*

"Hey." Dixon reached out and caught Corinne's hand. She looked down. Unconsciously, she'd unraveled a whole line of the tablecloth's stitching; a long red thread dangled to the floor. "Evan didn't want to worry you," Dixon said gently. "And neither did I. You've been working so hard. And really, the chef here is going to kill it—in fact, there he is now." His gaze moved past Corinne, toward the back of the restaurant. "He wanted to introduce himself."

Corinne turned toward the bar and watched as a figure in chef's whites walked toward them. At first his face was in shadow, but then he walked into the light, offering them a mild smile. Corinne took in his broad frame, his chiseled face, his slender nose and deep-set eyes. He had dark, wavy hair, some stubble on his face, and the kind of smile that seemed slightly teasing, like he knew something you didn't.

Corinne's jaw dropped. She actually felt herself shrink down in her chair. It was a man she hadn't seen in years but had never forgotten. His face was less tanned, his hair longer, his body a little more toned, if that was even possible.

For a second she was transported back to that summer in Meriweather, when Dixon had broken up with her and she'd felt so lost, realizing for the first time that no matter how much she planned, no matter how *right* they were together, she couldn't force him to want her back.

She'd gone out with Poppy in town one evening, drinking too much rosé at a bar overlooking the water. When they finished a bottle, another appeared, then another, all gratis; Poppy had that effect on people. The hours went on in a blur of silly conversations with guys who stopped by to meet her cousin, a blend of laughter and inside jokes that would never be as funny again. But whenever she looked up, there was someone watching her. Will Coolidge, he finally introduced himself. But it wasn't until he was leading her under the dock, the Atlantic lapping at the sand, that she realized he had been waiting for her the whole night.

She kicked off her loafers; the sand was cool and grainy under her feet. Dizzy with wine, they leaned toward each other and kissed. It felt strange for Corinne to kiss someone new after only being with Dixon for so long. And the kiss was so *different* from Dixon's. She wanted more, but she restrained herself, breathing hard and staring at him. "I don't do things like this," she'd announced.

"Neither do I," Will said.

Corinne laughed. "You seem like *exactly* the type who does."

Will shook his head. "You don't know who I am."

"You don't know who *I* am," she challenged.

Will had stared at her. "Yes, I do. Everyone does." And then he'd kissed her again.

"Hello, Miss Saybrook."

Corinne blinked, suddenly back in the dim light of the restaurant. She unthinkingly spun her wedding ring around so that the yellow diamond faced the inside of her hand. "H-hi."

After so many years together, Corinne sometimes thought Dixon could read her mind. But when she looked across the table, he was only smiling bemusedly, oblivious to her discomfort. "You *know* each other?"

Will glanced at Corinne, then looked away sharply, angling his body more toward Dixon. "Yes. We do."

"Well, that's even better." Dixon extended his hand to Will. "Thanks so much for helping us out, man. You're all for this, right, Corinne?"

Corinne swallowed. The scar on her torso started to itch. But she couldn't just sit there, saying nothing, so finally she looked at Dixon and smiled. "I can't believe you kept this a secret."

Will gazed steadily at Corinne. "It's amazing what secrets people can keep if they want to," he said.

And then he nodded and returned to the kitchen.

6

Later that evening, Rowan fumbled with the lock to the penthouse apartment on Horatio and Greenwich Avenue she'd owned since graduating from law school. She collapsed on the cognac-colored leather couch in the living room, her head buzzing from the two Maker's on the rocks she'd had with a guy from her running team. Greg was in great shape and could run a sub-3:30 marathon, but his conversational speed was slower than her grandmother's. She'd ordered the second drink just to get through it, James's words looping through her mind all the while: *You have to give people a chance*. But she simply couldn't help comparing Greg with James and coming up short. Poppy always said that more dates increased the odds of finding someone great, but Rowan feared that more failed dates just proved that she would never find someone who measured up.

A large shape darted into the living room, claws clacking against the wood floor. "Jacks," Rowan groaned as her one-hundred-pound Bernese mountain dog, Jackson, jumped into her lap. Bert, the Chihuahua, appeared next and yapped at her feet. Rowan gently kneed Jackson back down and patted Bert's head. Both animals took off down the hall and started barking in the bedroom.

Rowan shut her eyes, knowing they were dying for a walk. She could have paid someone to do it in the evenings, but she liked going herself. Hudson River Park was so peaceful at night, and she could let them off leash. But it was almost ten, and she was too tired.

A light shone from Rowan's office, which was off the living room. The computer monitor was still on, probably from her housekeeper Bea's dusting earlier in the day. Even from her couch, Rowan could tell that the Blessed and the Cursed was on the screen. Bea swore she didn't read it, but Rowan knew better. The lure of the site was like passing a traffic accident—you couldn't *not* pause and look.

Rowan rose, walked to her office, and peered at the screen. Pictures and gossip items about her family members took up the entire page. "Aster Saybrook Is Out of Control," read the bold-print headline at the top. "This girl's life is most definitely cursed," a comment said beneath the article. "I'd bang her," stated another; two hundred and six comments followed. Below that, there was an article about Corinne's upcoming wedding: "Sink or Swim: New Coxswain Chef to Navigate Waters of Meriweather Wedding." After that was a photo of Rowan's twin brother, Michael, on his way to his dermatological practice in Seattle, and a shot of her other brother, Palmer, with his family at their estate in Italy, where Palmer headed up marketing for the Ferrari Formula 1 team. The website speculated that Rowan's brothers didn't work for Saybrook's because Papa Alfred didn't think they were smart enough, but that wasn't true—they just weren't interested in jewelry.

There was also a segment that cited new evidence in the plane crash that had killed Poppy's parents two summers before. *Bullshit.* If the experts had finally found the black box in the depths of the Atlantic, Rowan and her family would be the first to know, not this idiotic blog. And finally, at the very bottom, was a piece about Rowan herself, jogging in the park. "Ro on the Go."

She clicked on the link, enlarging the photo. Her face looked confident, and her legs were strong and supple. Whenever she saw paparazzi pictures of herself, she felt as though she were looking at someone else altogether—someone more glamorous, more together than she actually was. She closed out of the site, wishing she could turn off the public's fascination with her family with the same ease.

The doorbell rang, and the dogs barreled back into the foyer. Rowan hurriedly shushed them as she walked to the door. A familiar face appeared in the peephole. "James?"

"Hey, Saybrook." Poppy's husband offered a boyish smile when she pulled open the door. His hair was unkempt in a messy-hipster way, and his nails were bitten to the quick, something he used to do before his old band, Horse and Carrot, performed.

Rowan looked past him into the empty hall. "Where's Poppy?"

"Actually, it's just me." James shifted his weight. "I came from work—I had a late night finishing up on a launch." He was a creative director at a tech company. "You mind if I come in for a sec?"

Rowan stepped aside so he could enter. Jackson bounded up and put his paws on his shoulders. "Oh, Jackson," Rowan scolded.

"He's fine." James patted the dog's fluffy head.

Rowan walked into the living room, and James followed. He sat down on the couch and looked around. The grandfather clock in the corner ticked noisily. "Did you redecorate?"

"Two years ago," Rowan admitted.

"It's very you."

Rowan tried to see her apartment through his eyes. She had several leather pieces and distressed-metal side tables. There was a large propeller from an old Charles Lindbergh–era plane on the wall, and an antique metal plaque for a defunct brand of cigarettes hung near the window. Compared with Poppy's feminine touches in their own place, Rowan's apartment looked like the inside of a cigar bar.

She cleared her throat. "Can I get you something to drink? I have water, lemonade, beer—"

"What about Scotch?"

She held his gaze for a moment, then crouched down to the antique cabinet where she kept bottles, as though this were all completely normal. There was a half-drunk bottle of Glenfiddich; she grabbed that and two crystal tumblers. The amber liquid burned her nostrils as she poured them both a few fingers' worth.

She handed one to James. "So what's going on?" Rowan asked casually. Her heart, she realized, was pounding, though she wasn't sure quite what she was anticipating.

James cocked his head. "Can't an old friend come see his buddy?" He shifted on the couch. "It was fun hanging out at Skylar's party. I miss you."

Something inside Rowan wrenched. She raised her glass and clinked it to his. "Well. Cheers."

James slugged it back. Then he raised his head and wiped his mouth. Rowan handed him the bottle, and he poured more. A few moments of silence ticked by. "Remember that time we skipped the bill at the Plaza?" James suddenly said.

Rowan blinked at him. "That was years ago."

James shut his eyes. "I forgot my credit card. And you were like, Hey, let's ditch! I've never laughed so hard in my life."

"It was your idea, not mine," Rowan chided. A bartender, dressed in a tuxedo and tails, had dashed out after them. James and Rowan looked at each other, and each swore the other had paid. After the bartender left, cash in hand, they doubled over in laughter, imagining the headlines in the paper the next day.

"Heiress Dines and Dashes?" James said now, clearly thinking the same thing.

Rowan snorted. "Ro-Ro Has No Dinero."

"That old guy could move fast, though." James took another slug of Scotch. "Though not as fast as Jell-O Shot Alex."

Rowan groaned. "Jesus. Are you *trying* to kill me?" Alex had been in the philosophy department at Columbia and had asked Rowan to a party he was throwing. Despite the fact that he could debate the pros and cons of Foucault and Derrida, he'd downed a batch of Jell-O shots in under a minute and then tried to grope Rowan.

"I don't know why you went out with that guy," James scolded.

Because I didn't have the courage to go out with you, Rowan wanted to say, taking a drink instead.

She thought back once more to the night she threw the party for him at Meriweather, when she almost *had* said something. Poppy had found her in the bathroom. "You're missing all the fun!" she'd said, bursting in as Rowan sat on the edge of the tub, trying not to cry. Poppy had leaned over the vanity to touch up her makeup, but then she seemed to sense Rowan's distress. "Are you okay?" she'd asked, blinking hard. "Am I hogging James?"

"Of course not," Rowan sputtered.

Poppy got on her knees on the bath mat and looked straight in Rowan's eye. "Ro. *Is* he just a friend?"

Rowan swallowed hard. Had Natasha said something? Was it obvious? It was humiliating, suddenly, especially because James clearly wasn't interested in her. Rowan wasn't the kind of girl who pined. And she wasn't the kind of girl who came in second.

A hard shell formed around her, blocking off her feelings. "Of course he's just a friend," she said firmly, returning Poppy's gaze. And that was that. She'd made her choice.

Now she and James drained the bottle of Scotch, and Rowan found some red wine in the kitchen. As she poured them glasses, they talked about how they'd once crashed a girl's bachelorette party and wound up in her limousine. They reminisced about James's band and their most memorable gigs, including the time they rented an inflatable bounce house to sit next to the stage. "Ah, the sex hut," James said, clasping his hands behind his neck. "One of my best ideas yet." A faraway look crossed his face. "That bounce house was like a water bed."

Rowan flushed. They hadn't talked about James's conquests in years; she was out of practice. "Ew," she said, mock-disgusted.

James grinned. "*She* didn't think so. Until I punctured the thing."

"*You* punctured it?" Rowan recalled how the bounce house had leaned left toward the end of the night, one of the castle turrets limp. *Like a penis*, had been the joke.

"My keys were in my pocket," James explained. "The thing almost swallowed me up. I had to hunt for my pants butt-naked."

Rowan pictured James trapped inside the bounce house without any clothes on. Then she felt a guilty twinge. Was it a betrayal to talk about James's player past like this? She wasn't sure Poppy knew about it—she had never asked, and Rowan hadn't shared. Rowan wasn't sure why she hadn't told, except that it seemed manipulative, as if she was hoping it would make Poppy like James less. Besides, he had changed because of Poppy; she'd made him better, as she made everyone better.

A renewed sense of drunken euphoria swept over Rowan, and she decided she was making too big a deal about all of this. She looked at James and blurted: "I forgot you were like this."

"Like what?" James cocked his head. "A great deflator of bounce houses?"

"Well, yes. You tell a good story."

"Well, *I* haven't forgotten that you can hang," James said, leaning forward and placing his hand on her thigh.

Rowan stared at his hand, thinking how she used to marvel over his long, slender fingers. She swallowed hard and reminded herself that he wouldn't be touching her right now if he weren't drunk.

But then he leaned toward her. A sizzle darted up Rowan's spine. Out of the corner of her eye, she spied a photograph of herself and Poppy on the mantel, their arms around each other's shoulders, ecstatic smiles on their faces.

She pulled away. "I think we're wasted."

"I'm not." James's voice was suddenly sober. He placed his hands on his knees, a pained expression on his face. "Rowan . . . I think Poppy's cheating on me."

The temperature rose a few degrees. "What?"

James ran his hand through his hair. "She's been so distant. It's like I don't exist." He sounded unglued. "I mean, look. I know the signs. *I've* done it to people. Something is really wrong with us."

Rowan thought back to Skylar's birthday party. Poppy *had* seemed a little standoffish. She hadn't noticed when James disappeared into the bathroom, and she wasn't looking for him when they reappeared. "She's overwhelmed. She has a crazy job, two little kids, and the press is still talking about her parents' accident," Rowan said, thinking of what she'd read on the Blessed and the Cursed.

"She's always handled it before. Now, there are times after work when she's just . . . *missing*," James explained. "I'll call her, and she doesn't pick up. And I've caught her making secret phone calls. Hanging up fast when I come around. It's why I didn't go back there tonight. I just couldn't handle it anymore. I had to tell someone." He grabbed Rowan's hand. "I almost said something to you about it at Sky's party. Do you know what's going on?"

"Of course not!" Rowan cried. She stared down at her hands, her head spinning. James's fingers were entwined in hers. Slowly she pulled them away. "This is all in your head. Poppy would never do that."

"You'd be surprised what people do."

"Not *her*," Rowan insisted. "And not to you. You're a wonderful father and an amazing husband. You're amazing . . . in *general*."

The sentence hung there. James met her gaze. Rowan pressed her lips shut, horrified she'd said it.

A surprised smile appeared on James's face. "Do you mean that, Saybrook?"

The Scotch felt thick on the roof of her mouth. "Maybe," she whispered.

"*How* do you mean it?"

He stared at her. Rowan swallowed hard, a door opening. All at once she couldn't lie. Here, drunk, at eleven o'clock on a Thursday night, maybe she could tell the truth.

"I mean it . . ." She shut her eyes and turned away. "In every way."

James's lashes lowered. Then, with one confident movement, he pulled her toward him. His mouth closed around hers. He ran his hands through her hair. She touched the back of his neck. She drank in the smell of his soap, his strong grip, the deftness with which he touched her. God, she had wondered about this for *years*. Every time he met another girl, every time he told Rowan he'd slept in someone else's bed, she'd *wondered*.

In minutes they were in her bedroom. "This isn't right," Rowan murmured as he laid her on the mattress.

"Yeah, it is, Saybrook. This is probably the most right thing we've ever done." He kissed her neck. "I knew you wanted me. I wanted you too."

Rowan stared at him. "No, you didn't." But the look on James's face said that perhaps he had.

James caressed her face, his breath quick. "I think even *Poppy* knew how we felt, deep down." He sank onto one elbow. "You are so smart. And beautiful. And *cool*."

"Stop," Rowan said bashfully, but he pulled her in again before she could say anything else. His words washed over her, again and again, until they were the only refrain in her mind, the only thing that existed between them.

For a few precious hours, she finally got everything she'd ever wanted.

ROWAN OPENED HER eyes. She was lying on top of her duvet in a merlot-colored silk camisole she didn't remember buying. The ceiling fan whirled over her head; outside, she could hear the soft hiss of the city waking up. Judging by the dull light streaming through the window, it was probably right before dawn. Her head pounded from the Scotch and wine. James lay beside her, unconscious. A figure stood over the bed. It had hollow eyes, a downturned mouth, a shapeless body. "Shame on you," a raspy voice whispered.

Rowan cowered back. But when she lifted the covers from her eyes again, the figure was gone. The digital clock blinked 5:50. Sunshine streamed in from the tall casement windows.

Rowan heaved a breath. *A dream.* There was nothing in the corner except for a pile of clothes. Her jeans. Her T-shirt. And black men's loafers.

"Oh my God," she whispered. James *was* here.

But he wasn't in the bed, as he had been in the dream. Rowan rose, walked to the door, and listened. James's muffled voice floated out from the living room. He stood in his boxers, his strong, tanned back facing her. His cell phone was to his ear.

"I know, I know," he whispered. "But I told you, something came up." He shifted. "I'll see you tonight, okay?"

Rowan tried to escape silently, but she stepped on a creaky plank in the floor. James turned. His eyes widened, and he hit the END button on the phone.

"I'm sorry," Rowan whispered, a lump in her throat. He had to have been talking to Poppy. Lying about why he hadn't come home last night, consumed with regret.

Rowan couldn't even *think* about her guilt, it was so overpowering. She couldn't look at her hands, knowing that they'd touched James everywhere. What had she *done?* She thought about how the future would unfold: she'd blurt it out to Poppy for sure. There was no way she could face her cousin as though nothing were the matter. Poppy might forgive Rowan, but there would always be an abyss between them—at every dinner, during every holiday celebration, every time they saw each other, they both would remember what Rowan had done.

And then, quietly, Poppy would tell the other cousins, explaining that she understood why it happened, in a way—poor Rowan had been single for *so* long, and James *had* been her friend, and really, could anyone blame her?

She backed out of the room. James dropped the phone on the couch and ran toward her. "Hey. Where are you going?"

He tried to wrap his arms around her waist, but Rowan arched away, almost feeling as though the future scenario she'd mapped out in her mind had already happened. "Oh, God, James. What the hell *happened*? What did we do?"

He leaned back and stared hard at her. "Calm down. It's going to be okay."

Tears filled her eyes, hot and salty. "How can you say that? *Nothing* will be okay."

He tried to kiss her, but she ducked her head to the side so that he got her ear. "I have to get out of here," she said, glancing at the clock. It was 6:03; she had a conference call with the Singapore office at 7:30. She dared to glance at James. Just looking at him, she felt an undeniable pull toward him. "You should go home," she ordered. "Work things out with Poppy. *Please*."

James shook his head. "I think we're past that. I'm serious. I'm telling her it's over."

Rowan felt the blood drain from her face. He couldn't do *that*. "Okay, so stay here and think. Sober up. You'll change your mind. You'll see how wrong this is."

"Saybrook." James stepped forward and took her face in his big hands. "Just slow down for a minute, and maybe you'll see how *right* this is. It will be messy, yeah, but you are my closest friend. You know me better than everyone. I *love* you. This should have happened years ago."

He pulled her close and kissed her. Rowan shut her eyes. If only it felt dreadful, two shapes fitting together badly. She struggled to pull away, her lips feeling toxic. "I have to go," she muttered.

It was six thirty by the time she showered, dressed, and gathered her keys, while James languished in the bed. Rowan avoided looking at James for fear of another tidal wave of shame—or desire. Was it even right to leave him here? But if they walked out of the apartment together, someone might see them, and that would be worse.

Rowan's head swam as she stopped at the Starbucks on the corner. She barely noticed the loud grinder, the pounding world music, or the woman with the Staten Island accent in front of her. After waiting in a long line to get coffee and a muffin, she decided to eat in a little park near her apartment. She was in no hurry to get to work and face her cousin.

As she sat, pedestrians streaming past her, her mind ebbed and flowed over what had happened. Did James actually love her? And was Poppy really having an affair? Rowan couldn't imagine it, but she supposed anything was possible. It didn't make what Rowan had done more forgivable, of course. But it certainly explained why James had turned to her.

Finally, when she couldn't put it off any longer, Rowan stood and made her way down Hudson. Twenty minutes later she turned onto Harrison—and stopped short. NYPD sawhorses blocked the intersection at Harrison and Greenwich. The Saybrook's building, a gleaming slab of gray limestone and glass that looked particularly beautiful against the bright blue sky, sat at the corner. Yellow police tape surrounded the front entrance, and several ambulances and fire trucks were parked crookedly in front, lights flashing.

Rowan walked cautiously along the sidewalk, her heart speeding up. The police tape cordoned off a small rectangle on the pavement just outside the building; paramedics stood over something covered by a sheet. She looked up. Across the street, people stood on their balconies, men in shirtsleeves and women in spring dresses, their hands over their mouths, staring at the ground.

Corinne swam out from among the crowd, her face ghost-white. She ran to Rowan and clutched her arm.

"What's going on?" Rowan cried.

Corinne stared at Rowan as if seeing through her. Then she

collapsed in Rowan's arms and started sobbing. The church clock a few blocks down bonged out the half hour.

"Corinne, what?" Rowan stared into her cousin's face. "What is it?"

Corinne looked at Rowan with wet red eyes. "It's Poppy," she said hoarsely, her voice breaking. "She's dead."

"Corinne!" called a voice as Corinne emerged from her parents' town car on Monday morning. "Can you comment on your cousin's suicide?"

"Aster, does she have a history of drug use?" another asked, training a camera on Aster. "Was she mentally ill?"

Corinne pulled her black satin clutch closer to her body, grasped her mother's hand, and hurried faster up toward the Cathedral Church of St. John the Divine on Amsterdam Avenue. A newsstand stood at the curb; Poppy's face was splashed on every front page. "Carat, Cut, Clarity, Calamity," read one headline. "City Mourns a Flawless Diamond," read another. "A Fall from Grace." There was a photo of Poppy at a gala at the Met, staring off into space, her eyes large, her mouth puckered, and her jaw tense. Another paper showed a photo of Poppy's lumpy shape under the sheet on the sidewalk outside the Saybrook's offices.

Corinne couldn't get the morning of Poppy's death out of her mind. She'd arrived at Saybrook's just six minutes after Poppy jumped, still reeling from seeing Will Coolidge the day before. There had been a crowd of people around the entrance, and at first she'd been annoyed. But then she'd noticed a paramedic leaning over someone on the sidewalk.

Corinne had pushed through the throng when suddenly a Saybrook's guard grabbed her. "Stay back, Corinne," he said in a firm voice. It was a sweet Irish guy, Colin, who always invited Corinne and Dixon out with him and his buddies to drink on Saint Patrick's Day.

"What's going on?" Corinne had demanded, her heart thudding against her rib cage.

Colin had looked at her. And then he'd mouthed the name. *Poppy*.

Years ago, at an amusement park on the Cape, Poppy had talked Corinne into going on a ride called the Rotor, a barrel that spun and spun until, abruptly, the ground went out below your feet and the riders stuck to the sides by centrifugal force. That was how she'd felt, seeing Poppy's body splayed across the sidewalk. It had been several days now, and every morning she expected to wake up and see an e-mail from Poppy, or a missed call. It has to be a mistake, she kept thinking, even as it became painfully clear that it was not.

"Rowan! Was there a business scandal?" another reporter shouted to Rowan, who was behind Corinne. "Trouble in her marriage?"

"Was she depressed about her parents' death?" another reporter screamed.

"Did she leave a note?"

Corinne's heart wrenched. Police had gone through Poppy's office, and there it had been, typed in a Word document on her computer screen. "I just can't handle it anymore," it read. "I'm sorry. Good-bye." Proof that Poppy, the most together-seeming of their cousins, had taken her own life.

As soon as everyone was inside the airy, high-ceilinged cathedral, away from the press, Corinne drifted to Rowan and gave her a huge hug. She looked deathly pale; Rowan hadn't been to work all week, and now Corinne wondered if she was taking it harder than the rest of them. Aster stood next to her, her gaze on the floor.

Corinne touched her sister's arm. "Hey," she said gently, her voice breaking. Now their fight seemed so petty.

Aster looked up. Her lips parted. Corinne opened her arms, and Aster fell into them. "It's so awful," Aster sobbed in Corinne's ear. "It makes no sense. She had *everything*."

"I know," Corinne whispered.

Variegated light streamed in through the stained glass windows inside the cathedral. Mourners in black stood in small clumps, some checking their phones, others dabbing their eyes with handkerchiefs. A large birdbath-like structure bearing holy water was off to one side; several people dipped their fingers in and crossed themselves.

The Saybrook family wasn't religious, but the cathedral's high ceilings and cool, dark space always made Corinne feel calm and at peace. It was less flashy than St. Patrick's, where Steven Barnett's memorial had been five years before.

The memory of Corinne's grandfather's funeral here came back to her. It had been at the beginning of what was already proving to be a horrible summer—Dixon had announced that he was going to London to intern at FTSE Group, and, oh yeah, he was breaking up with her. Two weeks later, still completely unmoored, Corinne got the news that her grandfather had suddenly died. She'd just seen Alfred at Meriweather a few days before. He'd given her a pair of three-carat diamond teardrop earrings; when Corinne asked what the occasion was, he just smiled and kissed her cheek. "Simply because you're my sweet girl." She could still smell his cigar-and-soap-scented skin. She could still hear his gravelly voice. She could still smell the lime in his gin and tonic.

Her grandfather's casket had been closed, so Corinne hadn't been able to kiss him good-bye and tuck those earrings under his satin pillow. A picture of Corinne crying had appeared on the Blessed and the Cursed the following day. Someone had actually sent in an image from inside the church.

Now an usher handed Corinne a program and pointed her through a door. Corinne walked, zombielike, toward the front, her gaze flickering over the sea of mourners crowding the entrance. There were people from work, colleagues from other jewelry empires, models, actors, musicians, and designers. A fashion editor from *Vogue* stood along the wall, next to a serious-looking blond woman in a business suit.

Mourners rushed toward Corinne, offering words of sympathy. Winston and Sullivan, her teenage cousins from California, hugged her hard. Their mother, Aunt Grace, who almost never came to New York, approached next, hugging Rowan tight. Rowan's brothers, Michael and Palmer, who'd flown in, pulled her in for bear hugs. "It's such a tragedy," said Beatrice, Poppy's twenty-five-year-old second cousin on her mother's side. Her words seemed especially hollow; Corinne wondered if it was because Poppy had passed her over for a promotion several months ago.

Corinne hugged a few more people from Saybrook's, and an accessories editor from *Vogue*. People streamed past her, their faces blending together. Danielle Gilchrist gripped her hand. "I'm so sorry—I can't believe it," she murmured. And Danielle's mother, Julia, stood next to her, her eyes full and sad. Corinne hadn't seen Julia in years, since she'd divorced her husband, but she looked as though she hadn't aged a day.

"My condolences," Julia told her. "Call if you need anything," murmured Mrs. Delacourte, Poppy's old nanny, who had to be almost eighty. "Just horrible," sniffed Jessica, Edith's personal assistant, before scuttling toward the front of the church, where Edith was sitting.

"Oh, honey," Deanna said next, squeezing Corinne tight. "If you're up for it, we should talk afterward," she whispered into Corinne's ear. "About some interviews. But only if you feel ready."

"I don't," Corinne said, pulling back. That was Deanna—she was part Jewish mother, part relentless workaholic, always thinking about the media's reaction. There would be a *People* special about the family's curse, and *20/20* would create a story without a single source. But at this point, Corinne didn't see the point in doing interviews. She'd already given a brief statement that she had no idea why Poppy might have done such a horrible thing. She had nothing else to add.

Then another hand touched Corinne's back, and she stared into

the face of Jonathan York, president of Gemologique Internationale, one of Saybrook's biggest competitors. He had also once been
Corinne's uncle by marriage, but he and Aunt Grace had divorced
years ago. Jonathan was tall and trim in his dark suit, with salt-and-
pepper hair and steely blue eyes. His trophy wife, Lauren, wasn't on
his arm—Corinne had heard they'd split recently. It surprised her,
actually, that he was here. He was the one person Poppy never quite
managed to get along with. They occasionally had to do business,
and more than once after a call with Jonathan, Poppy showed up in
Corinne's office flustered and angry.

"Corinne," Jonathan said now, touching her hand. "I can't imagine what your family is going through. It's such a tragedy."

Corinne smiled tightly. "Thank you for your sympathy."

She tried to move on, but he gripped her hand. "Healing takes
time," he added, his mouth close to her ear. "The business will always
be there. I wish I had been able to tell Poppy that. I know she was
struggling."

He stared at her patiently, as if she was supposed to know what he
was talking about. Struggling . . . with what? Her parents' death? And
was he suggesting that Corinne—or Saybrook's in general—just let
business *drop*? Gemologique would love that. Maybe she should just
wrap up their market share with a neat little bow and hand it over.

Corinne moved down the aisle. Most of her family was at the front
of the church. Edith, Mason, and Penelope sat in the first pew along
with Natasha's parents, Candace and Patrick, who were sobbing.
James sat there too, watching blankly as Briony waddled down the
aisle. One of the nannies, Megan, chased after her. Skylar sat politely
next to James, a numb look on her face.

Corinne slid into the second pew, her heart physically aching. She
pressed a hand to her sternum, understanding where the word *heartbreak* came from; that those little girls would grow up without their
mother, and that she would grow old without her cousin, seemed

impossible. Corinne remembered traipsing around Poppy's family's farm, renaming all the potbellied pigs and Belted Galloways. Poppy was so diplomatic, allowing each cousin to take turns picking a name, all the way from Natasha up to Rowan, but hers were always the prettiest. Corinne could still remember a lot of them: *Briar Rose. Hadley. Elodie.* Poppy's mother had given them poster paints and allowed them to decorate a wall of the barn with all the new names; as far as Corinne knew, they were still there.

Dixon was waiting for her at the end of the bench, his hair slicked back from his face. He wore a black suit and loafers. As she moved next to him, he wrapped his arm around her shoulder and pulled her tight. "You okay?" he asked softly.

"No," Corinne said miserably. She looked down at the program. There was a picture of a funereal bouquet of white roses on the cover. Inside was a recent shot of Poppy, a few wisps of her blond hair blowing across her face, and underneath, her birth and death dates. Corinne's throat felt like it was on fire.

On the other side of Dixon, Natasha leaned over and peered at Corinne. Her eyes were wide, her dark hair was mussed, and her fingernails were bitten to the quick. Melodramatic tears streamed down her cheeks, and she looked as if she hadn't slept. The same program was in her lap too. "Hey," she whispered.

"Hey," Corinne answered stonily, staring straight ahead. After years of absence, it felt almost intrusive that Natasha was here now.

Years ago they'd all been so tight, making up dance routines on the sand at the private beach, rehearsing pretend Saybrook's commercials in the attic, giggling over the older boys that came to the family parties. An only child, Natasha had clung to Corinne, confiding that she saw her as a big sister. And Corinne saw Natasha as the little sister she'd wished Aster had been. But all that had changed when Natasha disinherited herself. She wanted nothing to do with the family—not even Corinne. She didn't answer

Corinne's calls and started giving negative sound bites about the family to the press. Corinne had taken it personally. What had *she* done to Natasha?

At the same time, Corinne could practically hear Poppy in her ear, telling her to give Natasha a chance, coaxing her to include Natasha in her wedding party, as Poppy had done. "We're family," Poppy had insisted. "One day you'll reconcile, and you'll regret that she wasn't standing by your side."

"It's unbelievable." Natasha's voice was choked.

"Umm-hmm," Corinne murmured.

"I can't believe the note . . . ," Natasha went on.

Corinne nodded faintly. It hadn't even sounded like Poppy.

"Did she reach out to you?" Natasha hounded.

Corinne stared at her cousin over Dixon's lap. "No, Natasha," she said, hearing her voice rise. "Because if she had, I would have helped her, and she would still be here."

The organ music began to play, and the clergy at the front of the church indicated that everyone should rise. Corinne did so, watching as the rest of the congregation around her did the same. And then they began the process of saying good-bye to the most flawless Saybrook of all.

TWO HOURS LATER, after a reception at the University Club, Corinne and the other cousins, including Winston, Sullivan, and even Natasha, tumbled out of town cars at Seventy-Third and Park Avenue and walked up the stairs of Edith's Queen Anne revival mansion.

The forty-foot-wide town house was faced in brick and marble, with a regal-looking, peacock-blue front door. Today, though, Corinne barely noticed it, nor did she pause to smell her favorite peonies in the front garden, admire the sweeping staircase in the foyer, or ogle the enormous antique crystal chandelier that, secretly, she hoped one day to inherit. The room offered a floor-through view to the back of the property, which opened into a stunning garden and a glorious two-story waterfall, but Corinne saw none of that, either, as she walked through the hall and into the grand parlor, where everyone had gathered.

Megan was trying to corral Skylar and Briony near the first of the grand parlor's two marble fireplaces. James sat next to them on a long couch, looking dazed. Corinne's mother and Rowan's parents were squashed in next to him, cupping mugs of coffee. Natasha's parents sat across from them on a settee. A blond woman in a suit stood near the window, nearly swallowed in Edith's massive silk curtains.

"Who is that?" Corinne whispered to Rowan, realizing she'd also seen her at the church. Edith had asked the Saybrooks to gather here, stressing that it was family only.

"No idea," Rowan said, her face ashen.

Corinne, Rowan, and Aster sat on the couch opposite James and Rowan's parents. Winston and Sullivan slumped against the wall, fiddling with their popped collars and their shaggy blond surfer-boy manes. Natasha settled on a silken slipper chair near the room's second fireplace. She pulled out her cell phone and studied the screen while everyone got settled.

Finally Edith rose from her wing chair at the head of the room, wrapped her fur tightly around her, and dismissed one of her servants, who'd been pushing a silver drinks cart. "I know I'm not the only one who's had questions about Poppy's death," she said gravely. "I've brought you all here to tell you that Poppy didn't commit suicide. She was murdered."

James quickly jumped up and signaled to Megan, who whisked the children into the back parlor. Aunt Grace glanced at Winston and Sullivan and swished them out of the room too. For a moment, everyone was silent.

"Mother," Mason said feebly from the couch. "We've been through this."

Edith set her jaw. "I'm not the only one who believes this." She turned to the blonde by the window. "She's going to prove it."

The stranger stepped forward. She was a little older than Corinne, with wide blue eyes and an athletic figure. "Katherine Foley, FBI," she said in a confident voice. Then she reached into her pocket and revealed a shield-shaped badge.

Mason winced. "Mother, you *didn't*."

Edith's eyes flashed. "I most certainly did. And anyway, I trust Miss Foley. I know her."

Everyone squinted. "You do?" Aster asked.

"How?" Mason piped up.

"I'm sure I do, but . . ." Edith looked scattered.

Agent Foley cleared her throat. "I'm afraid Mrs. Saybrook might have me confused with someone else," she said delicately. "But you're in the best hands."

She pulled a Chippendale chair from the corner next to Edith and opened a laptop. "Edith came to me the day Poppy died, and I had my team look into things, including the note itself."

She typed something on the laptop, then turned the screen to face the circle. It was Poppy's note; next to it was a dialogue window. "The electronic signature on the file shows that Poppy wrote this note at 7:07 a.m. However, several witnesses say that Poppy's body was on the ground at 7:05. A security camera on the building across the street that caught the lower part of her fall registered that time as well."

James lowered his coffee cup. "What does that mean?"

Edith raised her palms. "A woman can't write a suicide note after she's dead."

Mason looked skeptical. "Could the clocks have been off?"

Foley turned the laptop back to face her. "We checked that, but the clock on Poppy's computer matches the security camera across the street exactly. We have to entertain the possibility that someone else wrote that note to make Poppy's death look like a suicide."

Aster shot forward. "Wait a minute. What?"

"Someone pushed her?" Rowan asked, and for a moment Corinne wondered if she sounded almost relieved.

"We don't want to make any rash conclusions," Foley said. "Unfortunately, the security camera from the building across the street didn't extend high enough to give us a view into Poppy's office. There were no witnesses."

Rowan's brother, Michael, touched his forehead. "Not one person?"

"We're still asking around. It's early yet."

"What about the autopsy?" James asked.

"The full report isn't in yet, but so far there's nothing conclusive either way," Foley said. "Poppy fell from about fifty feet, and that's all the findings show. But the discrepancy between her time of death and the time of the suicide note is concerning. One might argue that a bystander was in her office the whole time and typed the note at Poppy's request after she jumped. But why wouldn't that person come forward? It doesn't add up. And because of that, we're officially opening this as a murder investigation."

"I knew this wasn't a suicide," Edith said tightly. "But who would hurt our Poppy?"

"We have to figure out what exactly happened to Poppy the morning of her death. Who was in her office? Why were they there? Do we know if anyone might have been mad at Poppy for any reason? Someone inside the company, for instance? Or perhaps a business rival?" Foley asked.

Corinne's skin prickled. Jonathan York's smarmy smile. *I know she was struggling.*

"I'm not assuming anything," Foley went on quickly. "Unfortunately, Poppy's office doesn't have a camera in it, and the camera in the elevator bank didn't show anyone getting off the elevators around the time of Poppy's murder. But whoever it was could have taken the stairs, where there are no cameras."

Rowan cleared her throat. "Didn't the guards on the floors notice anyone coming out of Poppy's office?"

"It's a skeleton crew before actual business hours. Most people, including many of the guards and all of Poppy's assistants, weren't at work yet, so we don't have a complete picture. We're looking into electronic data from keycards used to get into the building and onto certain floors. We'll interview anyone who was in the building at that time."

Corinne frowned. "What about the surveillance video from the lobby?"

Foley pulled at her collar. "We haven't finished going through it yet. But we'll match the people seen there to the keycard data as well."

"What about fingerprints from Poppy's keyboard?" Natasha piped up, her throaty voice surprising everyone. "If someone else typed her note, they'd be there, right?"

Foley nodded as if she'd anticipated the question. "We dusted the keyboard. But the only match was Poppy's fingerprints. No one else's. The killer could have worn gloves, though. That would indicate the murder was premeditated—the killer might have anticipated killing Poppy before going into her office. It's not exactly glove weather." She gestured at the sunny sky outside, then cleared her throat. "Based on all of this, I'll need to speak with each of you separately."

Natasha looked annoyed. "But I don't even work at Saybrook's." Corinne could hardly process everything she was hearing. Poppy hadn't killed herself; she'd been murdered. Whoever had done this had been inside the Saybrook's office, and had known Poppy would be at work unusually early.

"You don't think *we're* suspects?" Corinne heard herself ask.

"Of course not," Foley said, but she didn't look any of them in the eye. "But I do need to know where you all were that morning, just for due diligence. I also want to hear if you know anything about Poppy that might indicate why someone would want to hurt her. If she made mistakes at work—or if she dabbled in drugs, got mixed up with dangerous people who might have a motive to hurt her."

"Poppy?" Rowan sputtered. "Poppy was . . . perfect," she finished sadly.

And she was, Corinne thought. She imagined Poppy here, her ghost flitting from seating area to seating area, thanking everyone for coming, remembering the smallest details of everyone's lives—names of pets, summer plans, the old yacht Natasha's father was rebuilding.

"You never know," Foley said. "And I don't mean to worry all of you, but there's also the possibility that this could be personal to the Saybrooks."

Mason frowned. "Meaning?"

Foley cleared her throat. "You're a prominent family. A lot of people are envious of you. Someone might want to hurt you because of your power, your wealth, your influence—or perhaps just to knock you down a few pegs."

Mason waved his hand. "Please."

"I would take this seriously," Foley warned. She typed something else into her laptop, then spun the screen around again. A familiar website appeared. *The* website.

Foley scrolled down the page. Below the banner with the site's name was a large headline that took up the whole screen. "One Heiress Down," it read. "Four to Go."

The room fell silent. Corinne's stomach sank to the floor, and her mind went blank. The only sounds were thumps from the back parlor, where Poppy's children were playing.

"W-who wrote that?" Rowan stammered.

"We don't know," Foley said. "We're trying to figure that out. We've tracked the website's latest update to the IP address for a computer at the New York Public Library. They don't keep thorough records of who uses the machines, but we're trying to get video feeds of the rooms to see if that yields anything. This could just be public speculation, someone's idea of a sick joke. But it could also be much more sinister."

"Are you saying that we might be next?" Corinne whispered.

"I'm saying to take this seriously, and if it is a threat, we'll keep you safe," Foley said, and then closed the laptop with a solid *click*. She turned to Edith. "Thank you very much for welcoming me into your home, Mrs. Saybrook. I'll be in touch."

Mason, Penelope, Edith, and Rowan's mother, Leona, jumped up to follow the agent out. James slipped out of the room to check on his children. Soon the only people left were the cousins. Corinne's head whirled.

One heiress down, four to go.

Finally Rowan breathed in. "Who would want to kill Poppy?"

"Who would want to kill *us*?" Aster whispered.

Natasha was staring, unblinking, her face set with determination. All at once, something she'd said to *People* when she disinherited herself crossed her mind. *The Saybrooks aren't what they seem. I need to surround myself with more trustworthy people.*

Natasha finally lowered her eyes, but Corinne was still shaken to the bone. She couldn't wrap her mind around any of this, but one thing was clear. Someone had murdered Poppy. And one of them might be next.

8

A few days later, Rowan stood at James's door in the hall of the Dakota. When she'd been here for Skylar's birthday, the air had been festive and happy. Now someone had left a bouquet of flowers for Poppy on the doorstep. Rowan scooped them up and rang the bell.

James opened the door, his hair standing up and dark bags under his eyes. He wore a fitted T-shirt and dark denim jeans, and was barefoot.

"Thanks so much for coming," he said. He'd called her fifteen minutes ago in a panic, saying the nanny had a family emergency, Briony was sick, and Skylar needed cupcakes for preschool the next day. A thrill had run through her—of everyone in his life, James had called *her*. Instantly, though, she'd felt horrified that such a petty thing had crossed her mind, and she'd lapsed back into the guilt and grief that had consumed her all week. Her cousin was dead, and Rowan had betrayed her in her final hours.

She didn't make eye contact with James as she swept into the apartment toward the kids in the living room. A Disney cartoon was on the flat-screen; glitter and paste littered the heavy wooden coffee table. Briony was sitting on the floor, staring listlessly at an electronic toy that was singing the ABCs. Skylar was on the couch, dressed in a pink satin princess gown and a silver tiara, and holding a silver magic wand. Tears ran down her cheeks.

When she saw Rowan, Skylar ran to her and carefully hugged

Rowan's legs. Even at three years old, she was a little heiress in train-ing. "Aunt Rowan, I've *missed* you."

Rowan picked her up. The little girl wrapped her arms around Rowan's shoulders tightly. Another wave of sadness overtook her as she realized that Skylar would never get a hug from her mom again.

"Did Daddy tell you I need cupcakes?" Skylar said when Rowan put her down. "It's my turn!"

"How about we go to Magnolia Bakery?" Rowan suggested. "Or Crumbs?"

Pink blotches appeared on Skylar's cheeks. "Mommy always makes them."

Rowan's heart stopped. She kneeled to Skylar's level and looked in her eyes. "Well, I'll make them today too. I'm the best cupcake maker this side of the Hudson River."

She reached forward to tickle Skylar, which usually sent the little girl into a fit of giggles, but this time Skylar just squirmed away. "Where *is* Mommy?" she asked, her three-year-old voice high and innocent.

Tears pricked Rowan's eyes. She glanced at James, but he was staring at his hands.

"She had a very bad fall," Rowan fumbled. "But she's always watching you. And if you talk to her, she's always listening."

Skylar's little face registered an incongruous blend of obedience and confusion. "My daddy said we could paint my toenails if I want," she said after a moment.

"Well." Rowan took her hand. "I think that sounds nice. Maybe I could give you a makeover too."

"*You?*" James snorted. Rowan shot him a look, and he shrugged. "Sorry. Skylar, Rowan will give you a *wonderful* makeover."

This seemed to cheer Skylar up, and she walked into the kitchen with Rowan. James trailed in last and stood at the island, staring at an unopened box of cupcake mix. He looked so helpless and confused.

Rowan wasn't sure she'd ever seen him like that, and she was seized with the desire to take care of him too.

She turned to Briony, who had followed them in and was pressing a flushed cheek to the stainless steel refrigerator door. "You okay, sweetie?" Rowan said softly, and swept the little girl into her arms. Briony koala-beared her legs around Rowan and started crying. "It feels like she has a fever," Rowan said over her shoulder to James.

James nodded. "I gave her Tylenol ten minutes ago."

Rowan nodded. "I'll hold her until it kicks in. And *tickle* her!" She shoved her fingers into the fold between Briony's chin and neck until the little girl finally cracked a smile.

On the counter, James's phone rang, a sharp run of piano notes bleating through the apartment. The device was sitting closer to Rowan on the island, and she subconsciously glanced at it. A 917 number popped on the screen. "Do you need to grab that?" Rowan asked him, shifting Briony higher in her arms.

James glanced at the number, then hit IGNORE. "Nah. We're in the middle of a cupcake emergency, after all," he said with a wan smile. "It can wait."

Rowan looked at the box James was holding. "You were losing it over *this*? We only need three ingredients, and one of them is water."

James opened the fridge and stared inside. "My head isn't screwed on straight." He sighed.

"That's fine, because *my* head is exactly where it should be." Rowan looked at Skylar and pretended to adjust her head on her neck. Skylar offered an amused smile. Rowan picked up at the Duncan Hines box again. "Okay, Dad. Get us some eggs. You remember what those look like, right? Round, white? Come from chickens?" She looked at Skylar again, tucked her fists in her armpits, and made chicken-wing-flapping motions. Skylar snickered.

"These?" James pulled out a tub of butter, joining in on the joke.

"Those aren't eggs!" Skylar cried.

James looked at them mock-confusedly. "I could have *sworn* they were eggs." Next he yanked open the crisper drawer and pulled out a cucumber. "Is *this* an egg?"

"Daddy!" Skylar cried, marching to the fridge herself. "*Those* are eggs!"

"Really?" James seemed astonished. "Skylar, you are the smartest girl *ever.*"

Rowan hid a smile and took the carton from James, then taught the little girl how to crack three of them in a bowl.

Once the cupcakes had been spooned into their little wrappers and were baking in the oven, she glanced in the fridge. It was piled full of stuff in Tupperware, takeout boxes, and Dean & DeLuca packages—from neighbors and family, she guessed. She pulled out a white box and inspected what was inside. Three marinated chicken breasts and a side of garlic mashed potatoes. Perfect.

Turning on the second wall oven, she passed Briony to James and placed the meal on a baking sheet. James hung back, but she felt his gaze on her as she moved around the kitchen. He didn't answer his cell phone when it rang again.

James pulled out a chair and said, "What do you think, Sky? Should Aunt Rowan stay?"

"Yes, please!" Skylar clasped her hands together, her eyes begging.

Rowan thought of her own quiet apartment and sat down in the empty chair—Poppy's chair.

It was easier than Rowan would have imagined to keep the kids entertained. She did her balance-a-spoon-on-her-nose trick. James made various coins from his pockets disappear. Rowan sang "Itsy Bitsy Spider" in the Donald Duck voice she and her brother Michael had spent hours perfecting. Both kids laughed happily and ate well. The oven dinged, and Rowan pulled out the cupcakes and, after they cooled a bit, frosted them with Skylar's help.

By the time the sun had set over the Hudson, Briony had fallen asleep in Rowan's arms on the couch. Rowan gently placed her in her crib, only to find Skylar behind her, begging that she read her a Madeline book—a first edition, signed to Adele, Poppy's mother, from the author. James eased Skylar into bed. "Aunt Rowan in bed too," Skylar insisted, and James stepped back, allowing Rowan to climb in. She tucked her legs under the covers, her heart breaking at the fussiness of Skylar's lacy sheets and how tightly the little girl clung to a stuffed turtle Poppy had bought for her in Meriweather last year.

"Are you okay, Aunt Rowan?" Skylar asked.

Rowan looked over at her, realizing there were tears in her eyes. She had been staring at a page of the book but hadn't started to read. "I'm great," she said quickly, swallowing the sob. "I'm just happy to be here with you."

Finally Skylar fell asleep. Rowan carefully settled her head on the pillow, pulled the blanket up to cover her shoulder, and tiptoed out of the room. James was waiting in the hall, his arms crossed over his chest. "*Thank* you."

Rowan lowered her eyes. "It was nothing." She walked into the kitchen. There was a pile of dishes in the sink.

"The kids seem okay, all things considered," she said as she filled the sink with bubbly water.

James moved next to her. Rowan could smell his familiar peppermint soap. "Well, Briony doesn't really get it, and I'm not sure how much Skylar understands, either. But she really misses her mom."

Rowan nodded. "Of course she does." And that would never go away. Even at thirty-two, Rowan still called her mom several times a week and tried to visit her childhood home in Chappaqua at least once a month. It was important to Leona that the family stay in touch, especially with her two sons so far away. Just that morning, Leona had called to report that her lilac tree out back was beginning to flower.

James moved away from the sink, wiping his hands on a towel. "I looked around the memorial service for, you know. *Him*. Anyone who seemed . . . unfamiliar."

Rowan's head snapped up. "You still think she was having an affair?"

James ran his hand through his hair. "I know I shouldn't be thinking about it right now, but I can't stop. I just keep imagining her whispering on the phone. There were so many nights when she didn't come home." He gazed out the window. "I was *this* ready to say something to her."

There were no dishes left to wash, but Rowan kept her hands in the water anyway. "Did you say anything to the FBI about it?" she asked. She'd spoken to Foley yesterday.

"Yes. I thought they should know."

"Oh." Rowan swallowed hard. "Did you tell them . . . where you were that morning?"

James took a dish and dried it. "I didn't tell them where I woke up. I didn't think you'd want me to."

Rowan felt a lump in her throat. Keeping her eyes on the spout at the sink, she nodded faintly. "Yeah." She tried to sound tough and unaffected. "I mean, after all, it wasn't like it . . . *meant* anything."

She hadn't told Foley, either, simply telling the agent that she'd been walking to work when it happened. She might not have pushed her cousin, but Rowan hardly felt innocent.

A siren blared outside. Rowan winced, worried it might wake up the girls, but there were no sounds from their bedrooms. James picked up a little glass bird from the windowsill. It was a souvenir from James and Poppy's honeymoon in Thailand—they'd found it in their suite, and Poppy thought it would bring them good luck.

He made a small noise at the back of his throat. "It's just so fucked up," he said in a choked voice. "How could this have happened?"

Rowan's chest tightened. "I don't know," she whispered. A plastic sippy cup in a wire rack next to the sink suddenly tipped over. When she looked up again, James was quietly staring at her from across the sink. He took a breath, and then said, "How are you doing with everything?"

Rowan's gaze instantly snapped to the floor. "You shouldn't think about me in all this."

"I shouldn't?"

The words hung there. The possibility fanned out in so many different directions. But when Rowan looked around, all she saw was Poppy—her collection of takeout menus and wineglasses and organic cookbooks. Pictures of Poppy and James and the girls. Grocery lists and reminders in Poppy's neat script.

"I should go," she blurted, shooting across the kitchen in seconds flat. She reached the door and began to unlock it, struggling with the latch. James, who had followed her, leaned in and did it for her easily.

"Thank you so much for helping with the kids." His voice cracked.

Rowan slung her bag over her shoulder. "Of course. Anytime."

He stood, hands in pockets. After a beat, she started out into the richly carpeted hallway. *Tell me to stay*, she willed silently, surprised at the ferocity of how much, despite everything, she suddenly wanted that.

But a few seconds went by, and James didn't say a word. "Okay," Rowan said, brushing off her hands. "See you soon, James."

"See you soon," he said quietly.

The elevator dinged and swept open. James still didn't shut the door, and Rowan still couldn't ask the question. And so she gave him a clumsy little wave, rode the elevator all the way to the bottom, and then went back to her apartment, alone.

9

On Wednesday morning, Aster, dressed in a lace minidress with bell sleeves, stepped out of her town car onto Hudson Street. Men in bespoke suits carrying crocodile briefcases swept busily past, not giving her a second glance even though the dress showed off her Pilates-toned legs. The air had a crisp, fresh quality about it, and everything buzzed with an unfamiliar sense of purpose. Aster realized why it was so foreign: she hadn't been up this early in years. Everyone was rushing off to a job—something she'd never had to do.

Until today.

She stomped along the sidewalk, glowering at the other worker bees headed to their offices. She glanced around for reporters too. The police had just released the details of Poppy's murder to the press that morning, and Aster knew it wouldn't be long before the circus began.

Murder. When Aster shut her eyes, she kept imagining the grotesque scene of someone bursting into Poppy's office and shoving her over the balcony. She tried not to think about it, but her brain kept pushing the scene further, imagining Poppy's spine snapping when she hit the pavement, her organs exploding, her beautiful eyes popping from their sockets. Someone so good, so beautiful . . . destroyed.

That message on the website stayed with her too. *One Heiress Down, Four More to Go.* What if someone was after *them*, all of them?

But why? Out of jealousy? And how on earth could the cops not know who was running that site? Wasn't *everything* hackable, these days?

Something cold brushed Aster's arm, and she screeched and whipped around just in time to see someone in a trench coat disappearing through a metal door in an alley. Her heart pounded in her ears. Had that person touched her intentionally? Was she walking around Manhattan with a target on her back?

When her phone buzzed with a text, she jumped again. But it was only Clarissa. *Good luck today!* it read. *You okay?*

Of course I'm not okay, Aster thought. What a ridiculous thing to ask. But instead she just wrote, *I'm holding up*. It was sweet of Clarissa to check in, at least.

Do you get a lunch break? Clarissa replied. *We could do Pastis?*

Aster's heart sank. Poppy had been planning to take her to Pastis today. *Maybe*, she typed back, just as her phone started to vibrate with an incoming call. She frowned at the name on the screen—Corinne. Taking a breath, she hit answer.

"Good, you're awake," Corinne said in a clipped voice.

Aster took a few steps toward the Saybrook's building. "Unfortunately."

"Are you at work yet?"

So this was a motherly reminder about coming to work. "I'm just outside," Aster snapped.

"Okay. Just making sure," Corinne said, and Aster gritted her teeth. "I should warn you," Corinne went on, another phone ringing quietly in the background on her end. "The vibe here is a little . . . weird."

"Weird?" Aster stared up at the stone building that had housed her family's business for almost seventy years. The spot where Poppy had fallen was still blocked off with yellow tape. Someone had left flowers just outside its borders. Trying to shake the image of Poppy's broken body, she pushed through the double doors—and froze in place. The lobby was bursting with NYPD officers and police dogs. Everyone seemed stiff, alert, and very on edge.

"Christ," she whispered into the phone.

"The police are keeping reporters away from the building for now." Corinne's voice was solemn. "But we'd better get ready for a lot more questions." She sighed. "Good luck today."

"Thanks," Aster said, caught off guard by Corinne's rare touch of kindness. She hung up and headed to the turnstiles that led to the elevator, only to learn that she couldn't pass through them without an ID card. Aster had no idea that their office, that any office, was so secure. Did they actually think people would try to sneak *into* work? And how could someone have broken in here to kill Poppy?

"It's okay, Miss Saybrook," said the security guard, scanning his card to let her through. "I'll make an exception for you." Aster gave him her best model smile in thanks. He must have recognized her from the ad campaign that was still plastered everywhere.

She stepped into the elevator and rode up to the eighth floor, where she was supposed to meet with HR so they could tell her where she was actually working.

"Aster?"

Danielle Gilchrist stood in the foyer, wearing a white, green, and orange color-block dress and expensive-looking wedges. Her red hair hung straight and shiny down her back, and a jumble of chunky bracelets lined her arms.

For a moment, Aster wondered in confusion what her old friend was doing here. Then she noticed the purple-and-silver folder with the Saybrook's logo on the front. "Welcome to the Saybrook's family!" Danielle chirped. Of course—Aster remembered now. Mason had gotten Danielle a job in Saybrook's HR after she graduated from NYU. The thought made her stomach churn.

"I'm already in the Saybrook's family," Aster said, taking a step back.

Danielle colored for a moment, then recovered. "Right. It's just a figure of speech." She turned on her heel. "Well, come on. Might as well get started."

She opened the door to a big conference room that overlooked the Hudson. On the walls were pictures of old Hollywood celebrities wearing Saybrook's diamonds. Aster remained in the doorway, finally understanding what was going on. "Wait. *You're* doing my orientation?"

Danielle nodded as she logged in to the computer and pulled up a PowerPoint. "Yeah, it's company policy. Everyone has to go through orientation. Even an actual Saybrook." Then she smiled. "You were at Badawi the other night, weren't you? I *love* that place."

Aster shut her eyes. She'd avoided interacting with Danielle for so long. She turned the other way if she saw her on the street, steered clear of parties if Danielle was on the guest list. Anything to avoid thinking about that summer. But all at once, a memory flooded back to her.

"Hey, Aster." Thirteen-year-old Danielle Gilchrist sauntered up to Aster on the beach in Meriweather. Aster had always known Danielle—she was the caretakers' daughter—but this summer she was different. "Got any Robitussin?"

"Why would I carry that around?" Aster asked haughtily.

"Because it gives you a great buzz," Danielle answered. "You've never tried it?"

Now it was Aster's turn to feel stupid. She shook her head. Danielle turned toward the shore. She was pretty, Aster suddenly realized—tall and thin, with long, wavy red hair and blue eyes. "I'm going to steal it from the drugstore, I guess. Want to come with?"

They drank Robitussin that night, and Aster got loaded for the first time. They snuck into Corinne's bedroom to read her journal, which was as boring as they thought it would be. "She's very . . . organized, isn't she?" Danielle asked, glancing around the fussy bedroom with a smirk. Aster giggled. "You mean anal." It felt good to laugh about her sister. Corinne might have been Aster's protector when she was younger, but as they grew older, she had begun constantly telling on her. And it wasn't as if Aster could talk about Corinne with any of her cousins.

Danielle slept over that night, and the next morning she was scribbling furiously in a notebook. "What are you doing?" Aster asked.

"I always write down my dreams," Danielle said in a matter-of-fact voice. "And then I analyze them for symbolism."

As the summer wore on, Danielle introduced Aster to vodka, prank calling, and how to get a fake ID through the mail. They spent every night whispering secrets and dirty jokes and watching French films that made Aster blush. They snuck over to Finchy's, the bar across the island, and claimed to be sisters, letting scruffy older guys hit on them and buy them shots of well whiskey that burned their throats. They stayed in touch all the next year, texting about boys they had kissed and parties they had gone to, and their grand plans to live on Bleecker Street together when they turned eighteen. When they both got into NYU, they signed up to be roommates.

But then Saybrook's needed a new face for its brand, and Aster seemed just the girl. Mason was enthusiastic about it, which was enough to persuade Aster—maybe *this* was her path. A week before she set off for Europe for the photo shoots, she was back at Meriweather with Danielle, on the beach outside the estate. Danielle took a sip of the vodka-lemonade Aster had mixed for them in her family's kitchen. Then she said, "My mom told me the weirdest thing today. It made me think twice."

"What was it?" Aster asked awkwardly. She always felt uncomfortable talking about Danielle's parents. They fought constantly—Aster could hear them yelling from the estate—and this summer the fights had grown even more heated. Danielle was certain they were headed for divorce.

"Just weird stuff," Danielle said, tracing a blue-painted toe through the sand.

"Come to Europe with me," Aster blurted out. Why hadn't she

thought of this before? "I'll be going to Paris, London, and Milan. I'll pay for everything, just come. You could use some time away from here for a while."

Danielle's eyes were hard to read behind the Gucci shades Aster had bought for her. She twirled the diamond tennis bracelet Aster had given her as a birthday gift around her wrist. "I don't know."

"Come on," Aster begged. "We can drink sangria by the bucket, hook up with European men, tan in Saint-Tropez . . ." She trailed off as something up the bluff caught her eye. Aster's father was standing at the edge of the patio, gazing at them.

Aster half waved, thinking her father was looking for her. But Mason seemed to peer right through her. Aster glanced up again and realized he wasn't looking at her at all—he was staring at Danielle. She turned to her friend and realized that Danielle was wearing nothing but a skimpy string bikini. Danielle had untied the top strap while they were tanning, the fabric precariously clinging to her chest.

An oily feeling filled Aster. But by the time she looked up the bluff, Mason was gone.

Now Danielle cleared her throat. Aster shot up. The past didn't matter; it was a long time ago. "Let's get this over with," she said flippantly, walking into the conference room and sitting down. "Do your thing."

Danielle plopped the folder on the boardroom table, then looked at Aster as if she wanted to say something. Aster pointedly turned away.

After a beat of awkward silence, Danielle cleared her throat and launched into a speech about Saybrook's employee policies. Then she dimmed the lights, and a movie came on the screen. Classical music played as the words "Saybrook's: A Family Legacy" appeared. "I'd like to walk you through the rise of the late Alfred Saybrook," Donald Sutherland's voice intoned. "His father, Monroe, opened Saybrook & Browne's Jewelers in Boston, Massachusetts, in 1922. It was a local establishment, mostly dealing in gold. Monroe never had plans to expand."

Up popped a picture of the store that Aster's great-grandfather opened near Beacon Hill. The 1920s storefront was modest, with old-fashioned script in the window and impossibly tiny diamonds in the display cases.

Aster glared at Danielle. "I already *know* all this." Her grandfather used to tell this tale all the time.

Sorry, Danielle mouthed, but she didn't stop the DVD.

"Monroe died from tuberculosis in 1938," Sutherland went on. "Alfred was forced to take his place." Next appeared a photo of Alfred in front of the store. A very young Edith—a teenager, probably—stood next to him, her arm looped through his elbow. Even though the photo was black and white, it was clear that she was a blonde, and that she was wearing dark lipstick. "But before long, World War II began, and Alfred bravely volunteered to fight."

In the next photo—the same photo Mason kept in his study—Alfred was in a military uniform, standing with his friend Harold. "Edith kept the store running in the States as best she could, though times were tough—no one wanted to buy diamonds during the war. And then things changed. While Alfred was overseas, he found . . . *this*."

A yellow stone appeared on the screen. Yeah, yeah, Aster thought. Not that she didn't adore the giant, canary-yellow Corona Diamond, which her grandfather had found at a bazaar in Paris. But she'd practically come out of the womb knowing about it.

The video went on to discuss how the Corona Diamond elevated the company to a new stratosphere. Alfred opened a flagship store on Fifth Avenue and office space down in TriBeCa to grow the business. Soon Saybrook's Diamonds became *the* place to go for engagement rings, anniversary bands, and tennis bracelets. Celebrities flaunted their diamonds on the red carpet. Dignitaries bought jewels for their wives. There was a famous shot of Jackie Kennedy wearing a Saybrook's pendant to a presidential ball, and a quote of her saying that Saybrook's was the only place worth going for something precious.

"Alfred Saybrook's death rocked the international jewelry community," the voiceover said, showing a picture of Alfred shortly before his death five years earlier, wearing his trademark black suit and wing tips and little round glasses. "But now, the business is stronger than ever, and Saybrook's stands by Alfred's principles of integrity, quality, and craftsmanship."

Then the screen went dark, and the lights came up. Danielle cleared her throat. "Um, I hope you found that informative."

Aster stared at her. "Are you serious?"

"I'm sorry. It's in my HR script." Danielle ran her hand through her long red hair, her expression unreadable. "Look, I know you don't want to be here, but it really is a good company to work for. And I'm sorry about Poppy," she added.

Aster made a small noise at the back of her throat.

"And I heard about . . . you know." Danielle's eyes darted back and forth. "That it might be a murder. I'm usually at work early, but I had food poisoning the day . . . it happened. If only I'd been here, maybe I'd have seen something." When Aster didn't answer, she sighed. "I hope it didn't have anything to do with the issues at work . . ."

Aster cocked her head, wondering what Danielle meant. But she didn't want to owe her anything, so she stood. "So where am I working again?"

Danielle glanced at Aster's paperwork. "Private client group," she said, directing her to the elevators. "It's the by-appointment end of the business for high-net-worth clients looking for one-of-a-kind pieces. You'll be working for Elizabeth Cole." A strange look crossed Danielle's face, but Aster decided not to ask about that, either.

Private Clients was one flight up and demarcated by transparent double doors. Inside, the music was a little louder, and there was a well-stocked bar cart and several crystal snifters in the corner. Nice, Aster thought, inspecting the spread. They had Hendrick's Gin and Delamain cognac and three types of infused vodka. Aster inched over and began to unscrew one of the lids. A little nip would definitely take the edge off what had already been a very crazy morning.

"Don't even think about it."

A woman with ash-blond hair, narrowed gray eyes, and a fitted black suit marched toward Aster. There was something familiar about her, Aster thought. She'd probably met her at a Saybrook's party. She'd met most everyone in the Saybrook's world at some point or another. "I think I'll take this too." She plucked the iPhone out of Aster's hand.

"Hey!" Aster protested.

"No cell phones at work." The woman started back to what must be her office. "I also don't tolerate overly strong perfumes, leaving early for any reason, or outfits like *that*." She glowered at Aster's lace dress, fixating on its short hem.

Aster pulled her knees together. "It's Valentino."

The woman stared at her. "I'm Elizabeth Cole. As of today, you're working for *me*, and I don't care what your last name is."

Elizabeth marched into a large office decorated in white and gray, all clean lines and sharp angles. Three walls were lined with pictures of her posing with various high-profile clients—mostly stuffy businessmen Aster didn't recognize, but Steven Tyler was in one, and Beyoncé in another. Dramatic floor-to-ceiling windows behind the desk looked out over the Hudson River, which was gray right now, under an overcast sky. It matched Aster's mood perfectly.

Elizabeth slammed down a pile of papers, picked up a coffee flask, and thrust it into Aster's face. "Skinny latte, no foam, and a gluten-free muffin from the bakery on the corner of Greenwich and Harrison."

Aster stared at the mug. "You want me to get you coffee?"

Elizabeth's brow furrowed. "There are a lot of qualified girls who actually *want* this position. Not socialites with daddies who get them jobs. If you aren't here to work, please see yourself out."

Aster wanted nothing more than to go home and spend the rest of her life under her Frette duvet. But something kept her from moving. She was already here. She'd gotten up early, faced the painful memories of Poppy and the surprise appearance of Danielle Gilchrist, and she was still standing. She thought of Poppy, who had been so certain she would succeed. "You're smart, Aster," Poppy had said after Mason cut her off. "Smarter than you give yourself credit for. You can do great things, I just know it."

"I'm staying," Aster said firmly.

Elizabeth raised her eyebrows and offered a quick nod. "Fine." Then she whipped around, shoved past Aster, and walked down the hall again. Halfway down, she swung back and stared at her. "Are you coming?"

Aster blinked in confusion, holding up the carafe. "What about your coffee?"

"After," Elizabeth snapped.

She led Aster into a tiny cubicle with a low desk and a dusty computer. A tall, lanky guy with unkempt hair and Clark Kent–style glasses was typing something and squinting at the monitor. Aster wondered if she'd have to sit on his lap.

Elizabeth glowered at him. "You're not done yet, Mitch?"

The guy scooted forward on the chair. "The server's acting weird again."

Elizabeth pressed her hand to her forehead, then looked at Aster. "Well, when he's done, I want you to start on this." She gestured to a large pile of papers on the edge of Aster's desk.

Aster lifted the cover sheet and stared at a page. It was a list of names, addresses, phone numbers, and other pertinent information. "What is it?"

"Our client list. I'm going to need you to manually enter it into Excel." She frowned at Aster's blank stare. "You *do* know how to use Excel, right?"

"Of course she does," the IT guy said quickly. Aster whipped around and stared at him. She'd never actually used Excel, but she knew better than to admit that now.

Elizabeth marched back into the hall. "Don't go into my office when I'm not there. And don't ever call me. IMs only, got it?"

Aster blinked. "Pardon?"

Elizabeth sighed. "Mitch, please explain to the heiress how a computer works." Then she eyed Aster ominously. "Girls like you always get what's coming to them in the end," she added before turning on her heel. Aster winced at the sound of her door slamming down the hall.

"Wow. She just went all evil Disney villainess on you." Mitch, the IT guy, turned and faced Aster. He had brown eyes, blondish hair, and a cute bump on the end of his nose. Unlike everyone else at Saybrook's, he wore Vans sneakers and no tie.

"Wait, I know you!" Aster cried. "I met you at last year's Christmas party, didn't I?" The company Christmas party was usually boring, but Aster remembered that last year she'd flirted with a cute geek. *This* cute geek.

"Good memory." Mitch's eyes lit up. "Welcome to the company. And"—he paused to cough into his fist—"I'm sorry about your cousin. She was well liked around here."

"Did you know her?"

"A little." Mitch shrugged. "She was nice to me. Some people brush off tech guys." He cocked his head, shifted his gaze, and pointed dramatically at the door to Elizabeth's office.

Aster riffled through the papers on the edge of her desk. The stack was thicker than a phone book. "Do I do this *before* I get her coffee, or after?"

"Definitely get the coffee first. That inputting will take *days*."

Mitch stepped closer. "Excel is a spreadsheet program, by the way. It's not hard to figure out. I can help, if you want."

"Thanks," Aster said, trying to smile. But she felt tears at the corner of her eyes. She was so out of her element.

"Hey." Mitch sidled closer. He smelled like laundry detergent and lemon. "You'll be fine. Seriously, I can help with anything technical. I'm pretty good with this stuff," he added shyly.

"I'll keep that in mind." Aster took a deep breath and turned toward the hall. "Okay, I'm off to get the coffee."

"Good luck," Mitch called out behind her. Aster sighed. She had a feeling she'd need it.

HALF AN HOUR and a coffee spill later, Aster raced back into the Saybrook's building and up to the ninth floor. There wasn't a bakery at Greenwich and Harrison, but Aster had found one at Greenwich and King that seemed cute. Hopefully it was the one Elizabeth had meant.

She knocked on Elizabeth's office door and, when no one answered, tentatively pushed it open. The office was empty. She quickly set the latte and muffin down on the desk and was turning to go when an image on Elizabeth's bookshelf caught her eye. It was a framed photo of Elizabeth in a wedding dress—which seemed odd, since Aster could have sworn she hadn't been wearing a ring earlier.

She stepped forward to examine the photo more closely. Elizabeth looked much younger, her skin smooth and her eyes unlined. Next to her was the groom, a tall man with slicked-back dark hair, an impish smile, and broad shoulders.

Aster's blood turned to ice. She knew that man. It was Steven Barnett.

This was why Elizabeth seemed familiar. Aster had always known Steven was married, to someone named Betsy . . . which was, of course, a nickname for Elizabeth. Elizabeth—Betsy—had surely been at the end-of-year party five years ago too. The one where he had died. The one where he was last seen alone on the beach with Aster.

"A*hem*. What did I say about coming into my office when I'm not here?"

Elizabeth stood behind Aster in the doorway, glaring. Aster quickly took a step back. "Um, I'm sorry," she mumbled, and turned awkwardly on her heel, but not before she saw Elizabeth's eyes flit to the wedding photo.

As she raced down the hall, she swore she heard Elizabeth chuckle ever so softly behind her.

10

After work a few days later, Corinne sat on the Louis XIV settee in the living room of her Upper East Side apartment. The settee was a period piece with intricate carvings on the arms and legs and brand-new camel-hair upholstery, but it wasn't entirely comfortable. It came from Dixon's great-grandmother, who had been French nobility and whom the family called *grand-mère*. Plenty of the other chairs and sofas in the large room were from the Saybrook side, along with a treasure trove of Tiffany lamps, botanical etchings, a Monet watercolor, and a vast collection of valuable porcelain and glass. Dixon wanted a picture of his family's Texas ranch in the room too, but Corinne's decorator, Yves, had insisted that the painting would ruin the room's nineteenth-century ambience.

Evan Pierce sat opposite her, a large leather binder in her lap. "So we've got hydrangeas and peonies for the altar," she repeated.

"That's right," Corinne answered, crossing her bare legs, which looked pale and cellulite-y next to Evan's smooth, whip-thin ones. "And I want to add lilies to the tables."

"Poppy's favorite." Evan sighed, tucking a black lock behind her ear and marking it down in the book in her spiky handwriting. Even though Poppy and Evan's friendship was one she had never quite understood, Corinne found comfort in knowing that Evan had been close to Poppy too.

Today Evan wore a large platinum ring with a huge onyx stone.

Corinne wondered who had given it to her. She wondered about Evan a lot, actually. She imagined her apartment as a movie set from the future, all white and hard lines. And what was it like to be so very single? Evan dated a lot, typically older men with a lot of money, but it was usually Evan who broke things off. And there was something about the way Evan moved, all slinky like a cat, that made Corinne think she was a ravenous lover.

"And you're choosing the wine tonight?" Evan said, still looking at her list. "The chef from Coxswain will meet you there."

Corinne's stomach lurched. Evan had arranged for a tasting at the St. Regis, where Will was friendly with the master sommelier.

"That's the plan," Corinne said shakily, then cleared her throat. "Actually, I'm wondering *why* you chose Coxswain."

Evan frowned. "It's *the* restaurant to watch. I thought you'd be pleased."

"I am," Corinne said quickly. "I just . . ."

She trailed off. What on earth could she say? *I don't want to use this restaurant because I had a secret fling five years ago with the chef?* It wasn't like Evan *knew*. Poppy would never have told her what happened.

Dixon strode into the room, freshly showered from the gym and with a fluffy white towel slung over his shoulders. His skin smelled like Kiehl's men's products, and his hair was slicked off his face. "Hey, lovely ladies," he crooned.

"I'm off," Evan said, leaping up. She kissed Corinne's cheek, then Dixon's, and strode toward the foyer. In moments, the front door slammed.

Dixon opened the media console and grabbed the remote from inside. After checking the markets on CNBC, he switched it to the World Series of Poker, which had been his favorite show since his fraternity days. "So listen. I'm really sorry, but I can't make it to the tasting tonight."

Corinne stared at him. "What? Why?"

"One of our deals went south. I have to make some calls, put out some fires."

Her thoughts scattered like marbles. "Can't someone else do it?" She wanted Dixon to come as a buffer with Will. She *needed* him to.

Dixon looked torn. "Babe, I'm sorry, but I'll make it up to you. What's the next appointment? Florist? Designer? I'll try on your dress for you if you want."

"I already had my final fitting." Corinne pouted, not wanting to joke right then. She almost thought she might cry. She couldn't go to this alone. She just *couldn't*. And worse, she couldn't even explain to Dixon why she couldn't.

Dixon inspected her face. "What's the matter?"

Corinne pressed her lips tightly together. Maybe she could tell him. It had happened so long ago; surely he'd had flings during that year too. But what if telling him meant explaining everything else?

"Why did you break up with me that summer?" she blurted. Then she blinked, surprised it had come out of her mouth.

Dixon lowered the remote. "Where'd *that* come from?"

Corinne kept her eyes on the carpet. "Well, I was just wondering. We never really talked about it, and we're about to get married."

She knew what she was doing. Seeing Will had stirred up a lot of memories, most of them unpleasant. She wanted to find a way to rewrite history, to twist things around until Dixon was responsible for everything that went wrong. *If he hadn't broken up with me, I never would have met Will. If he'd answered my calls, my life wouldn't have gone so wildly off course.* It wasn't fair. She knew that. What she'd done with Will had been her decision—including the aftermath.

Dixon stretched his arms behind his head. "I don't know if it's worth dwelling on, to be honest."

"Fine," she said haughtily, and plunged her hand into her handbag to get her Mrs. John L. Strong leather-bound day planner—she needed to enter the new appointments she and Evan had just discussed. She hadn't even had a chance to pencil in today's tasting, and she knew something would fall through the cracks if she didn't write it down soon. But the planner wasn't there. Corinne's gaze scanned the room—maybe she'd left it on the secretary desk in the corner? But when she walked over to it, the book wasn't there, either.

She frowned, then looked at Dixon. "Have you seen my journal?"

"You keep a journal?" Dixon looked amused.

"Was Margaret here this morning?" Their cleaning lady was meticulous about putting everything where it belonged.

Dixon shook his head. "I don't think so."

How strange—she never misplaced things. But perhaps she'd just left it at work.

"I must be losing my mind," she mumbled.

Dixon shrugged. "I mean . . . ," he said, with a playful smile.

She gave Dixon a weary wave. "I'll see you in a little while," she said, and then scuttled into the hallway.

LATER THAT EVENING, as the unusual-for-May humidity began to break, Corinne rushed past the shops in Rockefeller Center toward the St. Regis hotel. The sidewalk was full of tourists, an outdoor concert was taking place a few streets over, and the air smelled of fresh seafood from the restaurant in the Rockefeller skating rink. She glanced at her reflection in the windows of 30 Rock and frowned. Maybe she shouldn't have worn such a short skirt. At least she'd thrown on a sweater. Then she wondered if she was thinking too much about all of this. She shouldn't have changed at all. She was tasting wine for her *wedding*, not going on a date.

"Corinne!"

Natasha stood on the other side of J.Crew. She was dressed in yoga pants, a canvas tiger-printed bag slung over her shoulder. Her dark hair was tied back in a ponytail, and her pointed, pretty face was free of makeup.

Corinne blinked, looking for an escape, but Natasha had made it over too quickly for that. "How are you?" she asked, kissing the air beside Natasha's cheek insincerely.

"Oh, just fantastic. You?" Natasha asked, though she didn't wait for the answer. "You're going to a wine tasting, right?"

"Excuse me?" Corinne said. All sound fell away, even the loud, buzzing bass from the concert. "How did you know that?" Corinne asked shakily.

The smile was still on Natasha's face as she pulled out her phone and called up the Blessed and the Cursed. "How an Heiress Plans a Wedding," read the title. The first picture was of the cover of a leather-bound journal.

Corinne scrolled down, her eyes growing wider and wider. Every image was a page from her planner. There were lists of meetings with the florist and baker; deal points for a new office in Bangkok; her facialist's cell number. There were personal things too. Like the word *Lexapro* with a question mark next to it—her therapist had suggested she try it for anxiety. There were even lists of what she ate in a given day, and a message that said "Pilates Trainer Three Times This Week!" in commanding red pen. And on the last day, *today*, were blue-inked words: "Wine Tasting, 8:00."

Corinne nearly dropped the phone. It was in her handwriting, but she hadn't written the words yet. How had they so perfectly mimicked her handwriting? Or was Dixon right: *Was* she really losing her mind?

"Is everything okay?" Natasha watched her carefully. Realization settled over her features. "Oh my God. Deanna didn't arrange for those pages to be on the site, did she?"

Corinne shut her eyes, hating that Natasha, of all people, was witnessing her reaction. "No," she admitted. "But it's fine."

"Those animals. Aren't they sick of us by now?" But there was a strange lilt in Natasha's voice, almost as if this amused her. "Anyway, I should jet. Have fun at the tasting! And I'll see you next weekend for the bachelorette," she called out, getting swept up in the crowd.

Corinne blinked. *Go home*, said a voice in her mind. This felt like an ominous harbinger of what was to come. She should just get in bed, pull the covers over her head, and wait to wake up married. But she turned east, walking past Fifth Avenue to the St. Regis. She took a deep breath as she pressed through the gilded double doors into the glittering lobby. When she spied Will waiting for her by the concierge, she lowered her eyes and counted the checkerboard squares on the floor as she crossed the room. Her heart pounded hard.

"Sorry I'm late," she said to Will as she approached, trying not to look directly at him. He looked as handsome as ever. *Too* handsome.

Will glanced behind her. "Where's your fiancé?" He said "fiancé" the way someone might say "child molester."

Corinne swallowed hard. "Something came up." *Unfortunately*, she wanted to add.

"No problem," he told her smoothly—and somewhat impersonally. They started down a set of carpeted stairs, past the King Cole Bar, where Corinne had spent countless hours with Dixon and his buddies, and then down another flight of stairs, where they entered a small, grottolike private room lit by hundreds of flickering candles. Oak wine racks lined the walls around them, and the place smelled of grapes and oil and a tinge of cigar smoke. There was a bar set up at the end of the room; two stools beckoned.

Will looked at Corinne. "Welcome to your private tasting." He slid onto one of the stools. "I guess since Dixon couldn't make it, I'll help you out."

Corinne smiled nervously at a man who emerged from inside the wine cellar. He greeted Will with a fierce hug and shook Corinne's hand. "Andrew Sparks. I'm the hotel sommelier."

He proceeded to look at the menu Will had selected for Corinne and Dixon and disappeared back into the cellar to retrieve a few bottles. His body disappeared into the abyss of wine, and Corinne tried as hard as she could to keep her foot from jiggling.

Will looked at her. "I'm glad you approved the menu."

Corinne swallowed awkwardly. "Yes. I think it will be very good." At least he isn't freezing me out, she thought. She hadn't known what to expect, but after his iciness at the restaurant, maybe that.

Andrew reemerged and began pouring small glasses for each of them to try, an assortment of reds, whites, and rosés to suit each dish on the menu. Corinne sipped the first glass, a fruity chardonnay, then took another sip. She could feel Will's eyes on her again. Her gaze slid to a small cup on the side of the table meant for spitting out the tastes. But after her run-in with Natasha—and facing this long-forgotten past—she needed a drink. She grabbed her glass and quickly drank the rest.

"This one is lovely," she said as she set the empty glass on the table, already feeling lighter.

Will chuckled. "Long day?"

"Sometimes it feels like it's been a long few decades," Corinne said, surprising herself. She wondered how such an honest thought had escaped her lips.

Will shifted on the stool. "I was sorry to hear about your cousin. We only met a couple times, but I remember that you were close."

So. There it was. Corinne felt the knot inside her chest unfurl. Of course that summer wasn't a secret to either of them, but hearing him acknowledge it, she somehow felt as though a great weight had been lifted off her shoulders. She pictured Poppy then, dancing with one of Will's friends the night they met, never caring what anyone thought of her, and yet somehow managing for everyone to think only the best things. "Thank you," she said softly, a little bit calmer. This will go okay, she told herself. Just keep breathing. Just get through it.

Next, they tried a red from the Lagrein region, and then a heady Barolo, followed by some dessert wines. Before long, Corinne's posture wasn't as straight, and she wasn't dabbing her mouth after every sip. She stared at Will, who was talking animatedly to Andrew, firming up their final selections. An unexpected sensual feeling filled her. All at once, she could almost feel the cool sand between her toes, the salty spray coating her skin, the first night they met. And now, as she gazed at Will's pink, sensuous lips, she remembered distinctly what it had felt like to kiss him.

Andrew kissed her good night on both cheeks, and then left them with the unfinished bottles. Before long they'd helped themselves to another glass. Then another. Corinne's head was swimming; she felt as if she was floating. And though she knew she should get home, she couldn't exactly will her body to leave the stool.

Will turned to her and grinned. "You work at Saybrook's, don't you?"

"Yes," Corinne said, trying to remain poised. "I'm the head of foreign business."

"The head." Will didn't seem surprised. "Of course you are."

Corinne lowered her eyes, feeling as though she'd been too boastful. "Well, it helps if your last name is on the letterhead."

"Don't do that." He took her hand, the force of it surprising her. "I'm sure you deserve the position. Good for you. Ever think about working somewhere else?"

Corinne blinked hard. "I've never really thought of it."

"Really? Never?"

She was transported back to that summer once more. Not long after they'd kissed on the sand, Will had found Corinne again when she was shopping in town. He'd peered at her from across the street, and then walked over and slipped a note into her hand. "The boat-yard at Carson and Main. Midnight," it read.

It had been a warm and sticky night. Corinne had stood alone on the docks in a long skirt and way-too-expensive leather sandals. But then Will had appeared through the mist and took her hand, leading her to a small fishing boat halfway down the slip. Corinne hadn't asked whose boat it was; she hadn't even thought about it. She sat down in the hull. And then, instead of kissing her, he touched Corinne's house keys. The key chain was to the Meriweather Yacht Club. "You have a boat?"

"Just my family's." It wasn't just a boat, exactly—it was a massive yacht that slept twelve—but she hoped he didn't know that. He'd been so careful about his sneakers near the water, afraid to get them wet, whereas Corinne, who had been wearing five-hundred-dollar flip-flops, hadn't given it a thought.

"Of course. Your family's," Will said.

Corinne had held his gaze. It wasn't a surprise that he knew about her family; it surprised her, though, that he seemed to *care*. "I'm sorry. I don't mean to ask questions about your family. I don't want to know who they are. I want to know you. The *real* you."

The real you. It was a concept she didn't quite understand. There were the obvious basics. *I am Corinne Saybrook. I went to boarding school at Exeter. I had a 3.87 average at Yale. I play field hockey, lacrosse, and ride horses; I summer in Meriweather and go to Portofino or St. Barts over spring break. I've read every Jane Austen book twice. I just broke up with Dixon Shackelford, and starting next month, I will be working in the foreign business department of my family's company.*

And so she said all that—even the part about Dixon. Will had given her a searching look. "That sounds like a résumé. You're more than that."

Was she? But suddenly she found herself telling him things no one else knew. She told him that her first-grade teacher had it in for her for some reason—she never knew why—yet Corinne always told her parents she was the teacher's pet. She talked about how her mother used to make her walk around with a book on her head and made her go to every charitable event in the city, even though the other girls there weren't very friendly to her. She talked about how her father seemed to prefer Aster. She'd even admitted that there were rumors that her sister was getting in trouble in Europe, and told him how worried she was about her. But angry too.

She wasn't sure why she told Will everything. But she did, and that night a thought floated through her mind, unbidden. *I love you already*, something deep inside her had whispered.

Now, she looked across the bar at Will. He was still watching her. "I never thought about branching out because I never felt allowed to," she said, the confessional floodgates opening again. "I was always a good girl. I always did what my parents asked. That meant working for the family. It meant going to the right schools and wearing the right clothes and marrying . . ." She trailed off.

"What was that?" Will asked, cocking his head.

Corinne looked down. "Marrying well," she admitted.

Will stared at her, and for a long time he was silent. Then his fingers groped for his glass. "I'm sorry I was cold to you the other day," he said, his voice hitching on *cold*. "And this might make me sound like an asshole, but you never have to deal with me again after tonight, so I might as well say it." His lips trembled for a moment. Corinne's heart started to pound. "Life's too short to care about marrying well."

She clutched her wineglass. She wanted to defend Dixon, but all of a sudden, Dixon felt very far away. Corinne couldn't even picture his face—not the shape of his eyes, not whether he had dimples, not the way he smelled. On the other hand, she'd carried around a mental image of every contour of Will's face and body for five years. She could have sketched him perfectly if someone had asked. Maybe that meant something; if you could still draw someone when he was gone. If you remembered him perfectly. If you were his mirror, even after lots of time had passed . . .

She rubbed her palms against her eyes, smearing her makeup. What was she thinking? She balled a napkin in her hands and stood. "I think I've had too much to drink. I must look awful."

Will stood too. "You look amazing."

He placed his hand on her arm. Her head hummed. And suddenly it was as if she had floated out of her body and was watching from above, from some other plane. She pictured herself sitting in the front row of a theater, Poppy next to her, their hands in a bowl of popcorn, their mouths agape, as Corinne reached out for Will, pulling him toward her. He fell into her, his mouth hungrily searching for hers. Bumping against each other, they backed out of the private room into one of the cellars, a space dry and dark. Will laid Corinne down and gazed at her. He opened his mouth, as if to say something, but she covered it. He gripped the waistband of her skirt desperately.

The night on the boat washed over her once more. After Corinne had told him all her secrets, he'd taken her into his arms. It almost felt as if something was swelling inside her—and if it didn't happen right that moment, she would burst.

There in the wine cellar, Will kissed her neck as he tore off her sweater, and she arched her back against the surprisingly cold floor. He pushed her skirt up around her waist. And then they breathed into each other, their mouths tasting like wine. "Oh my God," Will kept saying, every so often pausing to stare at her. Tears formed in Corinne's eyes, though she wasn't sad. It was just that she remembered Will doing that same thing the first time they were together. Looking at her like that, as if he couldn't believe this was happening.

That first night, the boat had bobbed with their movements. Their sounds echoed across the bay. Corinne had never felt particularly passionate about sex, but with Will above her, blanketed by a canopy of stars, something happened. Something that felt very different. An aligning of the planets, maybe. A big bang, creating a universe.

And that was the thing. They had, in fact, created something that night.

They'd created some*one*.

11

Rowan sat at her desk at seven on Wednesday evening, staring blearily at a contract on her screen. It was still light outside, the evening hours stretching longer and longer as they moved further into May. A few phones rang in the bullpen of cubicles outside her office. Every so often, a paralegal or assistant swept by, but most people were packing up to leave.

She looked at her screen again, about to pull up a different document. But then the cursor began to drift toward the bottom right-hand corner of her monitor, though she hadn't touched the mouse. Rowan straightened up and rolled her chair back a few inches. She watched as the little arrow slowly migrated to the Windows icon in the bottom-left corner.

"Hello?" she called out, though to whom she wasn't sure. How had that happened?

There was a cough in the hall, then a small, shuffling set of footsteps. "H-hello?" Rowan called out, half standing. The office was suddenly *too* quiet, too empty. "Is someone there?"

Rowan jumped as Danielle Gilchrist poked her head in, her face flashing with worry. "Oh my God, I didn't mean to scare you."

Rowan smoothed down her hair. "I'm fine. What's up?" She offered a wobbly smile, taking in Danielle's long red hair and her modern-looking black-and-pink wool dress. She and Danielle worked together from time to time—as legal counsel, Rowan occasionally had to advise on hires and fires.

Danielle checked over her shoulder, then stepped into the room and shut the door. "Something has kind of been weighing on my mind."

"Sit," Rowan said, gesturing to the couch across from her desk.

Danielle perched on a cushion and folded her hands in her lap, a conflicted look on her face. A few moments passed before she spoke. "I've been thinking a lot about Poppy's murder and who might want to hurt her . . . and I had a thought. Something I'm not sure the FBI knows about."

A shock wave coursed through Rowan. "What do you mean?"

Danielle took a deep breath. "I used to be friends with Poppy's assistant, Shoshanna. You remember her, right? She basically ran Poppy's life? She was my hire. She came highly recommended."

"Sure," Rowan said. Plenty of times she'd walked into Poppy's office when Shoshanna, a lanky girl with curly black hair, a long face, and a predilection for baby-doll dresses, was briefing Poppy about something or other. "She left the company a few months ago, right? For De Beers?"

"That's right. She got a great offer in the PR department, better than what we could match." Danielle cleared her throat. "Before she left, though, she sort of let something slip about Poppy."

Out the window, a searchlight beamed around the sky. Rowan stared for a moment, then glanced back at her computer screen. The cursor hadn't moved again. "What did Shoshanna say?" she asked, turning back to Danielle.

"Maybe it's nothing, but she mentioned some . . . discrepancies in Poppy's schedule. Poppy started putting mysterious appointments in her calendar—vague things, like 'meeting,' without saying who it was with. And when Shoshanna asked—it was her *job* to know—Poppy said that she had everything covered. Shoshanna said she got kind of snippy about it."

"Okay," Rowan said, tapping the surface of her desk. None of that sounded so strange to her.

Danielle pulled her bottom lip into her mouth. "Or she would write things like 'lunch with James,' but then James would call *during* lunch, not knowing anything about a lunch. Shoshanna had to cover for her."

Rowan sat back. That *was* strange. But Poppy could have had the date wrong, or James might have forgotten. There were lots of explanations. "Huh."

"Shoshanna said she started taking these mysterious blocked calls too. And one time, Shoshanna tried to hop on the phone to take notes for Poppy and Poppy snapped at her to get off. She didn't explain who the calls were from or what they were about. But I think Shoshanna drew some conclusions." Danielle stuck her tongue in her cheek.

Rowan searched her face. The only sounds in the office were the little buzzes and clicks of Rowan's hard drive. Her brain seemed to temporarily short out, going black. Finally she said, "You think Poppy was having an affair?"

Danielle pressed her lips together. "I don't know. And maybe there's another explanation." She laid her hands in her lap.

Rowan considered the woman sitting across from her on the couch, for a second picturing the young girl who used to drive Edith around Meriweather in a golf cart. She'd been Aster's friend, not Rowan's, but Rowan had always found her entertaining. One summer, when they were all sitting on the beach together, they'd watched an older couple fighting as they walked along the water's edge. The wind had snatched away the couple's real words, but Danielle had adopted a high-pitched nasal whine for the woman and a phlegmy rumble for the man.

"I told you not to wear that Speedo," she'd said in a pinched voice.

"You worried about the competition?" she'd then rasped, holding her arms out at the same time as the old man.

Rowan knew the arguing couple—the Coopers were one of Meriweather's few year-rounders—and Danielle had mimicked their voices perfectly. Danielle's mother, Julia, had dashed by at that moment on her morning jog. "Be nice, Danielle," she'd admonished, her bright red hair flying behind her.

"Have you told the FBI?" Rowan asked.

Danielle shook her head. "They haven't contacted me. And instead of going to them directly, I thought I should let you know first. Especially since I don't even know if it *is* anything. I hope that was the right thing to do."

"Of course it was." Rowan shifted in her chair. "You did what anyone in the family would do, and I appreciate it." She shifted in her chair. "You don't have any idea who was on the other line in those blocked calls?"

Danielle shook her head. "Shoshanna might, but she didn't tell me."

Rowan stared out the window. Lights twinkled in the building across the street. "I wonder if Foley looked into Poppy's calendar. Maybe those appointments were a clue about who she might have been seeing," she murmured, mostly to herself, hardly believing the words coming out of her mouth. She'd assumed James's theory about Poppy's affair was just that: a theory. A thought that justified his own infidelity with Rowan. But here was another person echoing James's suspicions. The idea of Poppy having an affair still didn't compute, though.

A knock sounded at the door, and James poked his head in. "Oh, I'm sorry. Am I interrupting?"

"Oh, hi." She blinked confusedly at him. "Um, no, of course not."

"We were just finishing up." Danielle stood and smoothed her pencil skirt. "Well, if you need anything, call me, okay?"

"I will," Rowan said, and Danielle slipped out of the room.

Rowan turned to James. "So . . . what are you doing here?"

"I'm coming from work," James explained. He stuffed his hands in the pockets of his dark-wash jeans, looking suddenly sheepish. "The kids are with Megan. I thought you might still be here. I just . . . wanted to see how you were doing."

Rowan blinked rapidly, feeling disoriented. "How did you get in?"

James shrugged. "My wife was the president. They always let me in."

Rowan nodded. Of course.

She rubbed her eyes. "God, I'm sorry. It's just so *quiet* here. Kind of spooky." She wondered if he'd heard the conversation she'd just had with Danielle. But he looked guileless, one corner of his mouth lifted up in a smile, revealing the dimple she hadn't seen in so long.

She put her head in her hands and rubbed her scalp. Should she tell him what Danielle had said? Switched appointments, secret phone calls—that *did* seem to add up to an affair. Maybe the signs James sensed were really there. Suddenly Rowan felt somehow offended, as though *she* was the one who'd been betrayed. The woman she'd considered her closest friend felt as unknowable as a stranger at a bar.

Rowan's anger was a hot prickle on the surface of her skin. She stared hard at a picture of her and Poppy that sat on her desk, wanting suddenly to turn it facedown. Tears filled her eyes, and she immediately regretted her thoughts. Her cousin, her best friend, had been *murdered*. She couldn't be mad at her.

"Hey, everything okay?" James stepped forward and reached out as if to put a hand on her arm, then retreated, as though worried she'd brush him off.

"Yeah. It's just been a long day," she said, blinking back tears. "So how are the kids?"

"Briony's feeling better." James sat down on Rowan's couch.

"And how are *you*?"

James stared at her for what felt like forever. "You want the truth?"

"Of course."

He took a deep breath. "I can't stop thinking about you."

Rowan squeezed the sides of her chair. Her mouth twitched, and she could feel her face growing red. James stood up, crossed the room, and walked to Rowan's desk. He sat on the edge, still staring at her. Rowan was afraid to move, much less speak. She felt like two people: the Rowan who desperately missed her cousin, her best friend—and the Rowan who had slept with James . . . and who wanted to do it all over again.

Then his phone beeped. They jumped. "Do you need to get that?" Rowan asked.

James shook his head. "It doesn't matter."

"But what if it's the nanny?"

He waved her away. "It's not."

"It could be important."

A smile crept onto his face. He shook his head. "Saybrook, don't you get it? No one is more important than you."

Tingles washed down Rowan's spine even as she protested. "James, we shouldn't."

He stepped closer and ran a hand through his hair. "Yes, we should."

He pressed his lips to hers, and her whole body melted into him. James lifted her onto the desk, and one by one, he undid the buttons on her slate gray work shirt, exposing the lacy black bra beneath, kissing her everywhere. Within seconds her bra and shirt were off, his hands caressing her breasts.

"More," Rowan moaned, wrapping her legs around him and un-buckling his pants. He pushed her skirt up to her waist and in one swift moment thrust inside her, his lips and hands exploring her entire body. He started off slow, but soon he was moving against her with urgency, and she matched his rhythm, never breaking eye con-tact. "More," she told him again. *"Please."*

But it was over too quickly, and before long, James was pulling on his pants and tying his shoelaces. "Come over tomorrow," he whis-pered in her ear. He squeezed her hand once, gave her a lingering kiss, then slipped away.

He shut the door lightly, and Rowan stared around her office, her heart pounding fast in the sudden stillness.

A full minute went by before she noticed her computer. She must have accidentally launched the iMovie application; a small window showed the view from the top of Rowan's monitor, where her webcam was. A time clock was running, the camera still rolling. Rowan studied her image in the webcam, taking in her flushed skin, her mussed hair, her swollen lips. She hit stop with shaking, panicky fingers.

Then she rewound the video to the beginning. For a few moments, there was only heavy breathing, but then Rowan's head dipped into the camera view. Then came a slice of her bare breast, her naked torso, her arched neck. A man straddled her from above, his face hidden. "More," Rowan demanded breathlessly. *"Please."*

Rowan's cheeks blazed. She hit pause, embarrassed by her shameless display of passion. She moved the mouse to the top of the screen and, with a decisive, horrified click, deleted the video forever.

12

Aster exited out of the final Excel column and sat back with a sat-isfied sigh, lacing her fingers behind her chair and stretching her back to crack it. She couldn't believe it. After over a week straight of data entry, she was finally done. It hadn't been easy—Excel was miserable, but navigating Elizabeth was worse. Every interaction felt fraught with tension. Did she know about Aster and Steven? And how much?

She checked her watch: 6:00 on the dot. She would have just enough time to race home, throw some clothes into a bag, and make it to Teterboro in time to leave for Corinne's bachelorette weekend. Normally the prospect of three solid days filled with Corinne-planned bridal activities would have made Aster roll her eyes, but right now she wanted nothing more than to be at Meriweather. She couldn't wait to collapse in her canopy bed and sleep as late as she wanted.

She e-mailed the spreadsheet to Elizabeth, then stood up and started packing her things. "Aster!" she heard Elizabeth yell from her office. Aster quickly adjusted her blush-colored maxi dress—one of the few dresses she owned that fit Elizabeth's strict knee-length regulation—and scrambled to her boss's office, tripping over a pile of papers on the way.

"You're leaving, I take it?" Elizabeth asked, not even bothering to look at her.

"Yes, and I'm out tomorrow," Aster said, gritting her teeth. She'd asked for this time off her very first day, and it had been preapproved by HR. Elizabeth knew about this; she was just trying to goad Aster.

Elizabeth sighed melodramatically, as if Aster's taking off work on a Friday was the most ridiculous request imaginable. "Well, don't leave yet. I want to make our to-do list for Monday. Sit there while I look through my e-mail."

Aster perched on the chair, holding her notebook and pen at the ready, as Elizabeth glowered at her computer screen. Every night they made a list of things Aster needed to do the next day: schedule pickups and deliveries, return calls, book travel for important guests. Aster had never booked travel in her life. The first time Elizabeth asked her to do it, she'd tried to text the airline from her phone. She'd learned a lot in the last few weeks, she thought with an unfamiliar sense of pride.

Aster's gaze drifted to Elizabeth's desk. There was an open *Us Weekly* near her phone, with a full-page story on the rapper Ko folded back. Another magazine showed a photo of Ko and a pretty girl. With a start, Aster realized it was Faun, with whom she'd apartment hunted. She and Ko were dating? Since when?

"Are you a big Ko fan?" Aster asked.

Elizabeth's eyes flickered from the screen for a beat. "We're trying to design an engagement ring for his flavor of the month." She pointed at Faun's picture in the magazine, her mouth a thin line. "They came in a few weeks ago and basically said, 'Dazzle us.' Those are the worst kind of clients, the ones who have no idea what they want. They almost never end up buying what we design."

There was another knock. Mitch appeared in the doorway. "You mind if I take a look at your computer for a second, Elizabeth?" he asked. "I have to run a quick scan. It'll take one minute, I promise."

"Fine," Elizabeth snapped. "Aster, don't leave yet."

Mitch stepped into the room, shooting Aster a sympathetic smile. Aster smiled back. So far Mitch was the only good thing about this job. He checked in on her every day, sending her jokes and bringing her red Swedish fish—her favorite—to help her get through that bitch of a spreadsheet. He'd been the one to sit with her and patiently teach her Excel—and to recover the file when she accidentally deleted it. In Aster's old life, she would have held a party in his honor by now.

Elizabeth typed away furiously on her phone, clearly in her own world. Aster stared at the picture of Faun and Ko in *Interview*. They were in front of a step-and-repeat at the Chateau Marmont, one of Aster's favorite places in LA. "Faun comes from money too," she said, thinking aloud. "Her mom patented some new kind of plastic surgery technique that made them a fortune. She only died a few years ago. Faun's still devastated."

Elizabeth's head whipped up. "Where did you read *that*?"

"I didn't read it. She told me." Aster thought for a moment. "You know, her mom had one of the most insane jewelry collections I've ever seen. You should try to use that for Faun's ring. Maybe you could make a vintage-inspired piece that echoes something from the collection? I bet you could find an old photo in *Vogue* or something."

Mitch looked up from what he was doing, his head cocked. "That's a great idea."

Elizabeth made a swishing motion with her hands. "Stick to data entry, Aster. Leave the client management to the professionals."

"All done here," Mitch interrupted, standing back from the computer. He turned back toward the door, winking at Aster on the way out.

Aster glanced at her watch as Elizabeth logged back in to her e-mail, trying not to panic. Corinne would seriously freak out if she held up the plane. Or worse, she would just leave Aster behind, and Aster would have to take a *bus*.

"Aster." Elizabeth's voice was cold. "This spreadsheet isn't complete."

Aster sat up straight. "What?" she asked dumbly. She'd gone

over every data point multiple times; there was no way she'd missed anything.

Elizabeth tapped a French-manicured nail against the screen, the lines around her mouth growing deeper. "I don't see the past purchases anywhere on here."

Aster stared at her blankly. "You didn't ask me for past purchases."

"Well, you'll have to add it, then," Elizabeth said. "You can do that tomorrow."

"I'm not *here* tomorrow."

Elizabeth glared at Aster for a long beat, so long that Aster wasn't sure what she was supposed to do. "You think you can just come and go as you please, don't you?" she finally said.

"I'm sorry." Aster tried not to raise her voice. "I'm *trying*, I really am. I promise to tackle this first thing Monday. But I already told you I needed to use a vacation day tomorrow, so—"

Elizabeth raised a hand, cutting her off. "You think you're trying? That's a fucking joke, my dear." Her eyes blazed. "Your whole family is like this, but you're the worst of them all. You think there are no rules. You do whatever you want, no matter what happens to anyone else along the way."

"Then why do you work for us?" Aster shot back.

Elizabeth tilted her chin into the air. "That's none of your business."

Veins bulged in the older woman's neck. And then, suddenly, Aster got it. Elizabeth wasn't talking about work. She *knew*.

A few days before Aster left to model in Europe, she'd come back to Meriweather to see Danielle. She couldn't leave for the summer without saying good-bye to her best friend. Danielle didn't know she was coming; it would be a surprise.

The car tires crunched over the gravel on the long drive and came to a stop between her family's estate and the guesthouse. Aster closed the car door quietly behind her, clutching a Magnolia crumb cake— Danielle's favorite—in one hand and a bottle of prosecco in the other. She crept up the path, past Danielle's discarded bicycle and a bunch of empty terra-cotta planters, and was about to burst through the front door when two shapes shifted in front of the window. Aster had paused as she realized: Danielle had a *guy* over.

Aster had started to step forward and knock anyway—Danielle had interrupted her fair share of Aster's hookups, after all—when she did a double take. Danielle was in there with Mason; Aster's father's arms were wrapped tight around the redhead.

Aster stood there, frozen, for a long beat. She thought of how her father had stared at Danielle only a couple of weeks ago. What a fool she'd been.

She ran blindly toward the house, loud sobs erupting from her chest. *Her father and her best friend.* It was like something off a trashy talk show. How could she ever face either of them again? The answer, Aster decided after drinking the bottle of prosecco by herself and staring blankly at the kitchen wall, was that she wouldn't.

Aster lasted only a couple of months in Paris. All her pictures were outstanding, but most of the photographers had refused to ever work with her again. She couldn't really blame them, considering that she'd drunkenly insulted all of them, showed up high to almost every shoot, and almost set fire to one of the studios. When she landed back in the States at the end of the summer, she hadn't even wanted to attend the family's annual Labor Day party. She told her parents that she would be going to the Hamptons instead. To her surprise, Edith was the one who called and insisted that she be there.

"Aster," her grandmother had commanded, "I don't care what your reasons are for not wanting to come—you will be at Meriweather for the end-of-summer party. No excuses. We're celebrating Poppy this year. Come for her sake, if nothing else."

"Okay," Aster had said, cowed. No one could ever say no to Edith.

And so Aster had showed up at Meriweather, her stomach a nervous knot of dread.

What if she caught Mason and Danielle together *again*? Were they still seeing each other? Did anyone know?

Aster managed to avoid her parents for most of the party. But eventually Mason and Penelope had found their way to her. They were accompanied by Steven Barnett, the creative director of Saybrook's and Papa Alfred's long-standing right-hand man. Aster wondered if he was upset about Poppy's promotion; before her grandfather's death, a lot of people had thought he might be the next president. But he seemed happy enough, grinning widely and holding a glass full of bourbon.

"Well, well. Hello, Aster," Penelope said coolly, her eyes taking in Aster's very short white dress. She knew how badly Aster had screwed up in Europe. It was written all over her face.

Mason regarded Aster with a mix of confusion, hurt, and anger. "The bill at the George V was astronomical."

"I had a few get-togethers," Aster said stiffly, crossing her arms.

"Oh, you can afford it, Mason," Steven Barnett said, smiling at Aster. His words were slurred; Aster wondered just how drunk he was. "And you're only young once."

Mason just stared at Aster. She stared back.

"I need another drink," she announced, and turned to walk away from her parents without a second glance.

"Me too," Steven said, and to her surprise, he walked with her toward the bar. "So," he said in a low voice. "You can tell me the truth. Did you go wild in Paris because you were trying to get over a broken heart?"

Aster sniffed. "Sort of." It was achingly close to the truth.

"Poor, poor Aster," Steven murmured, his tone light and teasing. He stared at her for a long time. Aster knew that he was mentally undressing her—and to her surprise, she kind of liked it.

Wordlessly, they turned and started away from the rest of the party. "And what's this I hear about you quitting modeling?" Steven asked.

Aster played with the long necklace that had been dangling in her cleavage. "I wouldn't call it quitting," she said. "I would call it being asked never to model again."

"*Tsk*." Steven's breath was hot on her cheeks, and smelled of whiskey and Spearmint gum. "We didn't even get to work together."

The bass notes from the stage thumped loudly in her ears. Aster gave him a playful swat, but he caught her hand and held it hard. Her stomach swooped. When he reached out and touched the back of Aster's neck, she shuddered.

Steven gestured with his head toward the reeds. "Want to come see my yacht?"

"Do you say that to all the girls?" Aster giggled. She suddenly felt reckless and stupid, and she didn't give a shit, the way she'd felt in Paris after doing a line of coke. She reached for Steven's hand and took it, following him toward the beach as if she was doing nothing wrong. She heard someone gasp and faltered for a moment. Poppy stood frozen, a drink in hand, looking at Aster with a guarded expression. But then Aster thought of everything her father had done, and found that she didn't care anymore, not even if Poppy judged her.

Her heart pounded as she followed Steven to the beach. Yes, she decided, she would hook up with hot, older Steven Barnett, even though it was hideously inappropriate—maybe *because* it was hideously inappropriate. Her father and Danielle weren't the only ones who could do whatever they wanted and get away with it.

Now, in Elizabeth's office, Aster shut her eyes, trying to find her center. "We can cut the crap," she said. "We both know what this is about."

"By all means," Elizabeth said. "Enlighten me."

"The night with Steven." Aster stared at her. "You know that he and I—"

Elizabeth leaned back, suddenly cold and assessing. She didn't look surprised.

"I'm sorry, okay? It wasn't about Steven, if that helps. It was more about pissing off my dad, and—"

"Jesus Christ. *Stop.*"

Aster looked up. There was a strange smile on Elizabeth's face. "You think I care about that? You were one of many, my dear. And those were just the ones I *knew* about, the people around town."

Aster stared at the floor, not knowing what to say. "Oh, um . . ."

"To be honest, I'm glad my husband is dead. Your cousin did us all a favor."

Aster looked up. "Wait. What?"

Elizabeth cocked her head. "Your cousin Poppy did us a favor by killing Steven."

Aster blinked hard. "Excuse me?" Did she just say Poppy *killed* Steven? Aster burst out laughing. "That's crazy."

Elizabeth looked amused. "You didn't know?"

Aster ran her tongue over her teeth. "Steven Barnett drank too much and drowned."

"Oh, that's what the papers said. But I saw that crazy bitch standing over my husband on your family's marina the night of that party. He was most definitely dead . . . and she was the only one there."

"What?" Aster said slowly. Elizabeth just stared back at her, her expression grave. She meant what she was saying, Aster could tell.

But it couldn't be true. Aster grappled to remember that night. Steven had taken her down to the beach, where they'd undressed. She'd remained on the sand for a long time after he left, staring at the stars. Where had Poppy been during that time? Following Steven to his yacht? *Killing* him?

Aster blinked at her boss. "Did you tell anyone else about this?"

Elizabeth shook her head. "I'm the only one who knows, darling. I don't think your cousin went around telling people. And I'm sure if anyone in your family knew, they kept it a tight secret—the way you Saybrooks do." She chuckled nastily.

"Did you *ask* Poppy about it?"

Elizabeth snorted. "Poppy and I weren't exactly friends. But like I said, Poppy did me a favor. I'm glad he's gone."

Aster swept her arm around the room. "Then why do you still have your wedding picture up?" Something didn't add up here. A horrible thought struck her, and she scooted back from Elizabeth, suddenly terrified. "Did *you* kill Poppy?" she whispered. "Out of revenge?"

Elizabeth rolled her eyes. "No, Magnum, P.I. I was in Los Angeles that morning. And I'm not a murderer." She pointed to the wedding photograph. "I keep it as an homage, I suppose. Steven was an asshole, but I loved him once. And I love that I inherited everything."

Aster felt out of breath. "Okay. *Okay.* If what you said *is* true, why haven't you said anything to the police?"

"Jesus, you *are* slow." Elizabeth grabbed a pack of Parliaments from inside a desk drawer and shook out a cigarette. "I already told you I'm glad he's gone. I just wanted it over."

Her words sent a shiver down Aster's spine. "It sounds more like you might have killed Steven, not Poppy."

Elizabeth chuckled. "I wish. What your cousin did was brilliant, really—I would never have thought to just push him in the water and make it look like a drowning." Her eyes sparkled. "My schemes were always a bit more . . . graphic."

Aster stared out the window at the Hudson far below. "B-but why would Poppy *kill* Steven?" Poppy had just been promoted, after all. She'd met James that summer; not long after the party, they'd become engaged. She had so much to live for . . . and so much to lose.

Elizabeth took a long drag and blew a smoke ring. "Perhaps you aren't the only one in the family with secrets, my dear Aster."

"So you're saying Poppy was covering something up?"

Elizabeth shrugged. "Maybe. I guess now we'll never know."

Aster stood, her legs shaky. "I'm going now," she announced.

"Have a fun weekend with the *family*," Elizabeth said, somehow managing to make it sound like a dirty word. "You can fix this mess of a spreadsheet on Monday. Oh, and Aster?" she added. "I'd keep our little chat a secret if I were you."

13

To Corinne, it always seemed as though the compound in Meri-weather emerged through a thick wall of mist like a castle in a fairy tale, and it was no different when she and her cousins rolled up the driveway that evening for the bachelorette weekend. The mansion gleamed in the setting sun. The air smelled of salt and flowers. Brightly colored daffodils exploded from oversize planters. Someone had hung a banner over the front doorway that read "Happy Bache-lorette, Corinne."

Corinne felt pained. "Guys, you shouldn't have."

"Actually, we didn't." Aster shrugged.

"Oh."

Aster looked at Corinne for a beat too long, then hefted her mono-grammed duffel over her shoulder. Something about Aster seemed off today—there were circles under her eyes and a drawn look to her face, and she'd barely said anything on the flight up.

Maybe she was distraught that they were going to Meriweather without Poppy. Or maybe her abrupt change of lifestyle was taking its toll. Corinne wanted to reach out to Aster, but who was she to dole out advice? She'd just slept with an ex-boyfriend, weeks before her wedding. On the floor of the St. Regis wine cellar, she added to herself, as though *that* was what made it so shocking.

She'd walked home that night, stumbling up Fifth Avenue in her heels. The sidewalk was finally starting to cool, but the summer air was sticky and warm. What had she looked like to the doorman when she'd staggered through the lobby? Upstairs, she'd found Dixon asleep in his khakis and polo, a beer on the nightstand, lights on. Had he been waiting up for her?

But, as she undressed and showered, she couldn't stop thinking about Will, about his hands on every part of her. She shuddered. No matter how hard she scrubbed her skin, she could still feel where he'd touched her. The worst part was, she wanted it to happen again.

No, you don't, she willed silently. Or at least she thought she'd said it to herself—when she looked up, Aster, Rowan, and Natasha stood at the front door, staring at her in anticipation, as if waiting for her to finish her sentence. She smiled at them. If she kept pretending nothing was wrong, maybe she could convince herself it was true.

Fake it till you make it, she could hear Poppy telling her on her first day of work back in the city. *If you're confident, they'll forget about your name and trust you know what you're doing. Hell, maybe you even do.* She'd winked at Corinne—they both knew she was more than qualified for her job. She was well traveled and spoke several languages, but the last year had rattled her. While everyone thought she was in Hong Kong, she'd been holed up in Virginia, keeping the biggest secret of her life.

Now Corinne grabbed her bags, punched in the key code at the front door, and walked into the house. The foyer smelled like Lemon Pledge and lavender; even though the estate was mostly unoccupied during the off-season, the family kept a staff of four year-round. There was a bottle of wine waiting in the ice bucket, and a marble tray bearing cheese and crackers sat on the coffee table. There was a loud meow, and Kalvin, the estate's cat, slunk out from a back room and rubbed up against Corinne's ankles.

Corinne petted his orange-and-white fur, feeling a pang. Poppy had found Kalvin years ago on the side of the road near the family's farm and flown him here in her dad's private plane; they'd taken turns feeding him milk and bringing him to their beds. In fact, *everything* in this place—the velvet chair Poppy had curled up in with a book, the long curtains Poppy had hidden behind in games of hide-and-seek, the sweeping staircase Poppy had walked down on the day of her wedding—reminded Corinne of her cousin. She glanced around, noticing Rowan and Aster's drawn expressions. They were probably thinking about Poppy too.

"Okay, ladies," she said to her cousins and sister, shakily guiding everyone to the sitting room. "First things first. These are for you." She gestured to a bag she'd brought, full of wrapped gifts.

"That's so nice of you," Rowan said, her voice oddly melancholy, as though she were going to burst into tears.

Natasha sank down into a lounge chair. Having her here was jarring. When had they last been together—aside from funerals? A pang struck Corinne, as she remembered how cute Natasha used to be. One year, when Natasha was about seven, she'd decided she wanted to be an Olympic figure skater when she grew up. All of them, even Poppy, who was much older by then, put on fluffy skirts, took off their socks, and skated on the wood floor as her competitors, though it was unwritten that Natasha would win. "A perfect ten!" the cousins had crowed to the little girl, smothering her with kisses.

Now Natasha ripped into the package. "Pretty!" she whooped as she unveiled the pashmina wrap underneath. "Just like we wore for Poppy's wedding."

"That's what gave me the idea," Corinne said shyly. Poppy had gotten married at Meriweather four years ago. They'd sat in this very room before her wedding, and she had given each of them similar gifts. It was a December wedding, so those wraps were fur-lined. She'd also given the girls fur muffs and hats; they'd all boarded a horse-drawn carriage to go to the Old Whaling Church on the main island. The ground had been covered with crisp, untouched snow, the stars twinkled in the sky, and the church was already decorated for Christmas, silver and gold balls everywhere, the whole altar filled with amaryllises. After Poppy and James got married, they'd gone on a second sleigh ride back to the house, singing Christmas carols. Corinne and Dixon, solidly back together by then, had huddled close to keep warm.

Aster's eyes filled with tears. Rowan dropped the wrap in the box, her face twisted with pain. Corinne tried to breathe in, but it felt as if there were a load of bricks on her chest. She looked to the doorway, picturing Poppy stepping through, crowing, *Ha, ha! It was all a joke!*

Aster grabbed the wine bottle and poured four glasses. She picked up one and held it in the air. "A toast to Poppy. I don't know what we're going to do without her."

Corinne chose a glass from the remaining three. "To Poppy."

Everyone sipped quietly, the strange mood settling around them again. Corinne sucked in her stomach, hoping everyone would cheer up. Then Natasha's phone, which was sitting on the coffee table, bleated. On instinct, Corinne glanced down. A familiar 212 number was on the screen.

Aster was looking at the phone too. "Agent Foley?"

Natasha grabbed the phone and silenced it. "She wants to interview me. I wish she'd just drop it."

Aster flinched. "You haven't done your interview yet?"

Natasha shrugged. "Things keep coming up."

"But everyone else has talked to her already," Corinne said softly, irritated by Natasha's cavalier attitude, as if finding Poppy's murderer was just a big inconvenience.

Natasha turned her phone over. "To be honest, the FBI seems kind of useless. Don't you think? They don't even have a single suspect."

Everyone exchanged a glance.

"You don't know that for sure," Rowan said.

Natasha crossed her arms over her chest. "What about James?" Kalvin jumped on Natasha's lap and began kneading at her legs.

"You always hear that the husband is the first suspect? Maybe James had a motive."

"James didn't do it," Rowan said, dismissing the idea out of hand.

"I agree," Corinne said. James seemed so devoted to Poppy, so proud of all she'd accomplished. One time, when they were all at Meriweather, Poppy was being featured on the cover of *Time* magazine. James had gotten up at six in the morning to drive to the mainland's newsstand to buy the first copies the day it came out, even though the family had received advance copies the day before. He was so excited when he pulled back into the driveway.

Aster crossed her arms over her chest. "Let's talk about something else."

"Yes, maybe we should go through pictures?" Corinne said loudly. She wanted to choose some photos of the family to display at the wedding. *The wedding.* Even in Corinne's mind, she couldn't call it *her* wedding.

"How can you be so sure?" Natasha challenged, looking at Rowan. "Unless . . . you were *with* him?"

Shame flashed across Rowan's face. "As a matter of fact, I was, okay?" she blurted out. "He was at my apartment. In my *bed*. Are you happy now?" Rowan hid her face in her hands.

"Oh my God," Corinne heard herself say. The room was silent except for Kalvin's purrs. She met her sister's gaze; for once, she looked as shocked as Corinne felt. She cleared her throat and looked at Rowan. "I mean, how did it happen?"

With her head still down, Rowan explained how James had come over, convinced Poppy was having an affair. "We were so drunk, and one thing led to another," she said at the end. "And when I got to the office and Poppy was dead—I thought it was my fault. I thought James told her . . . and she jumped."

Corinne remembered how Rowan had seemed almost relieved to hear that Poppy was murdered. She couldn't imagine the guilt she must be carrying around with her. And she couldn't judge Rowan for sleeping with James. Not after what *she'd* done. You should tell them, Corinne thought, the notion pinging into her head.

Rowan's shoulders heaved up and down. "I don't know what to think right now. I just wish . . ." She trailed off, her gaze toward the stairs.

"Is it going to continue?" Corinne dared to ask.

Rowan stared at her with round eyes. She blinked once, then looked at the ground. "It happened again," she admitted, cringing as she said the words. "But if Poppy was with someone else, maybe . . . oh, I don't know." She shook her head. Corinne could see two ideas warring in her mind: that what she'd done was wrong and unforgivable, but that if Poppy had done it first, then maybe . . .

"Do you really think Poppy was having an affair?" Corinne asked.

Rowan nodded, explaining the reason for James's suspicion. She also told them about her old assistant noticing unusual appointments in her calendar. "She was sneaking around," she said. "Telling lies. I don't know."

"Do we have any idea who Poppy was with?" Natasha asked, her brow furrowed.

Rowan drained the rest of her wine. "No clue. I had no idea anything was going on."

"Me, neither," Corinne offered.

"Definitely not," Aster agreed.

"But say she *was* having an affair," Natasha piped up, gripping the sides of her chair. "Isn't that even *more* of a reason to suspect James? He thought she was having an affair. Maybe he even *caught* her. There could be more to the story."

Rowan stared at her hard, her mouth small. "He's telling the truth."

"Maybe you just think that because you're with him now," Natasha argued. "You have to look at the big picture."

The voice in Corinne's head grew louder. *You should tell them. You can't just sit here, pretending you're perfect.*

Rowan shook her head vehemently. "I left the house before James did. By the time I got to the office, Poppy was dead."

Natasha crossed her arms over her chest. "Well, did anyone see him leave?"

Rowan leaped up from the chair and paced over to the window that overlooked the sea. "He didn't kill Poppy, okay, Natasha? He just didn't."

"But—"

Corinne heard the voice again, and this time it was booming. *Tell them*, it said. *Tell them, tell them, tell them.* "I cheated on Dixon," she blurted, just to silence it.

All heads turned. Aster's mouth dropped open, her face like a charades clue for the word *shocked*. Rowan blinked hard, some of the color leaving her cheeks. Natasha's eyebrows knitted together.

"With *who*?" Rowan asked, walking back from the window.

Corinne took a long sip from the glass in front of her. "Will Coolidge." It was torture even to utter his name.

Everyone just stared blankly. It was Natasha who spoke first. "The guy from Coxswain? His name was in your journal."

Corinne gritted her teeth. Natasha must have really studied that Blessed and the Cursed post to have found *that*. "That's right," she said quietly. "I met him the summer Dixon and I broke up." She cleared her throat. "Only Poppy knew about us."

She peeked at her family, a hot flare of shame in her cheeks. Rowan looked stunned. Natasha had her arms crossed over her chest. And Aster was blinking rapidly, as though her vision had blurred and she was waiting for the world to right itself again.

"Now he's a chef, doing the food for our wedding. Dixon couldn't come to the wine pairing, and it just . . ." She trailed off. Then she looked at her lap, fearing the expressions on everyone's face. "I don't know what happened."

A small hand touched her knee. Aster was staring at her. "It's okay. We all make mistakes."

Corinne swallowed hard. "But *I* don't," she snapped, her eyes filling again.

Rowan returned to her seat and poured another glass of wine. "Okay, forgive me for saying this, but are you sure you want to get married? Are you sure Dixon's the person for you?"

"Of *course* he is," Corinne answered. "It was just cold feet. I had to tell you guys to get it off my chest. But now it's fine. It's over." She tried to take a breath, but it still felt like a pile of bricks on her chest.

Natasha leaned back on the couch. "Why did you and Will break up?"

The memory washed over her like a wave. It was the night of the end-of-summer party, the same night Steven Barnett died. Corinne stood barefoot on the cold marble floor in the upstairs Jack-and-Jill bathroom that straddled her and Poppy's bedrooms. Everyone else was downstairs on the patio, celebrating Poppy's promotion, but Corinne had retreated upstairs for privacy. She unwrapped a pregnancy test from its plastic and stared at it for a long time.

Her head had been spinning all day, her stomach had turned at the chicken salad the cook had prepared for lunch, her breasts had felt swollen for a week, and her period was late—*really* late. Earlier, she had taken the car out to a drugstore across the island, intending to purchase the test, but she'd been so freaked out about bringing it to the register that she'd slipped it into the pocket of her cashmere cardigan and walked out without paying. In one summer, she'd become a girl she didn't recognize.

She sat on the toilet, peed on the stick, and then stood up, the test wand in her hand. Slowly the dye filled the result window. The control line appeared, and the second line popped up immediately, the pink dye cheerful and bright. Corinne's heart pounded. Her ears felt wet and full, as they always did when she felt she might faint. Her fingers had started to shake. *Stupid, stupid girl.*

A particularly loud wave crashed against the rocks, and Corinne looked up. "I had this plan for my life. And everything had always gone according to my plan." *Until that summer*, she added to herself. "Will wasn't part of the plan. So Dixon and I got back together and I went to Hong Kong for work." Acid filled Corinne's throat, thinking of the secret she still couldn't say aloud. Of what happened next. "Poppy told him I was leaving. I was too busy to do it myself," she lied.

Aster was staring at her. "I have something crazy to tell you guys too. It's about my boss, Elizabeth. Steven Barnett's wife. She told me something . . . odd. Something about Poppy." She smoothed her dress. "Elizabeth said she saw Poppy standing over Steven's body the night of the party. She said *Poppy* killed him."

A jolt went through Corinne. "What? That's insane."

"Ridiculous," Rowan agreed.

"Well, Elizabeth seemed sure of it. And when I asked her what her motive was, Elizabeth made a reference to some sort of secret in the family. Something she thought Poppy was keeping. She said not to tell anyone, but I mean, you should know."

Natasha coughed loudly.

Rowan wrinkled her nose. "Steven drowned. There was no secret. And Poppy's not a murderer."

"Seriously," Corinne said shakily.

Poppy *killing* someone? It would be like finding out Edith drowned puppies in the bathtub. It simply wasn't something a Saybrook would do. But then she thought about that summer, and the year she'd stayed away from her family. The baby she'd had in secret and given away. The night she'd spent with Will. A Saybrook wouldn't do any of those things, either.

"Maybe it was an accident," Aster suggested. But then she frowned. "Poppy would have said something to the police, though."

Natasha tapped her foot. "What if Poppy *did* kill Steven? What if his murder had to do with Poppy's death?"

Aster cocked her head. "How?"

"Well . . ." Natasha thought for a moment. "What if someone close to Steven saw it happen? And what if that person wanted revenge?"

"Like who?" Rowan asked.

Everyone stared at one another blankly. Natasha stood up. "I don't know, but this seems like a really important piece of information. We need to tell someone."

Corinne shook her head, remaining seated. "It probably isn't true. For all we know, *Elizabeth* killed Steven."

"She said she didn't," Aster piped up, but then her eyes slid to the right. "But she *did* say she was happy Steven was dead."

"See? There you go," Corinne said, a story unfurling in her mind. "What if Elizabeth just told you that, expecting you'd go to the cops with the story? Remember, Poppy took Steven's job—deep down, Elizabeth could still be bitter. Maybe she blames Poppy for Steven's death—if he'd been promoted instead of Poppy, perhaps he wouldn't have drunk so much that night and fallen off the boat. But she tells you Poppy *actually* killed him in hopes of tarnishing her reputation. The cops would leak it to the media, our whole family would be embarrassed, and Poppy would be a disgrace."

Aster tilted her head. "Could you imagine the field day the press would have with this? Poppy, a secret murderer all these years."

"I'm with Aster," Corinne said. "We're not dragging Poppy's name through the mud."

"But what if this is a serious lead?" Natasha cried. "What if Steven *did* know a secret that Poppy needed to keep quiet?"

Rowan narrowed her eyes. "You seem awfully sure about this theory. Is there something you haven't told us?"

Natasha glanced away fast. "Why would *I* know anything?"

Aster stood too, and placed her hands on her hips. "If you're keeping something from us, Natasha, now is the time to tell."

"I don't know what you're talking about," Natasha growled impatiently. "It's just that everyone is so Pollyannaish about Poppy. She wasn't perfect. She was human. Look at what James said—she was cheating. Maybe she was lying about other things too."

Corinne bristled. Natasha was only there because of Poppy. "What did you have against her?" she asked. "She was so *nice* to you, although I don't really know why."

Natasha straightened her spine. "I'm just trying to get you people to take off your blinders. You're all like sheep. You go where you're supposed to go. You think what you're supposed to think. But you know what? Sometimes things aren't what they seem."

Rowan slapped her arms to her sides. "What the hell happened, Natasha? Why do you hate us so much? We used to be close, and as far as I can see, none of us did anything to you. Maybe you can enlighten me, because I'm pretty confused right now."

Natasha blinked. Her mouth hung open for a long beat. Then she lowered her eyes.

"There *isn't* anything, is there?" Aster demanded. "Did you cut yourself off for attention? Was this just your way of getting more press for yourself? You never could stand being out of the limelight."

A fierce look flashed in Natasha's eyes. All at once, Corinne couldn't handle it anymore. "We're ending this conversation right now!" she said loudly.

Aster and Rowan stopped and stared at her. "We are?"

"Yes," Corinne said shakily, feeling tears come to her eyes. All these horrible confessions . . . it was just too much. "And we're not saying anything to anyone," she added. "Not until we know something real."

Natasha sighed. "All right," she mumbled, trudging back to the center of the room and yanking her wineglass from the coffee table. "But I think you're making a big mistake."

Outside, seagulls screeched. Corinne tried to think of a way to change the subject, but what was there to talk about now? They'd already said too much. All at once, she couldn't believe what she'd admitted to them. She couldn't believe they knew about Will now. In two weeks, they would stand behind her at the altar, and they would know she was a fake. *I can't believe she's going through with this,* they'd think. *Poor Dixon.* Already she could feel their judging eyes on her back. She stood and gathered all the empty wineglasses. "You know what? I don't think this is the right weekend for a bachelorette party at all."

"What do you mean?" Aster asked.

"I mean I want to leave." Corinne marched to the kitchen and placed the wineglasses in the sink. Then she walked into the foyer and picked up the old worn monogrammed tote she always brought to Meriweather. "I think we should all leave."

"Corinne." Aster followed her to the door. "We just got here."

But Corinne was resolute. "We're going," she said, grabbing the keys and opening the door. "This is not how I want to celebrate my wedding."

She stepped out on the porch, sucking in the warm, humid air. A storm was rolling in, and the trees cut dark shapes against the cloudy sky. Branches scraped across the bricks, as high-pitched as wails. For a split second, Corinne thought she saw a shadow.

But then the door opened again, and her sister, Rowan, and Natasha walked onto the porch too. By the time Corinne glanced to that section of trees again, the branches had gone still. Or maybe they'd never been moving at all.

14

Aster hefted her bag on her shoulder and followed her sister down the freshly combed gravel path. Corinne walked with purpose toward the Navigator they kept on the island. "Corinne, please," Aster called out. "We should stay. We can still have a good time."

Corinne turned to look at her with red-rimmed, downturned eyes. "I just want to go," she said, her voice small.

Aster felt like Alice when she'd stepped through the looking glass and the world was suddenly upside down and backward. Poppy might be a killer, Rowan was sleeping with Poppy's husband, and perfect Corinne had cheated on Dixon. Aster couldn't imagine how hard that must have been for her sister to admit aloud. Not long ago, she would've felt satisfied that Corinne had finally cracked. Now she just felt bad for her.

"I'm sorry," she said, knowing the words were not enough.

"It's not *your* fault." Corinne paused to straighten out her roller bag, which she was pulling behind her.

"No. I'm sorry about . . . *me*. I haven't been there for you very much."

Corinne stopped and looked at Aster, a surprised smile on her face. She opened her mouth a few times, but no words came out. "Thank you," she finally said. "But I still want to get out of here."

"Okay," Aster said. "But the minute we get back to the city, we're getting disco fries." When they were little, Mason used to buy the two girls greasy diner fries, smothered in gravy and four kinds of cheese.

"As long as we can get them delivered."

"Done." Aster reached for her sister's hand, and Corinne squeezed in response, managing a feeble smile. They turned for the car, walking in step. Just as Corinne hit the unlock button, Natasha caught up to them. "I can drive," she offered to Corinne. "Please. You just sit in the back and rest."

Corinne looked at Natasha warily, then shrugged and handed over the keys. Natasha pocketed them and sauntered to the car. There was a *ping*, and she opened her phone to answer an incoming text, her fingers flying across the screen.

Aster stiffened. After all that had just happened, all they'd just confessed and argued over, Natasha was *texting*? "Who are you talking to?" she snapped.

Natasha stopped typing. "A client. Since we're leaving, I figured I could fit in a few private sessions tomorrow. Is that okay?"

Aster shot daggers at Natasha's back. After Corinne had been nice enough to invite her, she'd caused so much trouble that now they were leaving. And even worse, all of them had unburdened themselves . . . and yet Natasha had just sat there, Buddha-like, absorbing all of it, not revealing a thing.

Aster settled into the backseat with Corinne next to her, while Rowan climbed into the front. Aster looked longingly at the property as they pulled away. She hadn't even gotten to go upstairs and visit her old bedroom. Her gaze drifted to the caretakers' house across the lawn. It looked vacant, all the windows dark. She wondered if Danielle's dad still lived there; Danielle's mom, Julia, had moved away the summer Aster spent in Europe. Aster had always wondered if it was because she'd discovered Danielle and Mason's affair, or because her marriage had just finally ended.

The SUV rolled down the long driveway, which circled the shore, passed the tennis courts, and, finally, offered a view of the family's private dock. The *Edith Marie*, the family's sailboat, was the only vessel bobbing on the water, its masts bare and a large canvas tarp covering the hull. The rest of the dock was empty, the water lapping despondently at the shore. Aster stared at that strip of sand. She knew the others were too. It was where Steven Barnett's body had been discovered five years ago.

Natasha stopped the car for a moment. She didn't say a word, and neither did the other cousins, but it was clear what they were thinking. After a few beats, she faced forward again and drove on.

The only way to the main island was over the steel bridge that spanned the narrow sound. The bridge was empty as Natasha neared it. The sky seemed to grow even darker. The tall grasses on either side of the road swayed back and forth. Mist rolled in off the water, shrouding the car in wispy clouds.

"Turn on the lights," Aster called out uneasily.

Natasha found the switch for the lights and pulled onto the bridge. "Listen, I wasn't entirely truthful in there," she started to say, her voice strangely high and breathy. "There's something you need to know."

Aha! Aster thought, triumphant. "What is it?"

Natasha's throat bobbed. The car engine chugged. "It's about Poppy. And it's about—"

"Watch out!" Corinne yelled urgently, pointing at something in the windshield.

Headlights shone in front of them, suddenly very close. A car was driving right for them from the other direction, taking up the whole bridge. Aster's vision went white as the oncoming car careened closer. Before she knew what was happening, Natasha had yanked the steering wheel to the right, slamming on the brakes and laying on the horn.

Their car skidded, then fishtailed. There was a *crash* as something hit them, and then a *crunch*. Aster felt her body hurtling forward; her cheek slammed against the back of Natasha's seat. Someone screamed. Aster felt momentarily and unexpectedly weightless, and all at once, there was a loud boom and she jolted backward. Finally the car stopped, and everything was eerily quiet.

ASTER CAME TO on the floor of the backseat, her legs splayed above her. The interior of the car was dark. When she looked out the window, Aster saw . . . *bubbles*. She shot up, horrified.

They were in the water, and sinking fast.

"Hey!" she yelled. It was so dim inside the car that all she could see were gray shadows. "Is everyone okay?"

No one answered. When Aster reached out, she felt something wet. Blood? Her heart hammered fast, but she tried not to panic. "Rowan?" she cried. "Corinne?"

There was rustling in the front seat. "What happened?" came Rowan's voice.

"Oh my God," Corinne said, next to Aster. And then, more sharply, "Oh my *God*!"

"Where's Natasha?" Aster screamed, fumbling around in the darkness.

Leather squeaked as Rowan moved over. "She's right here," Rowan called from the front seat. "Natasha?" she yelled. "*Natasha!*"

No answer.

"Is she . . ." Corinne trailed off shakily.

Aster groped around more, then found the hard, flat glass of the windows. She pounded on them, but they didn't give. She felt water pooling around her feet. The car was filling up, water seeping through a break in the floor.

"Shit!" Corinne screamed.

Aster tried the door handles, but they didn't budge. She spun around—or at least what she thought was around—climbed over the backseat, and scrambled for the cargo area, her fingers searching blindly along the carpet. Finally she touched something hard, metal, and heavy. A tire iron.

"Everyone get back here!" she called out. "We need to break this window."

There were thuds from the front as her sister and cousin climbed over the seats. Rowan grunted loudly, dragging Natasha with her. Even in the dim light, Aster could see that Natasha's head hung back on her neck, limp.

Once everyone was in the back, Aster wordlessly handed the tire iron to Rowan, who was the strongest. Rowan heaved the thing over her head and thrust it at the back cargo door. It cracked against the glass. She took a deep breath, and struck the glass again. This time it broke.

Ice-cold water flooded into the car, forcing them heavily back. Aster gritted her teeth and strained against the flood, struggling to get through that window and out into the sound.

"Come on!" she screamed at her cousins, reaching to pull them with her toward the hole.

Together, they grabbed Natasha's limp form under their arms and clumsily hefted her into the dark water. Aster held tight to her cousin's calf with one hand and paddled furiously with the other. Her lungs instantly begged for air. She tried to open her eyes underwater, but all she saw was darkness. She felt Natasha slip from her grasp and grabbed her as tightly as she could around her waist. Rowan and Corinne were kicking below her, each of them holding one of Natasha's arms.

Finally, her lungs burning, Aster burst to the surface with a sputtering gasp.

The air was warm on her face. Waves lapped around them. Coughing, Aster looked up through the moonlit night at the bridge above. There was a large gash where the car had broken through the side rails. The bridge was empty.

Rowan popped up a moment later, Natasha deadweight in her arms. The three of them struggled to drag their cousin to shore and lay her down in the sand. She flopped on her back, her arms out-stretched. There was an eerie gray pallor to her skin, and her lips were blue. "Is she alive?" Corinne asked hysterically.

Rowan straddled Natasha's body and listened to her chest. "I think so." Her eyes were full of fear. "But we need an ambulance."

Corinne patted her pockets. "My phone's still in . . . *there*." She pointed at the bubbles rising on the surface of the water. The SUV was probably at the bottom of the sound by then.

"Mine is too," Aster whispered.

"Same here." Rowan looked like she was going to burst into tears. "Natasha!" she shouted at her. "Natasha, please wake up!"

"Natasha." Tears were streaming down Aster's cheeks. "Natasha, *please*." The last moments with Natasha swarmed back to her. How she'd started to tell them something about Poppy.

"Please wake up," Aster whispered.

But no matter how loudly they yelled, their cousin's eyes remained tightly shut.

15

When Rowan opened her eyes, she was sitting on an orange vinyl chair. A rerun of *Friends* played on a television hanging on the wall across the room. Next to it a clock read 11:30—p.m., presumably, as it was dark outside. Her cousins leaned against each other on a couch, wearing scrubs that read "Property of Martha's Vineyard Hospital."

Then she noticed a woman in a hospital bed a few feet away, with tubes up her nose and a breathing apparatus over her mouth. Her eyes were shut, her hands lay peacefully at her sides, and a monitor recorded her steady heartbeat.

Natasha.

Rowan swallowed hard. After they'd climbed ashore, another car had finally passed on the bridge, and they'd flagged it down and called for an ambulance. All of their clothes were soaked, so the EMTs had lent them scrubs.

Corinne rubbed her eyes and reached for a water bottle. "Did anything happen?" she said groggily, glancing at Natasha. "Is she . . ."

"No. She's still unconscious," Rowan told her robotically, peering at her unmoving cousin. She looked peaceful, almost as though she was just asleep. Still, Rowan couldn't shake the feeling that something was very wrong here. What were the odds that the *moment* Natasha said she had something to confess, a car hit them? Had there even *been* a car? It had all happened so fast, Rowan wasn't quite sure.

She thought she'd seen headlights. She was pretty sure she'd heard a horn. Only, was it *their* horn?

The door swung open, and Katherine Foley rushed toward them, dressed in a gray FBI T-shirt and khaki pants. Rowan shot up and shoved the phone one of the nurses was kind enough to loan her for family calls in her pocket.

"I came as soon as I heard." Foley stopped in the doorway. "Your car went over a bridge?"

Rowan glanced at her cousins. "That's right."

Foley glanced at Natasha and winced. "Was she the driver?"

"Yes." Corinne nodded.

"What happened?"

Rowan stared at the tiles on the floor. "I think another car was in our lane. Natasha tried to turn, but she lost control."

"What happened to the other driver?"

Rowan looked at the others. "We have no idea," Aster said.

"Did you recognize the vehicle?"

"It's all kind of a blur," Rowan admitted, realizing how pathetic that sounded.

Foley looked conflicted. Her gaze traveled back to Natasha. Aster cleared her throat. "Do you know where she was the morning of Poppy's death?"

Foley shoved her hands in her pockets. "I don't, actually. And now . . ." She broke off and curled her hands over the rails on Natasha's bed. "Well, I wish she had cleared that up."

Rowan's stomach churned at Foley's implication.

Foley looked at the cousins. "Where were you heading tonight?"

Rowan stood, careful not to get tangled in the wires that snaked from Natasha's body into the machines. "To the airport. We were at the house for Corinne's bachelorette party, but then we decided to go back to the city."

"Why did you cut the party short?"

There was a pregnant pause. "We don't—" Corinne started.

"I'm not—" Aster said at the same time.

All at once, Rowan couldn't hold it in any longer. "What do you know about Steven Barnett?"

Foley flinched as a machine started to noisily beep. A small heart icon indicated that Natasha's heart rate had dipped below sixty beats per minute. After a moment, it regulated and quieted down.

"What *about* Steven Barnett?" Foley asked, fiddling with a button on her jacket. "I thought he was dead."

"He is, but he wanted Poppy's job," Rowan said. "Steven was our grandfather's protégé. They were close, and he was very ambitious. There had been talk of him, not Poppy, becoming president. What if someone was angry at Poppy?"

Foley leaned against the wall. "That was five years ago, though. It doesn't seem likely that someone close to Steven would kill Poppy five years later over a missed promotion."

"We would have thought so too," Rowan said, looking at both of her cousins. Aster and Corinne nodded at her to go on. After what had just happened, they couldn't keep what Elizabeth had said a secret. "Until we found out Poppy might have killed him."

Foley's expression stilled. She didn't say anything, just blinked at them.

Aster recounted what Elizabeth had told her. With every word, Foley's face grew redder and redder. "Are you *sure* about that?" she blustered.

"We're not sure about anything," Rowan admitted. "And we'd rather you not make it public—both for Poppy's sake and for ours. Practically seconds after we started talking about it, a car hit us. Like someone wanted to keep us quiet." She swallowed hard. "I'm a little worried about even confessing this to *you*."

Foley frowned. "So you think someone was listening at the house? Did anyone know you were coming to Meriweather this weekend?"

Aster shrugged. "Everyone."

Foley shut her eyes and just stood silently for a while. Rowan exchanged a worried glance with the others. Maybe it was wrong to have said something.

Finally the agent looked up. "Well, thanks for that theory. It's definitely . . . interesting."

"Interesting?" Aster repeated, seeming confused. "What about scary? Or dangerous? Or plausible?"

"You're going to look into it, right?" Rowan protested. "What if this is why someone hit us?"

"We still aren't sure someone tried hit you on purpose." Foley's gaze was scattered, as if her thoughts were far away. "But I'll look into it. Try to get some rest, okay? I'll be in touch."

"Wait!" Rowan cried. Foley turned back. Rowan wanted more—to hear what she was thinking, what conclusions she was drawing, and what she thought about Poppy and Steven—but she didn't quite know how to ask the questions. "How much will the press know about the crash?" she asked instead.

Foley shoved her hands in her pockets, the dazed look still on her face. "The person you flagged down already called a local reporter. And obviously local authorities will report on the damage to the bridge. It's shut down right now, and it's the only way on and off the island."

Rowan shut her eyes. If there was such a thing as a Saybrook curse, it was the press. "Is there anything you can do to keep the reporters away?"

Foley tapped her nails against Natasha's bed rail. "Just don't comment."

And then she was gone. For a moment, the only sound in the room was the *Friends* theme song as the credits rolled on the TV. Finally Rowan exchanged a bewildered look with the others. "Is it me, or did Foley just act like a zombie?"

Corinne's eyes were round. "It was like she fell asleep halfway through the conversation."

"I guess she doesn't believe us about Steven," Aster muttered.

Rowan poked her finger through a small hole in her scrubs. "Then again, maybe we *are* jumping to conclusions a little quickly. This is *Poppy* we're talking about."

"So you think Elizabeth is making things up?" Aster bit a thumbnail. "I don't know. What if Steven threatened Poppy, and she fought back?"

"But I don't even remember *seeing* them together that night," Corinne argued. "Except at the very start of the party, when Steven congratulated her."

Rowan squeezed her eyes shut. She wasn't sure she'd seen Steven that night, either—but she'd seen Poppy plenty. Though she'd hung out with her brothers and a bunch of other guys that night, playing lawn bocce and poker, she seemed to have a keen radar for whenever Poppy and James swam into her peripheral vision.

Then she looked at Aster. "You were . . . *with* Steven that night," she said delicately. After Steven's funeral, Aster had confessed that she'd hooked up with him. It was sort of in the manner of *I hooked up with that guy, and then he turned up dead. How weird is that?* "Was he acting strangely? Did he talk about Poppy?"

Aster's cheeks bloomed red. "We didn't exactly talk much."

Rowan stared at a fluorescent bulb in the ceiling. "Okay. *If* Poppy did it, and *if* this has something to do with her murder, who was close to Steven? Who could have done this to her—*and* to us?"

Corinne gazed blankly ahead. "I don't know. A girlfriend?"

"When I talked to Elizabeth, she said I was one of many. Maybe someone else he had been with really cared about him. Maybe she was at the party too," Aster suggested.

"What about what Natasha wanted to tell us?" Rowan whispered, glancing at Natasha's silent shape beneath the blankets. Mist formed on the inside of the breathing mask whenever she exhaled. "What do you think she knew?"

"And where do you think she *was* that morning Poppy died?" Aster whispered.

Corinne gulped. "Maybe we'll never know."

Rowan leaned her head against the wall. "Or maybe there's a way to figure this out for ourselves."

"Figure *what* out for ourselves?" Corinne asked.

"Well, at least whether Poppy killing Steven is even plausible. I mean, there could be people who saw her somewhere else when Steven died. And we could try to find out who else cared about Steven. But if she did it, maybe she told someone else. Like your dad. Or Evan." Or James, Rowan thought to herself with a pang.

The others looked skeptical. "Dad might know," Aster said aloud.

Rowan nodded. "And I'll talk to James."

Corinne stood and stretched. "I suppose I could ask Evan—I'll be seeing her this week to go over final wedding details." She turned to the door, her shoulders sagging. "I need coffee."

"I'm going to check if Natasha's parents are here yet." Aster smoothed down her scrub shirt and checked her watch.

"I'll stay here in case she wakes up," Rowan said.

The door shut again. Rowan leaned back on the chair and listened to the wheezing sounds of the IV machines. Liquid slowly dripped from a bag into Natasha's veins. Her eyes remained closed, her eyelashes not even fluttering. Somewhere behind those closed eyes, a secret was locked away. Something so awful, someone might have run them off a bridge because of it.

Then Rowan's borrowed phone pinged, and she looked at the screen. She pulled up the e-mail through the Internet browser and a new missive came in. NEW POST ON THE BLESSED AND THE CURSED, read an e-mail. YOU'LL WANT TO SEE THIS! Rowan's skin prickled. How strange. She had never signed up to receive alerts from the website. She clicked on the link, suddenly filled with fear. What if it was a post about the crash?

The page popped up on the screen. But the top story was about something else. "Hard(Core) at Work," read the caption.

A QuickTime video loaded. With shaking fingers, Rowan pressed play, then yelped. There she was on her desk, arching her back and moaning "Yes" and gripping a man's taut back. Her nameplate, "Rowan Saybrook, Esq.," was clearly in view, along with the Saybrook's logo. James collapsed against her as they finished together, the camera never catching his face.

She stopped the video immediately. Goose bumps broke out on her skin. She'd deleted that video. Even deleted it from her trash. *Hadn't* she?

Something akin to a snicker sounded from across the room. Rowan did a double take at Natasha's sleeping form. Her hands were still at her sides, hair fanned out, and her feet pointed up. But one thing had changed. Now there was just the teensiest hint of a smile on her face now. It seemed teasing. Taunting.

Oh, you naive fools, she seemed to be saying. As if she was duping them all.

16

The following Monday, Corinne sat in her father's office, a huge corner room with two walls of windows, a vaulted ceiling, a separate entertaining area, and a small, elegantly appointed private bathroom off to one side. Rowan sat beside her, nervously jiggling her long, muscled left calf. Aster was on the couch next to Rowan, staring into a cup of coffee, and Deanna was perched on the edge of a leather chair against the window.

Mason sat behind his desk, his brow furrowed and his lips drawn. There were three empty Diet Coke cans next to him. Ever since Mason quit smoking—aside from an occasional cigar—he drank Diet Coke whenever he was stressed.

"I don't even know where to start," he said, pinching the skin between his eyes. "This accident isn't exactly what we need right now." He looked hard at all three of them.

"One of you will have to do CNN," Deanna piped up, staring at an iPad, a BlackBerry, and an iPhone on her lap. "But try not to talk too much about another car hitting you, okay? We don't need to fuel rumors of the curse. And don't give too many details about Natasha's condition."

"I'll do the interview," Rowan volunteered.

Mason's gaze shot to her. "No, *you* won't." His eyes blazed. "I don't even know what to say about you and that video. In the Saybrook's *offices*, Rowan."

"I know," Rowan mumbled, staring at her lap. She looked morti-fied. Corinne was embarrassed for her. She hadn't watched the video, of course, but she could only imagine.

Deanna flipped a page of her yellow legal pad. "Actually, Mason, maybe it would be good for Rowan to be our spokeswoman. She could apologize for the sex tape. It would humanize her. Maybe shed a little light on the mystery man—everyone is dying to know."

"Ex*cuse* me?" Rowan shrieked, looking as if she wanted to punch Deanna. Corinne stiffened too. Sometimes their publicist went too far.

"No, thank you," Mason said, his nostrils flaring. "Aster will do it."

"I will?" Aster looked surprised.

"Yes, you will." Then Mason glared at Rowan. "And if I catch you bringing another man into your office again, you're done. Got it?"

"Of course," Rowan said, blushing bright red.

"All right, everyone, get out of my sight," Mason said, making a shooing gesture with his hands. They stood and headed for the door. "Corinne, you stay," Mason called out when she was almost out of the room.

Corinne turned back and regarded her father. He had just opened a fourth Diet Coke, and he'd swiveled his chair halfway around to face the window that looked out on the Hudson. A few ocean kayaks were braving the water. The Colgate clock on the New Jersey side declared it was just past 6:00 p.m. Corinne slid her engagement ring up and down her finger, wondering what this was about. For a split second she worried that Aster had told him about Will, but she wouldn't do that—would she?

Mason turned around and looked at Corinne. "I just wanted to see how you were holding up."

"Me?" Corinne touched her chest. "Why?"

"Your wedding is soon. I know you don't need this stress." He gave her a sad smile. "It's why I asked your sister to do the inter-view instead."

"Oh." Corinne touched the collar of her silk blouse. She heard her new cell phone chime in her purse. The white screen lit up the dark satin lining. "Well, thanks."

"I'm proud of you, you know." Mason's voice was a little choked. "Juggling the difficulties of your job, planning for this wedding—you're everyone's rock. Especially now that Poppy is gone."

Corinne's throat felt tight. All her life, her father's affection had been rare. But Corinne had still needed him—and she'd needed more of *this*, him simply saying that he recognized how hard it was to keep everything together.

"Th-thank you," she said, trying to smile. Her phone chimed again. This time, she glanced at it. Two text messages had come in. *I need to see you*, the first one said. *Can you meet me?*

Will. Corinne's thoughts screeched to a halt. She couldn't go. Or maybe she had to go.

"Something important?" Mason asked, glancing at Corinne's phone.

"I think so," she told her father, standing quickly and hurrying out of the room before he could compliment her anymore. Because, she realized, she wasn't holding anything together.

She was tearing things apart . . . and she couldn't even help herself.

HALF AN HOUR later Corinne stood outside a nondescript apartment building on Bank Street. She stared at the gold numbers on the wall, and then at Will's name in the directory. Just seeing it horrified her, and she shot around the corner, trying to catch her breath. A coffee shop beckoned her across the street. She would go there instead. And think. And then go back uptown, where she belonged.

But her legs wouldn't move—or rather, they moved in the wrong direction, back to the apartment building. A woman in her twenties came out, and Corinne ducked out of the way, afraid she'd be seen. Her phone beeped. She glanced at the screen. Dixon.

She hit SILENT. Corinne had sent him a text saying she wasn't going to make dinner tonight, but she hadn't explained why. She couldn't speak to him right now. Her guilt would be obvious in her voice. She ran her hands down the length of her face. Squaring her shoulders, she turned to the buzzer panel and pressed the button for Will's apartment. The door unlocked, and she pushed into a vestibule with tiled floors, a blinking fluorescent bulb on the ceiling, and a line of small metal mailboxes along the wall. More mail sat on top of a radiator. A bike with a flat tire was propped against the wall.

After opening another door, she was confronted with a set of worn stairs. She started up them, the risers creaking. A line of doors greeted her on the landing, a motley mix of smells emanating from under them. She climbed another flight. Someone had drawn an anatomically correct woman on the hallway wall.

She imagined Dixon's face if he knew she was in a place like this. Her mother's judgmental gasp. She thought of what she'd told her cousins: *It's just cold feet.*

Still, she kept climbing.

Finally she reached the fourth floor. Will stood at his door. "Are you all right?" he cried, pulling her toward him.

Corinne stepped away, leaving an arm's-length space between them. "What do you mean?"

Will stared. "I read that you were in a car crash. I was so worried."

Corinne looked down. Of course. Every paper was talking about the crash. "I'm fine," she said woodenly. "It was just an accident."

"What about your cousin? Is she going to be okay?"

Corinne nodded weakly. There was no swelling in Natasha's brain, which meant she should wake up soon. Then again, some patients in this condition never regained consciousness.

There was a long pause. Corinne glanced down the carpeted hall, staring at a red door at the other end. "Well, come in," Will said awkwardly, stepping aside and gesturing Corinne into the apartment. Corinne ducked her head and followed.

They entered a small room with an exposed-brick wall. A modern-looking gray couch sat in the corner, flanked by two midcentury tables. Vintage cookbooks and hardcovers lined the built-ins along the brick wall. A pass-through window revealed a galley kitchen; knives were ranged along a magnetic strip on the wall, and pots and pans hung from a rack over the burners. It occurred to Corinne that most people in Manhattan would think Will was doing well for himself. Just not the people *she* hung around with.

On the back wall was a huge tin sign bearing the name of the local restaurant Will had worked for in the Vineyard, the Sextant. "Oh my God," Corinne blurted, letting down her guard for a moment. "Is that the road sign?"

"Oh." Will smiled bashfully. "Yeah."

"They let you have it?"

"Not exactly. I sort of . . . stole it."

Though the Sextant had been a staple of the island since nineteen-twenty-something, the only time Corinne had been there was with Will. It was the fourth time they went out together, the first time they dared to go somewhere in public—though it certainly wasn't anywhere Corinne would be spotted. Corinne remembered asking why the bartenders hadn't swept up the sawdust or the mussels on the floor, and Will had laughed and said, "It's *supposed* to be like that."

Now Will stared at the sign with a faraway look on his face. Corinne wondered if it reminded him of her. She liked the idea of his thinking of her while he was cooking. And then, instantly, she hated that she'd just thought that. Her emotions were so scrambled that she felt tears prick her eyes.

Will stepped forward. "What is it?"

"I don't know," Corinne said, tilting toward the wall. "I'm confused. And I lied to you."

Will looked up and blinked. "I know."

"About this weekend. The crash. I'm not fine." Then Corinne cocked her head. "Wait. How did you know I lied?"

Will raised one shoulder. "I sensed it," he said, his voice not quite steady. "Do you want to tell me about it?"

Corinne shook her head, wondering if she shouldn't have brought up the crash at all. Everything coming out of her mouth was wrong.

Will sat her down on the couch. "I heard the car started to sink."

Corinne's eyes filled with tears. "It all happened so fast. Thank God for my sister. She took charge." And then she told him about swimming to shore, running to find a passing car, the ambulances coming and taking them away. Will listened patiently, his gaze never leaving her face.

He cleared his throat. "There's all kinds of crazy talk, you know. After what happened to Poppy . . . and that website. Some people are worried that someone's after *all* of you."

Corinne flinched. "I don't want to talk about it anymore," she decided.

"You're safe now." Will reached out. "I'll keep you safe."

He said it so tenderly, and Corinne suddenly thought back to that summer, how she'd looked up at him—he was tall, much taller than Dixon—and felt safe in his arms. And she saw now how that tenderness would make him a good father. *Could have made him*, she corrected herself. It was like waking from a dream. My God, you haven't told him, she thought.

She had to get out of here. It was bad enough that it was a betrayal to Dixon, but there was so much more than that. She had betrayed Will too. She wanted more than ever to talk to Poppy, to ask her what to do. Poppy was the only person in the world who knew all of her—the part that loved Dixon, who knew she could be happy with him, their future predictable and pleasant. The part that had fallen for Will, that for a brief moment imagined a life that was completely unknowable. And the part of her that she had left behind in Virginia, the baby she had never gotten the chance to know.

She wanted to tell Will all of that; she wanted him to understand the complicated macramé of her life. But she also wanted to leave, to click her heels together and find herself back uptown in their lovely three-bedroom apartment, where each room was climate-controlled and everything existed in shades of gray and grège. But when she looked up again, Will's face was moving toward hers.

Just one kiss, Corinne told herself. Just one kiss good-bye.

"We shouldn't do this," she murmured—but she let him pull her dress over her head.

"No, we shouldn't," Will agreed, guiding her toward his bedroom.

Will's bed smelled like soap and sugar. He climbed on top of Corinne and began kissing every inch of her body. She shut her eyes and tried to numb herself, but she shuddered as Will's rough hands moved along her bare skin. He was fast with her, lustful and crazy, hard and desperate and needy. He didn't touch her C-section scar. More important, he didn't ask about it, either. She tried not to think of Dixon and that dark locked room of a secret inside of her. But before long, she didn't have to try not to think. All reason departed; only the physical was left.

Corinne kneaded her feet against the sheets, her legs shaking. It was as if Will understood inherently, without her having to say a word, what made her feel the best. It had set him apart from the other boyfriends she'd had when she was young—all of them had fumbled, asked too many questions, laughed when they shouldn't have. And Will—well, he just *knew*.

CORINNE OPENED HER eyes to find it was dark outside. She must have dozed off. Will's bed was empty, and she heard pots and pans clanging in the kitchen. She lay there for a moment, thinking about what she had done. What she'd done *again*, she reminded herself. But instead of feeling shame, the guilt that she'd tried to scrub off her last time, she felt relaxed. She felt as if she was glowing. Rising, she pulled on her clothes and padded in the direction of the sound.

Will stood in his boxers and bare feet over a pan on the stove. His hair was mussed, his skin flushed, and there was a look of concentration on his face as he flipped something over in the pan. When he noticed her in the doorway, he smiled. "I made us a snack." He slid a sandwich onto the plate. "Truffle grilled cheese."

"You didn't have to do that," Corinne said softly, accepting the plate. And though she knew truffle oil, brie, and bread were probably the worst thing she could do for her figure, she bit into the sandwich anyway and swooned. "Oh my God. This is *way* too good."

"Stick with me, and I'll make you one of these every day," Will said as he slid onto a barstool next to her.

"I'd weigh two hundred pounds."

"Then I'll make you one every *other* day." Will touched her chin, rotating her head so she was looking at him.

"You know it's not that easy."

"Tell me about it." He sighed. Will rose from the stool, walked to a messy desk built into the corner of the kitchen, and plucked a piece of paper from the top of the pile. "This is for you."

Corinne wiped her messy fingers on a napkin and studied the paper. "Invoice," it read at the top, next to Coxswain's logo. "Clients: Dixon Shackelford and Corinne Saybrook. Event description: Rehearsal dinner (175 guests) and wedding (260 guests) at the Saybrook family home in Meriweather, Massachusetts."

A hard knot formed in her chest. It was almost perverse to see her, Dixon's, and Will's names on the same piece of paper. She wanted to shift them around, make Will the groom, Dixon the hired help.

Will bit into his half of the sandwich. "Are you actually going through with this?"

Corinne's eyes burned with impending tears. "I don't know."

"Do you love him?"

A lump formed in her throat. "It's not just about that."

"Marriage isn't about love? That's new to me."

His voice was uncommonly stern. Corinne concentrated on the white plate on which the sandwich sat. She *did* love Dixon, but was that enough? Was it the kind of love you could build a life around? Was it a forever kind of love? "It's complicated." She laughed, a little bitterly. "I mean, obviously," she said, looking around.

Will paced back toward the stove. "I just don't get it. If you love him, why are you here?"

"I know. It's just . . ." She sighed and gazed out the window. "This would wreck my family." She thought about her father's choked voice earlier. *I'm proud of you.* "And it's who I am too," she added. "This is what I'm supposed to do. This is the person I'm supposed to marry."

Will's eyebrows arched. "It's not the Dark Ages, Corinne. Marriages aren't arranged anymore." Will crossed his arms over his chest. "There's something else, isn't there?"

Silence passed between them. Corinne looked away first. "No," she lied, the secret swimming inside her. She wanted to tell him, but how would she start? *I was pregnant that summer. We have a baby out there somewhere. You're a father.*

He moved closer. "Don't you want to live an honest life? Don't you want what you do and feel to be *real*?"

She hunched her shoulders, trying to hide. "I can't give you the answer you want right now. I need more time."

"You don't *have* that much more time."

Something in the kitchen crashed. It was only after the plate lay in pieces on the floor that Corinne realized that Will had shattered it. He stood there, his chest heaving, his shoulders and biceps and chest muscles prominent and powerful.

Corinne shot to her feet. "You're scaring me," she told him, suddenly unnerved.

Will looked back at her, his jaw hard. "Why can't you understand that you're not the only one with emotions?" His voice cracked. "That you're not the only person in this equation?"

"You're making me sound so selfish." She turned into the entryway, blinking back tears as she looked for her discarded shoes. "Is that what you think?"

Will didn't answer. Corinne unearthed her Jimmy Choo kitten heels and started to put them on, her throat tight. She couldn't fit her heel into the strap, so she let it flap free, as messy and undone as she felt. "I'm going," she mumbled.

Will started to walk her to the door, but Corinne marched a few paces ahead, refusing to look back at him. Will cleared his throat. "Corinne, stop. I'm sorry. I want to be with you. I think you want to be with me. It should be that simple."

Corinne stopped and turned. He stood in the doorway, a tortured look on his face. "Well, it's not," she whispered, and started down the stairs.

17

After an interview at the New York CNN studios, Aster returned to her tiny cubicle at Saybrook's, staring at a massive binder on her desk that listed all the Saybrook's stones still in company storage. The binder was categorized by color and then by carat and other features, like where the diamond was found and whether it was cut. Elizabeth had asked her to input all of the information and upload the images to a cloud server, whatever the hell *that* meant. But Aster needed a moment to breathe. She'd managed to hold it together during the interview itself—actually, she thought, she'd done a pretty fantastic job—but talking about Poppy must have affected her more than she realized. Afterward, she'd started crying on the way to the bathroom. She ducked into a stall and quietly sobbed for a minute, then carefully redid the thick, caked-on TV makeup before saying her good-byes and leaving the studio. Aster knew better than to let anyone see her cry.

Her phone buzzed, and she looked down. *New post on the Blessed and the Cursed*, read the message. Mitch had helped her sign up for these alerts a few weeks ago. Maybe it was masochistic to watch as someone aired the Saybrooks' dirty laundry all over the Internet, but Aster figured it was better to know what was being said than to be blindsided.

She took a deep breath to steel herself, then tapped the link. Sure enough, a new post had loaded. Two pictures were positioned side by side on the screen. On the left was a shot of a sheet-covered figure lying on a busy Manhattan sidewalk, a lock of blond hair peeking out from underneath the tarp, an elegant snakeskin pump emerging from another corner. Aster drew in a breath. *Poppy.*

The other photo was of Natasha lying in a hospital bed. Tubes protruded from her nose. Dark, curly hair framed her oval face, and an eerie smile played around her lips. Aster's mouth dropped open. How had someone gotten close enough to take a picture of Natasha?

"Two Heiresses Down, Three to Go," read the headline in bright red letters.

Aster immediately dialed Foley, but she didn't get through. Trying to remain calm, she scrolled down and looked at the comments under the post. Some of them condemned the message writer and demanded the blog administrator take the post down. Others said, "Can't you take a joke?" Still others wrote that Aster and her cousins deserved it. "Stuck-up bitches," an anonymous poster wrote. "What goes around comes around."

Aster's phone buzzed, startling her. The website had disappeared, and Clarissa's name appeared on the screen. Aster felt a flush of satisfaction—she hadn't seen Clarissa since before Poppy's death, but of course her friend would call in Aster's time of need.

"I'm guessing you saw me on CNN?" Aster asked instead of hello, still feeling shaky from the Blessed post.

"Why were you on CNN?" Clarissa's voice was husky, the way it always got when she smoked too many cigarettes. Aster wondered where she'd been last night. One of their old haunts, or a new club Aster hadn't even heard of?

"Because someone tried to *kill* me?" Aster said slowly, shivering at the sound of that. "There's a crazy serial killer leaving messages on my family's gossip site."

"You shouldn't read that site," Clarissa said. "You know it's all bullshit."

Except it hasn't been bullshit lately, Aster thought. Not all of it.

"Anyway." Clarissa yawned. "Are you coming tonight, or what?"

Aster clutched the phone tightly, startled that Clarissa had changed the subject on her. Being pursued by a murderer wasn't a big deal? "Um, where?"

Clarissa scoffed. "To Boom Boom, of course! Jake's going to be there."

Aster pulled up the Blessed and the Cursed on her computer. Poppy and Natasha's pictures were still front and center; she minimized the window. "Jake?"

"*Gyllenhaal?* Aster, I sent you the screenshots of his texts. Didn't you look?" Clarissa was sounding more and more disgruntled. She launched into a braggy story about how she'd traded texts with Jake and that they were meeting there at twelve thirty.

"I'd love to," Aster said, "but as I just said, my life's sort of in danger. I should probably lie low."

Clarissa snorted. "You sound a little Kim Kardashian overdramatic, honey. The people who post on that site are just doing it for fun."

And do you know this because you are one of them? Aster felt a stab of annoyance. Then she noticed a figure passing in the hallway. "I have to go. I'll call you later," she told Clarissa, and hung up. "Mitch!" she called out. He turned toward her, his face lighting up.

"Hey," he said softly. "How are you holding up?"

"I'm okay," Aster said. Mitch hadn't shaved that morning; the stubble made her notice how sharp his jawline was. He wasn't wearing his glasses, either. Aster had never realized how long his lashes were, longer than she had ever seen on a guy.

Mitch squinted at her, inspecting her features. "You know, *I* wouldn't be okay if I went through what you did this weekend." He glanced down the hall. "Has Elizabeth said anything to you about it?" he whispered.

Aster shook her head. "Not a word. She was pissed, actually, that I had to do an interview today." Elizabeth's door had been firmly closed when she returned to work, but she'd sent Aster an e-mail of things to do, everything in all caps. "She finds it an inconvenience."

Mitch sniffed. "I'd say *she* was the one to push your car off that bridge, but then she'd have no one to do her bitch work."

Aster had already considered the idea. Elizabeth clearly hated the Saybrooks—maybe she'd killed Poppy too, and was after the rest of the cousins next. But she'd checked Elizabeth's calendar this morning before the interview; her boss really *had* been away the morning Poppy was murdered. There were even receipts from the Four Seasons LA and Katsuya to prove it.

When Aster looked up, Mitch was still studying her. He shook his head. "Honestly, I don't know how you can even be here right now. If you need anything today, give me a call, okay? I can do your coffee run for a change," he added wryly.

Aster snickered. "Thanks," she said, then glanced at her computer screen again. "Want to figure out who runs the Blessed and the Cursed for me?"

Mitch frowned. "Isn't the FBI doing that?"

"Yeah, well." It didn't seem like they were working very hard.

Aster pressed her fingers to her temples. Her head was pounding, probably because she hadn't gotten a decent night's sleep since Poppy's murder. The last few nights, her mind had whirled overtime as she struggled to think of who could be after them. Natasha, perhaps—she hated their family so much that perhaps she was picking them off one by one, only her latest plan had backfired and injured her instead. Or a random girlfriend of Steven? Maybe Elizabeth. Maybe someone they didn't even know. And *did* Poppy have a secret? Why was Natasha the only one who knew about it?

"Mitch," she asked, getting an idea. "Have you ever looked through company e-mails?"

"I'm not sure if I should answer that honestly."

"I'm not going to get you in trouble. I'm just curious about Poppy."

She cleared her throat. "I sort of found out that she had . . . *struggles*." It was the same word Jonathan York had used with Corinne at Poppy's funeral. "And maybe a secret."

Mitch frowned. "You mean the jewelry thing?"

"*What* jewelry thing?"

Mitch looked conflicted, then slid forward in his chair. "I thought that's what you meant. A few months ago, HR was concerned that Poppy was . . . taking things."

Aster balked. "Taking things? What do you mean?"

"I saw it on e-mail. I think she checked out some pieces to show clients and never checked them back in. People were worried that she . . . stole them, I guess. And then maybe sold them."

Aster laughed incredulously. "Why would Poppy need money?"

Mitch shrugged. "I don't know. According to the e-mails, the jewels were never returned."

"So was she in trouble?" Aster asked, her mind moving slowly.

Mitch stared up at the ceiling. "I think it just went away. But I have no idea how it was resolved."

"Jesus." Aster's head pounded even harder now. Who was this new Poppy, and why had Aster never met her? She wondered if Rowan knew about the theft allegations. Probably not—she would have mentioned it. "I hate this," she whispered, feeling overwhelmed.

"Hey," Mitch murmured. "It's okay. It'll all be okay." He reached out as if to touch her shoulder, then seemed to think better of it and let his hand fall to the side. The silence stretched taut between them.

Finally Aster turned and started clicking randomly at her computer. "You'd better get out of here, or Elizabeth will push us *both* over a bridge."

"Right." Mitch looked a little disappointed. "See you later, Aster." He turned and loped into the hall. His shoe was untied, and he tripped over the laces, then turned back and shrugged goofily. Aster shook her head, smiling.

Her phone rang, and she jumped. Her father's extension appeared in the caller ID window. "Dad," Aster said shakily. "What's up?"

"I have something I need to talk to you about." Mason sounded very sober.

"Now?" Aster swallowed. Was he going to scold her about the CNN interview? What had she done wrong this time?

"Can you come into my office?"

Aster peeked into the hall. "I'm not sure Elizabeth would like that."

"I'll clear it with her. Come down now."

He hung up before Aster could reply. She rose and smoothed down her dress, a solid blue that would look good on camera and brought out her eyes. Maybe this was a good opportunity, actually. She could ask him about Steven.

She thought back to that night, at the end-of-summer party five years ago. It had been their point of no return. If she'd chosen differently that night, she and her father might have salvaged things.

But instead Aster had followed Steven away from the group, fueled with adrenaline and spiky anger. This was the perfect revenge against her father. If he could ruin her relationship with her best friend, then she could destroy one of his.

As for Danielle, all Aster had felt was hate. She'd thrown away their friendship to be with Aster's *dad*.

She and Steven pushed through the reeds and walked down to the beach. Though Steven had said he wanted to show Aster his yacht, as soon as they were out of view, he seized her around the waist and pulled her close to him. They sank down, and his hands traveled all over her body. In moments he'd unzipped the dress she was wearing and tossed it on the sand. Cool wind kissed Aster's bare skin. She undid the buttons on his shirt and loosened his tuxedo cummerbund. "Oh my God," he'd breathed into Aster's ear. "You are so wet." Aster didn't really feel like dirty talking, so in response she just unzipped his pants and yanked them down.

The moon had risen higher in the sky. Aster closed her eyes and pulled Steven closer to her, letting the anger fuel her movements in place of desire. His mouth was hot, and tasted like whiskey and lime. At one point she thought she smelled a cigar, but then the wind shifted and it was gone.

She didn't hear her father arrive until he was standing almost directly over her.

Steven scrambled away, yanking up his pants. Mason stood there like a wooden block, solid and firm, his arms at his sides. His eyes blazed. His body shook with rage.

"What the hell is wrong with you?" he growled at Aster.

She sat up, pulling her dress around her and crossing her arms over her chest, feeling steadier than she had in a long time. "If you can screw my friend," she said in a strong voice, "then I can screw yours."

Beep.

Aster turned her head back to her computer screen. The Blessed and the Cursed had refreshed, a new post appearing above the pictures of Poppy and Natasha. It was a picture of *her*, she realized, crying as she entered the bathroom at the Time Warner Center. Her eyes were closed, her makeup smeared as tears ran down her cheeks.

"Cry Me a River," read the headline.

Her heart skipped a beat. She hadn't noticed anyone in the hallway with her after the interview. How had the site gotten this picture?

She shuddered and closed the window, then turned and headed for the elevator bank. Whatever her father had to say couldn't be any scarier than this.

ASTER RODE UP two floors to where the execs and lawyers' offices were. She turned right, toward the big corner office. "Hello?" she called out softly, poking her head inside.

Her father's office was empty, his chair turned to face the window. Aster walked in and inspected his desk. There was no note saying he'd be back in a moment. She felt a familiar dart of annoyance. This was *so* like him—calling her down here, only to make her wait.

A web page with the Chase bank logo was on the computer screen. Aster started to glance away—then paused when she saw how many zeros were there. It was the confirmation receipt for a liquidation of company stock: "100,000 shares," it read. "In the amount of $10 million." Aster's mouth made a small O, and she leaned in a little closer. The transaction was from five years ago. She wondered why her father was looking at it now, and what it was for. Why had Mason wanted to unload so much stock all at once?

"Aster."

Her father stood in the doorway. "Oh, hey," Aster said, scuttling back to the couch and sitting down.

Another figure stepped out from behind him—Jonathan York, her once-uncle. He was wearing a well-cut gray suit and shiny loafers, and a large gold watch on his left wrist. There was a disconcertingly smug smile on his face.

"Oh, hi, Jonathan," Aster said, giving him a small wave. Back when he was officially a Saybrook, she'd never known how to deal with him. The family was full of strong personalities, but there was something about him—his silence, his hulking shoulders, his penetrating stare—that put her on edge. Rumor had it that he and her aunt Grace divorced because he was too controlling.

"Jonathan was just leaving." Mason turned to shake his hand. "I'll call you tomorrow." And then, offering a stiff nod, Jonathan was gone.

Mason slipped into his office and shut the door. "What was he doing here?" Aster asked.

"Oh, making trouble as usual," Mason said quickly, breezing past her to his desk. He spun his chair back around and sat. When he glanced at his computer screen, a guarded look flashed across his face, and he looked carefully at Aster. She kept her face blank. Then Mason reached over and shut the monitor off.

"So." Mason opened a Diet Coke. He took a long swig and swallowed audibly. "You did a good job on CNN."

"I did?"

"Yes, you did. Deanna and I are both pleased. As is your grandmother. We appreciate you doing it at the last moment."

Aster tugged at her collar, not used to praise. "No problem," she said in a small voice.

Mason drummed his fingers on the desk. "I also wanted to thank you for your good idea, about the engagement ring for Ko and Faun."

Aster frowned. "Pardon?"

"Making a ring like one Faun's mother used to have. Elizabeth told me about it this morning."

"Elizabeth *used* that idea? She told me it was stupid."

Mason coughed. "Well, she presented it to me earlier today. She tried to take the credit too, but Mitch Erikson was here, working on my computer, and he piped up that it had been your thought all along. I asked Elizabeth if it was true, and she admitted that it was."

Elizabeth had been upstaged? Mitch had stood up for her to her father? Aster smiled at the thought.

Mason leaned forward, his features softening. "I'd like for you to work more closely with clients. Apparently your background makes you a perfect consultant for some of their wants and needs. Maybe the last few years haven't been a waste after all."

Aster stared at him. "Are you promoting me because of my partying?"

Mason looked pained. "I'd rather not put it that way."

"I just . . . I didn't expect it."

"You're welcome," Mason said.

They stared at each other in silence. Aster hated it, but she missed her father. Missed having him cheer her on, believe in her, encourage her. "Aster, I'm your biggest fan," he always used to say. "Don't ever forget that."

But then she thought of him embracing Danielle, sleeping with her best friend and thinking he could hide it from her, and the window inside her that had opened a crack slammed shut again.

She cleared her throat. "I have a question." Mason nodded, and Aster forged ahead. "Do you know if Steven Barnett had a serious girlfriend before he died?"

Mason flinched. His fingers released the mouse. "What does that have to do with anything?"

"I mean, Elizabeth's my boss," Aster said quickly. She stared at him pointedly, waiting for a reaction. "Anyway, she's made reference to it," Aster went on. "I was just wondering."

"I try not to listen to staff gossip," Mason said brusquely. "Steven did a lot of things I didn't approve of."

"But didn't Papa Alfred pick him right out of business school? He always gave Steven so much credit for why the business was so successful."

"Yes, well." Mason restacked the papers on the side of his desk. "Not all of us thought as highly of Steven as your grandfather did."

Aster didn't dare push the subject further. But since the mood was already altered, she figured she might as well keep going. "Did Poppy steal jewelry?"

Mason drew back angrily. "Where did you hear that?" he demanded. "Was it on that site?"

"No. Is it true?"

Mason's fingers curled into a fist so tight that veins stuck out on the back of his hand. He breathed heavily for a few beats, his eyes downcast. "It's been taken care of."

She frowned. "What does *that* mean?"

"It means, *stop asking about it*."

"Why would Poppy do something like that? Does Foley know about this?"

Mason shot up from his desk. Aster pressed her spine into the cushion and made a small yelp. "What did I just tell you?" he demanded.

"I'm sorry." Aster breathed shakily. "I just . . ."

"I told you to *stop asking about it*!" Mason bellowed.

"Okay," Aster whispered, curling into herself.

Mason's nostrils flared. It looked as if he was going to say something else, but he was interrupted by the phone on his desk. "I need to take this," he said, giving a little wave of his hand as if to say, *You're dismissed*.

Aster stood and hurried toward the door, slamming it hard behind her.

18

On Friday, Rowan paused outside Scarpetta in the Meatpacking District. It used to be one of Poppy's favorite restaurants. Before Poppy married James, she and Rowan used to meet here after work and drink red wine that men at the bar would invariably buy them. "Let 'em pay," Poppy always said, tossing her blond hair over her shoulder. "It makes them feel needed—and it's a small price to pay to talk to someone as awesome as you are, Ro." Now, just seeing the awning filled Rowan with nostalgia and sadness.

But that emotion was swept away quickly as she felt someone's gaze boring into her back. She turned, and two men, several years younger, turned their heads quickly, pretending they hadn't been staring. The light changed, and they crossed the street. "Sex tape," Rowan heard one of them say.

She sighed. All of New York City now knew what she was like during sex. Deanna and the family's personal lawyers had sent multiple threatening e-mails to the Blessed and the Cursed, and the post had finally been taken down. But they still didn't know who was running the fucking site—or who was tipping it off.

The video was like a big X on her soul. Her brothers had called her about it, asking awkward, worried questions. Her mother, the feminist, had driven into the city to see Rowan. Over chickpea fries and quinoa salad at Peacefood Cafe, Leona had lectured Rowan about how she was thirty-two years old now and should be a little more careful about her romantic entanglements—not to mention that if she hadn't been working for the family company, she could have been fired. Even James had been freaked out, though Rowan had assured him again and again that no one knew it was him. The whole situation was mortifying.

Her phone rang, the volume so low Rowan almost didn't hear it over the sounds of Fourteenth Street traffic. Rowan checked the screen and saw a 212 number. When she answered, a young woman's voice said, "Rowan Saybrook? This is Shoshanna Aaron. I'm returning your call."

"*Hi*," Rowan said emphatically, cupping her hands around the phone. "Thank you so much for speaking to me."

A bus passed, drowning out Rowan's voice for a moment, but then she launched into the speech she'd rehearsed. "I won't take up much of your time. I'm the legal counsel at Saybrook's, and it's come to my attention that you might have pertinent information about Poppy."

Papers rustled on the other end. "What do you mean?"

Rowan pictured Poppy's old assistant. Long, dark hair, olive skin, a pretty face, a diamond-encrusted Chopard watch surely paid for by her father and not her assistant's salary. She had fit in well in the jewelry culture, always traveling with a gaggle of girls to lunch or happy hour.

"I spoke to Danielle Gilchrist recently, and she told me you noticed Poppy acting strangely before you left for De Beers."

There was a long pause. "I'm really sorry about Poppy," Shoshanna started. "I feel so guilty saying anything bad about her, you know?"

"I know," Rowan said quickly. "This isn't going on the record, either. I'm just curious about what exactly happened."

"Well, she was acting weird," Shoshanna said uneasily. "She asked me to get off a lot of calls. She scheduled appointments but didn't describe who they were with or where she was going. It made it hard to explain to Mason and other executives why she couldn't make meetings when I didn't know where she actually was. But what really made me wonder was the suite she booked at the Mandarin."

"What do you mean?"

"I got a call from the hotel confirming Poppy's reservation for one of their suites on a Wednesday. It wasn't on her calendar, so I thought it was a mistake. I was telling them to cancel it when Poppy broke in on the other line. 'Shoshanna, I've got it,' she said, and then told the reservations person that she would use her private card." Shoshanna coughed awkwardly. "Then I got off the line. But it seemed kind of . . . clear, you know?"

Rowan shut her eyes. "But you never caught a name? Never . . . *saw* anyone?"

"Oh, no. Nothing like that." A phone rang on Shoshanna's end. "Which means it might not be anything. I mean, I'm sure it's not." She swallowed audibly. "Poppy was a really good boss. I don't want you to think I'd ever, I don't know—*sell* this information."

"Of course not," Rowan said, though she hadn't even considered that.

She thanked Shoshanna, then hung up and walked into the restaurant in a daze. There it was, probably as close as she was going to get to proof that Poppy wasn't who Rowan had understood her to be. But as painful as Shoshanna's revelation was, it was also freeing. Staying away from James was being loyal to a ghost who hadn't been loyal to James. Poppy had moved on and found love elsewhere, and now maybe James and Rowan could too.

Corinne waved to her from a back table, and Rowan nodded and wove through the dining room to get to her. An iPad loaded with pictures sat in front of her cousin; Corinne was going through photographs to display at her wedding. When Corinne saw Rowan's expression, she cocked her head. "Did something happen?"

Rowan explained her conversation with Shoshanna. "So maybe Poppy and whoever the guy was had been meeting at a suite at the Mandarin," she concluded.

"Huh," Corinne said softly, though she didn't look like she quite believed it. "I wonder who it could be."

"No idea," Rowan said.

"Are you going to tell James?"

"I already told him what Danielle said." Rowan ran her finger along a groove on the wooden table. She'd finally mentioned her conversation with Danielle when she slept over at his place last night. "Well, that proves it, then," he'd said thickly.

James wanted to put it behind them; let sleeping dogs lie, he'd said. They had each other now. But Rowan couldn't let it go. What if the affair had something to do with Poppy's death?

A waitress set down two glasses of Corinne and Rowan's favorite malbec on the table, breaking Rowan from her thoughts. "So. How's the picture selection coming?"

"Eh," Corinne said miserably, flipping through a few images.

"What about this one?" Rowan pointed at a photograph of Corinne and Dixon a few years after they'd first met at Yale. They were at a Kentucky Derby party—Corinne was wearing an oversize hat, and Dixon was drinking from a silver cup. "It's really cute," Rowan added.

Corinne shook her head. "I look terrible in that one."

She scrolled through another perfectly good photo, nixing it too. Then another. Finally she let out a long sigh and ran her fingers through her hair. Rowan thought about what Corinne had confessed at the beach estate.

Rowan laid her hands on top of the iPad and gave her cousin a long, serious look. "Honey. *What* are you going to do?"

Corinne heaved a sigh and then dropped her forehead to the table. The part in her hair was a stark line splitting her head in two. "I'm going to get married," she said in a muffled voice.

"Do you *want* to get married?"

"Of course."

"People will forgive you if you don't, you know."

Corinne looked up, her mouth twisting. "What do you think Poppy would do?"

Rowan traced her finger around the top of the wineglass. "I honestly don't know," she said in a faraway voice. "I feel like she's a stranger these days."

"I know." Corinne swallowed hard. "First we lose Poppy . . . and then we lose who we thought Poppy *was*. I feel like I have to revise my whole history with her." A tortured look crossed her face, but then she sighed and seemed to let it go. She glanced down at the iPad again and smiled sadly at something on the screen. "Aw."

Rowan looked down too. The next photo was of James. He stood alone on the patio at Meriweather, wearing a seersucker blazer. Rowan remembered that blazer—shortly after he'd booked the house that summer, he'd arrived at her apartment in the city with a Brooks Brothers bag. "Do people really dress like this up there? Or am I going to look like a douche?"

Rowan had snorted. "You're asking *me* for style advice?"

James snickered. "Good point, Saybrook. You're as hopeless as I am." But he'd shot her a twinkly-eyed look as if to say, *We're in this together.*

She grabbed her phone from her purse and checked the screen. She'd sent James an I-miss-you text earlier, but he hadn't responded. Skylar had a parent-teacher conference tonight, and she wanted to hear how he was doing.

"You know, I really am happy for you," Corinne murmured softly.

Rowan looked up and touched her cousin's hand. "Thank you. But you don't have to be. I know it's strange."

Corinne shrugged. "In the grand scheme of things, after everything else we've learned, it's nothing." She touched the stem of her wineglass. "Have there been any more posts about . . . the video online?"

Rowan shook her head. "No, but I still don't understand who could have gotten it off my computer," she said worriedly.

Corinne nodded. "Do you think it was someone at work?"

"Maybe," Rowan said. "But . . ." Then she trailed off, noticing something outside. A man had walked by who looked exactly like

James. Same height, same build, same color of hair. Only Skylar's school was way uptown. She must have been mistaken.

But then she caught sight of him again in the windows along the west wall of the building. It was definitely James. His head was down, and he was typing something into his phone. On instinct Rowan looked at her own phone, anticipating a text, but one didn't arrive.

"What is it?" Corinne asked, noticing that Rowan had hitched forward to get a better view.

James had stopped and was staring at something across the street. He took a few steps forward, past where the window reached, seemingly toward someone. A smile spread across his face. Rowan's skin prickled. She recognized that smile.

She rose from the table, bumping her knee against the bottom. "Where are you going?" Corinne cried out.

"I'll be back in a sec," Rowan called over her shoulder. She would just walk out the door and see who it was. For all she knew, it was Skylar; maybe she'd misunderstood where he was tonight.

She brushed past the bar and stepped through the double doors onto the street, almost bumping into a quick-moving businessman going the other direction. Her heels clicked on the sidewalk as she walked to the corner and peered up the street, but James was no longer there. Rowan hesitated, then strode a few paces up the street; maybe he'd disappeared around a corner. She scanned the shops on the avenue: a dingy deli, a Duane Reade drugstore, and one of those New York frame shops that sold the same five Monet prints.

And then there he was, standing at the entrance of Dream Downtown. A dark-haired woman in a sleeveless dress held his hand, and the two of them walked toward the revolving doors. Rowan's stomach flipped. As the woman tilted her head toward him and brushed a piece of hair out of her face, Rowan realized she knew her too. It was Evan Pierce. Corinne's wedding planner. Poppy's *friend*.

Rowan was suddenly next to them without having known how she got there. Evan looked over first. "Oh!" she said pleasantly. "Hello, Rowan."

James stopped short at the sound of her name. He dropped Evan's hand, but didn't move away from her. "Rowan," he said, his voice taut. "Shit."

They had stopped right in front of the revolving door; a stream of people had to squeeze around them to get into the building. But Rowan couldn't move out of the way. "You're not with Skylar" was the only thing she could think to say. She hated how weak her voice sounded.

James stepped forward. "I know. But I can explain."

Rowan drew away from his touch. Evan crossed her arms over her chest, studying James quizzically. "Is everything all right?"

But Rowan kept her gaze on James. "Okay, then. Explain." Maybe they were here for a business meeting. Maybe Evan wanted to create a wedding-planning app. Maybe . . .

James's eyes darted back and forth guiltily. He shifted his weight and ran his hand through his hair. Rowan's heart sank. She recognized this look too. She'd lived through it countless times when James brought one girl to a party and left with another.

But she'd never thought he would do it to *her*.

"Jesus," she spat, a hard shell forming around her. Then she wheeled around toward the street, suddenly desperate to escape.

"Rowan!" James cried, darting after her. "Wait! Please!"

Her walk turned to a run. She sped to the end of the street, her eyes blurring with shameful tears. *Fucking idiot*, a voice inside her chided. And she'd thought James had changed. It was sickening how blindsided she felt, when really, she should have seen this coming from miles away.

"Rowan!" James's voice receded down the street.

She walked downtown, focusing on a forward point and nothing else. If she stopped walking, she thought, she might perish. If she stopped walking, she might start thinking about what had just happened. And she might crumble to sand.

"Rowan!" James screamed, a half block away. "Rowan, come back here!"

His words washed over her. She thought of a million horrible things she could say to him, but she couldn't imagine even looking at him right then. So she picked up the pace, turning off the avenue and zigzagging down a side street. Two small blocks later, she realized James's calls had ceased. She looked over her shoulder, and James was gone. She was filled partly with satisfaction and partly with loathing. He hadn't even bothered to keep up with her.

She turned a corner onto a street she didn't recognize. Abandoned slaughterhouses loomed above her like old iron carcasses. Rowan heard traffic sounds, but her head was spinning so manically that she couldn't tell which way Tenth Avenue was. Her heart started to thud. How was it that she had no idea where she was in her hometown?

She ran, her heels twisting, her arms pumping. When she stepped off a curb, her ankle turned. She felt her body launch into the air and screamed. Her knee hit the brick street first, and then her elbow. White-hot pain shot through her body, and she scrambled up as fast as she could. But then she felt a rush of wind to her left, and a horn honked in her ear. The headlights were bearing down on her as she turned her head.

"Rowan!" someone screamed behind her, and she felt a force pulling her back.

She stumbled up the curb again as the cab whipped past, the driver still laying on his horn. "Oh my God!" Corinne cried, spinning Rowan around and looking into her eyes. She pulled Rowan close and flung her arms around her.

"That car came out of nowhere," Rowan whispered, feeling her heart bang against her rib cage. She gazed out at the empty street. The cab's taillights disappeared around a corner. Thank God her cousin had been there.

Rowan began to quietly sob. Corinne might have been able to save her from a head-on collision, but who would rescue her from the free fall of a broken heart?

19

Corinne swept through the doors of her apartment building. "Miss Saybrook!" her doorman called out to her. Corinne turned warily. He was holding a large file folder in his hand. "For you. From that redhead."

Corinne breezed over and took it from him, saying a clipped thank-you. "Turkey—New Hires," it said in round handwriting on the front. She undid the closure and pulled out a few fat résumés. A pink Post-it was on the top one. "Sorry to hit you with work, but I need these approved by tomorrow. Thanks, Danielle."

"Is she single?" Markus called after her as she clicked to the elevator.

Corinne tucked the files in her purse. "I don't think so," she called over her shoulder. She remembered Danielle bringing an attractive man named Brett Verdoorn to the Christmas party last year.

She unlocked her apartment and dropped her keys on the enormous marble kitchen island. Dixon, still in his work suit and loafers, was sitting in the den, the TV flashing against his face. Four players sat at a poker table, trading cards out to the dealer. Corinne slammed kitchen drawers and cabinets open and closed, sighing loudly when she noticed that Dixon had left an unwashed bowl of melted ice cream in the porcelain farmhouse sink—couldn't he even wash a dish? She opened the fridge and pushed it shut again, hating its contents. She kicked off her shoes and didn't care that they went skidding across the marble floor.

"Hey, babe," he called out pleasantly, then slung an arm over the couch and tilted his neck back to get a view of her. "Where were you? More wedding stuff?"

Corinne plopped down next to him, irritated that he didn't seem to sense her distress. "I just saw something awful," she blurted.

Dixon crossed his arms over his chest. "Something on that website?"

"No. Worse." Corinne told him about finding James with Evan. "I just hope Rowan's okay. She's not picking up."

"Wait, wait. Evan Pierce? Holy shit." Dixon started to unscrew his cuff links. "I mean, that's fucked up. But why would Rowan care any more than the rest of you?"

Corinne bit the inside of her cheek. Sometimes she forgot how much she *didn't* tell Dixon. "They've been seeing each other."

Dixon's mouth dropped open. "Wait a minute. *James* is the dude in the video?" He reached for his gin and tonic on the side table next to the couch. A slice of lime bobbed cheerfully on top. "I mean, isn't that kind of messed up? Moving in on your dead cousin's husband?" He raised an eyebrow at Corinne.

"Dixon. *James* is the one who's at fault here," Corinne said. "They were consenting adults—Rowan wasn't moving in on anyone."

Dixon chuckled. "She sure seemed in charge in that video."

"She's my *cousin*, Dixon. Did you seriously watch that?"

Dixon shrugged good-naturedly. "Me and the rest of America."

Corinne shut her eyes, trying her best to let the comment go. "He's been sleeping with someone else. Poppy's best friend . . . *and* our wedding planner." She rubbed her temples, suddenly realizing something. "Does this mean I should fire her? I probably should, shouldn't I?"

"Whoa, whoa, whoa." Dixon held up a halting palm. "We're not firing Evan. The wedding is next *week*."

Corinne stood up and walked to the large fireplace in the back of the room. She didn't know why she was so indignant. She'd cheated on Dixon. She of all people knew how easy it was to do. How it could just happen.

"You're acting as if no one did anything wrong *except* for Rowan. What about James? At least tell me that what he's done is terrible. At least give me *that*." Even as she heard the words coming out of her mouth, she felt like she was in a play, acting the part of Corinne Saybrook.

Dixon sipped his cocktail. "Wasn't James always sort of a dog? Guys like that never change."

His gaze returned to poker just as one of the players—a smug-looking kid in a hoodie—won a hand and took a bunch of chips. Corinne pressed her hands against the cold marble mantel and tried to breathe, but there was a fire burning in her chest. "So that's how you rationalize it?" she asked shakily. "Rowan should have known better, so it's her fault."

Dixon set his glass back down. "Why are you picking a fight with me?"

"I'm not. I'm just—"

"Wait, wait." Dixon held his hand up, pointing at something on the screen. The players were placing new bids.

Corinne swallowed a scream and walked out of the room. She counted to five, but Dixon didn't follow her. She sank down into one of the high-backed wing chairs and laid her hands in her lap. But the chair wasn't comfortable. A crowd cheered on the TV in the other room. Dixon applauded exuberantly.

Corinne knew what would happen: in a few minutes, he would come in here and say, "Hey, let's go out," in an attempt to smooth it over. And then they would go somewhere loud and expensive, and they wouldn't talk about the argument because they *never* talked about their arguments, just like they never talked about anything real.

It hit her all at once: the whole time they'd been dating, she'd been waiting for him to *become* serious. Not serious as in I-want-to-marry-you serious, but serious in his own skin. Grown-up enough to have real discussions. Adult enough to want to spend a whole evening alone with her instead of inviting everyone along as though they were still in college. The more the merrier? Maybe it was because he had *nothing to say to her.*

And maybe she went along with it because she had nothing to say to him, either.

She stood up and pressed her hands to the window like a prisoner in a cell, watching the lights on Fifth Avenue change from red to green to yellow to red to green to yellow, the little don't-cross hands blinking in perfect tempo. It was beautiful, actually. A mini symphony of lights below her window, and she'd never noticed it before.

Don't you want to live an honest life?

Will's face appeared before her, and all at once, she thought she could. She felt stronger, suddenly, as if she could break from the mold of what she was supposed to be. Poppy had broken that mold, it seemed—and hell, so had Rowan and Aster and certainly Natasha. It felt as if they'd all broken an important contract that every Saybrook woman was supposed to uphold. They were *supposed* to be faithful and upstanding. They were *supposed* to set an example.

Why did *she* have to carry the torch for all of them? It suddenly didn't seem fair. And maybe Rowan was right: her family would forgive her for breaking it off with Dixon. Maybe not tomorrow, but they would—eventually. She was strong enough, she realized, to weather that storm. Because she would have Will.

But living an honest life meant coming clean too. Corinne took a breath, daring to consider what that meant. She pictured Will's face when she told him the whole truth. She imagined the questions that he'd ask. She imagined what he'd say—or wouldn't say. She had to acknowledge that he might not want to speak to her again. But if she wanted them to have a chance, she had to reveal everything.

She just had to do one thing first.

20

Saturday morning, Aster strode into the lobby of Elizabeth's apartment building, wearing a floppy hat, a sand-colored caftan, and gold sandals. It was a blisteringly hot day, and Clarissa had invited her to SoHo House later. Aster kept trying to muster up some excitement about going—normally she loved summer afternoons at SoHo House, sitting by the rooftop pool and sipping chilled rosé. But she was still irritated by Clarissa's complete indifference to what was going on with her family. Someone had killed Poppy and tried to kill the rest of them, and she was supposed to sit there and talk about Jake Gyllenhaal and whether he liked blondes or brunettes?

Taking a deep breath, she gave her name to the doorman and said she was here to see Elizabeth. "Is she expecting you?" he asked.

"I'm her assistant." Aster shifted nervously, wondering if this was a bad idea. What if Elizabeth wasn't home? But after tossing and turning all last night, haunted by nightmares about that stupid website and its headlines, Aster had woken up determined to get some answers.

The doorman picked up the phone, and after a moment, he gave Aster a nod. "You can go on up."

Taking a deep breath, Aster walked into the elevator and rode it all the way to the penthouse, staring at her reflection in the full-wall mirrors that lined the car. Something flashed out of the corner of her eye, but when she whipped around, the car was empty. She smoothed down her hair. She needed to stop being so jumpy.

The doors slid open, and Aster stepped tentatively inside. She'd dropped off countless packages for Elizabeth in the lobby, but she'd never actually been in the apartment before. A gourmet designer kitchen was to Aster's left, done up in exotic stone and dark wood. There was a living room full of angular, modern-looking furniture and an intimidating bronze stove shooting from the ceiling like a tongue. Sweeping views of the city greeted her from the enormous windows. On a far wall was a large display of photographs of Elizabeth and Steven together: the two of them walking down the aisle on their wedding day, in front of the Eiffel Tower, and in bathing suits on a tropical beach. Over the mantel was the same wedding photograph that Elizabeth kept in her office.

Elizabeth stepped out from what must be the bedroom, dressed in a long silk dressing gown and Louis Vuitton slippers, and with a bath towel wrapped around her head.

Aster flushed. "Oh, I'm sorry. I should have called first."

"Yes, you should've," Elizabeth said. "I was just giving myself a facial. But since you're here, you might as well tell me why you came. That hat is hideous, by the way," she added, turning back into the bedroom.

It's Hermès, Aster wanted to snap. But instead she just took off the hat and set it carefully on the kitchen counter.

She followed Elizabeth into the massive bedroom, where an extra-large king done up all in white presided over the space. Near the window were three mint-green chairs and an antique side table. A cart full of skin products sat on the Oriental area rug, as did a large machine with what looked like a vacuum hose protruding from a large white box. Elizabeth settled into the chair, squirted lotion onto her palms, and began massaging it over her face. "So, what did you want this morning, Aster?" she asked. "Are you here to hand in your resignation?"

Aster glanced out the floor-to-ceiling windows. She could see right into the apartments across the courtyard. Anyone could look in and see her and Elizabeth too.

Aster perched on the edge of the chair opposite her boss. "Sorry to disappoint you, but no. I was actually wondering if you could answer a question for me. About . . . your husband."

Elizabeth raised an eyebrow, but said nothing. Aster took that as permission to continue. "I wanted to know if he might have had an affair with anyone around . . . around the same time he was with me." She stared at the carpet.

"You know, jealousy doesn't suit you," Elizabeth chided.

Aster ignored the jab. "I just . . . with all this stuff connected to Poppy's murder investigation, I thought it might be important. What if whoever killed her was close to Steven? And killed Poppy for revenge?"

"If someone wanted revenge for Steven's death, why would they wait five years to push Poppy out a window?" Elizabeth asked. The machine beeped, and she moved the facial wand to her forehead as it started to buzz. "Someone could have done that the next day."

"I know it doesn't add up. But maybe this person wasn't sure Poppy killed him. Maybe she just found a final piece to the puzzle or something. Maybe you told someone else what you saw?"

A horn honked out the window. Elizabeth gestured to the facial machine. "Microdermabrasion." She sighed. "Tiny little knives are searing off all my dead skin cells. I love thinking about it like that."

"Look, do you know anything or not?" Aster asked, as impatiently as she dared.

Elizabeth pressed her lips together. "The only thing I can tell you is that my husband had a thing for townies. They looked at him like he was a god. He loved that. Sometimes I found things they left behind—name tags from diners, drugstore lipstick, a lifeguard whistle, even a pay stub once. I went into the fudge shop on Main Street, and this little blond thing ran into the back. That's when I knew Steven had nailed her too."

Aster glanced at the pictures of Steven on the mantel. He seemed to be smirking at them. The idea that she'd been with him suddenly made her sick. "And you never said anything to him?" she asked.

"What did I care? Better them than me." Elizabeth looked closely at Aster. "Steven wasn't all that great in the sack, as *you* know," she added pointedly.

Aster flushed. "No one deserves to be cheated on."

Elizabeth turned the hose back on and scoured her chin. "That's pretty rich, coming from you." She sighed. "Besides, we had quite the prenup. Poppy's way was much cleaner."

"We don't know for sure that Poppy killed him."

Elizabeth snorted. "Yes, darling. We *do*."

The sun came out from a cloud, sending a shard of light through the windows. "You said something before about Poppy having a secret. Do you think that's true?"

Elizabeth smiled knowingly. "Steven used to say Saybrooks were born liars."

"Do you know what he was talking about—specifically, I mean?"

Elizabeth looked at her for a long time. Aster flinched, anticipating a huge blow, but Elizabeth just stood up and removed the towel from her head. Her skin glowed. Her wet hair streamed down her shoulders. She reached for a glass of water on the table and took a long, slow sip. "You know, now that you mention it, there *was* a girl who seemed like she'd do anything for him," she said.

"Do you know where she worked? Or her name, maybe?"

Elizabeth balled the towel in her hand. "I never asked. But I wouldn't waste your time, honey—I don't think my husband's trashy ex-girlfriend killed your cousin. Personally, I think it was an inside job."

"Inside . . . what?"

Elizabeth smiled mildly. "Inside the *family*." Then she gently took Aster's arm and led her to the door. "Time to go now."

"What do you mean?" Aster asked as the doors swooshed open. "Why would you say that?"

Elizabeth practically shoved her outside. "My shrink is coming in a few minutes." She tossed Aster's hat to her chest. "My advice, dear? Go ask your father." She winked. "You can't be daddy's girl forever."

21

Monday morning, Rowan absent-mindedly bumped her bruised knee into a newly built cubicle and then burst into tears. It didn't even hurt that badly; it just felt like another mishap in a string of very, very bad luck.

"God, it's so creepy," Jessica, one of the paralegals, whispered as Rowan trudged to her office. "Two Saybrooks within weeks of each other."

"Natasha *still* hasn't woken up," Callie, a second paralegal, chimed in. "They're totally cursed."

"Is she still in that hospital in Massachusetts?" Jessica stirred her coffee, the spoon clanking against ceramic.

"No, I heard they moved her somewhere in the city. Lenox Hill, maybe?"

Beth Israel, Rowan wanted to correct them as she sat down at her desk. Natasha had been moved there a few days before so she'd be closer to her family. Rowan had visited her yesterday, sitting by her bedside and staring at Natasha's placid face. A few times her eyelids had fluttered, and she'd turned her head slightly, as if she was rousing from a dream. Rowan stood halfway in anticipation. She will wake up, and I will get the truth out of her, she'd thought. But then Natasha's features had stilled and she seemed to slip back into that dark, unknowable well, her secret locked inside.

Rowan put her head in her hands. It wasn't just Natasha she

was upset about. It was something far more trivial: heartbreak. But it was ridiculous. Of *course* James had cheated on her. She'd had a front-row seat for his cheating dozens of times. She'd always laughed at those stupid girls who thought there was something real between them. But she was the stupidest girl of all. She'd thought he'd changed, that Poppy had made him different. But he'd cheated on Poppy *with* her. What else had he done?

Taking a deep breath, she rolled her chair backward, opened a file drawer, and found a folder marked "Saybrook–Kenwood." Inside was the prenuptial agreement between Poppy and James that she'd helped draft years ago.

She leafed through it slowly. Sure enough, James would receive nothing of Poppy's estate if they divorced. Not a cent of her massive trust. Not a dollar of her sizable earnings as Saybrook's president. Rowan had argued with Poppy on this when they were putting the prenup together. "This is overly brutal," she'd warned Poppy.

Still, Poppy had been firm: the family had worked too hard for any of their fortune to just be given away. Rowan had been the bearer of bad news to James, but he'd taken it well. "I'm not with Poppy for her money," he said simply.

But if Poppy died—*when* Poppy died—he got it all. It wasn't unthinkable that a cheating husband would want to make a new life for himself. It wasn't implausible that someone would do anything to make that a reality, either.

Would James?

Rowan rubbed her eyes. Of course he wouldn't. Besides, James had an alibi: Rowan's apartment. She'd left before he had, and by the time she got downtown, Poppy had already jumped.

The air-conditioning whirred to life, blowing a stray piece of paper off the vent. Rowan opened her e-mail and tried to work, but her mind was still humming. She felt unsatisfied.

She returned to that first morning she and James were together. What if James hadn't remained at her apartment, as she'd thought?

What if he'd slipped out when she wasn't looking? She'd stopped for coffee that morning. Waited in that long line, then ate in the park. He could have left without her seeing. James *could* have jumped up as soon as she left, thrown on clothes, and gotten to Saybrook's in time. It was possible.

Awful, unthinkable, but possible.

She reached for the phone on her desk and dialed the number to her apartment building, her heart knocking against her ribs. Harvey, her doorman, answered in a chipper voice, and after Rowan identified herself, she asked, "I'm wondering if you could look up when someone left my apartment on a certain morning. You keep surveillance tapes, yes?"

"Of course," Harvey said. "Which day would you like me to check?"

Rowan gave the date of Poppy's death. If Harvey knew its significance, he gave no indication. "And who are we looking for, around what time?" he asked.

"A tall man, midthirties," Rowan told him. "Wavy, sort of longish hair. Striped shirt. Dark jeans. Sometime in the morning, after six thirty."

Harvey said he'd look into it and call her back, asking for a number he could reach her at. She gave her cell. Then she hung up, pressing the receiver deep into the cradle, her mind at a standstill.

"Knock knock?"

Rowan shot up. James stood in the doorway.

"W-what are you doing here?" she sputtered, jumping so abruptly she knocked over an empty coffee mug.

James leaned down to pick it up as it rolled across the carpet. "I want to explain."

Rowan thought of the phone conversation she'd just had—and was keenly aware of the prenup on her lap. Then something else hit her: *My wife was president*, James had said the last time he'd unexpectedly popped in on her in the office. *They just wave me in.*

Had they waved him inside the morning Poppy died too? His name wouldn't be on a sign-in sheet. There would be no evidence of him entering the building.

"Actually, I think you should leave," she said toughly, trying to mask how shaky she felt.

James flopped on the couch. "Saybrook."

"Don't call me that," Rowan almost shouted, covering her eyes. "At least not right now."

"*Rowan*, I made a mistake." He hitched forward. "I want to be with you. Really and truly. *You're* who I want."

His voice cracked. Rowan studied him more carefully. His hair was mussed, his skin was ashen, the lines around his mouth pronounced. This gave her a twinge of guilt, but then she hardened. He *deserved* to feel terrible. And for all she knew, it was just an act.

"The thing with Evan . . . it was a fluke," James went on when Rowan didn't respond. "She came by the apartment the other night to get a sweater she'd left there. We got to talking, had a couple drinks, and . . ." He puffed his cheeks and breathed out. "I don't know how it happened. And I never meant for it to happen a second time."

"You must have *kind of* meant for it to happen," Rowan said before she could stop herself. "Because you and Evan were walking into a *hotel*, James. I'm not an idiot."

James stood and walked toward her. He leaned over and placed his hand on her desk. "Tell me what we had didn't mean something."

Rowan did her best to look away. "I don't want to talk about this right now."

"Well, *I* do." James's voice was louder now. "I'm crazy about you, Saybrook. I *know* you're crazy about me." He leaned forward, his eyes wide. "I already lost Poppy. I can*not* lose you."

"Please." Rowan angled away from him. "I need you to go."

James took a step around her desk, toward her chair. Panicked, Rowan spun around so he couldn't see the papers, covering the top page with her hand. "Don't shut me out," he pleaded, catching the back of the chair and turning her back to face him.

The papers slipped from the sudden force; Rowan struggled to keep them on her lap, but a few fluttered to the ground. James cocked his head, his gaze drifting to the carpet. His name was on the top page. In bold lettering. A beat passed. The star-shaped Nelson clock in the corner ticked loudly. Rowan could almost detect the exact moment James realized what she was hiding.

"What are you doing with those?" James said in a tight voice Rowan had never heard before.

"Nothing," Rowan said quickly, scooping them up and shoving them behind her.

He shot forward to grab the papers. Blocking him with her body, Rowan shoved them into a desk drawer and slammed it shut hard. James's brow furrowed. He leaned over her to pull at the knob, half his weight on her.

"Hey!" Rowan cried out, pushing him away. "That's confidential!"

James leaned into her again, his eyes blazing. "I thought we were closer than that."

"We're not a *we* anymore," Rowan said firmly, shoving him off her once more. "Like I said before, James. *Go.*"

Slowly James stood up, never taking his gaze off her. His jaw was clenched, and his nostrils flared. There was something coiled and tense about him, as if he were a snake ready to strike. Terror washed over her. Maybe he'd come here to test the waters. And now, with her pulling out the prenup, acting so strange, he knew that she suspected him.

Rowan thought of the balcony off her office, the same as the one off Poppy's. All that separated her from Poppy's fate was the thin sliding-glass door behind her, the low terrace wall, and then the long fall to the street. Was that door locked? She couldn't recall.

James took a step closer to Rowan. Rowan rolled back, hitting her desk. James took another step, trapping her.

"Rowan, Rowan, Rowan," James said quietly, his breath hot on her face. He reached out and touched her cheek. Rowan flinched and squeezed her eyes shut, feeling his fingers graze her skin. Her jaw began to tremble. He wouldn't be so stupid as to hurt her right now. There were people just outside the office. But what if he'd cracked? What if he wanted revenge even if it meant he would be caught too?

"You're going to make me look like a cheating shithead so that everybody has an easy scapegoat, aren't you?" James whispered angrily.

"You're insane." Rowan's voice sounded stilted, not her own. "I'll call security." Her fingers inched toward the phone.

"No, you won't." James trapped her wrist against the desk with the flat of his hand. Rowan tried to reach for the phone with the other hand, but James grabbed that too. He had her pinned down in a Twister-like position, one hand crossed over the other. His nails dug into her skin.

"Please," she whispered, trying to wriggle free. Her whole body started to tremble. "That hurts. *Stop.*"

"Everything okay in here?"

Rowan looked up. James shot away from her, his hands at his sides. Danielle Gilchrist stood in the doorway, a folder tucked under her arm. Her head was cocked, and there was a crease in her forehead. Her gaze moved from James to Rowan. Rowan was keenly aware of how hard both of them were breathing.

"I was just leaving," James said, stomping across the office and pushing past Danielle.

Danielle watched James storm down the hall and then looked at Rowan, a worried expression on her face. "Do you need me to call security?" she asked in a small voice.

Rowan ran her hand over the back of her neck. It was sweaty. She was sure her face was flushed too, and her heart was still pounding. "Just make sure he leaves," she mumbled.

Danielle nodded slowly. Understanding seemed to pass between them, and then she turned in the direction James had gone.

A moment later, Rowan's cell phone bleated, startling her. Swallowing hard, she pulled it from her purse. On the screen was a familiar number. "Harvey?" she asked tentatively.

"Yes," answered her doorman. "Just letting you know that I looked at the tape. I have a recording of when your friend left."

Rowan glanced nervously at her office door. "What time?"

"Six forty a.m."

Rowan's knees buckled. She might have muttered "Thank you"; she didn't really remember. Six forty. Only ten minutes after she'd left.

And with plenty of time to get downtown before Poppy died.

22

"Virginia is for lovers!" a chipper stewardess said as Corinne pushed her way off a midsize airplane that same morning. "Thanks for flying with us!"

Corinne nodded and stepped onto the Jetway. The air was warmer and more humid than it had been in Manhattan, and the scenery around her was generic and utilitarian, all parking lots and signposts. She walked toward the airport exit, not needing baggage claim. The road outside arrivals was empty. Finally a clean white minivan with "Norfolk Kabs" emblazoned on its side rolled up. A friendly older man in a Hawaiian shirt smiled at her. "Where to?"

Corinne stared at the crumpled piece of paper she'd clutched through the whole plane ride. "Eighteen-forty Waterlily Road," she read off. It was an address she'd received a long time ago, the only thing besides her scar to remind her of what had happened. Corinne was amazed she'd even held on to it for this long. Maybe, deep down, she knew she'd someday do this.

The cabbie pushed Corinne's door closed and maneuvered around a Hertz Rent-a-Car bus. He followed signs for the airport exit and then pulled onto the main highway. Almost immediately there was a small tent at the side of the road. "Fresh strawberries, melons, broccoli," read a sign written on cardboard. And a second one proclaimed, "Fireworks!"

Watching the green scenery whip by her window, that fateful

night tumbled back to Corinne's mind once more. After the test confirmed she was pregnant, she'd stood up, wrapped the wand in toilet paper, and hid it deep in her purse, promising to throw it away far from there. Then she'd peeked out the window at the guests and tried to picture Will mingling with her family. It was so inconceivable; she could imagine him only as a waiter, or maybe a guest who was clearly out of place, like Danielle Gilchrist and her mother, two redheads standing at the edge of the group, awkwardly sipping white wine.

That whole summer she had felt like someone else, as if a different person had taken over her body, making her do things she'd never otherwise do.

And now she needed to undo them.

A half hour later she'd dared to enter the party, the nausea she finally understood rippling through her stomach. She spotted Poppy across the room talking to a few people from the GIA and strode toward her. Poppy must have sensed something was wrong because she excused herself and followed Corinne into the pantry off the kitchen. "What is it?" she said worriedly, wedging herself between the shelves of peanut butter and paper towels.

"You can't tell anyone what I'm about to tell you," Corinne said after shutting the door. The small room was dark.

"Okay." Poppy took Corinne's hands seriously, and when Corinne couldn't get out the words, she hugged her. "Whatever it is, it will be okay."

"I'm pregnant," Corinne whispered, barely able to get the words out. "But I have a plan," she added quickly. "I'm going to rent a place somewhere in another state. I'll get a doctor, and I'll stay there until it's done."

Poppy gently wiped the tears from Corinne's face. "Sweetie, you haven't thought this through."

"Yes, I have. I can't have a . . ." She couldn't manage to say the word. *Baby*. "But I can't *not* have it either."

"You're going to want your mom there."

The last thing she wanted was her mother. "Don't you get it?" she whispered. "I have to get out of here, and I can't have anyone know about this. . . . I can't have anyone *see* me like this. It will ruin my entire life."

Poppy drew her bottom lip into her mouth. "You're being so hard on yourself." She looked up at the ceiling. "And it's not like you'll be hiding for a month, you know—you'll be there for *nine months*. Maybe a year, depending on your recovery. How are you going to explain that to people?"

"I've thought of that too," Corinne said shakily. The idea had come to her so quickly, as if a dark place in her mind had been preparing for this day. "You can tell everyone you sent me to Hong Kong as my first order of business in foreign development. You're president now—you can do that, can't you?"

"What if someone wants to visit you there? What if someone catches you? I'll be blamed too, Corinne."

"No one will catch us," Corinne said desperately. "Just . . . please. I need out of here. I need you to do this for me."

Poppy's eyes lowered. She stared at the tile floor for a long beat. "But it would be the first Saybrook great-grandchild."

Corinne stared fixedly at a shelf full of soup cans, a painful lump in her throat. She tried to pretend Poppy hadn't just said that. All around her were jocular sounds from the party: forks clinking against plates, the thump of bass, her grandmother's voice rising over the other guests'.

"I don't know what else to do," she whispered. "I don't know who else to turn to."

Poppy nodded ever so slightly. "All right," she said in a low voice. "I just hope you're not making a mistake."

"I'm not," Corinne said forcefully. "I know it's a lot to ask. But you're the only one I can trust."

Poppy placed her hands over her eyes and stood like that for what seemed like a long time. "All right," she finally said. "I'll mention Hong Kong to your parents tonight."

Corinne cleared her throat. "Can you do one more thing? Can you tell Will that I've . . . left? Be sure to make him understand." There was no way she could tell Will she was leaving herself. The secret would be plain on her face, or she would blurt it out when he asked why she was breaking up with him.

"Okay." Corinne peeked at Poppy. She was trying, Corinne knew, not to judge her. And for that, Corinne loved her with all her heart.

Shortly after that conversation, she'd received a phone call. She stared at the screen, astonished to see Dixon's name in the caller ID window. He hadn't called her in months; that he reached out that day seemed fated. "Hello?" she'd answered tentatively, hoping her voice didn't sound thick with tears.

"Corinne." Dixon's voice cracked a little. "Hey."

There was small talk—Dixon mentioned he had returned from London, Corinne said Poppy was now president of Saybrook's. The next thing she recalled was Dixon drawing in a breath. "So your messages. I just got them. My voice mail didn't work overseas."

"Oh." Corinne's mind went blank. She tried to remember when she'd even left those messages. Before Will, which seemed like several lifetimes ago.

"I didn't . . . ," Dixon said haltingly. "I missed you . . ." He trailed off and coughed. "I'm in Corpus right now, but maybe we could . . . I don't know . . ."

"I've missed you too," Corinne said. And she *did* miss him. She missed how easy it was with him. And she loved him. She loved that they'd never have to sneak around, that they understood each other's backgrounds. She could see the future she had once planned with him within reach again. All she had to do was grab it, let this year pass, never look back.

Yes, she would return to Dixon. The summer had been full of mistakes, but this would set some of those errors right.

"Okay, good," Dixon said with ease. Corinne could tell in his voice that he was smiling. "I'll visit you soon, then."

"Actually, that's not possible," Corinne said fast. "I'm leaving for Hong Kong."

"Oh." Dixon sounded surprised. "For how long?"

"Almost a year," Corinne answered. And then she'd told him that he shouldn't visit her, either—she would be busy day and night. She knew it seemed as though this was his punishment for blowing her off all summer. Good, let him believe that.

The e-mails she wrote to Dixon over the next nine months were some of the most heartfelt Corinne had ever penned. Dixon's replies were lighter, but he held on until she returned. Not once did she hint at what she was going through. Not once did Dixon ever guess—then again, he wouldn't have in a million years.

And as for Will? A day after arriving in Virginia and settling into the beach house she'd rented, she'd called Poppy to check in. "Did you tell Will I left?" she'd asked. "Yes, I did," was all Poppy said.

"Miss?"

Corinne opened her eyes. The cab had stopped in front of a pleasant, well-maintained split-level on a quiet street. Lace curtains hung in the windows. A basketball hoop was fixed above the garage. The front door was open; through the screen Corinne could see a jumble of dolls, Legos, and other kids' toys on the stairs. Her heart lurched.

"We're here," the driver said to Corinne.

Corinne pushed a few twenties into his hand and watched as he drove away. Panic overcame her as he turned at the intersection and disappeared. Maybe she should have told him to wait. What if this was the wrong house? What if she couldn't go through with this? What on earth was she going to *say*?

She faced the house again, took a deep breath, and walked up the concrete steps to the front door. A small wooden sign that read "The Griers" sat on a little plastic outdoor table on the tiny porch.

Before she lost her nerve, Corinne reached out and rapped on the metal screen door.

From inside the house floated the sounds of an afternoon talk show and a running kitchen faucet. There were footsteps from the bottom level. Suddenly a barefoot young girl appeared at the door and whipped it open, revealing a small landing and two sets of stairs, one going up to the kitchen and living room, the other descending to a basement. "Who are you?" the girl asked.

Corinne's own big blue eyes stared back at her. There was her small mouth, and Will's round ears and freckles. His button nose and square jaw. The girl had Corinne's little hands and long feet, even the slightly longer second toe. Her blond hair hung down her back in a snarl of curls, the same way Aster's used to.

A mixture of sadness and guilt rippled through Corinne. There had been so many times when she had wondered what her daughter would look like—and here she was, a perfect blend of herself and Will. *I gave you up. I gave you up. I gave you up*, a voice chorused in her head.

Corinne tried to smile. "Is . . . is your mom home?"

The girl pivoted halfway. "Mommy!" she yelled up the stairs.

The sound of the kitchen faucet ceased, and a woman appeared at the top of the split-level stairs. She squinted at Corinne, then slowly walked toward the screen. She wore navy sweats and had a small, heart-shaped face that looked nothing like her daughter's. She put an arm around the girl and opened the door. "Can I help you?"

"I'm Corinne Saybrook," Corinne said, offering her hand.

The woman just stared at her. "Sadie Grier."

"And this is?" Corinne glanced at the little girl.

Sadie looked at Corinne warily. Then she placed her hands on the girl's shoulders. "Michaela, why don't you go downstairs and draw? Mommy will be down soon, okay?"

"Okay." Michaela shrugged and slid down the stairs to the bottom level on her butt. Corinne's stomach sank. Her own child had looked through her. She had no connection to this girl; another woman was her mother. Her baby didn't love her, didn't know her, didn't feel anything for her. She was just a stranger at the door.

Sadie turned back to Corinne. "I know who you are. And I don't mean to be rude, but haven't we been through this?" She glanced toward the stairs. "I know you regret what you did, but you all can't keep coming here, interrupting our lives. She's too young to understand. We're her parents now. You and your boyfriend made that choice."

Corinne stepped back. "What are you talking about?"

Sadie narrowed her eyes. "I'm so grateful for what you did, but you have to leave us alone."

Corinne shook her head, not understanding.

"Your boyfriend was here just last month. On Michaela's *birthday*. He asked so many questions. And he was so pushy. We had to explain to Michaela that we weren't her real parents. How do you think that made her feel?"

"Wait a minute." Corinne clutched the railing to the porch stairs. "My *boyfriend*?"

"Tall guy. Curly hair. Freckles like Michaela's. Obviously her dad."

Suddenly she felt sick. "But that's impossible. I never told Will about her."

Sadie frowned. "Well, I guess someone did."

"Did he tell you who?"

Sadie threw up her hands. "That's for you all to work out." She nodded toward the front door. "But stop, okay? It's scaring us."

"*Scaring* you?"

"Mommy?"

Sadie's head turned toward the basement. "I'll be there in a second, honey."

Corinne tried to get another look at her beautiful child. "I've come all this way," she said in a choked voice. "Can't I at least talk to her?"

Sadie shook her head, her expression firm. "We're her parents now. I'm sorry."

And then she shut the door. Corinne stood on the porch and stared blankly. A trash truck had passed outside, its hulking shape rounding the next corner. An overturned garbage can rolled down the street. Corinne pressed her hand to her chest, feeling as if she was going to throw up. Will had known.

But how? *No one* knew she'd hidden out down here or had a baby. Not her parents, not Edith, not a single friend. Only Poppy. A conversation shortly before Poppy died fluttered into her thoughts. That day at her bridal fitting. Poppy had pulled her aside: "Tomorrow is May first. How are you . . . feeling?" And Corinne had said she felt so selfish for never telling. Poppy had said, "There's still time."

What if Poppy knew Will was in Manhattan? She could have stumbled upon him at Coxswain. She and Evan could have gone there together, in fact. Corinne pressed her hand to her chest again, feeling her heart thudding hard against her ribs. What if Poppy had kicked Pandora's box open . . . and told Will everything? She might have thought she was doing a good deed. Sadie said Will had visited one month ago, on Michaela's birthday.

May 1. Corinne had blocked out thoughts of her daughter on that date. Then, that week, she and Dixon had gone to Coxswain. She'd seen Will for the first time.

That next morning, Poppy was dead.

Stop scaring us. Corinne thought of Will's large frame. His sharp tongue from the other night. The broken plate. Any man would be furious about such a huge secret being kept from him for so long. Any man might get a little scary, a little out of his head. What if Will scared people other than Sadie? What if he'd scared the messenger?

Corinne shakily pulled out her phone to call the cab back to get her away from this place. She clutched the phone with both hands. Horrific images of what might have happened panned quickly through her mind, and she felt tears come to her eyes. "What if someone catches you?" Poppy had said. "I'll be blamed too, Corinne."

Perhaps Poppy *had* been.

The guilt she suddenly felt was overpowering. If Corinne hadn't asked Poppy to cover for her, if she hadn't made the mistake in the first place, her cousin wouldn't be dead now. Corinne studied the phone, then opened up a new text and began to type to Will, her heart in her throat.

I'm going through with the wedding. Good-bye.

23

The next night Aster's parents' live-in housekeeper, Livia, let her into the town house for dinner. "She'll be out in a moment, dear," Livia murmured before returning to the kitchen.

Aster's stomach felt jittery as she paced around the front parlor. Paintings of generations of Saybrooks stared down at her. In the corner was Edith; the artist had perfectly captured her disgruntled smirk. Next to her was Alfred, large hands folded at his breastbone. Aster felt a pang of sadness at the thought of her grandpa; she missed him. And in the center of the wall was a family painting they'd all sat for, her dad's siblings and their spouses lined up along the porch, all the cousins sitting on the lawn at Meriweather. Aster stared at each face one by one, her gaze finally landing on her father's. Mason stood at the back, his hand on Edith's shoulder, a smug smile on his face.

She could hear Elizabeth's voice. *I think it's an inside job. As in, inside the family.* And then . . . *Go ask your father.*

Why would she say that? What did Mason have against Poppy?

"Aster?"

Aster jumped and looked up. Danielle Gilchrist stood in the doorway, dressed in a cherry-red sheath dress and carrying a large yellow clutch. Her red hair spilled down her back, and she had a pair of Aviator sunglasses propped on her forehead.

"What are you doing here?" Aster snapped.

Danielle smiled sheepishly. "Your mom invited me."

"Yes, I did!" Penelope crowed, appearing from down the hall. "Welcome, Danielle!" She leaned in and kissed Danielle's cheeks, then looked at Aster. "I ran into her at Pilates. We have the same instructor." She glided across the room and adjusted a few flowers in the oversize vase in the middle of the table. "Anyway, I told Danielle she *had* to come to dinner so we could catch up."

A sour feeling filled Aster's mouth. Catch up? Her mother had been so wary of Danielle when the girls were younger. "She's a bad influence on Aster," she overheard Penelope say to Mason once. But now that Danielle worked for Saybrook's, now that she owned a pair of Louboutins and a Chanel handbag—and how had she paid for those things? Aster wondered. Certainly not on her HR salary— now she was acceptable?

Aster clenched her fists. It shocked her that Penelope had never figured out what happened all those years ago. She'd been so blind; Danielle was *right* there.

For a moment Aster thought of leaving, anger warring with the desire to figure out the truth about her father and Poppy. Sighing, she slumped into the dining room and fell into a chair. Let's get this over with, she thought. Then she noticed that there were only four place settings at the table. Edith was already sitting at one of them, and the spot Poppy used to occupy was deliberately empty. Aster looked away.

"Dad isn't here tonight?" she asked.

Penelope shook her head. "He has a meeting."

Aster nodded. Maybe that was for the best. The last thing she wanted was to see Mason and Danielle in the room together. "What about Corinne?" she asked, suddenly yearning for her big sister. She'd tried calling Corinne earlier today to tell her about what happened at Elizabeth's, but she'd gotten no answer.

"I haven't heard from Corinne all day." Penelope sat down and poured herself a glass of wine. "I imagine she's busy with final wedding prep."

"One more week," Edith chimed in.

"You must be *so* excited!" Danielle exclaimed.

Aster twisted a cloth napkin in her hands, trying not to roll her eyes. Like you care about my family at all, she thought bitterly. Her phone chimed, and she glanced at it, grateful for the distraction. *Guess I won't see you at Boom Boom tonight?* Clarissa had texted. *Nigel is here, btw. Just so you know.*

Aster almost laughed. She couldn't care less who Nigel dated; she'd honestly forgotten he existed. She hadn't thought of him once since he left her apartment the morning Poppy died. It's funny, she mused, sliding her phone back into her bag without replying. That whole scene felt worlds away.

Esme glided in with plates of roast lamb and root vegetables. Edith inspected it, as usual, and pushed the plate away. "So, Danielle, what have you been up to lately?" Penelope asked, pointedly ignoring Aster.

Danielle smiled sweetly. "Work has been really busy," she said as she began to cut her lamb. "We're hiring a lot of extra staff to cover the spring lines."

"And you have a boyfriend, yes?" Penelope asked. "What's his name?"

"Brett Verdoorn," Danielle said proudly. "He owns a PR company called Lucid."

"How wonderful. He owns the company himself?"

"That's right," Danielle simpered.

"Brett who?" Edith brayed, turning her good ear toward Danielle, and Danielle repeated his last name. Edith shrugged. "Never heard of him."

Ten points to Grandma Edith, Aster thought, hiding a smile.

"And what about your family?" Penelope asked. "How's your mom?"

"Um, pretty good." Danielle tucked a lock of hair behind her ear. "She moved back in with my father, actually. They're trying to work things out."

Aster paused with her fork halfway to her mouth. "Really?" she asked skeptically, remembering Julia and Greg's epic fights.

Danielle smiled. "I know—I was surprised to hear it too. I guess time heals all wounds."

"I'm happy for them. I hope they can make it work," Penelope murmured.

Aster stared down at her plate, annoyed at herself for rising to Danielle's bait. Time *didn't* heal all wounds. Not in their case, anyway. What Danielle had done was unforgivable.

Elizabeth's words fluttered into her mind again. *Go ask your father.* Aster thought about Poppy and Mason, fighting at Skylar's birthday party so soon before Poppy's death. Was it about Poppy stealing jewels? Or something else?

Suddenly Aster couldn't wait a moment longer. She dropped her napkin on the table and shot up. "Excuse me," she said, as if she was going to use the restroom.

She darted into the hall, past the powder room, and stood at the door of her father's study. Glancing quickly right and left, she nudged Mason's office door open wider with her toe. The light was off, but the computer screen glowed.

She crept past Dumbo the elephant and sat down at Mason's desk. There was an icon for the Saybrook's company e-mail system on the screen; Aster clicked on it. Mason had set the computer to log him in automatically. His work e-mails instantly loaded in Outlook.

"Poppy," she typed into the search box. Hundreds of e-mails from Poppy appeared. Aster scanned through them quickly, but none of them seemed amiss. They were all about meetings, marketing strategies, new clients—actual work stuff. Nothing about stolen jewels. Nothing about secrets.

Aster chewed on her lip. Then she noticed another icon on the desktop, for a Gmail account. She clicked on it, but the computer requested a password. Aster closed her eyes, trying to imagine what

Mason's password might be, but she had no idea. She simply didn't know her father that well anymore.

She dug into her purse and found her phone, only to realize she didn't have Mitch's cell phone number. She tried him at the office and crossed her fingers as it rang twice, three, four times. . . . Just when it was about to hit voice mail, he answered.

"What are you doing still at work?" Aster asked, momentarily distracted.

"Aster?" Mitch stammered. "Um . . . well, I might be using the work servers to host a giant World of Warcraft online tournament." Aster could almost see his ears redden through the phone. She smiled.

"I was wondering if you could help me with something," she whispered.

"Where are you?" Mitch joke-whispered back. "At church?"

"I can't explain right now," Aster said hurriedly. "But I need to know if you can help me hack into someone's personal e-mail."

There was a pause. "You really want to read Elizabeth's mail?"

"Not Elizabeth's. My father's."

Mitch made a noise at the back of his throat. "Aster, I don't—"

"You won't get in trouble. I just need to find out something really quickly, and I'm afraid to ask him. He's a little intimidating."

"Uh, *yeah*." Mitch laughed self-consciously. "Which is exactly why I don't want to get on his bad side."

"*Please*. I'll make it up to you." Aster glanced up, hearing a noise from the kitchen. It was only the cook washing dishes. "Anything you want."

"Anything?" Mitch repeated. "How about a date?"

"Done," Aster said, surprised at how quickly she'd agreed. Then she got an idea. "Actually, I can do you one better. Will you be my date to my sister's wedding?"

"Really?" Mitch sounded surprised. "I mean, I was just hoping for the dive bar on the corner or something."

"Come on," Aster cajoled. "There will be dancing, and the best cake you've ever tasted, and you'll get to make fun of me in my embarrassing maid of honor dress . . ."

"You had me at cake," Mitch teased, then grew serious. "But please, Aster. Whatever is happening with your father, just promise me you won't do anything stupid."

"I promise," Aster said.

"Are you near his computer?" Mitch asked.

"I'm sitting at it."

"Okay. I'm going to e-mail you a URL. Type it into Mason's web browser exactly, then download the application on the screen."

Aster called up her Saybrook's e-mail. Sure enough, Mitch had sent her a URL. He'd also e-mailed her something called a key logger application, which she needed to install on Mason's machine; it would give Aster access to anything Mason had ever typed—including his passwords. She downloaded both of them and installed them on Mason's computer. A string of type came up, including Mason's Gmail password: *Dumbo*. Aster felt a stab of guilt.

She typed the password into Gmail, and sure enough, Mason's personal mail began to load. Aster lurched forward, peering at the screen. "It worked," she whispered.

"I told you it would." Mitch cleared his throat. "Now uninstall those programs immediately. I don't want your dad noticing them on his machine."

Mitch walked Aster through how to remove the program and then said he had to go. "I won't forget this," Aster said meaningfully.

"You'd better not," Mitch quipped. "I expect lots of dancing at the wedding."

"Fine." Aster groaned, but she was smiling. "See you tomorrow. Have fun with your online tournament thingie."

She hung up and looked at her dad's computer screen. There were so many e-mails—updates from the country clubs and university affiliations he belonged to, as well as travel updates, receipts of purchase, and personal e-mails from friends. Nothing about stolen jewels.

On a whim, she went back to around five years ago, to the summer when Poppy was named president and Steven died. Her gaze caught on a transaction record, the liquidation of a huge number of stock shares. Aster paused. It was the same transaction she'd seen on her dad's computer the other day.

She clicked on the e-mail; it listed a few transaction details, but nothing about where the money had gone. What had Mason done with all that cash? Then Aster saw a second transaction receipt from the same day, this one for $1 million. There was nothing listed about the bank account except the initials GSB. Who was that? Aster racked her brain, but she had no idea.

Hands shaking, she returned to the in-box and typed in Poppy's name. Still nothing. *Think, Aster.* On a whim, she checked the Deleted folder—and an e-mail thread appeared. *Lying* was the first word she saw.

We need to come clean with this, Poppy wrote. *Especially the money. I'm tired of lying.*

Over my dead body. Or yours, Mason had replied. *Seriously, Poppy, stop pushing or you'll be sorry.*

Aster looked up, straight into the eyes of the elephant. Come clean about *what*? And what money? Whatever it was, it sounded like something *Mason* had done—not Poppy. So maybe it wasn't about the missing jewels at all. Maybe it was something bigger. What was Poppy trying to push Mason to tell? And to what lengths had Mason gone to keep her quiet?

Her thoughts tumbled like dominoes. She stood up, feeling dizzy. No. She was overreacting. Elizabeth couldn't be right. Aster shut her eyes, not wanting to consider the possibility.

Her mind returned once more to that night on the beach with Steven. The warm breeze kissing her bare skin, the sounds of the party in the distance, and the way Aster's heart had thumped when she'd turned around and saw her father staring. Steven had shot into the bushes to pull on his clothes; he might have been listening, but Aster didn't care. "If you can screw my friend, then I can screw yours," she'd snapped.

Mason's face had clouded with confusion. "What the hell are you talking about?" he barked.

"Don't play dumb." Aster's voice rose over the sound of the waves. "I saw you and Danielle together. I know what you're doing."

Mason's face paled. He glanced in the direction Steven had gone, then grabbed Aster's wrist, hard. "That's none of your business," he said into her ear.

"Yes, it is. She's my best friend. How *could* you?"

She tried to wrench away, but Mason squeezed her wrist harder. Aster felt her pulse throb under the skin. "If you know what's good for you, you'll turn around, go back to the party, and say nothing," her father said in a chillingly calm voice. "If you utter even a word of this to anyone, you'll be sorry."

"I'm not scared of you," Aster warned him.

Mason's eyes blazed. "Well, you should be."

He gave her a shove. Aster yelped, wheeling across the sand. Her heel got stuck in a divot and flew right off her foot. She lay where she was, waiting for her father to help her up and apologize profusely, but when she turned back around, he was gone.

It wasn't until the next morning that Aster heard the commotion.

"Aster," Corinne had said, appearing at her door. Aster blinked at the clock; it was barely six a.m. "Come quick." She didn't even bother to put on a bra, just ran downstairs in her Black Dog T-shirt and oversize boy shorts, following Corinne toward the marina. Her parents, Poppy, and several other guests and staff members were already down there, gathered around where the big boats docked at the slips.

"Stand back," Uncle Jonathan was saying, trying to manage the crowd. In the gray dawn light, the aftermath of the party showed in all its ugliness—the white tents sadly deflated, the ground littered with paper napkins that had turned to mush in the dewy grass. Everyone was standing in a clump at the edge of the water, but Aster managed to shove her way through. When she saw what they were looking at, she screamed.

A body lay facedown in the water. Waves lapped over his head, and his arms were splayed out at his sides. Aster recognized his pink oxford and his white linen pants, which were now translucent, revealing the white boxers beneath.

It was Steven.

Aster had started crying from the shock of it. He'd been so alive just hours before. She felt her cousins' presence around her, Poppy and Rowan and Corinne's faces blurring in her vision. Mason stood angrily on the sidelines, speaking into his phone in angry, hushed tones. Aster looked away, stricken by a sudden and terrible thought: her father had done this. He was so furious that Steven had slept with her that he'd killed him.

She wasn't sure how long she'd held on to that notion—a few hours at the most, because by that afternoon, the police had questioned everyone. Apparently *no one* had been near the docks that night. But one thing remained clear: Aster had found it conceivable that her father was a murderer. Some people didn't have it in them to kill, but she had felt deep within her gut that Mason did.

"What are you doing in here?"

Aster's father stood in the doorway. He was in a trench coat, and was clutching a briefcase in his hands in such a way that it seemed he might throw it at her. His shoulders were stiff with rage.

Aster shot up fast, logging out of his Gmail. "Um, my iPhone wasn't working, and there was a work emergency. Elizabeth is such a bitch," she added for good measure, skirting around him. She was so frantic to escape that she bumped her foot hard against the doorjamb. Wincing, she kept going, down the hall and past the dining room. Danielle and Penelope stopped eating, their eyes wide. "Aster?" Penelope called out, but Aster didn't answer her.

She hurried out of the town house as fast as she could. As soon as she was on the sidewalk, she fumbled to dial Corinne's number. Her sister answered on the second ring. "Where have you been?" Aster cried.

"Just . . . around." Corinne's voice caught.

"Can you meet me on the steps of the FBI field office in half an hour?" Aster said quickly. "I'm going to call Rowan—she also needs to be there. I think I've figured something out."

"I'll be there," Corinne answered. "I have something to tell you too."

24

A half hour later Rowan stood with her hands on her hips on the steps of the FBI field office in lower Manhattan. It was almost seven thirty, and the streets were clogged with people heading home from work, their briefcases swinging, cell phones glued to their ears. Every sound made Rowan's heart jump: the grumbling subway beneath her feet, the whoosh of the city bus as it passed, a snippet of a salsa song spilling from the open window of a car. She looked frantically for her cousins, hoping they'd arrive soon. Now that she knew what James had done, she wanted to tell Agent Foley before something else terrible happened.

Aster and Corinne arrived at almost the same time from two different directions. "I know who killed Poppy," Aster said as soon as they were all together.

Corinne blinked at her. "I do too."

Aster's jaw dropped. "You know Dad did it?"

"*Mason?*" Rowan cried, looking back and forth between them.

Aster nodded grimly. "I think he was trying to cover something up—Poppy knew about it and wanted him to come clean. He wanted Poppy out of the company, and he pushed her out—literally."

Corinne wrinkled her nose. "Cover up what?"

"I don't know. Something about money and work."

Corinne frowned. "Dad would never do that."

Aster looked conflicted. "You don't really know him, Corinne.

Because Dad . . . well, he had an affair with Danielle Gilchrist years ago. I *saw* them."

"Wait, *what*?" Rowan exploded.

"Danielle Gilchrist?" Corinne repeated, her skin turning pale.

Aster quietly recounted exactly what she had seen all those years ago—and then what she'd found in Mason's e-mail. Rowan stared at Aster, not quite comprehending. Corinne's face grew paler and paler. "I can't believe it," she whispered.

"I'm so sorry," Aster said, peeking guiltily at Corinne. "I didn't want to tell you. I didn't want to ruin your image of our family."

Corinne tucked her chin into her chest. "Does Mom know?"

Aster lowered her gaze. "I couldn't bear to tell her."

A few pigeons landed near a piece of discarded soft pretzel and began to fight over it. Corinne sniffled, then took a deep breath. "Despite all that, I'm not sure Dad did it," she said faintly after Aster had finished. "I think it was Will."

Aster squinted at her. "The guy you . . ." She trailed off. "Why?"

Now it was Corinne's turn to look tormented. "I didn't tell you everything about my time with Will all those years ago." She swallowed hard, and then explained the real reason she'd disappeared mysteriously for so many months that following year. When she uttered the words *pregnancy* and *hiding out*, Rowan felt her brain might burst. And then when she explained that she'd put the baby up for adoption, Rowan's heart broke. Corinne had a *child*, a daughter.

Corinne rushed on. "I think Poppy told Will the truth about what happened . . . and Will was furious," Corinne explained. "You know Poppy—she probably framed it like *she* made the decision to send me away, to save my reputation. Maybe he blamed her."

Tears ran down Corinne's cheeks. She glanced at Aster, who stood on the sidewalk, looking equally stunned. Corinne let out a sniff, her hands wrapped tightly around her waist. Rowan walked over to Corinne and gently hugged her shoulders.

"I hate that you went through that alone." Her throat tightened as she thought of her younger cousin hiding herself away for so many months, telling no one her secret for years. The weight of it must have been unbearable.

After a moment, Aster ran to her sister and hugged her too. "You'll be all right," she said gently. "I promise."

When they broke apart, Rowan looked at them. "I was going to tell Foley that James did it."

Corinne wiped away her tears. "But James was at your house when it happened."

"No, he wasn't," Rowan said, explaining that the doorman had seen him leaving while she was in the coffee line. "I've never asked James where he was. So I really have no idea."

And she certainly wasn't asking him now, either. Ever since the incident in her office earlier today, she'd been on high alert, half expecting him to grab her when she got off the elevator at Saybrook's or be waiting for her when she went home. Which was why she hadn't gone home.

She placed her hands on her hips and watched the traffic. A guy pedaling a rickshaw trundled up the avenue. Two overwhelmed-looking tourists sat in the back. Then Aster turned and faced the building. "Let's go. Maybe Foley is already onto one of these guys as it is."

They hurried up the steps. After quickly sending their purses through the metal detector and holding their arms out for the scanners, the three of them boarded the elevator to Foley's floor. The office still hummed with activity despite the late hour—phones ringing, people rushing back and forth, a printer spitting out papers into a large, organized stack.

The security guard looked surprised to see three Saybrooks in the lobby. She made a call to Foley's office and then announced, "She's still here. She'll see you now."

Everyone marched down a long gray hall and into an office where Foley sat behind a cluttered desk, squinting at something on a computer screen. Her hair was pulled back into a bun, her eyes looked tired, and her lipstick was slightly smudged. When she saw the three of them, she stood. "Come on in," she said hurriedly, gesturing them inside.

The three women filed in and sat down on a tweed couch. The room was decorated with flowers and quirky art prints. A pair of pink-painted deer antlers hung from a high wall. The generic metal blinds, so standard in other offices, had been swapped out for wood ones, as if they were in a Mexican hacienda.

Finally Aster cleared her throat. "We each have thoughts on who killed Poppy."

Foley folded her hands on her desk. "Is this more about Steven Barnett?"

They shook their heads and, one by one, told her their theories. As Rowan listened to her cousins speak, her hands trembled. Their suspects seemed as plausible as James was. It was hard to believe that three separate people might have wanted to kill Poppy. And she found herself frustrated with Poppy once again for the secrets she'd kept. For never coming to them with anything. She was supposed to be Rowan's best friend.

Foley's brow was knotted by the time they finished. "Do you think this has anything to do with the person who hit us in Meriweather?" Aster asked, turning to her cousins.

"I don't know," Rowan said, not having considered this. She tried to imagine James running all of them down, and her eyes burned with unshed tears.

Foley spun in her chair to face a tiny window overlooking a cluster of gray buildings. "Well, nothing you've told me is useful, unfortunately. I've interviewed all of those people, and they all have solid alibis."

Corinne dug her fingernails into the couch. "*Will?* How did you know to interview him?"

There was a trace of a smirk on Foley's face. "Because I'm an FBI agent, Corinne. I do my homework. I've had you followed. I know you've been spending time with him. I didn't know how that pertained to Poppy, but I did know that he used to live in Meriweather, and I thought there might be a connection. I spoke to Mr. Coolidge myself; dozens of people can vouch that he was at the Union Square market that morning."

Corinne's face paled. "You were *following* me?"

"I had to. It's my job to keep you safe."

"Does anyone else in the family know about . . . him?"

Foley straightened some papers. "No. Though I have to say, I'm getting a little tired of covering things up for you people." She glanced at Rowan.

Rowan felt a discomforting gust of emotion that she couldn't quite identify, at Foley's tone of voice. She leaned forward. "But what about James? I spoke to my doorman. James left just after I did the morning Poppy died—he could have reached the office and pushed Poppy in time."

"I spoke to James too," Foley said, shaking her head. "He also has an alibi for that morning."

"Yeah, my apartment."

Foley frowned. "Actually, *not* your apartment. He was somewhere else."

"Where?" Rowan demanded.

Foley didn't say anything for a moment, looking around at all three of them. Finally she sighed. "He was with a woman named Amelia Morrow."

Rowan's brain felt scattered. She knew that name . . . why? Then it came to her: Poppy's daughter's birthday party. The mom whose daughter had called biathletes "bisexuals."

"Oh my God," she whispered, clapping a hand to her mouth. He'd gone from one woman's bed right to another's? Had Poppy *known*?

Foley looked at Aster. "And before you even say it, your father didn't kill Poppy either. He was prepping for the Singapore call that morning, and dozens of people saw him. I don't know what that e-mail between Mason and Poppy meant—that's their business. Nor do I know about that transaction. That's for an auditor to figure out." She leaned back in her chair and stared at them hard. "I appreciate how much you care, ladies, but from now on, leave the police work to me, okay?"

Then she rose, which seemed like a clear signal for the others to leave. Rowan opened and closed her mouth, feeling slighted and patronized, but she didn't know what else to say. She strode numbly and quietly down the hall like a reprimanded dog.

Foley walked them all the way to the elevator, phone in hand. As she pressed the down button, Rowan cleared her throat. "If it's not any of the people we thought, do *you* know who it might be?" she asked desperately. "Any inkling at all?"

Foley's gaze didn't lift from her phone. "When I know something, you'll know something."

"Does that mean you don't know *anything*?" Aster cried. "What about Natasha? Have you found anything out about where she was that morning?"

"Have you even been interviewing people?" Rowan demanded. "Danielle Gilchrist told me you never contacted her."

"I spoke to Danielle on the phone. She didn't know anything helpful," Foley answered in a surly tone. "Seriously, guys, just let us do our jobs." There was a *ding*, and the car doors swished open. Foley practically shoved them all inside.

They rode down in silence. Aster scowled at the closed doors. "She didn't have to be so rude."

Corinne tugged at her collar. "I can't believe they were *following* me."

"They've probably been following all of us," Rowan said bleakly. Her face burned at the thought of agents watching her steal into

James's apartment and pretend to be a mother to James's children. They'd probably seen her find out about Evan too—in fact, they'd probably known about Evan long before she did. It felt like even more of an invasion than the reporters or the gossipmongers on the Blessed and the Cursed, probably because Foley was supposed to be on *their* side.

A garbage truck passed, bringing with it the foul odor of everyone's mingled trash. "Well, I guess we're back to square one," Rowan said bleakly, turning back to her cousins.

Corinne and Aster nodded. And then they parted ways, Rowan sliding into her town car. "Take me home," she mumbled to the driver. She supposed there was no risk now of James lying in wait for her. He was a cheater, not a killer.

But the fact that he'd been cleared made her more afraid than ever. It felt as if anyone could be after them. Anyone could be watching. Any one of them could be next.

25

On Friday evening Corinne stood in her old bedroom at the house in Meriweather, staring into a full-length, antique mirror on spindly legs. It was only a half hour before her rehearsal dinner would begin. Her dress, a satin floral print with an open back, fit perfectly. A stylist had arranged her hair in loose curls, and her makeup was flawless, evening out the blotchiness that had formed on her cheeks from days of crying. Her eyes looked bigger and were no longer red; her waist seemed smaller, probably from being too stressed to eat.

"Honey, you look wonderful," her mother said softly, pausing a moment to push a stray hair out of Corinne's face. Then she frowned. "Why aren't you smiling?"

Corinne looked away, hating that her feelings were so transparent. She had been over her conversation with Sadie Grier a hundred times. The idea that Corinne could have had something to do with Poppy's murder—that she had put her in danger and that Will had snapped—had rattled her, even if it wasn't true. And then there had been the wound of seeing Michaela, the daughter she had never even held. On top of all that, this new information about her father and Danielle felt like too much to handle. The skinny red-haired girl with the snarky mouth and the steel-trap mind. Aster's best friend. It turned Corinne's stomach just thinking about it. She could hardly look her father in the eye this afternoon when he carried in a crate of champagne.

She felt guilty too for being cold to Aster for so many years—now

Aster's blatant rebellion against her family made sense. It felt as if the world had changed overnight, but Corinne hadn't. If anything, it made her desperate for something solid. No more surprises, no more messes. She was getting married. She had to. It was as though she were in line to leave a parking garage; if she backed up now, her tires would go over the sharp spikes, causing irrevocable damage. After all, people had already gathered downstairs—she could hear them burbling happily in the parlor and on the lawn. The day had dawned perfect, warm and sunny, and if she were to look outside, she'd see the big tent set up for the reception and the seats arranged for the ceremony. Dixon was somewhere downstairs, mingling with the guests, and judging by the smell of lobster and cream and sautéed vegetables, Will was probably here too.

Will. Pain streaked through Corinne. After she'd sent that text, he hadn't replied. Though maybe that was for the best.

"I'm just nervous," Corinne answered finally, blinking hard to keep from crying.

"Why?" Penelope waved her hand dismissively. "All the details are in place."

"I know," Corinne said, her chin quivering.

"Are you sure it's not something else?"

Poppy's words from so long ago floated back to her: *You're being so hard on yourself, Corinne.* And Rowan's: *Everyone will forgive you if you don't go through with it.* Had she underestimated her mother? Perhaps she'd sympathize. Perhaps she wasn't as rigid and regimented as Corinne thought.

Then Penelope laid her head on Corinne's shoulder. "It's Poppy, isn't it? We all miss her. But I'm so proud of you, honey. You've been so strong through this. Such a shining example." She leaned over and kissed Corinne's forehead.

Corinne winced at the feeling of her mother's papery lips on her skin. Not long ago, those words had been all she strove for. But now they seemed sort of ridiculous. A shining example? Really?

"Mom, could you give me a minute?" she said, offering her mother what she hoped was a jittery-bride smile.

"Of course, darling." Penelope's fingers trailed along Corinne's arm as she glided out of the room.

Corinne listened as she walked down the stairs, then sat down on the bed. This was where she'd slept when she was a girl, and it was still filled with her favorite things: the Victorian dollhouse in the corner, the porcelain figurines of ballet dancers and princesses on the shelves, the plastic organizers full of her mother's old costume jewelry, which she festooned her dolls with before she made them all get married.

A memory swirled into her mind, pure and sharp: that summer she'd been with Will, she'd lain on this very bed, staring at the ceiling, reliving their moments together. Feeling so alive, her heart thumping fast, her breathing quick. She remembered calling him once, whispering, "I wish you could come over."

"I'll come if you let me," Will had answered. "I'll climb in your window."

"But it's on the third floor," Corinne had protested.

"So?" Will had laughed. "I'll climb a tree. I'll scale the side of the house. I'll get to you somehow."

A fresh round of tears prickled at Corinne's eyes. Will had wanted her, *really* wanted her. But now everything was ruined.

There was a knock on the door, and Corinne looked over, expecting that her mother had returned. But someone else walked in instead.

Will, who had on chef's whites and a Boston Red Sox baseball cap, walked carefully into the room and sat on a wooden chair near the window. "I'll just be a minute," he said, keeping his eyes on the ground. "I just wanted to catch you before . . . you know." Then he looked at her. "Can you at least explain?"

For a brief moment, Corinne felt as guilty as she had all those years ago when she'd left Will without telling him anything. But then it rushed back to her: he was a liar too. They'd both hidden something.

"I know you know," she croaked. And then, in a stronger voice: "I know you know about the baby."

The color rose in his cheeks. "Oh," he said in a gravelly voice.

"I went to see her. For the first time. I wanted to see her before I told you about it. And her mom told me that you'd already been there. That you knew." A lump grew in her throat. "Why didn't you tell me? Why didn't you say you saw her?"

"Why didn't you tell *me*?" He shook his head. "I was so confused that summer. You . . . *vanished*. And then you sent your cousin, who I didn't even really know . . ." He squeezed his eyes shut. "I thought what we had meant more than that."

"It did," Corinne croaked, humbled. "I shouldn't have just taken off."

She heard a creak on the stairs, shot up, and glanced into the hallway. Her mother was nowhere to be seen. She returned to her bedroom and looked at Will. "So when did Poppy tell you?"

Will squinted. "Poppy? I actually thought you sent the letter at first—it wasn't signed. But it explained everything, and had Michaela's name and address. I don't think I truly believed it until I went down there and saw for sure." He paused. "She looks just like us, Corinne."

Why would Poppy have left the letter anonymous? Corinne looked down. "You scared them, apparently. So much that Michaela's mom basically kicked me out before I could even see her."

Will frowned. "Is that what she told you? I didn't scare anybody. I just . . ." He trailed off, sighing. "I was so amazed at the idea of a daughter. And I mean, you *saw* her, right? She's perfect."

"I know," Corinne said faintly, Michaela's face clear in her mind.

"But I didn't do anything to scare them. I don't know what she's talking about." He winced. "Jesus, Corinne. If you'd handled this like a normal person, we might be able to see her. She might be *ours*."

Tears rolled down Corinne's cheeks, probably making rivers in her makeup. "What was I supposed to do? I had no choice."

Will stared at her crazily. "Maybe I'm not Dixon Shackelford, and maybe that's who you were waiting for, but you still could have done the right thing. You kept a daughter from me. A grandchild from your whole family. You lied to them as much as to me. Are you really that afraid of them?"

"I don't know what I'm afraid of!" Corinne blurted, her voice echoing hollowly through the room. "Of making a mistake, I guess! Of everyone . . . *judging* me. Do you have any idea what that feels like? Do you have any idea how *hard* it is to uphold this *image* for your entire family?"

Will blinked at her. "Why do you have to do it alone?"

"I don't know!" Corinne blurted, feeling unhinged. She covered her face with her hands. "That's what I've been realizing. I thought all of us, my cousins and I, I thought we *all* were trying to be perfect and good and . . . *examples*. But it turns out I was the only one. Or else I'm the only one who beats myself up so badly when I screw up." She looked up at Will through watery eyes. "It's just that striving for perfection is who I *am*," she admitted. "It's all I know. I don't know who I would be if I wasn't."

The confession sounded silly in the light of day. Corinne shut her eyes and listened to the string quartet warming up in the garden. She pictured Dixon and his groomsmen, tanned, big-toothed boarding-school boys like himself, horsing around in the boys' wing.

She looked up at Will, suddenly exhausted. "I wish I could take it back. I should have listened to Poppy—she didn't want me to go and hide. She wanted me to face things."

Will sighed. "I wish you had too. And believe me, since I found out, there have been days where I've woken up hating you—which is pretty complicated, since I keep waking up loving you too."

Love. There it was, hanging in the air. A huge weight pressed against Corinne's chest. "Everyone's already here. They're expecting me."

He moved closer to her. "So what? I'll sneak you out the back if I have to. Corinne, I love you and I want to be with you—no matter the consequences."

Corinne's eyes filled with tears. Even after everything she'd done— the horrible secret she'd kept, the awful lies she'd told—he still wanted to be with her. *He's so good*, she thought. *I don't deserve him.*

She turned away from him. "I think it's too late."

"What do you mean?"

Corinne bent over the bed, tears blurring her vision. "How can we trust each other after this?"

"We'll earn that trust." Will touched her back. "We'll work at it, day by day."

Corinne turned around to face him. He looked so gorgeous and heartbreaking that she suddenly grabbed his face with both hands and kissed him hard on the mouth. Will leaned into her, reaching his hands up over her shoulders. Every memory of their kisses rushed back to her in one sparkling tidal wave. Her whole body began to tremble, from the tips of her toes, rushing up her spine and all the way into her head. *Are we doing this?* She had no idea. A tornado had just struck her whole life, ripping up farmhouses and cows and cars. She was buried under the wreckage. She couldn't breathe.

She felt herself wanting to pull him down to the bed and let him tear off her dress, snapping off the delicate buttons one by one. Everything she'd told him was so raw and true and honest, more from her heart than anything she'd ever said or done. She pressed harder into Will's mouth, kissing deep. She wanted this to never end.

"Corinne, honey?" her mother called from the bottom of the steps. "The photographer is ready for you."

Corinne shot away from Will. "I'll be down in a second," she yelled, her heart racing. Her mouth felt swollen, her skin dirty, her face on fire. "I have to go."

She pushed past Will and staggered down the hall like she was drunk, the imprint of the kiss pulsing on her lips. But instead of going down the main stairs to the dining room, she fled to the back staircase.

It was dark and smelled like dust. She wrapped her fingers around the old wooden banister and walked down hurriedly but carefully, trying not to tear her dress. The stairs let out just behind the kitchen; pans clanged behind closed French doors. A side door led to a path that was obscured from the patio; Corinne rushed for it, not wanting anyone to see her right now. Not her family, not the photographer, and certainly not Dixon.

She navigated the stone path all the way to the beach. The sand was empty when she got there, the sky a perfect blue. A single-prop airplane loop-de-looped overhead, seemingly placed there just for her special day. She stared out at the crashing waves, craving them in a way she never had before.

I've been perfect all my life. I'm afraid not to be.

We'll earn that trust. We'll work at it, day by day.

The kiss throbbed on her lips. She glanced behind her, checking once more that no one was watching. Then she turned and ran as fast as she could toward the water. Without even hesitating, she pulled off her dress and her shoes, and waded into the water in only her undergarments, more naked than she'd ever been before.

26

Aster had been a little bit nervous, coming back to Meriweather after the disaster that was Corinne's bachelorette party. But she had to hand it to Evan—even though she was a backstabbing bitch for sleeping with James, she'd done a fantastic job. All of the grand living room's blue-and-white furnishings, ship's wheels, and scrimshaw carvings were perfectly arranged around the elegant tables and chairs that now filled the space. The windows had been thrown open, the heavy brocade curtains switched out for light, gauzy strips, and the enormous Baccarat chandelier taken down and replaced with a thin wire sculpture that held hundreds of votive candles. The room smelled like gardenias, a jazz band played in the corner, and the line at the bar was three deep.

"Here we are," Mitch said, sidling up to Aster and presenting her with a copper cup. "One Moscow Mule, extra lime."

"You're the best," Aster said, clinking her cup to his. After seeing Mitch so often in Vans and jeans, she was surprised at how grown-up and polished he looked in a suit. He'd gotten his hair cut—just for her? she wondered—he was clean-shaven, and his jacket broadened his shoulders and accentuated his slim waist. Aster liked too how he kept sneaking little peeks at her legs, which looked especially long in her blush-colored Versace dress.

"Let me show you around," she said, taking his arm to lead him down the hallway. She showed him the old seafaring artifacts her grandfather used to collect. "He would always try to find things like this at flea markets. He had insane luck, finding things that everyone else thought were worthless. We used to always say he should go on *Antiques Roadshow*." Her voice broke a little at the thought of her grandpa. She wished he could have been here to-night, for Corinne's sake.

"He sounds like he was a really special guy," Mitch said softly, reaching for her hand.

Aster laced her fingers with his. "Here's a picture of him," she said, pointing to an old photo of Alfred and his friend Harold in front of the Saybrook's flagship store in New York City, wearing matching derbies and wire-rimmed glasses.

"He looks just like he did in the indoctrination video," Mitch joked. Then he gazed through the crowd. "So where's the woman of honor?"

Aster frowned. "I don't know." She hadn't seen Corinne since that afternoon. Edith stood in the corner, chatting with the Morgans, a family who lived down the street and had made a fortune in natural gas. Dixon was schmoozing with some people from his investment firm; his father stood next to him, looking eerily like Dixon's older, slightly grayer double. Mason and Penelope clutched hands tightly, deep in conversation with Natasha's parents in the corner.

Aster's gaze remained on her father for an extra beat. He may have had an alibi for Poppy's murder, but he still had a lot of secrets.

"Aster!" someone exclaimed from across the room. A figure shot through the crowd, and Clarissa tackled her in an embrace. "How have you been, you crazy bitch?" She stood back and gave Aster a once-over. "You look so hot tonight. I hate you a little. And I especially hate you for bailing on me at SoHo House last week. Plus you missed a *great* night at Boom Boom."

Clarissa looked skinnier and tanner than ever. Her dark hair hung down her back in long tendrils, and she wore a beaded dress that barely skimmed the top of her thighs. For a second, Aster thought Clarissa had crashed, but then she remembered she'd invited her.

"Sorry," Aster said weakly, realizing that she'd never answered the text Clarissa sent her at dinner that night. That was the same day she'd broken into her dad's e-mail and gone to the FBI with Corinne and Rowan. "Something came up."

Clarissa put her hands on her hips and gazed around the huge room. "So this is where you spent your summers?" She wrinkled her nose.

"Yes. Why?" Aster asked, feeling defensive.

"Oh, no reason." Clarissa smiled sweetly. "It just seems . . . I don't know. Sort of like the *Addams Family* house." She looped an arm around Aster's shoulders. "Do you think there's any way we can snag your family's private jet and bust out of this thing early? There's an amazing party tonight at this record exec's loft in TriBeCa. And guess who's going to be there? *Nigel!* And he's single again!" She bumped Aster's hip and winked.

Mitch cleared his throat. "Uh, who's Nigel?"

Aster nervously grabbed his hand. "Mitch, this is my friend, Clarissa."

"*Best* friend," Clarissa corrected.

"We've known each other for a long time," Aster conceded. "Clarissa, Mitch."

Clarissa looked Mitch up and down. The slightest smirk appeared on her face. "What's your last name?"

"Erikson," Mitch answered.

"Of the Darien Eriksons?" Clarissa asked.

Mitch peered at Aster for help. "I have a great-aunt who lives in Stamford?" he volunteered.

Clarissa turned back to Aster, giving her an are-you-serious? expression. Aster bit down hard on her lip. So Mitch didn't exactly fit the mold of guys Aster normally went out with. But maybe that was a good thing.

Then Clarissa widened her eyes at someone across the room. "Holy shit, it's Ryan!" She pointed to one of Dixon's friends, then leaned toward Aster. "Remember when I made out with him at Lot 61?"

And with that, she was gone.

The jazz band launched into a rousing, up-tempo number. Aster glanced at Mitch, who was coolly sipping his Moscow Mule. "Sorry," she said. "Clarissa is kind of . . . intense."

Mitch raised an eyebrow. "*She's* your best friend?"

Before she could answer, Edith stepped forward into her field of vision. "Well, look who's here!" her grandmother crowed.

Aster turned, expecting Corinne to appear at the top of the stairs. But Edith—wearing her usual mink stole—had pushed forward to the front door. She laid her hands on a blonde's shoulders and ushered her inside. It took Aster a moment to realize that the newly arrived guest was Katherine Foley, clad in not her usual black skirt suit but a champagne-colored, tea-length party dress and tan kitten heels.

Aster rushed over to the agent. "Did something happen with Poppy's case?" she asked. "Did you find the killer?"

Edith frowned. "Good Lord, Aster. Miss Foley is here because I invited her."

Aster tried her best to smile at Foley, mumbling an apology. "Hello, Aster," Foley said. Her tone of voice was just as patronizing as it had been the other day at the station.

Someone else touched Aster's elbow, and she turned around yet again, feeling dragged in too many directions. This time Rowan stood behind her, looking feminine and soft in a pale gray goddess dress. Aster froze, taking in the panicked expression on Rowan's face. "What is it?" She knew Evan was here somewhere. Maybe James too. If they had done anything to hurt Rowan—

"Don't make a scene, but we have an incident on the beach," Rowan murmured between clenched teeth, gesturing with her chin toward the large windows at the back of the house. "Corinne's in the ocean."

"What do you mean, *in the ocean?*" Aster peeked over her shoulder. Mitch was listening, his face etched with concern. Aster felt a momentary stab of gratitude that he was such a good guy, and wouldn't go posting this to the Blessed and the Cursed like most people would have.

"She's just standing there, in the water, nearly naked," Rowan sputtered. "Out where anyone can see. What is going on?"

Aster winced. She knew *exactly* what was going on.

"I'll stall," Aster promised Rowan. "You go get Corinne." Then she grabbed Mitch's hand and shot into the crowd. "And you're going to help me."

"Is your sister okay?" Mitch asked, stumbling to keep up with Aster.

Aster hurried him past a table of canapés. "My sister is a little uncertain about getting married," she whispered. She rushed over to Evan, who was at the front of the room, speaking to a few guests. Aster wanted to slap the smug look off her face. *James has been with tons of women*, she was dying to say. *You're nothing special.*

Evan looked over and raised an eyebrow at Aster.

"Why don't we propose a toast—to Poppy?" Aster suggested.

Evan's eyebrows knitted together. "That doesn't feel appropriate."

"On the contrary," Aster said, pulling herself up to all of her five feet nine inches, "it's entirely appropriate. Poppy was supposed to be the maid of honor tonight. She deserves to be remembered." Seeing Evan's hesitation, Aster pressed on. She pictured Rowan coaxing a dripping Corinne from the water. "C'mon. It will bring everyone together."

Evan pressed her full lips together, then shrugged. "I suppose everyone *is* getting a bit restless."

"Thanks." Aster smiled sweetly. She clinked her spoon against a glass, and the room quieted down. "I'd like to propose a toast," she sang out. "The first one is to my lovely cousin Poppy, whom we lost far too soon. Would anyone like to say a few words?" She was surprised when the first person to approach the front was her father.

Mason cleared his throat, then gazed into the crowd.

"As you know, our family has suffered a few tragedies lately." He coughed and swirled his Scotch. "Tragedies that have shattered all of us. I didn't speak at Poppy's memorial, mostly because I wasn't sure how. And though I don't want to cloud this weekend's celebration with the tragedy of her death, I want to say how devastated we all are to have lost her. It's not enough to say that Poppy was gone before her time. It's not enough to say that we miss her, even. There is a huge hole in all our lives, one that will never be repaired. The only thing that's kept me sane since we lost her is my beautiful family—my wife, Penelope, and my two precious daughters, Corinne and Aster." He glanced toward Aster, then her mother. "I love you girls with all my heart."

A sigh rose throughout the crowd. Aster blinked, shocked. She'd never seen her father show so much emotion. Tears pricked at the corners of her eyes.

Mason took a breath. "I hope there's justice in this world," he said, staring out at his now-rapt audience. "Poppy didn't deserve the fate she was handed. And I want to make sure no one else does, either. So I want to make a toast to Poppy *and* to my other lovely niece, Natasha Saybrook-Davis, whose parents made the trip up here even though their daughter is still in the hospital. To Poppy and Natasha."

He raised his glass, and everyone else copied. Clinks sounded throughout the room. Aster glanced at Mitch and touched her glass to his.

He shook his head in disbelief. "The FBI still haven't figured anything out?"

Aster glanced at Foley, who stood in the shadows, drinking seltzer water. "I don't think so," she murmured.

"It's just crazy, given the number of sweeps they do and the level of security in that building," he went on. "I mean, I'm afraid to steal a pencil from the supply closet, there are so many cameras on me."

Aster nodded thoughtfully. "I thought they would have caught something too, though I guess Poppy's office is a little bit out of range from where the cameras are. And they said the surveillance tape from the lobby didn't show anything suspicious. But it's not like the killer apparated into the office and back out again. He or she *has* to be on there somewhere."

Mitch looked at her curiously. "Did you just make a Harry Potter reference?"

"Maybe." She shrugged, feeling a flutter in her stomach that she studiously ignored. "I just wish I could see the surveillance tape. Maybe she missed something." She jutted a thumb at Foley.

"You do know there's a backup file, right?" Mitch asked.

"Backup file?" Aster repeated.

"There's always a backup on the cloud," Mitch explained. "That way if something happens with the server, there's a safety net. In theory, you could look at *that*."

Aster's breath came quicker. "I could? How?"

Mitch drained the rest of his drink and set it on a passing waiter's tray. "It's not hard. I mean, I could probably access the files through the server."

"Seriously?" Aster asked.

"Of course," Mitch said without hesitation. "My laptop isn't here, though. It's at my hotel."

"Could you do it *now*?"

Mitch jingled his keys in his pocket, looking torn. "The only thing is, if I go now, I'll probably miss the rest of dinner."

"This is more important," Aster said quickly. "I mean, if you don't mind, that is . . ."

"Of course I don't mind." Mitch shuffled his feet. "And I mean, if you decide to go back to the city with your friend, that's cool too. To see that Nigel guy."

Aster stared at him a few moments before she realized he meant Clarissa, and her request to jet back to Manhattan that evening. Not long ago, it was exactly what Aster might have done: chances were the loft party would be way more fun than this dinner. But now she couldn't even think about doing that to Corinne—or anyone else in her family. She didn't want Nigel or any of the other smooth-talking guys at that party who would high-five one another later about banging the Saybrook heiress. She wanted the tall, adorable nerd in front of her, with his World of Warcraft tournaments and the painfully hopeful look in his brown eyes.

She glanced around the room. Clarissa was standing by the French doors that led to the patio; when she noticed Aster staring, she motioned her over. Instead, Aster slipped her hand into Mitch's. And then she edged in even closer, wrapped her other arm around his waist, and kissed him. Mitch hesitated for a moment, then opened his mouth to kiss her back. Aster leaned into the kiss, wrapping both hands around his waist and playing with the hem of his shirt.

At last Mitch pulled away, gently detangling her arms from around him. "Okay," he said, his breath a little ragged. "What was *that* for?"

"For being you," Aster said. She reached into his pocket, grabbed his keys, and handed them to him. "Now go. I promise I'll be waiting when you get back."

Mitch nodded, the dreamy look still on his face, and wove through the crowd to the front door. Aster leaned against the wall, listening to more toasts. She could feel Clarissa's gaze on her, but for once she didn't care what she thought. Her thoughts were elsewhere. On Mitch . . . and on that file.

Poppy's murder might finally be solved—tonight.

27

By the time Rowan made it to the ocean, Corinne had already climbed out of the water and was sitting on the shore. "Hello," she said pleasantly to Rowan as she hurried down the bluff.

"Are you all right?" Rowan cried, handing her a beach towel.

Corinne wrapped the towel around her body and robotically dried off her legs. Her hair and makeup were still flawless. "I just needed a moment. But I'm fine now."

She picked her dress up from the sand, marched into the house, and climbed the back stairs to her room. Rowan trailed behind nervously. "Is this because of Will?" she asked. "Or Dixon? Because there's still time, Corinne. You don't have to go through with this."

Corinne bent over her suitcase and found a new bra and panties. She buttoned herself back into the dress she'd been wearing before, a strange Stepford smile on her face. "I said I'm fine."

She kept the smile pasted on her face as she gave her hair a final fluff and descended the stairs into the party. The room smelled like a mix of cigars, sea salt, and lobster soufflé. "Finally!" Rowan heard Mason bellow, and everyone burst into applause. Corinne floated through the group, kissing cheeks and clutching hands, taking an extra moment to give her grandmother a big hug. Then she glided over to Dixon, who was sitting at a table with his parents. He stood to greet her, and she gave him a long, passionate kiss on the lips. Everyone whooped.

Rowan remained by the stairs, unsure of her cousin's decision. Was Corinne trying to prove something? And to whom—everyone else, or herself?

"What took you so long?" Rowan heard Dixon tease Corinne as he leaned in for another quick kiss.

Corinne smiled coyly. "A bride needs time to look perfect for her husband."

Rowan swallowed the lump in her throat and looked around the rest of the room, taking in the faces. Corinne's girlfriends from Yale sat at a table, a few of them with young children. Another knot of kids fiddled with Papa Alfred's ships in bottles, which were lined up on a shelf by the windows. Aunt Grace stood near the canapés with Natasha's father, Patrick. Uncle Jonathan—Corinne had had to invite him, she said, for business reasons—stood on the opposite side of the room, deliberately avoiding contact with his ex-wife. Grace and Jonathan's sons, Winston and Sullivan, mingled with some of Dixon's friends, trying to sneak sips of whiskey. Rowan's brothers, who'd flown in last night, joked with their parents by the fireplace. A gaggle of second cousins and cousins twice removed tittered by the floor-to-ceiling windows that overlooked the beach. Edith cackled loudly at something Mason said. Rowan spied Danielle Gilchrist and her boyfriend, Brett, shaking Corinne's hand and wishing her well.

Then a little girl streaked toward Rowan, the pink sash of her dress trailing behind her. "Aunt Rowan!" she cried, barreling into Rowan's legs. Skylar glanced up at Rowan with big blue eyes. "Where have you been? I miss you!"

"Oh, honey, I miss you too," Rowan said, bending down to hug her. "You look beautiful!" Then she sensed someone shifting behind Skylar, and stood up. And there, hands shoved in his pockets, was James.

Rowan's throat tightened. She gave Skylar a quick pat on the head, then edged away. "Uh, I have to go do something for your aunt Corinne, honey. I'll be back soon, okay?"

"Okay!" Skylar said, running toward Aster next.

Rowan walked down a long hall toward the back of the house and opened a door to the wraparound porch that overlooked the ocean. She staggered to the railing and held on to it tightly, taking deep, even breaths. It doesn't matter, she tried to tell herself.

But it *did*. Not so long ago, she and James were supposed to have come to this wedding together. They had discussed how they would explain to the family that they had been seeing each other, that they were taking things slowly, that they didn't want to confuse the children or cheapen what James and Poppy's marriage had been.

What a fucking fool she'd been.

The door squeaked open, then slammed. Rowan knew James was standing there, without even having to look. His footsteps drew closer, and then there he was, standing at the railing by her side.

"Please leave," she said in a low voice.

"Rowan." James's voice cracked. "I'm so sorry. I know I was crazy the other day. Ever since Poppy died . . . I've been out of my head."

Rowan just stood there silently, hugging her body tight.

James knocked back the contents of his ginger-scented cocktail. "If you're wondering about Evan, I haven't even spoken to her all night."

"I wasn't wondering about Evan." Rowan gazed out at the gray ocean in the distance. "To be honest, James, I was wondering about *you*."

She turned and took in his bloodshot eyes, his drawn face, and how thin he looked. "Foley told me about your alibi on the morning Poppy died. You left my house to be with a woman named Amelia Morrow. She's another one of Poppy's friends, isn't she?"

James's skin paled. He looked down. "Yes."

"Did Poppy *know* about her?"

His shoulders drooped. "I don't know. Maybe. Probably."

She brought her hands to her face. "Did you do this to her . . . a lot?"

James laughed bitterly. "Do you really want to know?"

"*Why*, James?" Rowan cried. "What is *wrong* with you?"

His hands fumbled for his drink. He tipped it back, even though the glass was already empty. "You know me. It's really hard to say no to someone at the bar at the end of the night. Or at work. Or on a business trip. I've always been that way. I just can't help it."

Heat rose to Rowan's face. "You have free will, you know. You can control yourself if you really want to. If someone matters enough." She shut her eyes. "So was I just some girl at the bar too? Was Poppy?"

"*No*," James said emphatically. He looked as though he was about to reach for Rowan's hand, but then he thought better of it. "It was real with you. It was always real with you. And it was real with Poppy." He took a breath. "I didn't deserve Poppy. And I don't deserve you, either."

"You're right," Rowan said stiffly, angling in her shoulders. "You don't."

She took a deep breath, feeling herself slump. She was supposed to hate him, but instead she just felt . . . *empty*. She'd held on to a fantasy of the man she'd believed James was—a Casanova who'd changed when he met the right woman—and losing that was as painful as losing James himself. She turned her head toward the pinkish clouds in the sky, a realization dawning on her: Poppy had known that James cheated. And she'd stayed with him anyway.

It was the most jarring discovery Rowan had had in weeks, somehow even more shocking than the thought that Poppy might have killed Steven Barnett. Poppy was the kind of woman who lived purposefully. She was in complete control—and she always had been. Why would she stay with a man who cheated on her again and again? She could have had anyone in the world, and yet Poppy had looked the other way.

Had she thought she *deserved* it?

Was that why she hadn't confided in Rowan or the others? Was that why she pretended to have a perfect marriage? Suddenly Rowan felt strangled by all the lies. Corinne and her fake smile as she kissed the fiancé she didn't truly love. Mason and Danielle with their secret affair. And Rowan certainly couldn't count herself out.

And what about Poppy? Who had she *really* been? Would Rowan ever know?

Unbidden, a memory floated to the fore of her mind. At the end-of-summer party when Steven died, the band had played "Nothing Compares 2 U," which Poppy had always loved. She ran to James and looped her arms around him, nestling into his shoulder. They'd swayed to the whole song, holding each other tight. Rowan had stood on the sidelines, envy throbbing inside her like a second heart. A sob had escaped from her lips, and she'd looked around, hoping no one had heard.

Only Danielle Gilchrist was around. She looked pretty and pink-cheeked that night, and when she saw Rowan's expression, she handed Rowan her full glass of wine. "It's not fair, is it?" Danielle had said softly, her smile sad. "Her life just falls into place, while the rest of us have to struggle."

Rowan nodded. She was so jealous of Poppy in that moment. Her cousin made things seem so . . . *effortless*. Rowan would have killed for just a little of that grace. For a little of that luck.

But was Poppy's effortlessly perfect life real? Or was it just an illusion she'd carefully cultivated and maintained?

James sighed next to her, and Rowan looked up at him. "So that means there's no way you and I . . ." He trailed off, his brows raised. There was a sheepish but hopeful look in his eyes. "I'll try to change, Rowan. I'll try as hard as I can."

Rowan wanted to believe him. But James had said it himself: he was who he was, and he couldn't help himself. She saw that now. She could take his hand and then look the other way when she found lipstick smudged on his collar or a suspicious text on his phone. Maybe that was what Poppy had done.

But Rowan wasn't Poppy. She had the choice, and she didn't want to fake it.

She touched the top of his hand. "I'm sorry, James," she said softly. "But I think I'm going to have to let you go."

And then, just like that, she finally did.

28

The sunporch in the house at Meriweather had always been Corinne's favorite place to hang out, probably because the room was mostly unused by their parents. Edith complained it smelled like mildew and salt and was full of bugs, but Corinne loved it. It reminded her of long nights on the slightly damp old wicker couches, the citronella candles lit all around, the various swings and chairs squeaking, and the sounds of the waves loud in their ears. She and her cousins used to tell secrets in this close, humid little room—about boys, fights with their parents, their dreams. Back then, their futures had seemed as limitless as their fortunes.

Strange to think of that now, Corinne mused as she lay on the porch swing late that night, her head on Rowan's shoulder. Through the years she had boxed herself in, little by little, the boxes getting smaller and smaller until her knees were bent and her legs cramped. Now it felt as if someone was placing a lid on that final box.

"It was a really nice rehearsal dinner," said Aster, who had changed into yoga pants and a long, fitted T-shirt. "Great band."

"Yes, everyone had a good time dancing," Corinne said lightly. "Especially the kids."

"Sky looked really happy," Rowan said. The little girl had been on the dance floor all night, finally falling asleep on James's shoulder as he carried her upstairs. Everyone had beamed at Skylar happily, but there was a sadness there too. She no longer had Poppy's parents.

She no longer had a mother. And what about a father? James was here tonight, but he looked totally vacant.

"Men are jerks," Aster mumbled, as if reading her thoughts.

Corinne wanted to agree, but all she felt was sadness. Dixon wasn't a jerk. Will wasn't a jerk. But it was what it was. She was getting married tomorrow. Anything else was too much. Too hard. She felt like she was looking down a long, straight road; no twists, no unexpected turns. She wondered how something could feel like relief and regret at the same time.

Aster's phone rang, a jarring bleep against the soft roll of waves and humming crickets. She sat up and glanced at the screen. "I'll be back," she whispered.

The screen door banged, and her footsteps creaked across the wood floor to the front of the house. Corinne stared into the room, which a cleaning crew had scrubbed after the rehearsal dinner. Not a single glass remained on a side table; the floor had been swept and the dining tables and chairs removed and folded up to be reused tomorrow, in the tent outside. The only indication that there would be a wedding the next day was a collection of silver-framed pictures of Corinne and Dixon on the mantel. Tomorrow, those images would greet the guests as they walked to the backyard. Corinne barely recalled the photos she and her cousins had chosen.

She wandered over to look at them, grabbing the whole assortment and carrying the photos back to the sunporch. The biggest one was of her and Dixon in New Haven, their junior year at Yale. She was on Dixon's back, her legs splayed out playfully. Dixon had just had an interview for Skull and Bones, Corinne recalled, and he'd been thrilled because the guys who'd interviewed him had made it clear he was a front-runner to join the group. They were both beaming. Corinne couldn't remember being that happy.

Another, in the left-hand corner, was taken at a party in this house's backyard overlooking the sea. There were shots of the two of them alone—a baby picture of Corinne in a cotton eyelet dress, a shot of Dixon on a horse, Corinne again on the back patio at yet another party, her gaze fixed on something out of view. Corinne squinted at that particular photo, recognizing the floral Lilly Pulitzer dress she was wearing. She'd worn that dress only once: the night she'd discovered she was pregnant.

Corinne was the only person in focus; a swarm of other party guests spun around her in the background. Mason chatted with Penelope. Steven, blurry, tipped his head back and laughed. A blond waitress served him a drink on a tray, her arm outstretched. A couple kissed in the background.

She showed it to Rowan. "Who picked this photo?"

Rowan squinted hard. "Not me. Why?"

"It's from the night Steven died," Corinne pointed out.

"Hmm." Rowan regarded it for a long time. "Well, you certainly look happy."

Looks can be deceiving, Corinne thought. Especially that night.

Aster's footsteps pounded back, and then she appeared in the doorway. Her face was flushed, she was breathing hard, and she carried an iPad in her right hand. "I have something to show you guys."

She burst onto the sun porch and sat down. "So my date, Mitch, was able to access the lobby surveillance video the morning Poppy died. It's on this, right *now*."

Rowan wiped her eyes. "Wait. Foley said the video didn't yield anything."

Aster shrugged. "So? Maybe Foley didn't know what to look for." She looked up at them. "What if this shows us everything?"

Corinne scuttled forward, her heart suddenly pounding with the possibility. "Open it up!"

"Seriously." Rowan sat upright.

Aster placed the iPad on the wicker coffee table, then touched an app icon labeled Remote Camera. A QuickTime video appeared. A clock in the bottom right-hand corner of the screen said that the video feed was from 6:30 a.m. on Friday, May 6—the date of Poppy's death. The screen split into four separate camera images, each of a different view of the Saybrook's building. One was a side door that went straight to a back elevator. Another was a side-street entrance for maintenance workers. The third was the main entrance, where employees swiped their IDs through a turnstile or signed in with a guard. The fourth quadrant was a set of emergency stairs that led to the street.

They kept watching, the picture black-and-white and occasionally speckled with static. In a few moments there was Poppy herself, walking through the main entrance. Everyone jumped. Corinne clapped a hand over her mouth. It was like seeing a ghost.

Poppy gave the security guard a distracted wave and walked through the turnstile. Corinne touched Poppy's face on the screen.

Rowan leaned forward. "She looks . . . good." Her voice was choked.

"Busy," Aster agreed. There were tears in her eyes. "But not scared."

"She doesn't know she's going to die," Corinne whispered.

Poppy got into the elevator, pressed the button for her floor, and disappeared through the doors. Corinne swallowed hard. There she goes, she thought. Poppy would never ride that elevator down.

She settled back to watch, her heart still pounding. Rowan gripped her knees. Aster didn't blink. No one passed through the lobby for a while, though a maintenance worker walked in the side entrance and a few unassuming-looking women in hairnets pressed the down button on the side elevator for the basement cafeteria. Corinne and Aster's father appeared on the video that showed the main entrance. A few other people Corinne didn't recognize swept past too, but they were employees of the other businesses in the building, going to the other elevator bank. A woman paused at the back elevator door, also pressing the down button for the cafeteria. Finally another woman walked in. Even though the image was black-and-white, Corinne recognized Danielle Gilchrist's profile and that tacky color-block dress.

"Danielle's at work early," she commented, watching as the elevator dinged and Danielle walked into the car.

"Suck-up," Aster muttered.

"Oh my God," Rowan said.

She was pointing at something on the main entrance feed. Another familiar face passed through, but at first Corinne couldn't place her. Then something in her brain caught—this person shouldn't have been in the building. Not yet, anyway.

"Is that—" Rowan pointed a shaky finger at the screen.

"I think so," Aster whispered.

Corinne paused the tape and slid her finger along the time bar, rewinding it so she could look again. The figure pushed through the revolving doors and nodded curtly at the security guard. The guard seemed confused, but then he was distracted with another guest signing in, and the woman pushed through, unchecked. Corinne leaned in close, her heart pounding hard. All sorts of alarms blared in her head. It was who she thought it was, all right. A light-haired young woman in a black skirt suit. Straight mouth. Furrowed brow. Her rigid posture all business, steely determination.

It was Katherine Foley.

Corinne sat back, spots forming in front of her eyes. "I don't understand."

But then something hit her. She grabbed the picture back from Rowan, the one of her from the night Steven died. She focused on two of the figures in the background, both of them a little out of focus. One was Steven Barnett. His face was in profile, his hand outstretched to accept a drink from a blond waitress. Now that she looked closer, there was a secret, conspiratorial look between Steven and the waitress; a shared little moment no one else saw.

Corinne had just seen those features, that same blond hair.

"What is it?" Rowan asked, rising to her feet.

Corinne hurried back into the sunporch and flipped on the light. The room flooded with fluorescence, and everyone squinted. "*Look,*" she cried, placing the picture on the table next to the iPad.

She compared the blurry image in the photo to the frozen face on the iPad screen. The faces were the same.

"Oh my God," Aster whispered. And Rowan sank back down to the chair.

Katherine Foley had been to Meriweather before. She'd been there the night Steven was killed. And she was there the morning Poppy died.

Maybe they'd been looking in all the wrong places. Maybe Katherine had been in the picture all along.

29

The cousins were silent for what felt like ages. Rowan's breath shook as she inhaled and exhaled. The weight of what they'd just discovered slowly sank in. She looked again at the two images, one from the surveillance camera and one from the party five years before, serving Steven Barnett a drink. *Smirking* at Steven Barnett, as though they shared a secret.

"Foley was at that party," Corinne whispered, falling back into a seat. "She knew *us*."

"She never let on that she did, though," Rowan murmured. "Why?"

Aster leaped to her feet, looking at the picture of Katherine from the party again. "Elizabeth *told* me Steven Barnett had a thing for girls around town. She even said that there was one girl in particular with blond hair." She pointed to Katherine Foley's face. "Look at the way they're staring at each other."

Corinne paced around the room quickly like a windup toy coiled too tightly. "Maybe Katherine was in love with Steven?"

"It's possible, right?" Aster said. "Maybe she was devastated when he died—but maybe she didn't know who did it. Maybe she somehow just recently figured out that it was Poppy . . . and she got her revenge."

Rowan nodded slowly. "And she took this case so she could control it. When she said the surveillance tape didn't show anything suspicious, we all believed her without questioning it because she's FBI. But she conveniently left out the fact that *she* was on it."

Aster clapped a hand over her mouth. "And think about how quickly she got to the hospital the night of our crash. What if she was *at* the house? What if she heard us talking about Steven and was worried we were getting too close to the truth?"

"And remember how weird Foley was after we mentioned Poppy killing Steven?" Rowan added.

"She could have bugged the house—and broken into our homes," Corinne whispered, her eyes wide. "She had access to Saybrook's, Rowan. Do you think she stole the video from your computer?"

"Maybe," Rowan said, suddenly thinking of the moving cursor on her work computer. "Or she could have found a way to remotely access my machine."

"But I don't understand why," Aster whispered, her gaze sliding this way and that. "We didn't have anything to do with Steven's death."

Rowan cocked her head. "No, we didn't. But maybe she thought we were in on it. We were so close with Poppy. She could have thought Poppy told us everything."

"Or she might be trying to cover up Poppy's murder," Corinne suggested. "Pin it on someone else."

Everyone exchanged a spooked glance. Aster leaped to her feet. "We have to tell someone."

"Who?" Corinne asked. "Not the FBI—she *is* the FBI."

Rowan climbed off the couch. "We'll go to the Boston bureau. There's got to be someone over her head—someone who will take us seriously." She slipped her feet into her sandals. "We should go. Foley could be listening to us right now." She glanced at Corinne. "You can stay here if you want. Rest up for tomorrow."

"Are you kidding?" Corinne draped a cardigan over her shoulders. "I'm not letting you guys go by yourselves." She flipped on a light in the main room and found the keys to their SUV. "Let's go."

They slipped out the front door and walked into the cool night. The air was thick with the scent of salt water, and the night was moonless and misty. The only light was from the porch and a single light in the caretakers' house. Rowan sprinted to the SUV in the driveway, feeling that if they didn't get out of here this moment, something awful might happen to them. Her head hummed with the terror of what they'd just pieced together. She thought of all the times she'd been in the presence of Foley. She'd been in their offices, their homes. Edith had even invited her to Corinne's wedding.

Rowan unlocked the door to the Range Rover and swung into the driver's seat. Corinne slid in next to her, while Aster climbed into the back. But when Rowan jammed the key into the ignition and turned it, nothing happened. Frowning, she tried it again. Still nothing.

"What's wrong?" Aster whispered.

"I don't know." Rowan tried to flick on the lights, but the drive-way remained dark. "Maybe it's the battery."

"You've got to be kidding me." Aster's hands fell limply to her lap. Then her eyes widened. "What if she drained the battery on purpose?"

Rowan reached over and locked the doors, suddenly afraid to head back into the house. "What are we going to do?" Her voice screeched with panic. "We have to get out of here!"

Suddenly there was a loud knock on the car window. Everyone screamed at the shadowy figure barely visible behind the tinted glass. *Foley*, was Rowan's singular thought.

"Hello?"

Tears ran down Rowan's cheeks as she tried the ignition again and again. "Hello?" the voice called once more. "Corinne? Rowan? Aster?"

Rowan blinked. Over her pounding heart, she suddenly realized it wasn't Foley's voice at all. She pulled the key from the ignition. "Who's there?"

"It's Julia."

"Mom?" called a voice outside the car. There were footsteps. "Rowan?" the voice called. "It's Danielle."

Rowan clicked her phone into flashlight mode. Two redheads

stepped into the light. Danielle and Julia Gilchrist. Rowan exchanged a look with the others, then rolled down the window.

Danielle was in a T-shirt, and her hair was messy with sleep. Julia wore yoga pants and a Sherpa hoodie. Both women peered at them worriedly. "Are you ladies okay?" Julia asked.

Rowan shook her head. "N-no."

"Our car won't start," Corinne blurted.

"Maybe it needs a jump?" Danielle offered.

"Or we could just give them a ride somewhere," Julia said uncertainly.

"Yes, *please*," Aster said, shooting out of the car. "If you don't mind."

"Of course." Julia gestured toward the caretakers' house. A Subaru sat under the porte cochere. "Just let me grab my purse."

The other cousins stepped out of the car and hurried across the driveway. A stiff wind knocked against Rowan's cheek, and she heard a rumbling sound in the distance. As they climbed into the vehicle, headlights appeared at the other end of the drive. Rowan's heart seized.

She leaned into the front seat and touched Julia's shoulder. "We have to get out of here," she said nervously. *"Now."*

30

Aster crammed into the backseat with her cousins. "Drive," she commanded Danielle. *"Please."*

Danielle gave Aster a circumspect look, then revved the engine. Julia leaped into the passenger seat and shut her door just as Danielle hit the accelerator, and the car lurched forward. The Subaru swept past another vehicle pulling toward the house. Aster stared into the front window, but she couldn't make out who was driving. A few of Dixon's friends had gone to a local bar to celebrate; maybe someone was bringing them back?

Or maybe it was Foley.

"Faster," Aster urged Danielle.

"Okay, okay," Danielle said, an edge to her voice.

The night was calm and still. Mist swirled ominously and big droplets of dew covered everything. As the car turned onto the main road, Danielle glanced toward the backseat. "Where to?"

Aster exchanged a worried look with Corinne and Rowan. Rowan took a deep breath. "The airport. We need to get to the Boston bureau of the FBI."

Aster pulled her lip into her mouth, still feeling prickly about involving Danielle in private family matters. But it wasn't like they had much of a choice. They needed help *now*.

Danielle's eyes widened. "Is it Poppy?"

Rowan shook her head as if to say, *We can't talk right now.*

Danielle searched their faces, clearly confused. "Okay," she finally said, lowering her shoulders. Aster wanted to throw her arms around her for so dutifully following orders.

Everyone was quiet as the car turned onto the winding road that bordered the sea. Aster touched her hand lightly to her lips, thinking about Mitch's kiss. She wondered if she should text him, to let him know what they'd found on the surveillance video. But by now she was pretty sure that Foley was reading her texts.

They passed a spot in the bluffs that led down to the sand—the very place Steven had led Aster the night he died, where she got revenge on her father for having an affair with her best friend. She looked at the back of Danielle's head, suddenly feeling a sharp nostalgia for the times she and Danielle used to hang out together. The last time they'd spoken, really spoken, was in this exact spot, the night Steven died.

Aster had remained on the sand after her father had shoved her and stormed off, needing to be alone. She'd rubbed her bruised arm, disgusted by her father's behavior. He didn't even seem sorry for what he'd done. It was like Aster and her mother didn't matter—as if their *family* didn't matter.

She'd heard swishing footsteps on the dunes and looked up, her heart lifting. Maybe her father had returned to apologize. But it was another face that appeared through the reeds. Danielle stood on the path, her hands at her sides, her eyes lowered demurely. She was wearing a striped beach dress and flip-flops, her hair loose around her face.

"Aster," was all she said at first. "I am so sorry."

Aster felt a sudden flare of anger and, underneath it, hurt. She hugged her knees tightly to her chest and stared at the waves. Sorry for *what?* she wanted to snap. *For sleeping with my father, or the fact that I found out?* Mason had probably gone knocking on the Gilchrists' door and sent Danielle over. What had he said to her? *Aster knows,* maybe. *She's freaking out. Make sure she doesn't tell.* He'd sent his mistress to do his dirty work.

Aster stared at her old friend, her eyes blazing.

"Aster." Danielle's voice cracked. "Don't you get it, Aster? You're like a sister to me. I can't lose you."

Aster's chin wobbled. "That's why it hurts so much."

Danielle took a step forward, but Aster retreated, throwing her hands up as a barrier between them. "Just go," she whispered.

Danielle had hung her head. And then, sighing deeply, she'd turned and done just that.

The car went over a bump, jolting Aster back to the present. She blinked at the dark, foggy road in front of them. Something nagged at her brain, a tiny barb she couldn't locate. She glanced at Danielle's bright red ponytail in the seat in front of her, thinking.

And then she remembered. During her orientation, Danielle said she hadn't been at work the morning Poppy had died. Food poisoning, she'd claimed. But now, given what they'd seen on the security tape, that didn't make sense.

Aster's palms began to itch. She leaned forward between the seats. "Um, Danielle? Did you say you were home sick when Poppy died?"

Danielle cocked her head, her gaze still on the road. "That's right. I ate some bad sushi the night before."

"How long were you sick for?"

Danielle met Aster's eyes in the rearview mirror. "About a day, maybe two."

"Are you sure about that?"

Corinne shifted her weight. Rowan looked over at Aster, but Aster kept her gaze fixed on the rearview mirror, waiting for Danielle to look up. "It's just that we saw you in the surveillance video from the morning Poppy was killed," Aster said carefully.

Danielle slowed the car ever so slightly. "That's impossible. It wasn't me."

"It *was* you," Aster insisted. Her heart was pounding at triple time. "It was your hair, your dress. I'm sure of it."

"I was at home, sick," she insisted. Danielle glanced at the women in the backseat, then at Julia.

Aster's head felt as if it was splitting in two. All at once pieces began to fall into place, pieces that had nothing to do with Katherine Foley. Danielle knew Meriweather; she certainly could have had a key to the estate. Working in HR, she had free rein in the building, and access to all sorts of personal employee information. She could have simply knocked on Poppy's door that morning, and Poppy would have let her in, thinking she had an innocent question. And then . . .

But why? Because Aster had rejected her? Because, perhaps, *Mason* had rejected her? Wasn't it enough that they'd been together in the first place? Wasn't it enough that Danielle had already gotten a job out of that affair?

"Seriously, I was nowhere near the office," Danielle said again.

Corinne looked questioningly at Aster. Aster closed her eyes. Reality seemed to twist on its axis. She had no idea what to believe. She looked out the window at the foggy night sky, and a chill crept up her spine. They were on the bridge out of town—the very same bridge they had plummeted off a few weeks ago. The bridge where they had almost died.

"Stop the car," she commanded. "Stop *now*."

Danielle hit the brakes. The car skidded. Everyone screamed as they lurched to the left. The car slid almost to the edge of the bridge, but the brakes finally engaged, and they stopped moving. For a moment, everything was silent. Then Aster wrenched the door handle, desperate to get the hell out of that car, away from Danielle. This felt all wrong suddenly. Something bad was going to happen.

"Not so fast," came a voice.

Aster froze, the door hanging open, and turned back to look

inside the vehicle. There was a flash from the front seat, a glint of silver winking in the overhead light. Aster gasped—a gun.

Only, Danielle wasn't the one holding it. It was Julia.

"Mom!" Danielle gaped at the gun. "What are you doing?"

"Everyone, please get. Out. Of. The. Car," Julia said very slowly.

Danielle fumbled for the door handle and shakily climbed out of the vehicle. Aster didn't remember actually moving, but she must have, because the next thing she knew, she, Corinne, and Rowan were outside on the bridge. Thunder rolled angrily overhead, and the sky was pitch-dark. Aster felt in her pocket for her phone, only to realize she'd left it in the car.

Julia stepped forward, aiming the gun at the three Saybrook women. "Against the railing, you three. *Now*. Danielle, you come over here with me."

Danielle's face was pale. "Mom. I don't understand." She stepped toward her mother. "Is this because of what Aster was asking me about that surveillance tape? I wasn't there. I didn't kill Poppy. I *swear*."

"Please, Julia," Rowan tried, using her calmest voice. "What's going on?"

"All these years, and you still don't know?" Julia challenged, pointing to Danielle. She looked at Aster. "Even you? You have no idea who Danielle is to your family?"

Aster stared at the gun, then at Danielle's face. Her old friend's bottom lip was trembling. *Danielle is my father's mistress*, she wanted to say, but suddenly she wasn't sure if that was the right answer. *You're like a sister to me. I can't lose you*. The words looped in Aster's brain on repeat. She looked up and met Danielle's eyes in the mirror—bright blue eyes, so much like Aster's. They used to love that; it was part of the sister act they would put on at bars.

She recalled the day she'd caught Mason and Danielle together. The way he'd held her . . . it had been so tender, loving. And then there'd been that earlier look, that day on the bluffs—the way he'd stared at Danielle with an almost ferocious intensity. But was it sexual? Suddenly Aster was no longer sure. Now that she thought about it, it was almost the same look that had been on his face tonight, when he'd mentioned his family in that speech about Poppy. An expression full of love, yes; but also protectiveness, and a little bit of regret.

"You were never having an affair with my dad, were you?" she said slowly. "You're his daughter."

"Ding, ding, ding!" Julia crowed.

Corinne's head whipped around. "Wait. *What* is going on?"

Julia grabbed Danielle's arm and pulled her close. She stared at Aster. "*My* daughter has known for five years."

Aster blinked hard, trying to wrap her mind around what was happening. She looked at Danielle again. "That was what happened between you and my father that summer. That was when you found out, wasn't it?"

Danielle's bottom lip trembled. "He told me not to say anything."

"That's because he didn't want it to be true," Julia interjected. "He was such a shit to her."

Danielle slapped her arms to her side. "He wasn't, Mom! He's been good to me."

"Really?" Julia growled, her voice taunting. "Wow, he let you live on his property, but not in his real house. He let you hang around with his *real* daughter, let her lend you clothes and grace you with her presence, and you're supposed to be so grateful? You should have everything she has!" Her voice rose to a high-pitched screech.

"I've made peace with that," Danielle begged. Tears ran down her face. "I understand why he didn't want to tell his wife the truth. I thought you understood, too. Mom, I thought you were done with him. I thought it ended when you moved out." She took a step toward her mom. "Can you please put down the gun?"

Julia sniffed. "It's kind of difficult to make peace after all I've done for that family. You don't know the risks I've taken for them, Danielle. I thought I could earn my place—and I did. I earned it in spades at that end-of-summer party. I got rid of someone who would have destroyed them. And they *still* rejected us."

Aster felt as though a bolt of electricity had shot through her. She exchanged a glance with Corinne and Rowan; they all seemed to be thinking the same thing. *End-of-summer party. Got rid of someone.*

"Are you talking about Steven?" Rowan ventured.

Danielle's jaw dropped. She took a step away from her mother. "That man who drowned?" she squeaked. "What did you—"

Julia looked over at her daughter, keeping the gun trained on Aster and the others. "It's not how it sounds, honey. Steven Barnett was a terrible man. He was holding something over Mason. If I hadn't killed him, it would have ruined the Saybrook family."

"What was it?" Aster couldn't help asking.

Julia's gaze swiveled to her. "You don't know? What about you, Miss Hotshot Lawyer?" She whirled on Rowan. Rowan shook her head, her eyes wide with terror, and Julia laughed bitterly. "How typically Saybrook. You don't even share your dirty little secrets with one another." She took a step forward, keeping the gun aimed high. "The truth is, I don't know, but I was still willing to kill for it. Doesn't that sound like loyalty to you? Doesn't that sound like someone who deserves to be part of your family?"

Aster glanced at her cousins. No one said anything. She suddenly felt foolish. Naive.

"It was that night, at the end-of-summer party," Julia said, launching into the story. She clearly loved the fact that she had a captive audience. "I was with your father, and *your* father too"—she jerked the gun at Corinne and Aster—"in his office, doing . . . well, you know." Aster shuddered. "Then, when someone knocked at the door, you know what he did? He shoved me into the fucking closet."

"Stop it, Mom!" Danielle said, twisting away.

"But I heard them talking," Julia went on. "Steven knew something—something *big*. He said he was going to expose it because he hadn't been named president. I didn't hear what it was, but from Mason's reaction, it had to be *terrible*." She turned to Aster and Corinne, a wicked glint in her eye. "I'd never heard your father worried like that, girls. He nearly lost his mind. Begged Steven not to do it. Tried to bribe him. 'This will ruin us,' he kept saying, 'the family, the company, all of us.' 'Good,' Steven said. 'I want to ruin you.' " Julia paused. "The Saybrooks screwed him over just like they screwed me and my daughter."

Aster shivered, trying to understand what Julia was saying. Next to her, Rowan was covering her mouth. Aster glanced at Danielle again, to see if Danielle had known about any of this. Her old friend was just standing there, sobbing quietly.

"I had to shut Steven up," Julia said in an even, rational tone. "I did it for you, Danielle, for your inheritance. It wasn't hard. I followed that drunk asshole later that night and pushed him in the water and held him there. Clean and simple." Her face hardened. "I thought Mason would be grateful—I had just solved a huge problem for him. And how did he react? He broke up with me! He *threatened* me."

"Mom, I—," Danielle started to say, but Julia just talked over her, her voice getting shriller.

"He promised to take care of *you*, of course. But he told me we were through, for real this time. That I had crossed a line. Well, I had, and I swore I would cross it again. I was going to make Danielle a Saybrook if it killed me—or if I had to kill again."

"You think I wanted in the family *that* way?" Danielle screamed.

Corinne stepped forward a little. "W-what did you mean when you said 'kill again'?"

Julia smiled sinisterly. "What do you think I meant?"

Danielle's mouth dropped open. Ice sluiced through Aster's veins. She glanced at her cousins, who were pale and still.

Danielle touched her throat. "It wasn't me in the surveillance video," she whispered. "It was you."

"It was necessary, honey," Julia explained. She kept the gun held up, reaching for her daughter with her other hand. "Don't you see? You deserve to be an heiress just as much as they do."

"But why Poppy?" Rowan asked hoarsely.

Julia turned back to them. "I wanted Mason to pay for dropping me, and refusing to acknowledge Danielle. At first I planned on killing *him*. That's how Poppy's parents died—Mason was supposed to be on that flight to Meriweather, but he backed out at the last minute because he had business to attend to. It was too late then. That plane was already going down." She shrugged. "Once I saw how sad he was about the accident, I realized this would be better revenge—killing his family, one by one." Julia's eyes gleamed in the moonlight. "I tried to hurt sweet little Penelope, the bitch who'd never move out of the way, but I didn't manage to kill her. So I moved on to Poppy instead."

"Why wait so long?" Corinne whispered.

Julia laughed. "Why not? It was so much *fun* being your curse. I submitted items to that site about you for years. I should write a thank-you note to whoever runs it. I sent Will that letter about your daughter, Corinne—I thought he *deserved* to know. And I sent angry letters from Will to the Griers, demanding to spend more time with her."

Corinne's mouth dropped open. "How did you figure that out?"

"It's not rocket science," Julia snapped. "None of you hide things very well. And technology makes it so easy these days. Right, Aster?" she asked, glancing over. "Just ask your little tech boyfriend." She smiled, aiming the gun straight at Aster's head. "I hated you the most, for the way you just dropped Danielle cold. But I never really had to do anything to you—you just crashed and burned on your own. And Natasha protected herself the day she disinherited herself." Julia shook her head. "Now I'm going to finish what I started." She waved Danielle over. "Stand by me, honey. We can take them down, one by one."

Danielle didn't move. Her chin was still wobbling. "You pretended to be me," she said slowly. "You wore my dress. You used my pass." Her eyes grew round. "The police could have linked it to me. You had no idea you wouldn't get caught, did you? But that was okay, because if you did, the cops would just pin it on me."

Julia scoffed. "You're being dramatic. Has anything happened to you? No. I made sure of it. I even called the FBI from your cell phone, pretending to be you. I knew they were interviewing everyone who was there that morning."

Danielle's hands shook. "I can't believe you. You don't know what the FBI is thinking. They could be looking into me right now."

But Julia just smiled. "The FBI, huh. Now that you girls have seen the surveillance video, your little agent friend has some explaining to do, doesn't she?" Her grin grew wider. "She was in Poppy's office before I was. They were talking, their heads bent together, all hush-hush. Strange Foley never mentioned it, hmm?"

She turned to Danielle. "Everything I did, I did for you, so you could have a better life."

Danielle's throat bobbed as she swallowed. "I *have* a good life," she finally said. "And if you had ever listened to me, you would have understood that."

Swallowing a sob, she turned away from her mother and walked over to where Aster, Corinne, and Rowan were huddled against the guardrail, and stood in front of them. Then she turned and faced Julia, tears streaming down her face.

Julia lowered the gun. "What the hell are you doing?"

"I'm sorry," Danielle said. "But this is coming to an end right now. If you want to kill them, you have to kill me too."

Julia's eyes blazed. The protective, loving look on her face dropped away, and she stared at her daughter with a cold, psychotic glare. "You *are* one of them. It's like I don't even know you," she said in a dead voice. There was a sharp click as she released the safety latch. "Fine, then. If that's the way you want it to be."

She took a step forward. Danielle, Aster, Corinne, and Rowan crowded together. Aster shut her eyes, her mind swirling with everything she'd learned tonight. Strange, that in her last few minutes of life, all she could think about was how wrong she'd been about her dad and Danielle. She reached for the other girl's hand, and Danielle took it. Aster gave her a squeeze. *I'm sorry*, she tried to convey through the touch. *I should never have jumped to conclusions. I should have let you explain, trusted in our friendship.*

And then, suddenly, a voice rang out in the darkness. Aster opened her eyes and immediately lifted a hand to shield them. Headlights blinded her, and tires screeched at the end of the bridge.

"Drop your weapon!" a man screamed, jumping from the SUV and advancing toward Julia. An agent from another SUV stepped forward as well, his gun pointed at Julia's head. Katherine Foley appeared from the front seat and ran toward the girls. She was wearing a bulletproof vest, and her eyes were bright. "Don't move!" she screamed at Julia.

Julia looked right and left, her eyes rolling wildly. She squeezed the gun in her hands, showing no sign of dropping it. She aimed it at the agents.

"Grab her!" one of the officers screamed.

"Mom!" Danielle yelled, her voice ragged.

Suddenly Julia rushed over to the edge of the bridge. None of the Saybrook women put out a hand to stop her. She climbed up onto the railing, her bright red hair blowing in the breeze. She still held tight to the gun, which gleamed in the bright headlights.

"Drop your weapon!" the agents bellowed again. "Hands up, or we'll fire!"

But Julia just grinned. And then a gunshot rang out.

Aster screamed and ducked her head. The noise reverberated through the air, piercing her eardrums. A second scream sounded from the edge of the bridge, and when Aster looked over, Julia's eyes were wide and stunned.

"No!" Danielle wailed, sinking to her knees.

Julia spun halfway around. Aster leaned forward, trying to see if the bullet had hit her. But before she could, Julia's legs went slack. A strange, mournful expression crossed her features.

"Good-bye," she said softly. And then she turned, opened her arms, and fell back into the water.

31

The hospital doors swished open, bringing with them the astringent scent of cleaning products. Rowan hurried across the marble lobby, ducking around patients in wheelchairs and harried doctors in mint scrubs. A gift shop bearing racks of candy, stuffed animals, and trashy magazines was on her left. The cover of nearly every tabloid and newspaper in the window bore pictures of Rowan, Corinne, and Aster shortly after their incident with Julia on the bridge. "The Curse Wears Kors," one headline screamed. Below it was that grainy image of Julia Gilchrist posing as Danielle in that color-block dress the morning she killed Poppy. What most of the papers glommed on to was the fact that Julia was still missing. The authorities had dredged the sound and found nothing. It had been so dark, and it had all happened so fast, no one knew whether the bullet had hit her.

Rowan turned away and hurried to the elevator bank, riding it to the neurological intensive care unit on the fourth floor. The last two days had been a whirlwind—first the police questioning, then the concerned hugs from family members, and then meeting with Deanna to decide how to spin the damaging story. In one night, everything the Saybrooks had worked so hard to create had crumbled, their dark secrets finally exposed.

The family's lawyers had been furious that the cousins hadn't consulted them before speaking with the FBI. As a lawyer, they said, Rowan should have known better than to implicate Mason. Rowan loved her uncle, but it was time for him to come clean. His affair had given new life to the curse, and too many people had already paid the price for his deceit. They were lucky Foley had discovered Julia exactly when she did—otherwise Rowan, Corinne, Aster, and maybe even Danielle would be dead too.

Rowan had spoken to Foley shortly after their rescue. Foley had explained that the headlights at the end of the driveway that night *had* been hers; Julia had been on her radar, and she'd wanted to speak to Danielle about whether her mother had access to her Saybrook's keycard. But when she got there, only Danielle's father was home.

"He said that Danielle and Julia had just left with you girls. And so I followed the car, and called for backup."

Foley had also apologized for lying to Rowan and the others for leaving out that she'd known Poppy, catered that party, and even had a brief fling with Steven Barnett. "My superiors knew," Foley explained. "But I didn't think it was necessary for you to."

"Did you ever think Poppy killed Steven?" Rowan had asked.

Foley shook her head. "It never sounded right. But I looked into it and discovered what really happened. That's what led me to Mason . . . and then to Julia."

Apparently Mason had paid off the coroner to falsify the autopsy results after Steven's death, reporting that his blood-alcohol level had been higher than it really was. All to make sure no one knew the real reason Steven died.

But Rowan hadn't been able to get Foley to admit why she'd visited Poppy the morning she'd died. An ongoing business matter, was all she said. "Was it always under secret cover?" Rowan asked, a thought striking her. "Did you ever go to the Mandarin Oriental?" Foley just cocked her head noncommittally, but Rowan's mind had whirled, suddenly realizing that Poppy might not have been cheating on James after all. But what *had* she been doing?

Now Rowan pushed through a door marked 414, a private room

that overlooked Manhattan. With Julia still unaccounted for, Natasha had been secretly moved to NYU from Beth Israel. Only the family knew about it; even the press hadn't gotten wind yet. If anyone found out, Natasha's family would move her again. Anything to keep her hidden and safe, especially now that she was awake. Just last night, the doctors had called with the good news.

Rowan expected Natasha to be propped up on the pillows, reading a magazine, but she was asleep, and a tangle of tubes and wires still snaked into her veins. Her chest rose and fell with each breath. Her eyelids fluttered ever so slightly, and then, beautifully, they opened. The trademark Saybrook-blue eyes stared back at Rowan.

Deep breath, Rowan thought. Before the accident, she'd suspected Natasha of killing Poppy. Their last conversation hadn't exactly been pleasant. But her cousin just smiled sheepishly. "Hi," she said in a gravelly voice.

"How are you feeling?" Rowan asked tentatively.

Natasha slowly lifted her IV-clad hand to her cheek. "Not too bad." She coughed loudly. "My parents were here before. They told me what happened. And they told me about Julia." She lowered her eyes.

Rowan nodded. "It's pretty unthinkable, isn't it?"

Natasha's head bobbed weakly. "I can't believe it."

Rowan couldn't, either. Julia Gilchrist. But the more she thought about it, the more it made sense. She had access as the caretaker, as well as through Danielle's job—and she had true motive.

It was still unclear how much havoc Julia had wreaked. Had she recovered the sex tape from Rowan's computer and stolen Corinne's journal? A picture of Julia had been handed out to the staff in all of the Saybrook's buildings, the ski resort where Penelope had been hurt, and the private airport Poppy's parents had flown from when their plane exploded. They were still waiting to hear back from most locations, but a concierge at the Four Seasons in Aspen had called to report that she'd remembered seeing a striking red-haired woman at the lodge when the accident occurred. There was no record of Julia staying there, but she might have registered under a false name.

The single-mindedness of it was what chilled Rowan the most. Julia had persevered for five long years after killing Steven. What would she have done next if Foley hadn't connected the dots? Would Rowan and the others be dead now?

"Did they find Julia yet?" Natasha croaked.

Rowan shook her head. "No." She awkwardly patted Natasha's leg. "You shouldn't worry about it, though. You need to concentrate on getting well."

The door creaked, and Rowan looked up. Corinne and Aster pushed into the room, holding steaming cups of coffee. Both of them gave Natasha tentative, awkward hugs.

Rowan cleared her throat. "Natasha knows about Julia."

Natasha nodded. "It's crazy."

Aster crossed her legs. "This might be a good time to . . . you know. Ask the other thing?"

Corinne frowned. "She just woke up," she whispered. "It's too soon."

"Yeah, I don't know," Rowan said tentatively.

"Um, hello?" Natasha's voice floated from the bed. "I'm right here. Whatever you have to ask, just ask it."

Everyone clamped their mouths shut. Rowan glanced at the others. Corinne raised her eyebrows, then gave a nod. Aster nodded too. Taking a breath, Rowan said, "Apparently there's a family secret. Mason knows it—and so did Steven Barnett."

"Julia said it was something that could have destroyed the family," Aster added. "You know what it is, don't you?"

Natasha nodded, her face full of uncertainty. She looked down at her hands. "Yes."

An alarm beeped in a hall, and a nurse was paged. Rowan set her coffee cup on the small table next to Natasha's bed. "Tell us. I don't care how devastating it is. We're family; we can get through it."

Corinne touched her hand and nodded.

Natasha was silent for a long time. Rowan worried they'd pushed her too hard, but then Natasha licked her dry lips. "Alfred's story of how the business started is a lie."

"What?" Rowan whispered, her heart beating fast.

Natasha moved her head to the side. "Are you sure you want to know?"

"*Yes*," they all said in unison.

Natasha took a breath. "After the war, Papa and Harold Browne, his friend from the war? Well they were in a battalion that sorted through plunder the Nazis had stored in the Musée du Jeu de Paume in Paris. They were supposed to take everything to a repository in Munich so the items could be cataloged and returned to their rightful owners, but I guess Papa and Harold found a few things they wanted to keep for themselves."

"Wait, what?" Rowan blurted. "You're saying the diamonds he brought back were *stolen*?"

Natasha nodded. "From families sent to concentration camps."

Rowan frowned. "But diamonds can be traced—especially valuable ones. He wouldn't have taken that risk."

"He was an amazing cutter, remember? He simply cut them to look different."

"What about the yellow stone?" Aster asked. "The Corona?"

"It was one of many, but that was the crown jewel. I guess he and Harold had a pact; they were going to take their secrets to the grave."

Rowan felt dizzy. "I think I only met Harold once. *Maybe*." When she was very young, she remembered her grandfather having drinks with a man his age on the patio in Meriweather. They'd talked about golf and their children, she was pretty sure.

"Well, apparently Harold had a change of heart about six years ago," Natasha went on. "His son contacted Mason and Alfred, saying it was Harold's dying wish to go public and right their wrongs. They refused, of course, and soon Harold died, but the son just wouldn't go away. They ended up paying him off, and making a large donation to the Holocaust Survivors' Foundation."

Aster's eyes widened. "How do you know all this?"

Natasha adjusted the pillow behind her head and sighed. "Mason went to my mom for help because he couldn't liquidate his company shares fast enough to pay off Browne's son—he needed my mom's approval. They had a huge argument in my father's study one night that I overheard. My mom begged me not to tell."

"Is that why you disinherited yourself?" Rowan asked.

Natasha nodded. "That money isn't ours, not really. I couldn't live with that on my conscience."

Corinne touched Aster's hand. "You said you found an e-mail thread between Poppy and Dad where he was trying to tell Poppy to keep quiet about something."

"That's right." Aster regarded Natasha. "*Did* Poppy know?"

"I think so," Natasha answered. "I thought you all knew, honestly, and were just keeping quiet. But about a year ago Poppy came to me and said, 'I know why you're so upset with the family.' It turned out she'd just discovered the secret. She was meeting with Agent Foley—she was helping to track down the families Saybrook's had stolen from and figure out a way to pay reparations."

Rowan nodded, letting it sink in. So there it was. The reason why Foley and Poppy were meeting. Poppy wasn't having an affair; she was trying to right an old wrong. She placed a hand on her stomach, sickened that she'd assumed the worst about her cousin.

She turned and watched as Corinne stared at her diamond bracelet, looking as though she wanted to take it off. Rowan recognized it: Alfred had given all the cousins matching ones years ago.

Their sweet grandfather. Rowan could still recall the feel of his leathery hand on hers. She pictured following his tall, straight back down the aisles of the Meriweather flea market, excited at the prospect of finding another Corona Diamond like he'd found in Paris.

But there hadn't *been* a flea market in Paris, had there? It was a childish lie, and they had been fools to believe it.

"I wonder if Steven knew because he was Alfred's protégé," Corinne mused.

"Maybe," Aster said, sinking into a chair next to Natasha's bed. "And if Julia is telling the truth, Steven was going to go public the night he was killed."

"Do you think that's why Mason promoted Poppy instead of Steven?" Rowan mused.

Natasha nodded. "It sounds as if Steven was questioning the liquidation of the stocks. They were making moves to fire him and needed to promote someone in his place."

"But Steven still managed to find out," Aster said. "And he was out for revenge for having been passed over."

Rowan paused to let this sink in. All this time, they'd all thought Poppy was promoted to president over Steven because she really and truly deserved it. That wasn't exactly the case. Rowan wondered if Poppy had known that all along. Maybe not *why*, exactly, but that she was a replacement, a quick fill to cover something up. *Jesus.* James's infidelity, the true reason why she got her job—there was probably so much that Poppy felt insecure about. Rowan would have never guessed.

Corinne looked at Natasha. "I can't believe you've had to carry this burden all these years."

Natasha slowly raised her tube-addled hand to push a stray hair from her face. "My mother begged me never to speak of it. She hated that *she* knew, let alone me."

"We thought *you* killed Poppy," Aster blurted. "You were acting so strange before the accident, refusing to meet with Foley . . ."

Natasha shrugged, looking shamefaced. "I just didn't see the point. She already knew about the diamonds, and I didn't have anything else to add. It was stupid of me."

"What are we going to do, you guys?" Aster asked. "Now we know. We can't just keep this to ourselves. My dad clearly knows—who else? And don't you think we should finish what Poppy started? Make amends, somehow?"

"Of course *Dad* knows," Corinne said bitterly.

"So do my parents," Natasha reminded her.

That was hard to swallow. Rowan shut her eyes and pictured Natasha's parents, landing on the memory of them hovering over baby Briony right after she'd been born. Poppy's parents had been gone by then, but they'd taken over the role as grandparents, taking late-night shifts, walking Briony up and down the halls to soothe her crying, delighting in her first smiles and laughs. They were so . . . sweet. Tender. All the while hiding a hideous secret and doing nothing about it.

Rowan looked at her cousins. Their family had always been surrounded by tragedy, and maybe they'd brought it on themselves. They wanted too much and gave back too little. They were like Icarus, flying too close to the sun and getting scorched: it was all their own damn fault.

"If it were up to me, I would tell," Corinne said. "The company will recover, or it won't. And if it doesn't, maybe we deserve it."

Rowan nodded, and then Aster and Natasha did too.

"I think," Rowan began slowly, "that we've all assumed too much over the years. But that stops now. We're family, and it's time we start acting like it. We have each other, and the truth, no matter how much it hurts."

Aster nodded, and Corinne took Natasha's hand. As Rowan looked around at her cousins, she felt buoyed again. It had taken an unthinkable tragedy and a loss of one of their own, but a new bond had formed between them. And that gave Rowan comfort and strength.

Corinne leaned forward, pulled four plastic cups from a stack on Natasha's little tray, and poured each of them a cup of ice water. "I think we should have a toast," she said. "To us. And to family."

Rowan raised her glass, and Aster followed. An impish smile appeared on Natasha's face. "Does this mean I can force you guys to watch my figure-skating performances again?"

"*No*," they all blurted at once, and Rowan smiled at the memory. Just like that, it seemed as if they had their old cousin back again— the cute, sprightly, utterly infectious Natasha. When Rowan looked at her again, Natasha was beaming, her expression placid and finally relaxed. Rowan had always known the expression "Weighed down by a secret," but she had never truly believed it until right now. Natasha seemed literally lighter and freer, as if she could finally live her life without lies binding her tight.

And maybe the rest of them could too.

32

A few days later, Aster and Mitch walked into her parents' town house, past the dining room to the slightly less stuffy living room. To Aster's surprise, the latest edition of *People* lay on the coffee table. Practically the entire magazine was about her family. She sat down on the yellow silk couch and flipped through it, even though she'd already read the whole thing cover to cover. Several times.

There was a story, of course, about their standoff with Julia. An exposé on Julia Gilchrist's past—apparently she had a degree from MIT, but she'd also spent several years as a stripper. How reporters found this stuff, Aster would never know.

Julia's husband, Greg, had come forward with an interview of his own—it had been odd, he'd said, that Julia wanted to get back together with him out of the blue, as they hadn't spoken in years. "My guess is that she wanted to get closer to the Saybrooks," Greg was quoted as saying. "She must have been planning to attack the rest of the girls at the wedding. It's truly unbelievable."

"You shouldn't be looking at this," Mitch murmured, brushing his fingers against Aster's leg. When she didn't reply, he sighed and flipped the page to the next story. Next was a two-page spread on Poppy. When he turned the page again, he gasped. "What's *she* doing in here?"

There was a picture of Elizabeth Cole looking glamorous in a black sheath dress, high heels, and red lipstick. "Saybrook's Insider Tells All," read the headline.

Aster reread the first paragraph.

Sometimes, a story about a dynasty can be better told by someone close to the family, and Elizabeth Cole, head of private client relations at Saybrook's Diamonds, has just that inside look. The widow of Steven Barnett, once the second-in-command at Saybrook's, Elizabeth has witnessed private, personal family moments that few others will ever see, and now she's ready to share her stories with the world in her new book The Curse of Plenty: My Life with the Saybrooks, *out this fall.*

Aster rolled her eyes. "I know. How typical. She has to make everything about her."

Mitch snorted. "No one will buy that book. I'll hack into Amazon and give it zero stars."

Aster leaned over and kissed Mitch in response. He pulled her legs up onto his lap, and she sighed, nestling into his chest and closing her eyes for a brief moment of peace. People *would* buy the book, she knew that. People bought anything with her family's name on it, good publicity or bad. But surely Elizabeth would be fired for writing a tell-all, right? Aster felt a little excited. That meant she would get a new boss.

She reached for the magazine again and flipped to the next page, which contained a story about Danielle. The image of her was a candid from her days at NYU, probably submitted by one of her classmates. "The Secret Daughter" was the headline. But there wasn't a single quote from Danielle; the reporters had built the piece around the public details of Julia's confession on the bridge, and little else. As far as Aster knew, Danielle hadn't said a word about anything.

She pulled out her phone and composed a new text. *I saw the story in* People, she wrote.

A few moments later, Danielle texted back. *Ugh, I know. Disaster.*

Actually, you look good, Aster replied. *And they aren't too mean.*

She and Danielle had been talking a little since the standoff, mostly in texts and e-mails. Aster didn't know what it meant or where it would lead, exactly; she still hadn't quite wrapped her head around the fact that Danielle was her sister.

In one of their first conversations after Julia attacked them, sitting at the police station before they gave their statements, they'd rehashed that night five years ago when Danielle had come to Aster on the beach. "Why didn't you just *tell* me who you were?" Aster asked her.

Danielle shoved her hands into her pockets. Her cheeks were still stained from crying, and her nails had been bitten to the quick. Aster was amazed she was even coherent—if *her* mother had just tried to kill her, Aster would be a complete wreck. "Your dad said not to say anything, but I thought you'd figured it out," Danielle said. "I thought that's what you were fighting with your dad about. And then, when you rejected me, I just figured . . . well, you didn't want me to be part of your family."

"I thought you guys were *sleeping* together," Aster repeated.

Danielle nodded. "I get it now. The look on your face when you put it together . . ."

Aster took a sip of the bitter-tasting coffee one of the officers had poured for her. "Do you remember when we'd sneak to that bar on the other side of the island? Finchy's?"

Danielle's expression grew wistful. "Of course."

"And all those guys were like, Are you sisters? And we would pretend we were?"

Danielle bit her lip. "Yeah."

"I used to fantasize about you being my sister," Aster said quietly.

Danielle made a small, pained noise. "I did too. And when I found out . . . I was so excited. That's why it hurt so much, when I thought you'd rejected me."

There was a cough from the back room, pulling Aster out of the memory. Her father opened the den door, clad in a robe and slippers even though it was three in the afternoon. His gray hair stood up in peaks, and there were bags under his eyes. Her stomach clenched.

"Aster," he said in a sticky, mumbling voice when he saw her.

Mason's downfall had been so fast, moving at the same whirlwind pace as everything else, and Aster hadn't had time to really decide how she felt about her father. He'd quietly stepped down as CEO of Saybrook's, and Natasha's mother, Candace, had taken over. The idea of him losing everything brought tears to her eyes, but so did the idea of him hiding an affair with Julia . . . and hiding Steven's death . . . and hiding that awful secret about the company. He'd felt like a stranger to Aster for so long. Where was the father she'd known as a child, the warm, encouraging man who'd help her through anything? Was he still in there somewhere? It was why she had asked him to meet with her today. It was time he finally answered some questions.

"Will you come into my office?" Mason asked quietly, his tone subdued.

"Sure," Aster said, sliding off the couch.

She looked back at Mitch. He reached out and squeezed her hand. She bent down and gave him a quick kiss. "Thank you again for coming," she whispered. When she pulled away, Mitch looked as surprised and delighted as he had when she'd first kissed him at the rehearsal dinner. Aster would never, ever get tired of seeing that expression.

Her father's office looked the same as it always had, the guns on the walls, the hunting gear dangling from hooks, that elephant staring glassy-eyed at nothing. But her gaze landed on other things too. Like a cotton-ball snowman that had lived at the top of the shelf for years and years. She didn't remember making it. Was it Corinne's or Danielle's? And what about that picture of Mason cradling a swaddled baby girl? Was that really Aster?

Mason sat down at his desk. He looked much less substantial in his chair. Suddenly Aster felt nervous. Here they were, face-to-face; and for the first time, they both knew everything.

"How is your time off going?" Mason asked. Saybrook's had given Aster two weeks of paid vacation, calling it "medical leave."

"Fine," Aster mumbled.

"Have you seen your mother?"

Aster fiddled with the cuff of her jacket. Naturally, Penelope had left the house immediately once the news about Mason's affair came out; she was staying with her sister in Connecticut. She had remained centered during the whole thing, poised to a fault. She didn't even have a comment about Mason's predicament. Then again, maybe she was too angry to comment.

"Yes, I've visited her," Aster said stiffly. "She's doing fine."

Mason nodded. Then he swallowed and looked at her. "I've really missed you, Aster. I've done a lot of thinking about how I failed you. I was supposed to be there for you during the important times of your life—especially that summer. Instead I let myself be distracted by things that shouldn't have distracted me. I just want to say I'm sorry."

For a moment Aster stared at him, slack-jawed. "You're *sorry?*" she snapped. "You think that's going to solve these problems?"

Mason's mouth opened and closed, like a fish. "I—"

"You ditched me that year," Aster pointed out. "You just dropped me like I didn't matter. Because you had to cover up the Danielle situation, and you had to deal with Julia and all your other secrets."

"I was trying to keep things together," Mason said. "Everything was spinning out of control. I didn't know what to do."

Aster turned her palms over, unsure of how to respond. "How did you find out about . . . the Nazi thing?"

After a long moment, Mason sighed, folding his hands. "Dad told me, back when I became CEO. He downplayed it, though. Only when Geoff Browne came to me did I realize the extent of what had happened." He shook his head and stared at the ceiling. "There were still stones in our collection from that time. But how was I supposed to know?"

"But instead of coming clean, like Browne wanted, you paid him off."

"Yes." Mason's gaze flicked back and forth.

"And you thought it was over, but then Steven Barnett poked around where he wasn't supposed to, right? He'd been close with Papa. He knew where to look."

Mason nodded. "He was being groomed to be the next president. He was looking over financials, considering our next moves. He saw that I'd liquidated a lot of company stock and started asking questions. I refused to tell him, which angered him. If he was going to be the next president, he said, he had to know. 'Well, then,' I told him, 'maybe you won't be the next president.' And we named Poppy instead."

Aster nodded. It matched Julia's story.

"But then Barnett figured it out anyway and came to me the night of the party." Mason glanced at Aster. "He made all kinds of threats. The worst of it was that earlier that night, I had seen him with *you*. I thought he was going to apologize for taking advantage of you. And instead he threatened to ruin me. I don't know what sent him over the edge."

"He didn't take advantage of me," Aster said, pushing aside the feelings of guilt that rose at her father's story. *None of us are truly innocent*, she thought sadly.

Mason folded his hands. "Well. It doesn't matter. His mind was made up."

"What would you have done if Julia hadn't killed him?"

Mason sighed. Suddenly he seemed decades older. "Honestly, Aster, I don't know."

"But then Julia came to you and told you what she did."

"That's right. But I would never have *killed* him."

"And what about Poppy?" Aster asked. "Where did she play into this? Because Elizabeth Cole was sure *Poppy* killed him."

"I got a hysterical call from Poppy, shortly after Julia told me what she'd done. It was probably—I don't know." He looked up. "Midnight? Poppy had walked down to the marina and discovered Steven in the water. She was panicking, wanting to call the cops, but I talked her down. I told her to leave Steven where he was."

"*Leave* him?"

Mason hung his head. "I know it wasn't right. But his body would be discovered eventually. And I couldn't help worrying that if she was the one who found him, Poppy might look guilty—and it might bring more unwanted attention to the family. To make sure, I paid off the coroner to punch up his blood-alcohol level."

Aster covered her face. "Oh my God."

"Poppy was always asking questions," Mason went on in a hollow voice. "She never believed Steven drowned. And then, not long after that, she found the same blip in the financials that Steven had. Only, when she asked about it, I told her the truth. She was family, after all—I knew I could trust her. Poppy wanted to come clean, though. She wouldn't let it go."

Aster let out a breath. That explained that threatening e-mail she'd found in Mason's deleted files. Then she thought of something else. "So what was the deal with the stolen jewels?"

Mason twisted his mouth. "She found out the extent of the jewels that had been stolen and realized, like I did, that some of the old pieces were still in our collection. She tracked down their owners' ancestors. And then she checked the jewels out of the vaults and returned them to the original owners without asking. Obviously, this raised all kinds of red flags with audit and security—they had no idea who those jewels belonged to or what Poppy was doing. She was trying to force my hand, make me come clean. But I managed to cover it up."

Aster groaned. "Dad, why didn't you just come clean?"

"I wanted to," he said, and sighed. "But I wasn't sure if the business could endure the blow."

"So it was all about the business, then. That was more important to you than anything else."

She met Mason's gaze. He looked away guiltily. Without Aster's mother in the town house, the place was oddly quiet—no classical music in the kitchen, no sounds of her voice as she talked on the phone. The place felt like a tomb.

She glanced at Dumbo, his trunk extended, his huge, bell-shaped ears fanned wide. All of a sudden she pitied her father. He's a coward, she realized. And he had been, his whole life. All he did was scurry around making excuses and covering things up. Transferring money to cover up old family sins, supporting illegitimate children, supporting Aster's partying lifestyle for years to keep her from telling her mom about Danielle. If that elephant had actually charged Mason, he would have run screaming.

"You used to be my hero," she said softly, feeling tears come to her eyes.

Mason's chin wobbled. "I loved when you thought that."

She felt tears run down her cheeks. "I'm sorry I turned you in, Dad."

And with that, Mason rose from his chair. Aster stared at him through blurred tears as he walked toward her and knelt down. His skin smelled like sleep. "Aster," he said firmly. "You did the right thing."

As he wrapped his arms around her, a sob rose in her chest. He wasn't supposed to be hugging her right now, and she wasn't supposed to hug back.

And yet she couldn't hate him. Even after all this, he was her father.

Then Mason pulled back and looked at her. "The mistakes I've made are mine to pay for, and I can't fix that now. But what can I do to fix . . . you? What do you want? You can stop working at Saybrook's. You can go back to your old life."

Aster blinked. "Just like that?"

She stared out the window at the building tops across the street and considered the prospect of no longer working. Waking up at noon, scanning Twitter and the party blogs to see what was happening that night. Taking off for weekends to far-flung islands to booze it up and dance all night and talk about nothing.

It all felt oddly far away. She hadn't gone out in weeks. Clarissa hadn't called. Though Aster was still on a group text that got sent around every early evening, throwing out hot spots for the night and gossiping about people they knew, her other party friends hadn't asked how she was, either. Thinking about it, what did she really miss? The thrill? This month had been full of enough thrills to last a lifetime. And it was clear her friends didn't miss her. The city was full of fabulous socialites, after all—and heiresses who'd foot the bill.

"You know, I don't know if I even *want* my old life." And as soon as she said it, she realized it was true. "I'm keeping my job," she said firmly.

Her father cocked his head. "Well. Good for you."

"But actually. There *is* something you can do." Aster stared at him closely. "I want Danielle to be part of our family. For real."

Panic flickered across Mason's face. He swallowed hard. "Do you mean . . ."

"I mean making her feel like she's one of us. You're her dad. And now she has no mom. I just think . . ." Aster closed her eyes. "I just think we should."

Mason was quiet for a long time. "All right," he finally said. "You do what you think is right."

Aster left her father's town house a few minutes later, feeling scooped out and emotionally drained. She held Mitch's hand as they walked down the sidewalk, knowing he was waiting to hear what had happened. But she wasn't ready to tell him quite yet. They walked block after block in peaceful silence, past the dog walkers who wrangled six dogs on split leashes, past other beautiful town houses and co-ops with marble lobbies and stiff-postured doormen. The air felt fresh, the day new. Aster felt new too—strangely reborn. A hopeful feeling she'd never experienced before filled her. She felt in control of her destiny, suddenly. She felt . . . *right*.

She pulled her cell out of her bag and called Danielle. "H-hi," Danielle said shakily when she answered, as if she wasn't sure whether Aster meant to call or if this was a pocket dial.

"Hey," Aster said in a strong voice, pausing at the corner to let a line of cabs sweep by. "Want to come to dinner with me tonight?"

"Really?" Danielle coughed on the other end. "Are you sure?"

The light turned green, and Aster pulled Mitch's hand across the street. "Of course," she said. "I'm positive."

33

One week later, dressed in a trench coat and a floppy hat that covered most of her face—both to avoid the sun and to give her at least a little privacy—Corinne pushed through the Bendel's revolving door and looked around. A salesgirl swept up to her immediately.

"May I help you, miss?" she asked, her gaze dropping to the six carry-alls in Corinne's hands. Then she looked at Corinne again, and her eyes widened. "Oh! You're . . ."

Corinne angled past her toward customer service. Yes, she was Corinne Saybrook, the woman who'd almost died on the eve of her wedding. Yes, she was also the woman who'd called off the wedding to Dixon Shackelford, the heir to the Shackelford Oil fortune. All she wanted was to return her gifts in peace and crawl back home to hide. She was annoyed that she even had gifts to return, after all the trouble she'd gone through to direct everyone to donate to charity. They'd all seemingly come from Dixon's side of the family, as though they knew she was going to call everything off and would have to slink to Bendel's, tail between her legs.

"Hello," the woman at customer service said evenly, then did the same double take as the perfume girl at the front. "Oh, *honey*," she simpered, pressing her long nails to her cheek. "I don't know what happened, but I'm *so* sorry. Are you okay?"

Corinne twisted her mouth into a polite smile. "I'm fine," she said. "Thank you."

It had been obvious, after their ordeal, that she and Dixon couldn't get married the following day—Corinne was too traumatized, the police needed them for questioning, and Meriweather's single bridge had been shut down while the police dredged the waterway for Julia's missing body. After that, Corinne stayed at Rowan's in the city, trying to collect her thoughts and not answering Dixon's calls.

But a few days after seeing Natasha wake up in the hospital, Corinne felt a mental clarity she hadn't experienced in a long time. She knew what she wanted, and she suddenly wasn't afraid of it anymore. She'd returned to her and Dixon's apartment, her nerves jumping, her lips dry. Dixon was waiting for her on the couch; he smiled at her as though they hadn't spent a week apart. "So I have good news," he said. "Since we're rescheduling, Francis at L'Auberge can cater for us again. Isn't that great?"

Corinne's lips parted. And then she just . . . said it. "I don't want to get married."

Dixon had blinked, looking almost childlike in his surprise. "Oh," he'd finally said, blinking hard before tears began to run down his face. Corinne was astonished: she'd never seen him cry. He put his head in his hands. His shoulders shook. "I'm an idiot," he said in a muffled voice.

"You're not," Corinne said, sitting down next to him and patting his back. "But, Dixon, look at us. Are you really happy?"

She'd stayed with him several hours after that, discussing how they would tell their families, even deciding to list their apartment—neither wanted to live there alone. After that, they reminisced about meeting at Yale, all the places they'd traveled, and how he'd tried to teach her to ride bareback at his family's ranch in Texas. It was actually pleasant, as if they were two old acquaintances catching up, knowing they owed each other nothing and that they probably wouldn't see each other again. After Corinne left, she cried for hours, astonished that she'd made such a life-altering choice. But every day that passed, she'd cried less, and today she hadn't cried at all.

The Bendel's customer service rep undid the box and peered at the gift. "Oh, how beautiful." She pulled out a crystal bowl. A tag fluttered out too—"Best of luck, Corinne! Love, Danielle Gilchrist and Brett Verdoorn."

Poor Danielle. A lot of gossip blogs had implied that she'd known what her mother was up to. Others said she'd been like a Svengali to her mother, encouraging her to kill the Saybrook heiresses one by one in the hope of Danielle finally capturing the whole pot.

But Corinne didn't believe that. She'd seen Danielle on that bridge; she'd been devastated to discover that her mother was a monster. It was possible Danielle had sensed that her mother was off-kilter, but she hadn't had any idea she was a full-blown lunatic. There was someone who had, though: Corinne's father.

Which was why she was barely speaking to him. She hadn't even called him after the news had come out this morning—on the Blessed and the Cursed, of course—that Mason was being charged with obstruction of justice in Steven Barnett's murder. No doubt he would pay someone and make it all go away.

Maybe someday Corinne would forgive her father, but now she just needed distance. It was the same way she felt about her grandfather. Person by person, her idols had been knocked off their pedestals. Everything had changed, it felt, and yet here she was, with no option but to keep moving forward.

The salesgirl placed the item behind her and typed on the screen. Corinne unloaded several more parcels and returned a cashmere blanket, a Versace tray for chips and dip, and a pair of crystal goblets with gold-tipped rims. All at once, she thought of the mismatched plates she and Will had used the night they were at his apartment. He'd bought them at flea markets for a dollar apiece, and they'd all had a story before Will got hold of them. That was far more interesting than a chip-and-dip tray for three hundred dollars.

Will. She checked her phone, but of course he hadn't called. Did she even want him to call? She'd been the one to tell him it was too late.

He had to know they'd called off the wedding. But did he care? Corinne dropped her phone back into her purse.

The salesgirl took the final item, and Corinne spun back around, inhaling the flowery scents around the salesroom. She scanned the directory, her gaze washing over the various departments and floors. She'd taken the day off, but she had nowhere to go, and there was nothing she wanted to do. She thought about visiting her grandmother, but lately Edith had stayed in. She claimed she wasn't feeling well, though Corinne believed that really she had no idea how to handle the truth about the business. The cousins had decided to call a family meeting to announce what they knew. Instead of nodding ashamedly, Edith had been shocked—it was clear she'd had no idea what her husband had done.

Fifth Avenue was a swarm of people and vehicles, and Corinne turned right, with nothing better to do than walk back toward the office. It was a bright June day, the sidewalks and windows sparkling in the sun. In a parallel universe, she would still be on her honeymoon with Dixon in South Africa. In a parallel universe, she'd be with Will, sitting at the bar of his restaurant.

In a parallel universe, she'd have her daughter too. And Poppy wouldn't be dead.

"Corinne?"

She turned. The sun was in her eyes, so at first the figure down the sidewalk was just a dark shape. She shaded her eyes. Will.

Corinne's hands went limp. "H-hello," she managed to stammer. "You're here."

Will walked toward her, a Trader Joe's carrier bag swinging on his arm. "I've been meaning to call you."

Her heart did a leap. "Yeah?"

The sun slanted against Will's features. He smiled sadly down at her. "Yeah. So. You aren't getting married anymore."

Corinne shook her head. "I couldn't go through with it."

"How did your family take it?"

Across the street, three pigeons perched high atop the Trump Tower. All of them looked like fat old men, set in their ways, as if this had been their perch for years. Corinne had braced herself to tell her parents that she'd broken it off with Dixon. Her mother's eyes had gone wide, her father was silent. But Aster hadn't cared. Neither had her cousins. And her parents hadn't even said they were disappointed—in fact, Corinne's mother had hugged her afterward.

"I guess it went okay. But I have no idea how to judge anything anymore," Corinne said, suddenly overwhelmingly tired. "I don't even know what I think about things. Maybe I never have."

"You know, you said it was too late for us, but I don't think it is. It's never too late."

"What do you mean?"

He took her hand. "Why don't we just start over? Begin everything again, right here, right now."

Start over? Just like that? She looked down at his hand, considering what he'd just offered her. There was something about the simplicity of it that brought to mind one of Corinne's favorite poems, "The Love Song of J. Alfred Prufrock." Edith used to quote part of it all the time, the line about preparing a face to meet the faces one needed to meet, but Corinne was thinking about the poem's first lines instead, the ones about a couple going off into the night as the evening spreads out before them. It sounded hopeful.

Pedestrians rushed busily past them. Those pigeons lifted off the top of the high-rise across the street, all at once the most beautiful sight Corinne had ever seen. She curled her fingers through Will's. She had no idea what the future would bring. But that was it: she would wait and see.

34

On a Friday evening, Rowan unlocked the door to Poppy's apartment and dropped the keys back in her pocket. "Here we are," she announced.

"I can't wait to see all my toys again!" Skylar exclaimed, pushing around Rowan to run inside.

Rowan exchanged a smile with Aster, Corinne, and Natasha, who were standing behind her. Corinne adjusted her grip on Briony, who was sucking madly on a pacifier, and gazed into the foyer. "Well? I guess we should all go in."

They filed in one by one. The living room was dark, the curtains drawn. There were slipcovers on the couches, the rugs still had vacuum lines across them, and all the kids' toys had been packed away, though Skylar was doing a good job of pulling everything out and flinging it around. Skylar and Briony had been staying with his parents while James was on a two-week business trip. While he was gone, he'd asked Rowan and the cousins to go through Poppy's clothes, jewelry, and other items, to decide which items to keep for the girls and which to auction off for charity.

"Let's get started," Rowan said briskly, turning toward Poppy's bedroom with a dart of apprehension. She didn't want to think about James sleeping there with women who weren't Poppy.

Yet when she swept into the room, she felt . . . *nothing*. No twinge of wanting James back. No memories of him flashing into her mind.

The only thing she *did* think of was a time when she and Poppy had hung out here by themselves after Skylar was born, when James had to go on a work trip. They'd piled on the bed, tiny Skylar in Poppy's arms, and watched Food Network programs for hours. Rowan got Poppy everything she needed and took Skylar when Poppy wanted to nap, gazing at Skylar's perfect lips, her smooth skin, her placid expression. At one point, she'd looked up and found Poppy staring at her. "You'll make a good mom, Ro," Poppy said.

And Rowan *would* make a good mother—someday, one way or another. And as for life beyond James, she was optimistic about that too. An old friend from law school named Oliver had called her several days ago, and they'd talked for almost an hour. Rowan remembered how cute he'd been; he'd asked her out a few times back then, but she'd always turned him down. She'd had eyes only for James.

But that was then. She and Oliver had made plans to go to wd~50 tomorrow night. For the first time in, well, a *long* time, she was actually excited about it.

The cousins pulled open Poppy's closet, and the overhead lights flickered on. Poppy's clothes hung in neat, organized rows. Her shoes were lined up on shelves on the ground, and she had special drawers for belts, small handbags, jewelry, hats, and other accessories. At the back of the closet were the gowns she wore to special events, the bright colors and shimmering fabrics like a line of rings in a jewelry box.

Skylar ran into the room too, and *ooh*ed softly. "I love Mommy's closet," she said in a polite, reverent voice.

"Don't touch anything, okay?" Corinne advised.

"Oh, I know." Skylar's eyes shone. "A good girl always asks before touching."

Rowan hid a smile. In the months since Poppy's death, Skylar had become serious, mannered, and almost . . . wise. It was as though she understood that someday the Saybrook mantle would be passed to her, and she'd best prepare now.

Rowan put her hand on Skylar's shoulder, feeling sorry for the little girl. She still couldn't fathom the idea of not having a mother during her childhood. But though James hadn't been a great husband, as far as Rowan could tell, he *was* a good father.

Natasha stepped forward, touching the front of a shoe box. Her breathing was labored. She'd only been released two days ago, but she'd insisted on coming to help. "Are you okay?"

Natasha nodded. "I will be." She smiled at Rowan and squeezed her hand.

Then the doorbell rang. Everyone looked at one another, but then a light came on in Aster's eyes, and she ran for it. Seconds later Danielle Gilchrist appeared in the closet doorway. Her red hair hung down her shoulders, and she wore an expertly tailored white shirt, pencil-straight black pants, and expensive-looking black leather booties. There was something classic about the outfit, Rowan thought; it was both unassuming and luxurious.

It was, she realized, exactly the way a Manhattan heiress might dress. After all, Danielle was in training too.

"Are you sure it's all right that I'm here?" Danielle said, gazing nervously around.

"Of course," Aster said eagerly, grabbing her hand and pulling her into the vast closet. "We were just going through some stuff. Come help."

They began to sift through the dresses. "Remember this?" Corinne asked, holding up a feathered and beaded Chanel gown Poppy had worn to a Metropolitan Opera costume benefit a few years ago.

Aster snatched it. "Ooh, do you think she'd mind if I kept that?"

Corinne gave her a look. "Where would you wear that?"

"To a Halloween party," Aster teased, slipping the dress over her thin frame. It fit her perfectly. Natasha straightened up. "I want to wear something too."

"And me, please!" Skylar volunteered, reaching out her arms.

Rowan found a floppy striped hat Poppy had bought for a trip to Saint-Tropez and gave it to her. Skylar placed it on her head, giggling. "Can we do a fashion show?"

"Oh, honey, I don't know," Corinne said cautiously, bobbling Briony up and down.

"Come on, it'll be fun," Aster decided.

"I'm game," Natasha agreed.

Corinne shrugged, placed Briony on the floor, pulled a robin's-egg-blue gown from the rack, and started to undo the clasp. "Okay, twist my arm."

"Yay!" Aster cried, pushing a long peacock-blue column dress at Danielle. "Wear this! It would look amazing on you!"

Danielle looked touched. "You want me to join in?" She ran her fingers along the silken fabric.

Aster waved her hands. "Stop asking that. You're one of us now. Now, come on."

You're one of us now. Aster was handling that so well—but then, that was Aster for you, always game for whatever life threw at her. Rowan glanced at Danielle again as she quietly unzipped the back of the dress. She wanted to like her new cousin. She wanted to embrace her as much as Aster did. But she wasn't sure she quite trusted her yet. Perhaps that had nothing to do with Danielle and everything to do with Julia—after all, Danielle was just as much of a victim as they all were.

Rowan selected a fringed black dress and put it on too, feeling a little bit like Poppy as she zipped it up. Moments later, when Rowan looked around, *all* of them had transformed into Poppy, their skin glowing, their eyes bright, their smiles confident. Even little Skylar in the floppy hat and a pink tunic of Poppy's that came to her ankles had a sudden je ne sais quoi about her. In the dull bedroom light, her face turned a particular angle, she looked so much like Poppy, it took Rowan's breath away.

Then she realized how ridiculous they looked standing in the middle of a closet in such ornate gowns and bare feet, and she burst into laughter. It felt suddenly as if they were little girls at Meriweather again, playing dress-up in their mothers' closets.

Aster ran to the stereo and put on dance music, bopping to the beat. Then she started across the floor, swinging her hips and pasting a confident look on her face. "Go, girl!" Rowan called out to her, swaying to the music too.

"Aster, you still have a great walk," Natasha admitted.

"You really do," Corinne added, which made Aster's face light up. "Have you ever thought about modeling again?"

Aster burst out laughing. "I'm sticking with Saybrook's. Haven't you heard? Boring is the new black." Then she looped her arm around Natasha's. "Maybe Danielle could recruit you too."

Danielle, who had finished pulling on the blue sheath—it *did* look amazing on her—looked up. "That could be arranged."

"It would be so much fun!" Aster cried, clapping her hands. "We could all be there. Have lunch every day, cocktails after work, take retreats on the company expense account . . ."

Natasha shook her head. "I don't think so. Actually, I've been thinking about getting out of New York for a while. Traveling somewhere remote, getting my head together."

Corinne looked crushed. "You're leaving?"

"It won't be for very long," Natasha promised. Then a sly smile crept across her face, and she shot down the hall, swinging her hips like Aster. At the end of the hall, she thrust her arms into the air dramatically, just as she used to do at the end of her dance routines or one-act plays. Everyone hooted with laughter.

"Rowan's turn!" Corinne called when Natasha finished.

Rowan looked at Poppy's dress. It was so long that it dragged on the ground. "I need shoes," she announced. She hunted Poppy's racks for good ones.

"Ooh, I know she has some silver sling-backs that would look great with that dress," Aster announced, dropping to her hands and knees too. She pulled a small step stool from the back and climbed up it to check the upper racks, producing the pair in question.

"My turn!" Skylar tugged on Rowan's skirt when Rowan finished her run. "Watch me!"

All of them cheered on Skylar as she pranced down the long hallway. The floppy hat fell halfway off her head, but she caught it with a flourish. After Skylar walked, Corinne took a turn, her cheeks shining. Then Danielle went. They sorted through more dresses, tried on more items, and even made fun of some of Poppy's impulse buys, including a pair of neon-green snakeskin platforms and a coat that looked as if it was made out of hair. Rowan sat back for a moment, watching all of them, feeling a moment of utter peace. Everything felt so good. So safe. And she realized, with a start, that she *adored* her life. Her cousins, her family, her integrity. It finally felt like enough. More than enough.

Across the room, her phone chimed loudly. Frowning, she glanced at it, then turned back to Aster, who'd pulled out a beautiful but totally impractical white dress that was see-through on the top and had a voluminous skirt that looked as if it was made out of hundreds of silken braids. "Even I couldn't pull this off," she said.

"It looks like a princess dress!" Skylar cried, reaching for it.

The phone bleated again. Rowan shot her cousins a quick smile, then rose and crossed the room. She pulled her phone from her bag and glanced at the screen. Her stomach dropped to her feet. *New post on the Blessed and the Cursed.*

The site had been eerily silent since Julia's disappearance. There hadn't even been a link to the story about the standoff on the bridge or a hint that Corinne had called off the wedding, or everything about Danielle, even though Page Six and Gawker had practically dedicated days' worth of bandwidth to all of those stories. Nor were there any candid pictures of them. No unauthorized videos. No overheard conversations. Was that proof that Julia, despite her protestation on the bridge, had been running the site? Or had she just provided the host with the juiciest tidbits?

Rowan pressed the link that took her to the page. Sure enough, there was a new post. Rowan blinked hard. Chunky words filled the page. Pictures, too.

"One heiress, two heiress, three heiress, four," it said, showing pictures of Rowan, Corinne, Aster, and Natasha. Rowan scrolled down a little.

"Five heiress, new heiress." A picture of Danielle. And then: "Do they know there's one more?"

Rowan's eyes blurred. She understood those last words individually, but not as a group. What was the site talking about? There had been another heiress: Poppy, but now she was dead. Or maybe it meant *heirs*? But there were four heirs: her brothers, then Winston and Sullivan. Somehow she didn't think it meant anything like that, though. Her fingers started to tremble. A metallic taste filled her mouth.

Danielle stuck her head out of the closet. "Are you okay, Rowan?"

Rowan shot up fast, covering the phone screen with her hands. Danielle's stare was intense. Knowing, maybe? Or perhaps Rowan was losing her mind.

"I'll be there in a second," she said absently, hoping she didn't seem anxious. "I just need to take care of this."

It means nothing, she told herself, taking deep, even breaths. Whoever had posted this was just fucking with them. There were no more Saybrooks. There were no more secrets. They knew everything they needed to know.

And yet she couldn't help but peek again. But when she gazed down at the screen once more, the page was blank. She hit refresh again and again, her heart pounding hard.

But just like that, the post was gone.

ONE YEAR LATER

It was late afternoon at the Saybrook family's annual end-of-summer party in Meriweather. Edith Saybrook stifled a cough as she strolled to the porch. Though the thermometer tipped almost eighty-five degrees in the shade, she felt an impenetrable chill. She pulled her fur closer around her neck.

Her granddaughter, Corinne, looked up from her Adirondack chair in alarm. "Are you okay?"

"Of course," Edith snapped, clutching her lime-flavored Perrier. "I'm as healthy as an ox."

Corinne took a sip of her lemonade. Her brand-new fiancé, Will, exchanged a worried look with her. They made a nice enough couple, and she certainly seemed happier than she'd been with that Shackelford boy. What a mess *that* had been, but it was over now. Not that the tabloids thought so. Reporters were still calling Edith to get her comment on whether Dixon and Corinne would reconcile. Let it go, she always thought.

Edith looked over the balcony at the party on the patio. Though they'd wanted the Labor Day party to be a small affair, mostly to celebrate Loren DuPont, a brand-new client Corinne's sister, Aster, had wooed, it had turned into a two-hundred-person bash. There was Aster now, wearing a silver cocktail dress, chatting with Loren herself, with that man she hung around with—Michael? Mitchell?— standing awkwardly by her side.

With that Elizabeth gone—Edith had never liked her—Aster had been promoted to associate client liaison, and she'd brought in a lot of new business. Of course, Edith had always seen that girl's promise.

Edith's other granddaughter, Rowan, glowing in a short white gown that showed off her athletic figure and holding hands with a tall man whose name she never could remember—they met on the *Columbia Law Review*, perhaps?—was letting Poppy's older daughter pet one of those filthy dogs she owned.

And then there was that new one, that redhead who used to live in the caretakers' cottage but now stayed here. It was sickening the way they all fawned over Danielle now. She was a grown woman, for God's sake. How could they be so sure Danielle hadn't been part of her mother's scheme? Edith had half a mind to go down there and give that Danielle a talking-to, once and for all.

But she felt so tired. And suddenly she couldn't remember the name of the granddaughter who'd gone to India shortly after she'd recovered from her injuries. She was still there—hadn't she just sent a postcard a few days ago of a child on the side of the road? It was that black sheep, the one who for so long pretended like she was too good for the family.

"Grandma?" Corinne peered at her curiously again.

It popped back in: Natasha. Of course. "I told you, I'm *fine*." Edith was keenly aware that Corinne might have been sent up here to baby-sit. "Good Lord, I'm just getting over the flu! You people are acting as though I have the plague."

Corinne and what's-his-name exchanged another secret glance. Edith pulled her fur tighter around her, suddenly struck with paranoia. Could they know? Might they suspect this wasn't the flu? They couldn't. She was keeping up such good appearances.

Still, in her mind's eye, she pictured that doctor, an impertinent upstart named Myers, displaying her MRI scans on a glowing screen. "It's such an unusual path for this type of cancer," he'd told Edith.

She'd visited him alone that day, just as she'd gone alone for the blood draws, and the MRI too. "Usually these sorts of lesions are slow-growing, easy to catch. But this . . . well . . ."

He'd outlined all the medications and the treatments they could try, though he didn't sound very optimistic about her prognosis. Whatever this was, it had spread. Edith had stood up, livid. "I'm getting a second opinion. Don't you know who I *am*?"

The doctor looked startled. "Ms. Saybrook, cancer doesn't play favorites."

It sounded like something one might put on a bumper sticker. Edith stormed out of the office, nearly slipping on the hard linoleum. But in the elevator, she'd pressed every floor just to get a few moments of peace. A quiet, dooming voice whispered seductively in her mind. *You knew it would come to this. Deep down, you knew everything.*

Did she? *Could* she have? Oh, she'd wondered plenty after her granddaughters revealed what Alfred had done. Mason knew. Poppy too . . . and Natasha, and Candace and Patrick, and he was only family by marriage. And then everyone had looked at her, expecting her to be in on the secret too. And she'd sat there, poker-faced, but inside she just felt . . . shriveled. Punched. Good Lord, she'd thought. Here it was, after all these years. Laid out like a corpse.

She remembered when Alfred came back from the war as if it were yesterday. How proud he'd been to show her the diamonds he'd found! "I got this at a bazaar in Paris," he said excitedly, holding up the large yellow one to the light. God, it was as big as a baseball. "Oh, Edie, isn't it beautiful? We're going to make a killing."

But something had bothered her about the story. A bazaar in Paris? What were they doing having flea markets at a time like this?

And where had he gotten money to buy stones? Toward the end of the war, whenever Alfred went on leave, he complained in his letters about barely having any money for a movie and a beer, pretty much forgetting that Edith was struggling at home trying to keep his jewelry store afloat. And she'd heard the whispers too. Less-than-moral things happening over there by the Allied soldiers. Thefts from people who'd already had their dignity stripped from them. They rationalized it, Edith supposed, because they felt they were owed something for their sacrifice. And so they took . . . and they didn't tell. But her Alfred wasn't like that, was he? Wasn't he a good man, an honest man?

Still. She'd asked, in a roundabout way, just to make sure. Alfred told her again and again that everything was legitimate. "Just be happy," he told her on his way to auction that morning. "And get ready, because our whole life is going to change."

And then it did. That stone sold for a mint. Alfred gained national recognition for it, and he invested the money he earned from its sale into the store.

Saybrook's grew. Alfred cut and sold the other diamonds he'd "acquired" while overseas, expanding the store again and again. He made connections with better mines and dealers. With some of the profits he was able to buy better, clearer diamonds, turning them into higher-quality jewelry. Soon people from New York were coming to Boston to see him. And shortly after *that,* the decision was made to move to Manhattan.

Every time a Saybrook died tragically, Edith wasn't one hundred percent surprised. But to admit it was karma, a curse? Buying into that, agreeing with the press that the family was cursed—well, that meant admitting that they'd done something to deserve it. And so she'd dismissed it as nonsense.

Now Edith shut her eyes. That was a long time ago. And what Edith was suffering from probably just *was* the flu, not some garish, amorphous tumor assailing her from the inside out. She certainly didn't deserve this illness for keeping her mouth shut all those years. She didn't believe in curses. That was that.

A strange noise startled her awake. She opened her eyes, not having been aware she'd even dozed off, and looked around. The two chairs next to her were vacant now. The music had stopped. Guests froze, cocktails in hand.

A scream rose from the beach. Edith stood. Who was that? Then Patrick emerged from between the pines. "Help!"

Everyone started to move. Though still disoriented, Edith made it downstairs and across the lawn. She searched frantically for her granddaughters, but she didn't see a single one. A few men pushed through the group, offering their services. But where was Aster? Where was Rowan? Edith called out to them weakly, but her voice didn't carry.

There was a small circle around a body on the sand. Edith's heart lurched. "Call nine-one-one!" a voice bellowed. Patrick dropped to his knees over the body. "Is she breathing?" someone yelled. "Is there a pulse?"

"Who is it?" Edith screeched, clawing furiously to get through the crowd.

A stranger she'd never seen before whirled around and widened her eyes. "It's one of yours."

It hit Edith like a blow to the chest. The stranger stepped aside so Edith could get through. She knelt down on the sand, touching a girl's bare foot. Patrick loomed over her, trying to do CPR. "*Move*," Edith growled at her son, crawling on top of the body. She stared into the girl's face, recognizing those signature ice-blue eyes, that sloped nose, the oval-diamond pendant Edith had given each of her granddaughters on her eighteenth birthday.

"*No*," she bellowed, collapsing against the girl. It couldn't be. Not another one. Wasn't her tumor enough? Couldn't she be the sacrifice?

The tide rushed in, hitting Edith with a shock of cold. People rushed to and fro, shouting panicked instructions. Edith stared into the trees, suspecting that someone was watching. Julia Gilchrist had never been found. Could it be her? Could it be someone else?

Or maybe it was some*thing* else. Maybe it had been something else all along.

An ambulance screamed up the walkway. People ran up to the EMTs, directing them to the body. But Edith's gaze remained fixed on the woods, waiting for whoever—or whatever—it was to show themselves. All at once, she knew it for sure: the curse was here again.

Or maybe it had never left.

ACKNOWLEDGMENTS

It was such a pleasure and privilege to be given the opportunity to dabble in this world and the lines of these fascinating, complicated characters for more than a year. Every book I get to write is a gift, and *The Heiresses* was a particularly exciting one. My unending thanks to Jonathan Burnham at Harper for making this possible, and to Les Morgenstein, Josh Bank, Sara Shandler, Lanie Davis, and Katie McGee at Alloy Entertainment for their brilliant insights, for their masterful sense of plot and characters, and for their continued support of me. Thanks also to Natalie Sousa and Liz Dresner for their tireless efforts and amazing designs. Huge hugs to Maya Ziv too—I was so thrilled to work with you on this project, and your guidance of what this book should be transformed it into something really special.

Also thanks to Jennifer Rudolph Walsh and Andy McNicol at WME for helping to make this project happen. And my best to the team at Harper: Robin Bilardello for your savvy cover insights, and Kathy Schneider, Katherine Beitner, and Katie O'Callaghan for your enthusiasm. It's hard to get a book out into the world, and this wouldn't have been possible without all of you.

Thanks to Ted and Lindsay Leisenring and their daughter, Chase, for hosting me in their lovely home, where I spent many hours writing and editing. Thanks to my father for his insights on vintage hunting attire and how to rig planes to crash. Thanks to my mother and her knowledge of the glamorous life (and some of the New York City haunts mentioned on these pages). Thank you, Yuval Braverman, for the sneak peek into the world of diamonds. Thanks to Ali and Caron for our many stays in New York, and even though you can't read and your vocabulary mostly has to do with construction vehicles right now, much love to Kristian, my favorite little guy. Please don't be like James when you grow up.

And much love, Michael, for definitely not being like James except for your easygoing coolness. Thanks for enduring the many frustrations that come with writing a book and for coming up with get-rich-quick ideas involving Bruce Springsteen. I'm glad I was able to work some Texas references into these pages too.

ABOUT THE AUTHOR

SARA SHEPARD graduated from New York University and has an MFA in creative writing from Brooklyn College. She is the author of the bestselling young adult books *Pretty Little Liars* and *The Lying Game*, as well as the adult novels *The Visibles* and *Everything We Ever Wanted*. She lives in Pittsburgh.